DOUBLE GOD

It was the simplest of errors and also the most lethal. The kind of mistake anyone in their position could have made. All they did was forget to re-set the time lock, and Double God was let loose upon the world . . .

'I am the Double God. I make the world and unmake it with these hands,' he whispered . . .

Her eyes snapped open onto the darkened room. Behind her the house creaked yet again. As she lurched forward, moved by an impulse to run, she felt something or someone snatch at her throat.

DOUBLE GOD

Veronica Hart

Mandarin

A Mandarin Paperback
DOUBLE GOD

First published in Great Britain 1995
by Mandarin Paperbacks
an imprint of Reed Consumer Books Ltd
Michelin House, 81 Fulham Road, London SW3 6RB
and Auckland, Melbourne, Singapore and Toronto

Copyright © Veronica Hart 1993
The author has asserted her moral rights

A CIP catalogue record for this title
is available from the British Library
ISBN 0 7493 1648 9

Printed and bound in Great Britain
by Cox & Wyman Ltd, Reading, Berkshire

This book is sold subject to the condition
that it shall not, by way of trade or otherwise,
be lent, resold, hired out, or otherwise circulated
without the publisher's prior consent in any form
of binding or cover other than that in which
it is published and without a similar condition
including this condition being imposed
on the subsequent purchaser.

For the Lord thy god is among you, a mighty God and terrible.

Deuteronomy 7:21

How dreadful is this place! This is none other than the House of God and the Gate of Heaven.

Thomas Traherne, *Centuries of Meditation*

Contents

Prologue	9
Part One	1
Part Two	29
Part Three	83
Part Four	117
Part Five	165
Part Six	223
Part Seven	241
Part Eight	315
Part Nine	363
Part Ten	405
Part Eleven	429

Prologue

And Miserie's increase
Is Mercy, Pity, Peace.

William Blake, from the *Rossetti Ms*

It was the simplest of errors, and also the most lethal. The kind of mistake anyone in their position could have made. All they did was forget to reset the time-lock, a task they usually carried out every Sunday evening.

They thought of the time-lock itself, a straightforward release mechanism, as a form of insurance, though not so much for themselves.

'Suppose something happened to us and we couldn't get back here,' he argued, when they first discussed its installation. 'I mean ever,' he added.

'But if we were gone away and ... and the door opened ...' she began nervously.

'What if it stayed closed?' he interrupted her. 'Wouldn't that be worse?' And when she had no ready answer: 'A life's a life, say what you like. They're all precious in their own way.'

So it was that the time-mechanism was installed. A humane gesture of sorts; at least that's how it looked from their point of view.

Then once, and once only, for they were given no second chance, they forgot to reset it.

It must be said that as oversights go, theirs was fairly

understandable. That particular Sunday, after all, was an anniversary, a mournful one at that. A day spent at the cemetery grieving over what they thought of as a double bereavement.

'They're gone!' she had sobbed, kneeling in the rain at the graveside. 'My two dear babies, lost to us forever.'

And he had been so taken up with comforting her, both there and later when they reached home, that the time for resetting the lock somehow slipped past unnoticed.

Naturally they had allowed themselves a safety margin. Two days to be precise. How was it, then, that they didn't pick up on their mistake during the Monday or Tuesday? That's less easily explained. Maybe they had been dealing with the matter of the door for so long, week in and week out, that they genuinely believed they had seen to it. In their circumstances, one week may well have merged into another. Or maybe a renewal of the old grief — reminding them, as it must have done, of happier times and far gentler bonds — made them less wary, less mindful of their own safety. Whatever the reason, the fact remains that their forgetfulness continued into the ensuing week.

The first she knew of their fateful error was when she glanced up on Tuesday evening and saw an unwelcome guest standing in the kitchen doorway, the flames licking about its head. It looked at her with the good side of its face, the half she had always loved, and for a few blissful seconds she was sure that all would be well; that one of the wounds in her heart was about to be healed. Then it turned its head and showed her the blank side, where the flames clung thickly and the mouth was a jagged scar; where the one blank eye, unseeing, fixed itself upon the space where she crouched in ready submission. And she remembered that although her husband had been working at the bench outside the door, she had heard nothing. No greeting. No cry of alarm.

The figure swept across the kitchen towards her, its tread like the pulse of invisible wings.

'I come as a thief in the night,' it hissed.

'Mercy!' she pleaded, a hand to her breast.

Though she knew well enough that as gods went, this was not a merciful one.

PART ONE

She went out in Morning, attir'd plain and neat;
'Proud Mary's gone Mad,' said the Child in the Street.

William Blake, 'Mary'

1

Mary's trouble...

Or should we say rather the trouble with Mary? Either way, it began when she was nearly sixteen. Before that she gave no sign of being out of the ordinary. Like most teenagers she could be moody or cheerful as the fit took her, and she was blessed with a reasonable share of brains and good looks. About the only thing that marked her off from the average was her size. She was tiny, so short and slight that she looked almost fragile; a fact that didn't worry Mary in the least. Or anyone else come to that. As everyone who knew her agreed, she had enough noisy energy for someone twice her height and weight. Not the strength, however, and that proved to be important. Just *how* important she was not to discover until one morning shortly before her sixteenth birthday.

She was at that stage still at high school, and had for some time been earning extra pocket money by doing odd jobs about the neighbourhood — cleaning cars, watering people's gardens while they were on holiday, and such like. Two jobs in particular had become regular features of her life. One was taking care of a toddler every Saturday morning, a little boy called Josh; the other was walking a neighbour's dog several times a week.

The dog, a fully grown bull terrier, answered to the name of 'Terror', because that was what he made people feel when they first saw him. With his stocky build and broad chest, his pinkish slit-eyes and powerful head, he was truly a terror to behold. Most of the neighbours gave him a wide berth, but not Mary. Where she was concerned he was as gentle as any lamb, slobbering lovingly over her with jaws properly designed for mortal combat. Together, within the confines of their quiet Sydney suburb, the two of them became a familiar sight, with Terror literally dogging her heels, guarding her fiercely against even the friendliest of approaches. During their visits to the local park, for instance, if anyone so much as ventured near he would growl and start to bristle; and if ever she happened to pass his gate without calling in, he would sit in the middle of the concrete drive and howl dolefully for half an hour or more afterwards.

Josh, too, regarded her as his own special property. 'Mewwy!' he would crow when she arrived on Saturday mornings, and clutch onto her with small greedy hands. At other times, chancing to see her in the street, he would grow red in the face and scream if she failed to stop. He was always at his worst if she was with either of her two brothers. Perhaps sensing Mary's special fondness for them, he would descend into an orgy of thwarted rage, his strident cries, like Terror's, often pursuing her for a block of more.

There can be no doubt that in their separate ways both Josh and Terror were genuinely devoted to her. Each, according to his limits, loved her with a possessive and jealous love that brooked no rivals. And therein lay the problem. One that came to an unexpected head on a morning that would otherwise have been as pleasant and ordinary as Mary herself; a morning on which the relative calm of her suburban existence was shattered by an obsessive fury that . . . Well, let's just say that it left her different. Another person entirely. Someone unmoved even by the tender concern of her once beloved brothers.

The day in question was a Saturday — Josh's day — a morning of fine spring weather. Far too fine to be spent cooped up either in the house or within the narrow orbit of the garden. Or so Mary believed.

'How about a walk in the park?' she suggested — the self-same words she used on the days she went to collect Terror.

'Park!' Josh echoed her enthusiastically, already tugging at the door of the cupboard that held his stroller.

She detained him only long enough to comb his soft brown hair back from his face. (A simple action she would recall with bitter clarity in the hours and days to come.) And minutes later they were bowling along the street together, past her own front gate and on towards Terror's.

She was given no warning of what was to follow. She heard no jealous growls; detected no danger signs at all. As she drew abreast of the opening a white blur of sheer frenzy struck the side of the stroller, tore it from her grasp, and sent it flying. Josh landed half across the road and was still rolling over and over when he was taken by the head and shaken like a stringless puppet, his arms and legs flapping free.

'Terror!' she wailed, the true meaning of the word breaking through in the high resonance of her voice.

The dog became still for a moment, as if displaying his handiwork, and even as she rushed forward she was amazed that his jaws could stretch so wide, the top of Josh's head wedged in the hard angle of teeth and mottled skin. One of the teeth had punctured the child's eye, which was oozing a mixture of fluid and blood. The rest of Josh's face was livid, the same as when he clung to the palings of the garden fence and screamed out for her attention. He had sucked in his breath, but was unable to expel it, and in the growling silence she could hear the dog's molars grinding on the fragile skull.

'Terror!' she cried again, with authority now, in the pathetic belief that a single word, spell-like, could bind the unruly world to her will.

She learned then for the first time how small and powerless she really was, and how useless was her pathetic supply of words. She also glimpsed a furtive truth about physical strength: how it can take on almost godlike qualities in the absence of pity or remorse. For Terror did not simply ignore her. Using the child's body as a flail, he knocked her aside effortlessly as she tried to snatch Josh from him.

Dazed, she rose slowly from the gutter. Terror was

still once more, watching her, the body hanging limply from his gaping jaws.

'In the beginning . . .' those jaws seemed to be saying. Not in words: this was another language altogether. And he, Terror, master of this new and undreamed-of tongue, was standing there like a careless god caught in the act of rearranging her familiar universe.

'In the beginning . . .' the jaws insisted.

But she refused to listen. *Would not!* Unready as yet to believe him, even less to accept her own powerlessness. Didn't brains, intelligence, being human, count for something? Didn't they?

She put her own question to the test by lunging past Josh and grasping at Terror's head. One hand clenched onto the slack skin of his ruff, an 'ouf' breaking from her lips as she and Josh were slammed into a parked car. She groped desperately with her free hand, searching across the broad, bony cranium for the eyes. A fingernail lodged in a narrow slit and met with jellied resistance. She was slammed against the car a second time, another 'ouf' sounding from somewhere out there in the sunlight. She had lost the slit, but soon found it again. The same jellied resistance as before, which burst into warm submission as her finger pushed through.

Can gods cry out? she asked herself afterwards. And knew they could, because she'd heard him. A single sharp yelp as he released Josh long enough to turn on her. A god and a betrayed lover at one and the same time, who slashed downwards and laid her arm open from the shoulder to the elbow.

Then he had Josh by the head once more. Merciless

now, he tightened his grip and the head sponged out of shape, the plates of the skull grating together and splintering.

'O Lord, how great are thy works.' That was what she had been told. In church with her family on peaceful Sunday mornings, the minister's familiar voice ringing through the silence. Yet surely his words couldn't have meant this!

'Please!' she sobbed, giving in to him — to Terror — who continued to shake the lifeless body in an unanswerable display of power. 'It's enough! Please!'

She could hear running footsteps, her own name being called by a voice she had once cared about. But none of that counted for anything. Terror, a one-eyed and unforgiving god, was the only arbiter here.

'Please!' she repeated through her tears, pulling ineffectually at both tiny heels.

With a last vicious tug, Terror took what he clearly regarded as his due. A trophy. The whole of Josh's scalp, which tore free along the hairline. The rest he hardly glanced at. His mouth crammed with the soft brown hair that she had combed for precisely this outing, he abandoned them both; turned in what she now regarded as his lordly might and ambled back through the gate.

Her elder brother, Bob, was the first to reach her. She was sitting propped against the side fence, her mouth and eyes tight-shut, Josh's dead body cradled in her arms. The top of the flayed head, a bloodied mess with glints of white bone showing through, rested in the vee of her young breasts.

'What in God's name . . . !' Bob burst out.

'Terror,' she answered him softly, and pushed her tongue resolutely against her palate, an action that signalled her loss of faith in the power of words and marked the beginning of her long silence.

2

Mary lay on her bed, heavily sedated, and listened to a dog barking in the far distance. Terror, she thought drowsily, and visualised him in all his magnificence. They were walking together in the local harbourside park, and he had just found a dead seagull down near the water's edge and deposited it at her feet. A ruined thing with limp wings and muddied feathers, so soiled and abused that it was hardly a bird at all. Now he was circling about them both — her and the bird — springing stiff-legged into the air and landing on his toes. His head was thrown back, though not in laughter, and his tongue flapped crimson from the side of his mouth, as crimson as the headless ring of the bird's neck.

'This is how it's done,' he seemed to be saying at every bound. 'Like this . . . like this . . .'

She understood what he was telling her, but was unable to move, locked there in the circle with the bird. Too mesmerised by his one gleaming eye and snapping jaws even to remember the word that described what he was doing as he leaped about her. You've taken all the words! she wanted to shout. You've eaten them! Her mouth opening onto silence while he continued with his circling, his movements keeping time to the dull background throb of a drum.

She came half awake, roused partly by the throbbing pain in her freshly stitched arm, and partly by the sound of raised voices.

'She was supposed to be looking after him!' she heard a woman cry out. 'He was in her care!'

The voice was disturbingly familiar, and she made an effort to concentrate, to bring a particular face into focus. She regretted it immediately and would have retreated into sleep, but her father's rumbled reply held her there, his typically gentle tones drifting up from below in broken fragments.

'What more could she ... against a brute like that ... ? ... risked her own life to ... mauled in the process ...'

'Mauled?' The voice too shrill to be shut out. 'A scratch on the arm and you call that mauled? When Josh ... when Josh ... !'

And her mother, only slightly less distraught: 'We're sorry, Carol! We all are!'

'Sorry?'

There was the crash of a door being slammed shut, followed by urgent, muffled talk. It was too far off to be made sense of, going on and on, and Mary had again begun to drift away when a last wailing cry sounded through the house.

'Forgive? *Never!* You don't know what you're asking. It'd be like dancing on his grave!'

Dancing! Mary reached hazily for the idea and hugged it to herself, carrying it like a secret password back to the park where Terror still circled the decapitated bird. Yes, that was what he was doing, she remembered now, a kind of dance, savage and carefree. He must have seen the recognition in her eyes because he barked loudly, as though inviting her to join him. She lacked the courage to refuse and, abandoning the bird, she stepped clear of the circle out into the abruptly darkened park. With her own head thrown back, one eye closed in ready sympathy, she did her feeble best to copy his extravagant leaps and turns, his quick pouncing steps and sudden crouches — her bare feet, in the faraway waking world, twitching spasmodically beneath the bedclothes.

The room was dusky when she next returned, the far wall faintly illumined by a flickering light. She thought at first that Josh's mother had disturbed her with another of her wailing cries, and then realised that what she could hear was a siren. Groggily, she rose from the bed and staggered over to the window. From there she had a clear view of the lower end of the street, the end closer to the park. Unconsciously she had vowed never to look in that direction again, but now she couldn't help herself, because of the flames. She didn't have to work out where they were coming from. She knew. By the way they danced, the way they twisted and twirled in savage abandon, snatching cruelly at the dark evening one moment and sinking down in mock submission the next.

As far as she was concerned only one thing could dance like that. Him! Terror! And ducking below the windowsill so the light from the flames couldn't touch her, she crawled under the bed and lay curled up in the dusty corner.

She was still hidden there when her father looked in soon afterwards, her soft whimpers giving her away.

'Come on out, sweetheart,' he coaxed her — a big man down on his hands and knees, stroking her hair with one silky-hard palm. 'It's just the fire engine you can hear. And they've finished now. It's all over.'

'What is it, Doug?'

Tess Warner appeared in the doorway, small and fine-boned like her daughter, but taller. Seeing her husband crouched beside the bed, she clicked her tongue in distress and pushed past him, squirming in under the bedsprings until she was close enough to take Mary in her arms.

'There's nothing to be scared of, love,' she murmured. 'It's finished and done with. He can't hurt you any more.'

The whole family had crowded into the room now. Her two brothers were over by the window, where they could watch the firemen coiling their hoses and preparing to leave.

'Come and look, Med,' her younger brother, Harry, called encouragingly. 'You can see where the kennel was. Half the garage has gone too. Carol poured petrol over it — that's what they reckon — and it went up like . . .'

'That's enough!' Tess Warner said sharply, because Mary had stiffened in her arms, more resistant than ever.

'But if she knows he's dead . . .' Harry protested.

'I said that'll do!' Tess broke in. 'This isn't the time

or place. She's not ready for it, and she doesn't believe you anyway.'

That much was true: Mary had not the slightest doubt that they were lying, trying to pretend everything could go back to normal. Well she had learned otherwise. Hadn't Terror revealed to her who he really was? Hadn't she seen him dance? How could any of that be stopped? Finished? And what did their words matter, she reminded herself, pushing her tongue back against her palate? Hadn't Terror taught her what words were worth too? Just worthless sounds borne by the wind, with no power to control or change anything.

'But we could prove it to her,' Harry insisted, cutting across her secret thoughts. 'We could take her down there and let her see what's left . . .'

'For God's sake!' Tess broke in again. 'Will you get them out of here, Doug? She needs quiet. You heard what the doctor said as well as I did.'

Her husband stood up heavily, his thickly jowled face red from leaning over, and placed a hand on Harry's shoulder. 'Come on, boys,' he advised them both in a whisper. 'Let's leave her to your mother.'

After they had filed out, Tess made only one attempt to lure Mary from under the bed. When that failed, she reached for the tablets and glass on the bedside table and administered another dose of the sedative.

'There, that'll help,' she said. 'And I'll be here,' she added, settling herself in the confined space, 'so you have nothing to worry about.' With one hand she dragged down a loose rug and spread it over them. 'Sleep now, baby,' she whispered soothingly. 'Sleep . . .'

And Mary, feet again starting to twitch, floated back to the darkened park where the whiteness of Terror's coat shone far more brightly than any moon or star.

She surfaced just once in the course of the night. Her mother was breathing deeply and evenly beside her, and she raised her head slightly so she could see the rest of the room. A pencil-thin stream of light spilled in from the passage where the door stood ajar. Exactly like the gate to Terror's house, she recalled, which someone must also have left ajar. And quickly, in a reflex attempt to forget that remembered opening, she clicked her eyes shut.

When she looked again, peeking fearfully through the strands of her mother's hair, the door had swung inwards, the band of light had broadened, and she could see someone out on the landing. A hunched shape, down on all fours. There was a sharp hiss as she sucked in her breath and waited.

But it was only Harry. Careful not to make a sound, he crawled into the room and placed something on the floor close to the bed. Even in her sedated condition she understood what he had brought her and why. His proof, he might have called it, but of what? Wasn't it still intact? A perfect circle, unharmed by the dancing flames? If it proved anything at all, it was the very opposite of what Harry had intended. It showed that Terror had survived the fire, never mind what anyone said; it showed that nothing could hurt him. And with her new-found faith unshaken, she let herself slide back into the enduring place. A parkland that had become as overgrown as it was dark; an ancient jungle through which she groped her uneasy way.

She was the first to wake in the morning. Peering over her mother's sprawled hair, she examined the leather collar that Harry had left for her. Although fire-blackened and cracked, its studs and buckle stripped of their chromium plating, there was no mistaking whose it was. A sign, as if she had needed one, of where her duty now lay; a wordless message to her from the owner of those godlike jaws.

Gingerly, she disentangled herself from her mother's arms, eased aside the rug and squirmed down to the foot of the bed. Raw sunlight cut a dusty path across the room. She shrank from the soft warmth of its touch, determined never to be beguiled by such things again, and stooped for the collar. The buckle was stiff, but she struggled with it as she knew she must, and the whole collar creaked open at last, like the little-used gate to Terror's house, where he still awaited her. Hastily, she drew it about her throat and pulled the leather tongue through the buckle with sore fingers. Fastened at the innermost hole, it fitted her surprisingly well — another of Terror's secret signs, that she could not ignore — and she was just about to start moving her feet in the patterns of his dance when something else attracted her attention.

Her mother's eyes, watching her from beneath the bed.

'What are you doing, Mary?' Her voice caring, but also coolly suspicious.

She didn't answer. Couldn't. Had foresworn that

other language, having heard her own words billow out into emptiness, blown like leaves by Terror's hot breath; had pledged herself from here on to respond only to his unspoken commands.

'O Lord, how great are thy works.'

'I'm talking to you, Mary. Why have you put that thing around your neck? Why?'

But she had no reasons to give either. He had taken those from her too: plundered them with one scythe-like sweep of his jaws. Her mind blank from remembered fright, all she could do was push one finger through the metal loop attached to the collar, her arm hanging down as if it were a living chain.

3

Bob was calling her from downstairs, his voice gentle, the way everybody spoke to her now.

'Time to go, Mary. We're missing the best part of the day.'

She was completely dressed except for the collar, and she knew Bob wouldn't let her wear it around her neck. None of them would.

'Thirty seconds, Mary, that's all you've got before I come up there for you.' His tone playful to mask his determination. 'You're not going to disappoint me again.'

If not on her neck, then where? Because she didn't dare leave without it. Never mind anyone else, *he*, Terror, would notice. And then . . . and then . . . She looked around desperately, as though the secret of what she must do were hidden somewhere in the room.

'You can't stay locked in the house forever.' Bob's footsteps sounded on the stairs, mounting steadily. 'You're beginning to look like one of those battery hens, d'you know that?'

Where? Her mind skittered back to its previous thought. *Secret! Hidden!* Yes, of course. A place where nobody else would see it. That only *he* would know about. Which was all that mattered.

'Blast-off time, Mary.' The footsteps had reached the landing. 'No more delays.'

She pulled up her skirt just as he knocked. One swift movement and she had wound the collar about the very top of her thigh, where it wouldn't show. She was still struggling to fasten it when the door opened behind her.

'Oops! Sorry about that.'

There, it was done, the leather snug against her skin. She smoothed down her skirt and went over to the door.

'You look great,' Bob said, and led the way downstairs.

She followed him as far as the front gate, but baulked at the sight of the open street.

'It's all right,' he assured her, and took her hand. His own hand, although leaner, had the same feel as her father's — the same silky hardness that came from working with wood. She had trusted it once; reached for it at scary films or if she was upset. Even now it was capable of coaxing her through the gate, out into the exposed street. Where anything could happen. *Anything!*

Turn left, she willed him silently. Left ... left ... *LEFT!* No! Not that way! No! With a quick turn of the wrist, she pulled free and clung to the gate.

He didn't complain, didn't make fun of her.

'Look at it,' he said, pointing at the street with its rows of Sydney red gums and parked cars. A street she had been familiar with all her life, that she had once thought she knew. 'There's nothing dangerous about it, nothing here to hurt you. Just trust me, okay?'

But she had trusted *him* too. Terror. Let *him* slobber her arm with his massive jaws, lick the backs of her fingers with his crimson tongue . . . until he showed her the truth.

'We needn't go far.' Bob pried her hands gently loose. 'The important thing is to make a start.'

He had her hand in his again and was sauntering on ahead, pretending not to notice how she hung back.

'You're doing fine,' he encouraged her. 'You can easily make it to the next corner.'

Next? Meaning the intersection on the other side of the street? No, he was urging her past that, towards . . . ! She risked a quick look ahead: glimpsed the familiar gates, the blackened end of the garage where the flames had danced. Then she dug in her heels, just as *he* had done on those mornings when she'd brought him back from the park, his collar rucking up the loose skin of his neck, his paws dragging on the hard pavement. She could feel the collar now, tight about her tensed thigh, and her shoes were making a similar scraping noise.

'The garden's empty,' Bob was saying, tugging and tugging, just like her in those far-off days. 'The kennel's gone. Just a burnt-out shell. Take a look for yourself.'

She braced her toes against a join in the pavement, but Bob, who was almost as big and heavy as her father, forced her onwards; she grasped at the hedge with her free hand, but was left with a fistful of leaves.

'Nearly there,' Bob panted, laughing, trying to make a joke of it. 'You'll be glad afterwards. You'll see.'

She risked a second look. The gates were open, as

they would always be, and almost within reach. A few shuffling steps and Bob's shoulder was level with the gatepost; a few more and . . . !

She turned on him then, just as Terror had instructed her: clamped her teeth about his wrist and held on. Not so fiercely that she broke the skin, but hard enough to make him cry out in pain and surprise. Growling deep in her throat, she shook her head from side to side, worrying at him, tightening her hold until he stopped hitting out at her and slumped to his knees.

'Enough!' he sobbed. 'Enough!'

And she released him with a final warning, the merest nip — her front incisors closing on a ridge of bruised skin and leaving behind a tiny fleck of blood.

❋

She wasn't nearly so gentle two days later, when she was persuaded to join the rest of the family on an outing. That's what they called it, 'an outing', not mentioning the arranged interview with the counsellor.

'An hour or two by the sea will do you the world of good,' Tess said by way of enticement, urging her step by step towards the car.

And they did in fact drive first to Bondi, where Mary walked listlessly along the beach while her brothers swam. Eyes half-closed against the glare, one hand pressed firmly to her right thigh to stop the wind lifting her skirt, she showed no interest in the rush and sparkle of the waves or in the shouted laughter of the bathers. After all, hadn't *he* once splashed happily along the water's edge, retrieving sticks and soggy tennis balls? And what had all that come to in the end?

She showed the same indifference when, on the way home, they stopped off to see the counsellor.

Words, nothing but words, she thought as she sat back in the easy chair beside the window, not bothering to listen to what the counsellor had to say; not bothering even to look at the woman's face. What was the point? *He*, Terror, had already told her all she needed to know; revealed to her the one abiding truth behind the misleading face of things. Unreasoning strength, the rule of tooth and claw, that was all she believed in now. And surreptitiously, so the woman wouldn't notice, she brushed her thumb across the hard ridge of collar that pressed up through her skirt. It felt solid and real. Far more real than all this talk that counted for nothing; than all these questions that washed over her in an endless stream, hardly penetrating her silence.

To while away the time, she imagined what Terror might do in this situation. How, she wondered, would this earnest, middle-aged woman react to *him*? Mary smiled at the idea and ventured further. Suppose, just suppose, that the door behind her had been ajar all along, and that *he* was waiting out there, ready to rush in on them.

Like before?

The smile froze on her lips, and she clenched her eyes shut. But having once been invited in, *he* refused to be banished. There was a faint noise somewhere in the background. Her parents? Her brothers? No, too furtive for that. More like . . . like the scrabbling of claws on a cement path!

Mary leaped to her feet, hands splayed, her whole body tense and still, listening.

'What's the matter, Mary?' The woman was there beside her, one arm around her shoulders. 'Was it something I said?'

The scrabbling grew louder, nearer, Terror's distinctive odour pervading the room.

'Was it the part about the dog?' the woman asked anxiously. 'Is that what's upsetting you? Is it Terr . . . ?'

Mary lunged straight for the throat, but missed as the woman flinched aside, her teeth biting down hard at that point where the shoulder slopes towards the neck. Only the thick material of the woman's business suit prevented her teeth from meeting. All the shouting and pleading were just so much noise. With an impatient toss of the head, she tore the cloth away, and was about to lunge again, onto the bare flesh, when hands grabbed her from behind.

'No, sweetheart!' her father protested. 'No!'

She swung towards him in turn, with the same fixed sense of purpose, but Bob had her by then. One of his hands twisted into her hair, the other cupped firmly beneath her chin, he forced her head away — he and her father together holding her still until the growls died in her throat and her lips eased back over her teeth.

4

Ruth Close, her cheeks flushed, her jacket torn, faced Tess and Doug Warner across the heavy wooden desk. Even with Mary in the next room being looked after by her brothers, she felt safer having the desk between her and the door.

'I don't need to tell you that Mary's a very disturbed girl,' she said quietly, doing her best to sound calm and unruffled. 'She's been wounded inside, and it'll probably take her a while to heal. In the meantime . . .'

'But she will heal eventually,' Tess cut in, her voice tight with concern. 'That is what you're saying, isn't it?'

Doug Warner, bewildered and out of his depth, reached for his wife's hand, as much for his own comfort as for hers.

'It's too early to be sure . . .' Ruth began hesitantly, and then saw the stricken look on the couple's face. 'But yes, the chances are she will. On the other hand that isn't what we need to talk about right now. Our immediate problem is Mary's behaviour. We can't have her attacking people whenever she pleases.'

'But she's always been so gentle,' Doug muttered in a

dazed voice, and ran a hand distractedly down his heavy features.

'She wasn't being exactly gentle with me ten minutes ago, or with your son the other day.' Ruth directed the remark mainly at Tess who, despite her strained expression, seemed more in command of the situation than her husband. 'What if that were to happen again, with some stranger maybe, who won't be so understanding? What then? Wouldn't it be wiser to do something now, before anyone else gets hurt?'

'You mean lock her up?' Tess asked pointedly. 'Put her into one of those places for the dangerously insane?'

'We'd only consider that as . . .'

'No!' Tess leaned forward, her face narrow and intent. 'I'd rather move. Take her out of Sydney, to some place where there aren't any people around for her to harm.'

'What I was trying to say,' Ruth went on in even tones, 'is that physical restraint would be a last resort. I was thinking more in terms of medication.'

'No!' Tess said more vehemently than before, and slapped her hand down on the desk with a fierceness that made Ruth rear back, reminded suddenly of how Mary had leaped at her. 'I won't have anyone turning her into a zombie either. That's just another way of locking her up.'

'It needn't be like that, Tess.'

'It sure as hell won't be, will it, Doug?' Jerking at his sleeve while he gazed from her to Ruth with troubled eyes. 'The last thing anyone's going to do is scramble our daughter's brains with drugs. Because I meant what I said. If we have to, we'll get her away from people.

We have our own cabinet-making business, so we can live anywhere as long as it has a good work area.'

'Listen, Tess,' Ruth said, purposely keeping her voice low, professional, though at that moment she felt more like Tess, tense and on edge. 'I'm not telling you how to act. All I'm trying to do is offer you a less drastic option.'

'Less drastic?' Tess rejoined hotly. 'You talk about medication, about filling her up with mind-bending substances, and then you call it less drastic? My God!' And as much out of frustration as anger, she brought her hand down on the desk once again — a sharp, aggressive sound that produced an immediate reaction from the neighbouring room.

There were a few muffled crashes, of people lurching against furniture, followed by something that was a mixture between a yelp and a howl, a distinctively animal cry that brought them all to their feet, their faces turned towards the door.

For a minute of two none of them moved — Ruth standing there with one hand raised to her bruised shoulder; Doug, despite his size, clutching onto his wife's arm as though for protection. Tess, her face drained of anger as well as colour, had the shocked look of someone woken halfway through a dream.

After that, there seemed nothing else worth saying.

'Well, maybe you'd like to think it over for a few days,' Ruth added lamely.

*

Tess did. She thought especially hard on the day they

drove home along the lower road, the one that joined their own street at the end nearest the park. As they were passing the spot where Josh had been attacked, Mary gave another of her yelping cries, scrambled up from the back seat and sank her teeth into Doug's beefy neck. His shirt and jacket were soaked in blood before she could be dragged off.

And Tess thought harder still on the day she took Mary to the supermarket. Nothing could happen there, she told herself. Nor did it, until her attention wandered for a few moments. They were standing together at the meat section and Tess was looking at the racks over to her left, trying to decide what cuts to buy. When she glanced back, Mary hadn't moved from her side, but she was eating something, bloody drops running down her chin and staining the front of her dress.

It was that sight more than any other — of her daughter's mouth crammed with raw meat, her teeth tearing the last bloody fragments from the bone — that finally made up Tess's mind.

Part Two

I fled Him, down the labyrinthine ways
  Of my own mind.

    Francis Thompson, 'The Hound of Heaven'

5

Ann Guthrie prided herself on being able to read a customer, and when the Warners had walked into her office she'd felt certain that they were desperate to find a house. So desperate that they'd take almost anything. Yet here she was, at the end of a long day, and nothing had seemed to satisfy them.

'We need privacy,' Tess Warner had stressed, and Ann had shown them houses perched on hills and others hidden away in valleys.

'Not enough space for a workshop,' Tess had said in each case, sometimes with regret.

'Plenty more to choose from,' Ann had responded. (Always stay cheerful, that was the secret, never let your impatience show.) And she had driven them off to places with everything from stables to shearing sheds erected in the grounds.

But of course none of these was ever private enough. Always the neighbours or the road or something or other were too near. On one memorable occasion they'd even been put off by the sound of barking dogs. What did they expect, for God's sake, with Sydney barely two hours away? A monastery?

Now they were looking over the last of the vaguely suitable properties she had to offer, and she could tell from their expressions that she'd drawn another blank. Oh well, you couldn't satisfy every customer. Still, in the Warners' case she could have sworn she was going to make a sale. They just didn't have the look of people who'd be hard to please.

In which case . . . ? A sudden thought occurred to her, and on the pretext of having to contact her office, she walked briskly back to the car and put through a call to a rival firm.

'Is that you, Mike? Ann here, Ann Guthrie. Listen, is the Clements' place still on the market?'

'Is there a God in heaven?'

'So you won't mind if I show some people over it? The usual deal.'

'Be my guest. Though frankly I think you're wasting your time.'

'No, these are Sydney people. They're not up with local affairs. They probably wouldn't be put off anyway. They have that any-port-in-a-storm look about them.'

'Even so, the place is in a hell of a mess. Worse than when we first got it. Some derro decided to take up residence. He actually opened the door to me, can you believe it? Put his eye to the crack and asked me what I wanted. "I want you out," I told him. But you should see how he left it!'

'Can't you get it cleaned up?'

'The estate's not interested. There's only one beneficiary, up in Queensland, and he won't even answer the lawyer's letters.'

Ann thought for a moment, her chin resting on the mouthpiece.

'I think I'll give it a try just the same. Okay if I call in for the key?'

'Go for your life.'

The Warners were walking back down the drive as she replaced the phone.

'I think we're in luck,' she told them brightly. 'The house I have in mind . . . well, it's not a palace, but it may be just what you're after. Plenty of workspace, with a wonderful easterly light, and views right across to Sydney. It's up on the Bells Line of Road, high above all the heat and smog and set on ten acres. That's quite a lot around here.'

She continued to chat pleasantly (keep it cheerful!) as she ushered them into the two cars, hoping all the while that for once the daughter would go with the father. It was disconcerting having her there in the back seat, never saying a word, always staring straight ahead with her blank face that made her look as if she'd seen the bogeyman. But as usual Tess Warner wasn't letting her out of her sight, clucking over her like a mother hen. And it wasn't as though the daughter was a child. Small, yes, tiny even, but around fifteen, sixteen maybe. Not that you'd know it from the way she acted. Mentally defective, most likely. Never mind, Ann consoled herself (taking care to keep the smile in place), however things went this would be the last trip of the day.

Half an hour later, having collected the key, she was leading the way up into the Blue Mountains, the other car following hard behind. Fortunately Tess wasn't difficult to talk to, unlike the daughter.

'Try not to be put off by first appearances,' Ann explained as she navigated the long bends. 'Underneath all the mess it's a good solid house. And the space . . . !'

She swung off the main road and stopped at the gate. My God, the place was far more private than she remembered, a great pyracantha hedge right across the front, and thick bush behind.

'Is this what you had in mind?' she asked, unnecessarily, because a quick glance sideways had already told her that Tess was more interested than she had been all day.

Taking her time, so as to get the full benefit of what was obviously a good first impression, Ann climbed out and opened the gate. Then, as luck would have it, just as they were driving in under the trees, the bellbirds started up. All around the property! So many that their high, crystal calls echoed each other and overlapped.

'What a welcome!' she laughed, concentrating on keeping to the overgrown track, but conscious all the same of Tess's rapt expression. 'You'd think the place had been waiting for you to arrive, wouldn't you?'

The house itself, though, was a disappointment. She had to admit that. A heavy, block-like structure set deep into the hillside. And clearly uncared for. The easterly windows on the lower ground floor, which she'd referred to earlier, were barely visible through an untidy screen of bushes; and the view she'd boasted of was virtually non-existent because of the height of the surrounding trees. In fact it was no good pretending, the house was just about grown-in, which was probably what made it look so dingy. The only reasonably open space was to the south, where a creek marked off the boundary. Even that was lined with willows and she-oaks, but compared with the dense tangle of growth everywhere else it appeared almost light and airy.

'A good chain-saw would make the world of...' Ann began, and stopped, taking her cue from Tess whose face still wore the same rapt smile. 'On the other hand,' she went on, correcting herself effortlessly, 'you could just leave it as it is. Regard it as an ultimate form of privacy. Your own totally private hideaway only a stone's throw from Sydney. Not easy to find these days.'

She let that idea sink in while the other car drew up alongside and everyone climbed out. The father, as always, was looking bewildered, but Ann had already discovered that he wasn't the one who really mattered. It was mainly Tess who made the decisions. She was the one to watch.

'Now, as to the house...' Ann announced lightly, and ran up the front steps.

This was going to be the hard part, she had no illusions on that score. The important thing was to get them in and out quickly, before the effect of the garden (could she actually call it that?) wore off. So, how best to manage it? To joke about the mess? To ignore it? Or to shake her head sadly and treat it as a minor tragedy?

She was still debating with herself the pros and cons of the tragic approach when she turned the key and stepped inside. Instantly all thought of sales strategy was forgotten. She had been anticipating a certain amount of disorder, but not on this scale. A derro — isn't that what Mike had called whoever had squatted here? Whereas this was the work of vandals. Or of madmen. From where she was standing, she could see through the living room to the dining room and on into the kitchen, and within her line of sight every piece of furniture, every door, every fitting, had been ruthlessly smashed. Nothing was left intact, as though someone (the derro?) had hated the house itself and set out to take personal revenge on it. Some revenge! she thought ruefully. This was more like an act of God! One of those natural disasters they talked about on insurance policies. A natural disaster for her, too, with her potential sale well and truly fallen through.

'Look, I'm sorry,' she said, turning in the doorway, 'I had no idea it was in this state.'

But Tess was already squeezing past her, the others crowding in behind.

'Who did all this?' Tess asked as she picked her way across the debris-stricken floor.

'A derro probably. A squatter anyway. This was his answer to being thrown out.'

'And before him?' Tess had disappeared into the passage, her voice drifting back. 'Whose house was it?'

'No one's for a while. It's a deceased estate.'

'Deceased? Deceased how?'

Keep it simple, Ann warned herself.

'Car accident,' she called out. 'A middle-aged couple, both dead.'

'Any children?'

'No,' she answered shortly, restricting herself to the precise truth. 'Only one relative, somewhere in Queensland, and he couldn't care less.'

Tess had reached the front bedroom. Her heels made sharp clicks on the once polished floors as she moved deliberately from one side of the room to the other, and all at once it dawned on Ann that she was actually inspecting the place. She was still interested. Her husband must also have thought so because he had begun rapping on the walls, peering up at the ceilings, his face not at all vacant or foolish now he was doing something practical.

'What about the workspace?' the elder son asked, and although he looked like the father, big and slow moving, Ann noticed for the first time that there was a lot of the mother's sharp, perceptive quality in his voice.

'Er . . . there's a stairway leading down from the kitchen,' she said, quickly regaining her presence of mind.

She had her smile firmly back in place as she showed them the way: on into the kitchen (littered with smashed dishes and scores of empty food cans), through a shattered doorway and down into a huge room that was half lower-ground floor and half basement. High-set windows ran the length of its outer, eastern wall; but the inner wall, where the house slotted into the natural curve of the hillside, was a blank screen of sectioned concrete with a tall wooden cupboard at one end. Down here the vandalism appeared even worse than upstairs, if that were possible, with the entire floor buried centimetres deep in rubble, as though the avenging force had found this portion of the house particularly detestable. It also looked much gloomier than Ann had expected, partly because the windows were filthy, partly because they were blocked off by the outside growth.

'Why didn't he smash the windows as well?' the younger boy asked unexpectedly.

Yes, why? Ann wondered. The upstairs the same.

'I expect he didn't want to be found out,' she improvised. 'He wanted everything to look normal from the outside so he could get away.'

That probably *was* the reason, she concluded privately, but still felt surprise at the boy's perceptiveness. Until then she had lumped him in with the father and brother. Not big and ponderous like them, but just as dull. Now, seeing the keen, questioning look on his face, she was forced to think again. About him and the whole family, none of them nearly as dull as she had supposed.

None? Did that include the girl? Were appearances equally deceptive in her case? No. Her face was too blank, her listlessness went too deep. There just wasn't anyone at home. In all likelihood, if it weren't for the younger boy, who since their arrival had taken upon himself the job of minder, she wouldn't have been able to find her way out of the car. That, however, was their problem, not hers, Ann decided with relief.

'Well, what do you think?' she asked in her bright professional manner. 'Can it be rescued?'

She was immediately aware of everyone turning towards the mother — everyone except for the girl, that is. Even Ann's eyes were drawn towards Tess, who simply continued with her inspection of what was, after all, a disaster area, allowing the silence to lengthen, and then lengthen some more. It was an impressive performance, Ann had to admit, the way Tess left the question hanging in the air until it had all but faded. Only when the merest ghost of it remained did she respond.

'Rescued?' she queried. 'At the right price it can.' And there was an undisguised toughness about her voice that explained in full why the rest of the family deferred to her.

'Any reasonable offer . . .' Ann answered vaguely.

It was the usual pat reply, trotted out on all such occasions. Meanwhile she was asking herself why she had ever thought these people would be a pushover. For on consideration it wasn't only Tess who was tough. It was the whole family unit. In their own peculiar way they were quite a formidable proposition. Ann could see that now. Tess was the leader, yes, the decision maker, but her real force derived as much from the others as from her own strength of personality. From that lump of a husband who, Ann felt instinctively, would have supported her no matter what; from the two boys whose eyes flew as readily to hers as birds to their nest. And from the girl? Did she also support the mother? With her silence perhaps? No. Definitely and finally, she was out of it. Dead wood in an otherwise healthy . . .

Ann's thoughts were interrupted by Tess.

'Depends what you mean by "reasonable".' She pushed disdainfully at a heap of rubble with her toe. 'Personally, I wouldn't say this property's in a *reasonable* condition. Would you?'

Touché! Ann thought with a flash of wry humour.

Never let the agent get the upper hand. And she was about to answer in kind — to remind Tess of what the house *did* have to offer — when something about this semi-underground room made her pause. It wasn't simply its gloominess. That was easily fixed by clearing away the growth from the windows. There was something else, a closed-in, oppressive feeling. Or was it possible that she had picked up the vibes from the girl? *She* certainly had an oppressive look about her; her face oddly brooding and at the same time empty, as though she were locked inside her own skull.

Ann shook her head, rejecting such dark imaginings, and surprised herself by giving a truthful answer — a rare occurrence, she observed with another flash of wry humour.

'If I owned this place, I'd snap up any offer that was even half reasonable.'

She had a moment's misgiving. Could that, by any stretch of the imagination, be called representing the best interests of the vendor? But then who the hell was the vendor? Some faceless nobody up in Queensland who had discarded his relatives long before the accident, at a time when they'd probably needed him most. So what did she owe to him? Or to this family either, come to that? Not that there was any going back on what she'd said, for already she'd felt them close ranks; seen the silent nod pass from Tess to ... what was his name? Doug? that was it ... and on to the elder son.

'If you'll excuse us for a few minutes,' Tess said formally, and the three of them trooped upstairs.

So, a sale! Or half a sale after she'd shared the proceeds with the original agent. She had a strong suspicion he wasn't going to be too impressed by the offer, but he'd probably try and push it through, thankful to get rid of the place. Memories were long in country areas, even this close to Sydney, and nobody wanted this sort of listing.

In the meantime, she reminded herself, this wasn't a family you could rush, no matter how desperate they might seem. Better to let them take their time, and she sat down on the bottom step, trying to ignore the chaos all about her.

It didn't appear to bother the girl, she observed. Not at first anyway. Mary, they called her. So innocent sounding. She was standing in the very darkest corner, over by the inner wall, her face tipped upwards, eyes closed, as though listening. To what? Voices in her head? Unseen spirits hidden somewhere amongst all this rubble? Whatever she could hear troubled her suddenly because her face twitched and her forehead creased into a frown. Her lips formed themselves into a silent 'Oh!' of distress that brought the boy quickly to her side. Taking her hands in his, he began whispering intently to her, the words indistinguishable, but the tone gentle, soothing; an all-is-well kind of murmur that even an infant would have been able to understand. The two of them so close together, so private, that on impulse Ann rose silently and stole into the protective shadow of the stairs.

She was glad she had. A few seconds later, and for no apparent reason — some forbidden word spoken by the boy maybe — Mary clutched at her thigh and then lunged at him, teeth bared. He must have been ready for her, forewarned somehow, because he leaped back in time, the small white teeth flashing harmlessly past his jaw. But he was off balance, stumbling and then falling onto a heap of smashed timber and glass. When he stood up his hand was bleeding. He held the whole arm away from his body while he groped unsuccessfully in his pocket for a handkerchief, several full red drops splashing down onto a bare patch of floor.

'It's all right,' Ann heard him whisper gently to the girl, who had grown dull again, her eyes open but unseeing. 'No one's going to be angry. I promise. Just wait here for me, I'll be back in a minute.' And without spotting Ann, who had shrunk back further into the shadows, he ran up the stairs.

Ann was on the point of following him when the girl came abruptly alive. That was the only way Ann could think to describe what happened to her. Her face lost its empty mask-like quality, her shoulders straightened, and a new tension flowed into her limbs. From being listless, almost somnolent, she grew into someone purposeful, someone filled with a restless, nameless energy. And all within a few seconds. Working hurriedly, kicking and scraping at the rubble, she cleared a larger space around the bloody patch on the floor. That done, she glanced swiftly, warily, towards the top of the stairs, and then began to dance.

Again that was the only word Ann could think of — dance — the only word that fitted. A dance that was more animal than human, and more primal than either.

A series of prancing leaps and sudden pounces that were unnerving to watch; that conveyed a weirdly religious fervour, carrying Mary round and round the bloodstain in an ever-diminishing circle — the pallor of her face, her bare arms and legs, shimmering like cool fire in what little light struggled in through the high-set windows.

Ann Guthrie didn't wait for the end of the dance. The moment Mary's back was turned, she emerged from her hiding place and fled upstairs to the comparative sanity of shredded mattresses and wildly slashed upholstery and curtains.

*

Had she lingered just a little longer, she would have seen how the circle of the dance closed in upon itself and touched its own centre. One final, telling pounce and it was all but over, with Mary crouched and still, her cheek pressed to the floor a mere tongue's-flicker from the bloodstain. Opening her lips, she pushed her tongue out once ... twice ... three times, gathering in the bloody drops, until the floor was clean, a moist patch of bare concrete in the midst of chaos. Slowly she straightened up and swallowed, her eyes closed in what could have been an ecstasy of joy or pain. Then, a final action before stepping clear of the circle, she let out a wolfish cry, a summoning bark almost, soft and low enough to be contained by the ill-lit room.

She looked around when she had finished, head half-bowed in submission, as though awaiting the approval of some unseen watcher whom she knew to be there.

And if there *had* been such a watcher? Morbidly fascinated eyes peering at her through the gloom? Someone other than ourselves, looking in on the forbidden secrets of her life? What would such a person have made of her strange performance? How would it have appeared? As a beginning perhaps? As a first tentative step into the most profound darkness of them all?

Perhaps.

6

Slow footsteps along the passage woke her. Tess rolled over and squinted at the clock in the half light.

'Is that you, Mary?' she called.

No answer, which meant it must have been Mary. Oh well, at least she was wandering around and not just sitting in one place with a blank look in her eyes. That was an improvement, surely.

Tess settled herself comfortably, all further prospect of sleep gone. Now that she came to think of it, quite a lot of things had shown signs of improvement since they'd decided to move here. Not that she was over-fond of the house itself. It was too . . . too what? Hard to say, except she didn't feel altogether easy with it, as though it were trying to intrude upon her instead of just being passive, a place to live in, like their other house back in Sydney.

That aside, there was no disputing how good the house had been for them. Mary's bouts of violence had grown less frequent from the day of their initial visit; and since actually moving in, she'd become far more active and alert. Restless even, the way she prowled around the house at all times of the day and night, working off some of her natural sixteen-year-old energy. Yes, all in all, it had been worth the effort of shifting up here.

And had it really been so much of an effort anyway? With a smile, Tess recalled the real estate agent's face when she'd opened the front door for that first inspection. Her expression had said it all. Disaster! Not fit to be lived in! When she should have seen at a glance that the damage was only superficial; that whoever had smashed up the place had been more interested in the contents, in the things that touch people personally, than in the house itself. People, that's who the unknown vandal had wanted to get back at, not bricks and mortar.

Tess smiled again, the firm lines of her face softened by the early morning twilight. Thanks to the agent's incompetence, they'd managed to settle for a rock-bottom price. The kind of price you paid for a wreck, whereas this house had needed very little fixing.

How long had it taken? Two days for the garbage contractor to clear out the debris; six or seven days for Doug and Bob to replace the doors and frames and some of the fittings in the kitchen and bathroom; and several days more for someone to sand and seal the floors and make other incidental repairs.

While that was going on, she had seen to the workshop herself, cleaning the main windows across the front and cutting back the bushes outside. What a difference it had made. A transformation! So much fresh spring light flooding in. She had almost resented the electrician's insistence that they install strip lighting for overcast days.

Altogether, then, no more than two weeks to make the house presentable. Why, setting up the workshop had taken longer than that. Of course there was plenty left to do. The jungle of growth flanking the house, for instance, that would have to be seen to eventually; and she was looking forward to changing the interior colour-scheme. But all in good time. They'd only moved in a few days ago; and as Doug pointed out, in a house as modern as this (surprisingly, he seemed to think it was only five to ten years old), it wasn't likely to . . .

The jangle of the alarm broke off her train of thought. Doug stirred beside her, groaning softly as he slowly surfaced.

'Take an extra five minutes while I see to the kids,' she whispered in his ear, and slipped out of bed.

Because Harry had to catch the early bus to school, she went first to his room.

'Time to get moving, love,' she said, kissing him.

He woke with a rush, like her, the sleep clearing from his eyes even as he sat up. 'I had this dream,' he said thickly, and ran a hand through his hair. 'There was a dog that wouldn't stop barking. I could hear it going on and on.'

A dog? Barking in the distance? Hadn't she also . . . ? No. She shook her head, blaming it on dark imaginings.

'I think we'll all be plagued by dreams for a while,' she said. 'It's natural enough after what happened. You mustn't let them get to you.'

'It wasn't scary or anything,' he explained. 'It was just there, this noise in the background.'

'And I'm just here in the foreground, telling you to

hurry up,' she replied, making light of it. 'What's more, I *am* scary, so get a move on.'

She went next to Bob's room, but didn't knock because she could hear him moving around inside. No need to wake Mary either, she thought, remembering the footsteps in the passage earlier, and was walking back past Mary's half-open door when something caught her eye. The pale glow of the bedside light, still on.

'Mary?' she called softly, and poked her head around the door.

The room was empty, the curtains drawn, the bed unslept in.

'Mary!' she repeated, in a louder, panicky voice, and ran through the house checking every room.

'What's going on?' Doug and Bob were trying to push past each other in the narrow passage as Tess emerged from the basement.

'It's Mary. She didn't sleep in her bed last night. She's disappeared! She could be miles away by . . . !' Tess paused, collecting herself. 'Wait a minute, I heard her round about dawn. How long ago is that? An hour? An hour and a half? She couldn't have got too far.'

Bob, who was already dressed, made a dash for the front door. 'I'll take the ute and check the highway,' he yelled back.

Doug, flustered and puffy-eyed from sleep, blundered back into the bedroom for his clothes. Tess didn't wait for him or Harry. Grabbing a coat and a pair of slip-on shoes, she ran down the front steps just as Bob drove off.

The morning was cool, the sun not yet showing above

the trees. Beyond the drive, a small patch of rank grass glistened with dew. Where . . . ? she asked herself frantically. And then saw the two sets of tracks: dark, parallel lines that curved away through the dewy grass. Two? She didn't stop to think about that. She was already running down the slope, the wet grass cold against her bare ankles.

The tracks petered out beneath the trees, but by then she was sure of where they were leading: over towards the willows and she-oaks that lined the creek. Drawing her coat about her, she hurried through the early morning shadows, with sharp arrows of sunlight flickering across her face and uncombed hair. The creek, luckily, was low. Three . . . four splashing footsteps and she was across and labouring up the opposite slope.

Here the trees had been cleared, giving way to an open paddock, the short-cropped grass already dry and free of tracks. At the top of the slope she could see two houses: a big old-fashioned wooden homestead with a green-painted roof; and a little lower down, a much smaller dwelling.

She was out of breath by the time she reached the main house. Close up, it looked almost dilapidated — the verandas rickety, the paint peeling off, the spouting rusted through — yet someone obviously lived there because a plume of smoke rose lazily from the kitchen chimney. Tess ran around to the back section and hammered urgently on what had once been a glass-panelled door — most of the gaps now patched with pieces of rough-sawn timber.

From inside there came a shuffle of footsteps, and the

door was opened by a woman in her fifties or thereabouts. She had a mop of unruly hair that half hid her face, and she was wearing a grubby chenille dressing gown, stained across the front.

'Yes . . . ?' She pulled a lock of hair aside, to reveal watery grey eyes; eyes that had a veiled, untrusting look about them.

'It's my daughter,' Tess explained. 'Have you seen her around here this morning? A girl of sixteen? Short . . . small for her age.'

'Lost, is she?' the woman asked.

'Yes. She left the house an hour or two ago and may have come this way.'

'Sixteen, d'you say?' the woman queried sceptically. 'That's a bit old for gettin' lost, in broad daylight and all. Unless she's . . .' — she tapped her temple with one finger — 'you know, on the slow side.'

Tess was about to make a hot denial, but changed her mind. 'Not really slow. Just confused. She won't talk and . . .' She gave up her hasty attempt at explanation. 'Listen, we live next door, in the house across the creek, and it's important that I find her. Has she been over here at all?'

The woman pondered the question for a few moments. 'From the new house, are you?' she said at last, her voice giving nothing away. 'Related to that last lot, I suppose.'

'No, we have nothing to do with the previous people,' Tess answered impatiently. 'We never knew them. And all I'm interested in at the moment is my daughter. Where she could have got to.'

'Yeah, these youngsters are a worry,' the woman agreed conversationally. 'Always disappearin' somewhere or other. Our Kev's the same. We wake up one mornin' and he's gone, and that's the last we see of him for months. Till he runs out of money and work, an' then he's back again, touchin' us for a few dollars. My Ted, he reckons . . .'

'Look, thanks for your help,' Tess broke in, and was about to turn away when the woman raised one hand as if something had occurred to her.

'Now you come to mention it,' she said thoughtfully, 'there could've been someone about earlier, because I heard the dog. Usually he's with us, but when Kev shows up he takes him over to . . .'

'Dog?' Tess interrupted her again. 'You have a dog?'

'That's what I'm trying to tell you,' the woman went on evenly. 'He's with Kev right now, down at the shack. An' he was really goin' at it earlier, like there was a possum in the roof or somethin'. Or it could have been your daughter, I s'pose. Anyways, he woke us both with his noise.'

As if summoned by her mention of the dog, there was a series of ringing barks directly behind Tess. She swung around, startled, and found herself staring at a big Doberman. It was standing at the end of the kitchen wall, its head jerking forward at each bark, its jaws snapping at the air. Even in those first few seconds of surprise, Tess couldn't help noticing its collar: a thick band of black leather embossed with heavy studs.

'There y'are,' the woman added, as Tess stepped hastily into the doorway beside her. 'That's just how he was carryin' on. Don't mind him though, love, there's no real harm in him. He's all talk. Say boo and he'd run a mile.' To prove her point, she waved her hand dismissively. 'Go on, you bugger, get out of it!'

The animal fell silent just as a tall, heavily-built man appeared around the end of the kitchen. He was no longer very young — Tess placed him in his mid-thirties — and he was dressed in a crumpled Driza-bone, with a shotgun over one arm. Tess didn't have to be introduced to realise who he was: the same veiled, untrusting look in his eyes as in the woman's.

'This is our Kevin,' the woman said. 'An' I'm Doris Briggs, by the way. You'd be . . . ?'

'Tess . . . Tess Warner.'

'Glad to meet you, Tess.' And to her son, who hadn't so much as nodded, 'Tess here's from next door. She's lost her daughter. A little slip of a thing from what I gather, an' a bit slow up top. Doesn't talk much, is that right, Tess? Yeah, well talkin's not everything. Ted reckons there've been times when he wished I'd . . .'

Tess cut straight across Doris's ramblings. 'Have *you* seen her his morning?' she asked Kevin directly.

And he hesitated! She was sure of it! The way he knuckled his forehead, scooping the gingery hair aside, and fidgeted with his gun before answering.

'Not that I've noticed,' he mumbled vaguely. 'If she'd been hangin' around here, Rory would've heard her.' He fondled the dog's head as he mentioned his name.

'Your mother did say he was barking earlier on,' Tess pressed him.

That same brief hesitation as before. 'At a couple of

maggies, that's all. You know what the bastards are like this time of year. Dive-bombin' everyone in sight.'

Tess glanced from him to the dog and back again, and remembered the two sets of tracks curving across the dewy grass. Two! One beside the other, both heading in the same direction. His and the dog's? Who else could have made them?

'I think you're lying,' she said deliberately. 'I think you were over on my property with your dog, shortly after dawn, and that you scared her.'

'Hang on a minute . . .' Doris began, and was cut short by Kevin.

'*Your* property, lady? What would I want over there?'

He sounded too self-righteously indignant for Tess to believe him.

'You tell me, Kevin.'

'Our Kev wouldn't go near it,' Doris began again. 'Who would, after what went on . . . ?'

'I'm talking to Kevin,' Tess insisted.

'I'll tell you what, lady!' Kevin almost shouted, waving his gun and making the dog bristle. 'You can piss off from *our* property for starters! And after that you can bloody well . . . !'

'That's enough!' A scrawny-necked man, unshaven and in baggy, striped pyjamas, pushed between Tess and Doris. Although nearly a head shorter than Kevin, he shoved him roughly in the chest, and then swiped at the dog when it dared to growl. 'Shut it, d'you hear?' he warned them both.

'Christ, Dad!' Kevin protested. 'She's the one making

trouble, not me. Bargin' in here and sayin' I know where her bloody daughter is, when I don't.'

Didn't he? The evidence of those tracks through the dew was still too damning for Tess to doubt, despite his denial. So damning that she didn't care what these people thought of her, just as long as she found Mary. Whatever happened, she wasn't going to let this... this countrified thug stand in her way.

'Look, I didn't come here to complain,' she said to the older man, forcing herself to speak calmly, slowly. 'All I want is information. Kevin must have seen my daughter earlier on. I need to know where she went, where she might be. That's all.'

The man rubbed the back of his neck and gave his son a strangely accusing look. 'Yeah, well that sounds reasonable to me, Kev. So why not tell the lady what she wants to know?'

''Cause she's crazy, that's why!' Kevin answered. 'And 'cause I've already told her, I didn't see her bloody daughter!'

'I still say he's lying!' Tess said as deliberately as before, her lean face not flinching when Kevin again waved the gun in the air.

The man snatched the gun from him and turned towards the doorway. 'You better put me in the picture here, Doris.'

'Tess is from the Clements' place,' she answered shortly.

She said nothing more, yet it seemed to Tess that those few words were somehow explanation enough for the man because straight away his attitude changed.

'You the new neighbour?' he asked in a guarded voice. She nodded.

'And you've lost your daughter, you reckon?'

She nodded again. 'Early this morning.'

He drew the palm of his hand around his chin in an obviously embarrassed gesture, the thick stubble making a rasping sound. 'Well there's not much we can do for you,' he muttered, and glanced warily at his wife. 'Nor Kev neither.'

Tess turned to Doris, who was biting nervously at her thumb, and back towards Ted.

'What's going on?' she asked, genuinely bewildered. 'Why should our being neighbours change anything? And what makes you so sure Kevin hasn't seen Mary?'

Ted shrugged, no less embarrassed, both he and Doris refusing to look at her. 'Kev's right,' he said. 'You'd be better off on your side of the boundary.'

Their closed attitude, although it baffled her, served only to make her more suspicious. And also more stubborn. 'I'm not leaving till Kevin tells me what he knows,' she said, planting her feet firmly on the doorsill.

'You be careful who you're accusing,' Kevin blustered.

Ted cupped his hand around her elbow, trying to ease her from the doorway. 'On your way, love.'

'Leave me alone!' she cried, and pushed him off angrily.

'Hey! This is my place!' he warned her.

'And Mary's my daughter!' she half shouted, close to tears now — the painful bitter tears which were all she was ever capable of. 'Go on, ask him! Ask him where she's gone!'

Ted had a firmer hold on her arm, but again she broke free.

'Come on,' he muttered, his face turned away as if he were ashamed of what he was doing. 'We've had enough of this.'

In the background, Kevin was grinning slyly to himself, one thick, work-hardened hand fondling the dog's ears.

'But he *knows*, I tell you!' she yelled, unable to control her tears any longer. 'He and the dog were on the far side of the creek. I saw their tracks.'

Ted had manoeuvred himself so that he stood between her accusing finger and his son. 'This is none of our business,' he told her quietly. 'It never has been. Not now, nor before.'

'Before?'

'Leave her to me, Dad,' Kevin said with a laugh. 'Me and Rory'll soon see her off.' And he flicked the dog on the rump, urging him forward.

That was more than Tess could bear. 'You bastard!' she cried, her long-held resentment of Terror centring on this dog before her now — determined in that moment of blind anger to kill the animal if she could.

And all at once she and Ted were struggling desperately for possession of the gun, their faces only centimetres apart as they pushed and shoved at each other, their hands clasped around the barrel and the trigger-guard.

'Let go, you silly cow!' Ted panted, pulling so hard that he almost broke her grip.

She tightened her hold, and with a deafening report

the gun went off, the recoil tearing it from their combined grasp. They both staggered back, too white-faced and shaken to do or say anything. The others were equally silent. Doris had covered her eyes with the grubby flap of her dressing gown; and even Kevin had shied away, one arm raised protectively. Rory, after letting out a frightened whimper, turned and scampered off.

In the ensuing hush there was a sound of approaching footsteps and Harry, badly out of breath, dashed around the side of the kitchen.

'We've . . . found her,' he gasped. 'Down in the . . . the workshop . . . behind the benches . . . Dad said I must . . . must come and . . . and tell you.'

'Thank God for that!' Tess burst out, her initial relief overriding any feelings of embarrassment for all the trouble she'd caused here.

And oddly, in those first moments following Harry's news, she gained the distinct impression that Ted and Doris were almost as relieved as she was.

*

'I feel so ashamed of myself,' Tess confessed.

She was sitting in the kitchen of the old homestead, a room as dilapidated as the rest of the building, with a sagging floor, cracked paint on the walls, and flowers of damp and mildew blossoming on the low ceiling. Really, she considered, looking about her, it was little more than a hovel; a place hardly fit to live in. So why did she need to feel so . . . ?

No, she recognised that attitude for what it was — snobbery — and rejected it out of hand. What she'd done had been inexcusable, never mind this house or the fact that she still didn't like Kevin. He'd gone off in search of the dog, thank goodness, and left her with his parents. Tess, too, would have been happy to leave and to take her sense of shame with her, but Doris had insisted that she stay for a cup of tea. 'To steady you off', was how she'd put it.

Now Doris was bustling over from the old wood stove, a steaming kettle in both hands. 'Don't go losin' any sleep on our account, love,' she said, pouring boiling water into the teapot. 'We all make mistakes. An' when it's your own flesh and blood that you're frettin' about, well . . .'

'Dot's right,' Ted agreed, nodding vigorously. 'Don't give it another thought.'

He was still wearing his pyjama top, but in response to Doris's earlier demand to 'make yourself decent, why doncha', he'd buttoned it up high around his skinny throat and pulled on a pair of work trousers.

'You're both very kind,' Tess said. 'Though the truth is, I shouldn't have been so hasty. You see there were these two sets of tracks through the dew, leading in this direction, and when I saw Kevin and the dog, I couldn't help . . .'

'It's only natural,' Ted butted in. 'Considerin' what you've told us about your girl — you know, how she's scared of dogs and a bit on the slow side — what else were you supposed to think? If y'ask me, anyone in your position would've jumped to the same conclusion.'

'Specially if they lived on a property like that one,' Doris added darkly.

'Doris!' Ted growled by way of warning.

She drew a lock of grey hair over her eyes, as though hiding from his disapproval. 'Well it's true, isn't it?' she muttered. 'A place like that'd make a saint suspicious. Look at what it did to the Clements.'

'There's a world of difference between the Clements and their bloody land,' Ted pointed out.

'Says you,' she answered with a sniff.

'What Dot's trying to say,' Ted explained diplomatically, 'is that the Clements weren't the luckiest people around.'

'I'm saying no such thing,' Doris corrected him. 'It's the property I'm talking about. That's where it all started and finished.'

'Where *what* all started and finished?' Tess asked, curious.

Doris took her time before answering. She first poured three mugs of tea and pushed one across the old pine table to Tess.

'Some might call it bad luck,' she said at last, 'but not me. There was more to it than that. The place itself, that's what it came down to in the end.'

Tess paused, the tea almost to her lips. 'Surely you don't believe there's some connection between how the Clements died and where they lived?' she asked incredulously. 'From what I heard, it was just an ordinary car accident.'

'There was nothin' ordinary about it,' Doris came

back at her. 'A fireball, that's what they called it in the paper.'

'Yeah, a terrible business,' Ted added with a sigh. 'They come off the road down near the Richmond bridge. No one worked out why, not for sure. A bit of a curve there, but not one of them black spots you hear about. Anyway, before they could get out — whoosh! — the whole bloody lot goes up. Burned to a cinder, both of them.'

'An' when the autop-thing was done,' Doris went on, 'there was parts of . . .'

'I reckon we can spare Tess here the grisly details,' Ted broke in. 'She's already had one scare too many this mornin'.'

'No, I'm all right, really,' Tess said, sipping at her tea. 'It sounds a terrible story, but when you've never met the people involved . . . you know, it's hard to get too upset.'

'My sentiments entirely,' Ted agreed. 'Look after your own, that's what I say.'

'What I still don't understand, though,' Tess insisted, 'is what any of this has to do with the house and land.'

'Nothin' at all,' Ted said hastily, patting her shoulder. 'It's all past history. The place'll be different again with you there. A new broom sweeps clean and all that. Am I right, love?' he added, appealing to Doris.

She repeated her earlier action of hiding behind her hair. 'I know what I know, that's all,' she murmured stubbornly. 'I went over there enough, didn't I? Twice a week for more'n a couple of years.'

'Dot cleaned for the Clements at one stage,' Ted

explained. 'It was handy money for us while it lasted.'

'An' I felt it many a time,' Doris went on, 'this kind of . . . close feeling, like a storm brewin' up. You felt it too,' she added, pointing accusingly at Ted, 'so don't say you didn't.'

'Not in the *old* house I didn't,' Ted responded.

'Old house?' Tess asked.

'The one that burned down,' Ted said quickly. 'About seven, maybe eight years ago. Nice old wooden place, and in good nick. A sight better than this. No, there was nothin' wrong with that. A happy sort of house, that's how I'd describe it.'

'Maybe so,' Doris conceded. 'But what about after? When they built the new house? Don't tell me you were happy about the place then?'

'Oh, come on, Doris,' he protested. 'I hardly went over there. The Clements only kept you on for another coupla months at the most.'

'You went there enough to know what I'm talkin' about,' she pressed him.

'Yeah, well . . .' He hooked a finger into his collar uncomfortably. 'It wasn't the same, I'll grant you that much.'

'An' not just the house,' she continued, oddly relentless in her quiet way. 'You said yourself you didn't like crossin' the creek.'

'Nor did I,' he admitted. 'Yeah, that's when their run of bad luck started — when they lost the old house. Mind you, that's all it was,' he said emphatically, 'bad luck and nothin' else. So don't give me any more of that stuff about storms brewin' up and all the rest. D'you hear me, Doris? The bad feeling came from them, not from the property. And that's the last word on the subject.'

There was an uncomfortable silence during which the couple glared at each other across the table — Ted with his thumbs hooked self-righteously into his braces; Doris gazing out through a fringe of hair with her untrusting eyes.

Tess put down her empty mug. 'Well I'll tell you something,' she said light-heartedly, trying to ease the tension. 'Regardless of what happened to the Clements, that property's going to be *good* luck for us. I can feel it in my bones.'

'I'm sure you're right, love,' Doris said non-committally, and carried the mugs over to the sink.

Tess stood up and only then, with the worry of the morning behind her, did she realise how she must look — her hair uncombed, her nightdress barely reaching to the middle of her thighs, and to top it all off, Doug's old parka hanging down around her like a half-collapsed tent. And to think she'd been snobbish enough to object to the run-down appearance of this room! She reddened at the memory.

'Just look at me!' she said, laughing. 'You must think a family of derros have moved in next door.'

Which reminded her: sometime she must ask Doris and Ted about the derro who'd wrecked the house while it was empty. But not now. It was time she got back.

'You look fine to us, Tess,' Ted said, laughing with

her. 'I'm no bloody oil painting meself. And that dressing gown of Dot's . . . what would you say about that? Out of one of those Vogue magazines, maybe?'

'Get away, you silly old bugger,' Doris said, giving him a good-natured shove, their recent difference forgotten. And to Tess: 'You know where we live now, so don't make yourself a stranger. There's always a cup of tea if you've got half an hour to spare.'

Tess thanked them and made her way back to the creek. As she splashed through the narrow skim of water that snaked across the sandy bed, she was mindful of what Doris had said about there being a time when Ted hadn't wanted to cross it. Well, *she* didn't feel like that. Already, despite her slight reservations about the house itself, she felt almost at home here. Peculiarly free after the close confines of inner Sydney. All this land — and it belonged to them! To her and Doug. And to the kids too. This was where Mary was going to get well, she was sure of it; here, in the peace and quiet of the bush, with space enough for her to roam in.

Tess looked appreciatively about her, aware of how much she would have liked this place when she'd been as young as Mary. Or younger come to that. The bush so thick in parts that it blocked out the sun. Perfect for hiding in, or for just being private. The kind of place you could withdraw to, without any fear of being spied on. Over there, for instance. She peered into a dense tangle of trees and undergrowth . . . and glimpsed someone in the shadows, watching her! She gave a start and looked more closely. No, it was just a trick of the light. What she had mistaken for a crouching figure was merely a tumbledown cairn of stones, the clay that had once bonded them now largely washed away.

She smiled at her own folly and moved on up the slope, trying to recapture her former sense of contentment. But that one brief moment of fright had unsettled her, leaving her vaguely uneasy. So that when she reached the strip of lawn bordering the drive, she recalled once again those twin tracks through the dew. Clearly, they had been made by Mary, not by Kevin and the dog, Rory, as she had first supposed.

Or had they?

The doubt popped into her mind, unbidden, as did the image of the dog's studded collar — a broad band of black leather that was sickeningly familiar to her.

Tess faltered at the very edge of the lawn, struggling to banish both her sudden doubt and the unwanted image. The sets of tracks, she repeated firmly to herself, had belonged to Mary. To no one else. One set showed where Mary had left the house shortly before dawn (hadn't Tess heard her footsteps in the passage?); the other showed where she had returned.

But then if that were so, what had Mary been doing out at night on her own? A girl too troubled even to talk, to voice aloud her lingering terrors. And how did she, Tess, feel about her daughter wandering around here, unprotected, in the unfriendly dark?

These were questions that Tess could not so easily push aside. Her first impulse was to resolve on locking Mary up at night. She'd speak to Doug and they'd make sure Mary stayed indoors from now on, where no harm could possibly befall her. Except Mary wasn't a child, and she'd be unlikely to get well if they treated her as one. Also, locking her up would defeat their main purpose in moving here, which was to give Mary space and freedom, to ensure she wasn't shut away in any sense. If they policed all her comings and goings, they'd merely be exchanging one kind of imprisonment for another. Wouldn't they?

Tess hurried across the lawn and drive as though trying to leave all such questions behind. But about halfway up the front steps she couldn't resist the temptation to turn and look out over the property. The areas of bush, she noticed unexpectedly, didn't grow quite as haphazardly as she had supposed. (Why hadn't she spotted that before?) Rather, they hugged the boundaries and any dips in the land, effectively preventing anyone looking in from outside. What's more, although dense, most of the growth wasn't particularly high. A good deal of it may well have been planted recently. Ten years ago perhaps? Or even less. Say, seven or eight years, which dated back to when, according to Ted, the old house had burned down. Had all this been done since the fire then, she wondered; had the Clements, for unfathomable reasons of their own, decided to turn the place into a kind of . . . ?

She baulked at the word 'fortress', refusing even to consider it, conscious all at once of how far her imagination and her anxieties had led her.

'Nonsense!' she said aloud, and with a rueful smile, her natural confidence restored, she called out cheerfully that she was 'home' as she re-entered the house.

7

Tess was disturbed twice in the course of the night. The first time when Bob came home late. She heard his ute cruise cautiously up the drive, a sound followed soon afterwards by the click of the front door and the whisper of his bare feet along the passage. She imagined him creeping past their room, shoes in hand, so as not to wake her or Doug, and was swept by a wave of fondness for him.

Lying there in the dark, listening to his furtive movements, she considered how like Doug he was. The same big gentle body, the same quiet thoughtfulness, the same total dependability. It was right that he and Doug now worked together; it made sense in a world which, according to Tess, was not particularly sensible or even sane most of the time.

Why, even she was capable of a kind of madness. She saw no point in pretending otherwise. Like most other people she was subject to sudden crazy impulses, moments of insanity when everything flew out of kilter and right and wrong didn't seem to matter any more; when she acted as though she were God, able to make up the rules as it suited her.

That incident over at the Briggs' sprang instantly to mind. She and Ted wrestling for possession of the gun; pushing and grunting like a couple of crazed animals. And if she'd managed to wrest it from him? What then? Would she, in the heat of the moment, have used it? Have shot Rory? Or even Kevin? She stiffened at the prospect, her body registering an unsettling mixture of dread and desire.

Reluctantly, listening to the house creak in the gathering coolness of the night, conscious of her family all about her, she had to admit that if Bob took after Doug, then Harry was temperamentally closer to her. He shared her volatility, her tendency, at moments of crisis, to step abruptly from the known path, out into the waiting dark. Like that night he'd crept secretly from the house in order to sift through the smouldering ashes of the kennel. Tess recalled with a shudder how he must have eased the collar over what was left of the dog's head, because the buckle had still been fastened when she had seen it lying there on the bedroom floor. She could hardly pretend *that* had been a normal thing for him to do, and yet she knew in her heart that she might well have done the same if the idea had occurred to her — if she had thought it would help Mary.

And what of Mary? There had been a time when Tess had half believed that in spite of her daughter's diminutive size, in spite of her froth and bubble, she was really like Doug. Tess knew better now. Under stress, something wild and fearful had broken from Mary; something Tess dimly discerned in herself. The same primitive and instinctive identity that had surfaced in the struggle for the gun; or in Harry's unholy search though the smouldering heap of charcoal and roasted flesh. Except that in Mary's case the primitive self seemed to have taken over completely.

Thoughts of Mary, plus her own wakefulness, prompted Tess to get up and make her second check of the night. (It isn't really policing her, she'd tried telling herself several nights earlier, when she'd begun this regimen, it's just ordinary motherly concern.) As silently as Bob before her, she padded down the passage and into Mary's room. The merest click, and the sudden wash of yellowish light from the bedside lamp eased her lingering anxiety. Mary was lying there in the bed, still asleep, her hair fallen softly across her face, her hands clasped beneath her chin. Exactly as she had looked when Tess had last . . .

On the point of dousing the lamp, she saw it. A suggestion of something black, alien, showing between Mary's fingers. Carefully, so as not to disturb her, Tess slid the bedclothes down past her shoulder and then, with a quick intake of breath, down almost to her waist. Nestled in the curve of Mary's body was the blackened collar, the buckle section clutched tightly, possessively, in her clasped hands.

'Jesus!' Tess moaned, and sank to her knees beside the bed, as though momentarily winded. Leaning closer to her daughter, she whispered despairingly, 'Let him go, baby. Forget about him.'

Mary didn't stir, her face closed and still, until Tess tugged gently at the collar. She made a low growling noise then, deep in her throat, and her feet twitched beneath the covers.

'Give it here, love,' Tess pleaded, and tried unfolding her fingers one by one, but Mary only tightened her hold, the growl growing into a muted snarl.

There was a rustle of movement near the door as Bob, attracted by the light, looked in on his way back from the bathroom. One glimpse of Mary's sleeping face and he was at Tess's side.

'Leave her, Mum,' he warned, ready to yank her backwards if he had to.

She released the collar unwillingly, her shoulders trembling between his hands as he led her out into the passage.

'She wouldn't have bitten me, would she?' she wailed softly.

She could no longer see his face, but his silence was answer enough. Somewhere off in the shadows the house creaked and groaned, as it often did in the cool of the night, making her jump and lift her hand to her throat, as though Mary were there, unseen, about to lunge at her.

'That damned dog!' she grated out. 'I swear to God I'd have killed it myself if I'd had the chance.'

She was still trembling, with suppressed anger now, still muttering to herself, when she groped her way back to bed. Beside her Doug slept on, but for her sleep proved elusive. On the verge of drifting off, she would hear again Mary's low growl, and the hated image of Terror would rear up before her in the darkness. Once, as she tossed and turned restlessly, the house gave another of its creaks and seconds later she heard muffled footsteps in the passage, but the tread was far too heavy for Mary and she guessed that it was Bob, creeping along to make sure she was all right. That touched her, soothed her slightly, and soon afterwards she dropped into troubled sleep.

Not surprisingly, she dreamed of Terror. He was chasing Mary, barking and leaping up at her as she ran silently from the house and down the moonlit slope towards the trees. Tess herself was unable to move, her limbs strangely nerveless. 'Get away from her!' she wanted to shout, but the words came out in an ineffectual whisper and were all but obliterated by Terror's repeated barks and yips. She could see his pale body from the bedroom window, his stubby legs pumping madly, his jaws snapping at the shadowy figure that fled before him. Then they were both swallowed by the thick line of bush, their footsteps receding until all Tess could hear was Terror's barking, somewhere off in the distance, the nagging persistence of the sound so enraging her that she surfaced with a rush.

'Wha'?' she cried in alarm, because someone was looming over her: a black shape with a knot of tousled hair and heavy hands.

'Mary's gone!' It was Doug's voice; his hands urging her awake. 'I've looked downstairs, but she's not in her usual place.'

Tess realised then that the barking wasn't restricted to her dream: it was still there in the background, a savage, staccato sound that came from lower down the hill.

She glanced at the glowing figures of the digital clock — four a.m.! — and jumped out of bed, fumbling in the dark for clothes, shoes, anything that came to hand. It didn't seem to occur to either of them that they could switch on the light. Doug, already dressed and equipped with a torch, waited for her in the doorway. On the point of following him outside, she turned and ran down to the kitchen for one of the big knives she used for chopping vegetables. The blade flashed in the brief burst of torchlight he sent in her direction.

'We don't need that,' he told her, a note of quiet disapproval in his voice.

'*I* need it!' she answered wilfully and brushed past him — one part of her mind cautioning her not to act rashly, another part urging her on, careless of the consequences.

She paused at the foot of the steps to get her bearings. A cool breeze had sprung up, making her shiver. It was swishing the tops of the trees, carrying the night sounds this way and that, so it was impossible to tell where exactly the barking was coming from. As she darted off down the slope, with Doug lumbering along behind, a bank of dappled cloud drifted across the moon, creating an uncertain, shifting pattern of dim light.

'Mary!' she called.

Doug echoed her far more loudly: 'Mary! Can you hear us?'

The barking faltered for a few seconds and began again.

They had reached the trees, which stood like a high wall of darkness before them. With the knife clutched in both hands, Tess plunged forward, slashing at whatever stood in her way. Sticky strands of spiders' web and fragments of severed leaf whispered against her bare arms, while Doug, struggling to keep up, sent the torchbeam flickering after her. Its circle of roving light faded as the moon appeared briefly between puffballs of cloud, and strengthened again moments later, picking out a ghostly lattice-work of drooping branches. She ducked beneath them and pressed on, ignoring Doug's mild curses and his plea for her to slow down. She was at the very limits of the torchbeam now, hidden from the moon by the trees' thick canopy. Confronted by an inky patch of darkness, she slashed outward and down and felt the knife blade sink into something soft, resilient — something with the quivering resistance of flesh. Simultaneously, her feet and shins crashed against something hard, rocklike, which brought her stumbling to her knees.

Doug was still struggling to get through the dense undergrowth. 'Have you found her?' he panted.

For the space of a few panicky breaths, Tess feared she had.

'The light!' she shrieked at him, dropping the knife with a clatter.

The beam, criss-crossed with hair-lines of shadow, wavered and dipped in her direction, down towards her kneeling figure, instead of higher up where she was groping blindly; where her fingers plunged into soft, sticky warmth.

Hastily, instinctively, she drew her hands towards her mouth, and tasted a salt-sweet flavour, rank and familiar.

'Higher!' she moaned, and as the beam arched upwards, uselessly spotlighting the canopy, she reached out once again, driven by dread alone.

Her fingers encountered fur this time, and a body far too small for Mary's. It swung away, pendulum-like, under the pressure of her touch.

'What on earth . . . !'

Doug was directly behind her, steadying the light on the swinging figure that eluded her groping fingers. It was a dead possum, strung from a high branch by its hind legs. It had been gutted, slit open from the anus to the throat, and judging from the bright red drops of blood that still glistened on the cut edges of fur, it had died within the hour. The top of its skull had also been opened and scoured clean, a glint of off-white bone showing where the brain had once nestled. One eye, peeking out from a fold of peeled-back fur, glistening moistly, as though alive and watching them — a fish-eye lens in which their shocked faces, caught in the wash of torchlight, appeared ghoulishly distorted.

Tess rose and stepped back in a single movement, her shoulders slamming against the solid warmth of Doug's chest. Her hands and face were both smeared with blood, but for the moment she hardly cared.

'Who the hell could have done something like this?' Doug breathed out.

For Tess is was like the last stages of her dream. The same frustrated anger swelled up in her; anger tinged now with a despair she dared not confront or even acknowledge.

'Who do you think?' she almost shouted, tears prickling at the back of her eyes. 'There was only one person out here! Unless you think that damned dog did it!'

It continued to bark, almost hysterically, as though scenting them in the darkness; and grabbing the torch from Doug, Tess headed purposefully towards the sound, only to crash once again into the stony object at her feet. Wincing from the pain, she turned the light on what she mistook at first for another possum, its bulging eyes starting up at her. She blinked hard, because instead of fur it was covered with clay.

Clay?

She blinked again and realised that she was staring at a model, a lifelike version of the poor gutted creature suspended overhead. Its eyes were clear glass marbles set into a make-believe face; and where she had blundered against it in the dark, part of its body had crumbled, revealing a core of rocks and sticks. Unlike the dead animal, it had obviously been placed there some time before — perhaps days earlier — because its outer coating of clay was dry and hard.

'Why would she . . . ?' Doug began in a mystified voice, and Tess cut him short.

'Shut up, Doug!' Her own voice matching the hysteria of the dog whose barking now seemed to fill the night. 'Just shut up and let me think!'

But think about what? The cairn of stones she had glimpsed beneath the trees the other day, on the way back from the Briggs'? Had that been the remains of another model? Or of something much bigger? In which case, why had Mary — because it had to be her, there was no one else — why had she . . . ?

As Tess's thoughts came full circle, the dog reached a howling crescendo and Tess remembered abruptly that Mary was still out there somewhere, and alone. Hurriedly, she searched the undergrowth for a glint of steel. There! She snatched at the knife and ran on, leaving Doug to catch up as best he could.

Even with the torch to light the way, she was scratched about the arms and face by the time she reached the clearing. On the far side lay a narrow fringe of bush, and beyond that — she could tell by the distinctive background shape of the willows — was the path that led to the creek. The dog had to be close now, probably somewhere in the creek-bed, because its hoarse voice reverberated on every side. She paused, hoping to spotlight it with the torch, but the moon appeared, reducing the beam to a pale circle that barely penetrated the nearer line of bush. Dousing the light altogether, she stole across the clearing and was almost to the other side when she detected a faint movement over to her left. She spun around and glimpsed a tall figure flitting silently between the tees. It disappeared before she could raise the torch, obscured as much by the fading moonlight as by the bush itself, but she had seen enough to guess who it was.

Her initial feeling was one of utter thankfulness, that it hadn't been Mary after all who had butchered the possum — a feeling followed instantly by a sense of outrage.

'Kevin, you bastard!' she cried, flinging the knife after

the departing figure and hearing it twang against one of the trees. 'You get off this property and stay off, or I won't answer for what I'll do! You'd better believe me, Kevin!'

There was a splash of footsteps in the creek, and the dog let out a final series of whooping barks that grew steadily fainter as it dashed off up the far slope. Before they faded altogether, someone else scrambled away through the shadows over to Tess's right, heading back towards the house. Again she was slow with the torch, but there was even less chance of mistaking this figure, which looked too small and slight to be anyone but Mary.

Tess didn't call out to her, didn't try to follow, mindful of how frightened she must be already.

'Run, my baby, run,' she murmured, nodding her approval as she pictured to herself the grisly remains of the possum — something that anyone in their right mind would run from.

She was searching amongst the trees for the knife when Doug emerged into the clearing.

'It was the halfwit from next door,' she explained, 'down here with his dog. That abomination back there in the bush' — she jerked her thumb in the direction of the possum — 'must be his twisted idea of hunting.'

Despite the darkness, she saw the same thankfulness in Doug's heavy-featured face as she had experienced moments earlier.

'And Mary?' he asked hopefully.

'She may be home by now. She was heading that way.

Can you check while I hang on here? Just in case she circles back.'

He half turned and hesitated. 'What are we going to do about him? Call the police?'

She shrugged. 'What's the good? It'll just be his word against ours.'

'It might scare him.'

'And it might not. Anyone who can butcher a dumb animal like that must be pretty sick. He may not be very scarable.'

He ran his thumb down a crease in his cheek. 'So what'll we do if this happens again?'

Again? She repeated the word silently to herself, recalling the cairn of stones she had seen before, hidden amongst the trees.

'This may not have been his first hunting trip,' she suggested vaguely.

'It's the next one I'm worried about.'

'There'd better not be a next one!' she said with sudden vehemence. 'If there is, we'll do something about him ourselves.'

He shook his head, and for all his size he struck her at that moment as a little boy, an innocent almost, standing lost and alone in the drifting moonlight.

'That isn't our way, Tess,' he said uneasily.

There was a break in the cloud, and she had to shield her face from the flood of silvery brightness so he wouldn't see her expression; wouldn't see how outraged she really felt. Or how worried she was by the mere idea of Mary's becoming involved with someone like Kevin.

'Is it "our way" to let that bastard walk all over us?' she responded. 'Hasn't Mary been traumatised enough already, without him coming over here with his dog? Without his sick hunting practices?'

'Well, we'll see,' he muttered, made uneasier still by the bitterness of her tone, and he pushed through the fringe of bush to the path that led up to the house.

Left alone, Tess continued to look for the knife. Yet it was not really the knife that was on her mind, and after some minutes she abandoned her search and made for the creek. Yes, there were Kevin's footprints leading straight across the damp, central portion of the sandy bed; and close beside them, on the far side, the deeper, splayed paw prints of the dog. The only odd thing about the human prints was that they'd been made by bare feet. Why, she wondered, had he taken off his shoes? Did it all tie in somehow with the slaughtered possum? Did Kevin come over to their property in order to carry out some kind of primitive hunting ritual? Had he perhaps been naked altogether, his face and body painted like a savage?

These were not pleasant thoughts, but how else could she explain his bare feet? Crouched there on the open creek bed, she peered nervously about her, examining the trees on either bank and wishing she had found the knife after all. As a precaution she switched off the torch and bent lower, so that she blended into the shadow-streaked sand. And what if she was right, she asked herself, what if he did cross the creek in order to indulge in strange hunting rituals of his own, how did the sculptured model of the possum fit in? Or that other, cruder model she had spotted days before? What had he made those for?

Partly because she felt too exposed out there in the open, but also to appease her own curiosity, she stole back across the sand and began probing the bush on either side of the path with the torch beam, working her way steadily up towards the house. It didn't take her long to find the cairn of stones, though a closer examination of it told her little. Originally, this could have been a model of almost anything: a kangaroo or wallaby, the kneeling figure of a human being, even an inanimate object like a building. Without its covering of clay, which had long since been eroded by the weather, it was impossible to identify. Only one thing was clear: it had been made by the same hand that had fashioned the possum, because the same construction method had been used — an identical mixture of sticks and rocks bound together by clay. But as to its purpose . . . ?

Tess clicked off the torch and, in the abrupt darkness, without the figure there to distract her, she remembered something. An article she had read, or a radio or television program perhaps. About some Aboriginal tribes and other hunter-gatherer peoples. How they had painted likenesses of the animals they wished to hunt in the belief that the paintings gave them power over their prey. Was that why Kevin made his sculptures? Because he believed they gave him the same magical powers?

Maybe. But true or not, as far as Tess was concerned he could practise his magical rites somewhere else. She and Doug would see to that. Yes, even soft, gentle Doug, provided she pushed him hard enough. And she would if she had to, for Mary's sake.

With that resolution made, she strode up the path to where Doug was waiting for her at the top of the front steps, his bulky figure silhouetted against the lighted doorway.

'She's down in the workshop,' he explained in a whisper.

'Why didn't you bring her back to her room?'

'She was pretty scared so I thought it better to leave her there. I've made up a bed for her on the floor.'

'On the floor?' she said impatiently, all the nervous tension of the night breaking out of her suddenly. 'She should be in a bed, for God's sake! She's not just another animal for that bastard to . . .'

The words were almost out of her mouth before she realised what she was saying — what, unconsciously, she had begun to think. Something far worse than anything they had had to cope with so far. Not just a matter of Mary being frightened by a dog. Mary being hunted down, that was the issue now. Mary as a possible prey. A *sexual* prey, maybe. In her mind's eye Tess saw her daughter fleeing before the Doberman much as she had fled, in the dream, before Terror; but now with a *naked man* padding along behind.

'What is it?' Doug asked, concerned by her desolate expression, and he put his arm comfortingly about her shoulders.

She shrugged him off. 'I want to see Mary!' she cried, and ran along the passage ahead of him.

Only one of the striplights was on in the workshop,

over near the high front windows. Mary she found lying on a mattress in the shadowy area beyond the wooden benches at the back of the room. She wasn't curled up, as Tess had expected; not closed in upon herself, which was how she usually slept. She had thrown off the rug Doug had draped over her and flattened herself against the concrete wall, as though its massive, immovable quality offered her the security she had failed to discover in the living world. Although the night was cool, a line of perspiration showed around her hairline, a speckle of tell-tale droplets that glistened in a beam of light that arrowed between the benches.

Tess drew the rug back over her. 'It's all right, love,' she murmured, stroking her hair. 'He can't hunt you now, not while you're here with us.'

'Hunt *her*?' Doug queried incredulously. 'You mean Mary?'

'Why not?'

'A possum's one thing, Tess, but a human being's . . .'

'He's a savage!' she broke in. 'If we're not careful, Mary could be his next victim.'

'Look, let's not get this thing out of perspective,' he began, but she waved his reasonableness aside.

'You saw that possum!' she said fiercely. 'What he did to it! Someone like that's capable of anything. Well so are *we*!' She paused, letting her emphasis on the word 'we' take effect. 'So are *we*!'

PART THREE

O fools, he was God, and is dead.

Algernon Charles Swinburne, 'Hymn of Man'

8

Mary liked it best behind the benches, close to the concrete wall that had no windows; the wall that closed off the inner part of the workshop, forming a solid unbroken surface except for the tall cupboard in the corner. Every few paces along the wall there were vertical lines where the separate sections of concrete met, each section fitting so tightly against the next that when she'd tried sliding a hacksaw blade into one of the gaps it had refused to go. She was pleased about that. It meant that even *he* — even Terror — couldn't get through. The wall was like a promise that the Other One had yet to keep.

The Other One. Not Terror, nor Terror's likeness whose summoning bark called regularly to her from beyond the creek. This was a different One altogether — a man of sorts — whom she heard at night, outside under the trees. Who followed her through the dark, treading where she trod, stopping when she stopped, always keeping the same distance between them. She had never seen him clearly, only as a shadowy outline, but she knew that he wore no clothes, no shoes, his whole body naked except for the painting which she glimpsed once in the moonlight. And he was big, bigger even than Bob, and as solid as the wall. The Other One and the wall, both of them there to keep her safe. Or so she hoped. So she often believed until *he* — Terror's likeness — started barking again.

It was different then. The same as it was different at the far end of the wall, where the cupboard stood. She was scared of the cupboard . . . well, not so much scared as wary. *He*, Terror, was the only one who really scared her. The cupboard was more like . . . like a weakness. Yes, that was it, a weak point in the armoury of the wall; a space *he* might force his way through one day. That was why she kept away from it, so as not to show *him* where to look. Just in case.

She stayed away from it now, crouched in the shadow of the furthermost bench. Bob was working above her — Bob, who had also made her feel safe once, though that was before, when she'd still gone to discos and to films and made the daily trip to school. She smiled at the memory, the way people smile sometimes at images of their childhood, immature experiences that they've left far behind. She'd learned so much since then. About the night especially. How it was the real time, not the day; and how it was a lie what she'd learned in church on Sundays with her family. God saw the light and thought it was good, the minister had said. But it wasn't true. Terror had taught her that. *He* called to her most nights, just to remind her *he* was still there, hidden away beyond the creek — beyond the half-open gate. Waiting. Watching to make sure she was true to *him* and all the things *he'd* taught her.

So why did she hope the Other One — the man — might be able to protect her from *him*? Because she did hope sometimes, in secret, when she thought *he* wasn't watching. It was stupid, she knew, but she couldn't help it. The same as she still couldn't help wanting to smile at Bob. Like now, as he looked over the edge of the bench and grinned down at her — Bob, the person she found it hardest to ignore because he'd been her favourite.

'You okay, Mary?' he asked in a voice that was only happy on the surface, like everything.

She knew she was expected to respond with a frown, or to show her teeth perhaps. Instead, she let her face go blank — at least that wasn't smiling — and inched a little nearer to the wall.

'What you need is a new hairdo, to cheer you up,' he suggested jokingly, and started planing a piece of wood, lifting his arms so high after each stroke that the shavings cascaded down onto her hair and shoulders. 'There you are,' he added, and his grinning face appeared over the edge of the bench once again. 'A blond wig. It suits you.'

The curled shavings had the clean fresh smell of resin, and she was tempted to thread her fingers through them, to wear them like golden rings. Then she remembered that they were only wood, dead things she could crush in her hands. Or in her teeth, exactly as *he* had shown her, with *his* jaws wrapped around the tiny skull. She put a shaving into her mouth now, and bit down hard on it, and Bob left her alone for a while after that.

She wished her mother would also leave her alone.

'She needs some contact with the outside,' she'd heard Tess telling her father one night, soon after their arrival.

Her parents had been lying in bed together and Mary crouched in the passage listening.

'I thought we were going to keep her away from other people,' Doug had objected mildly.

'I'm not talking about letting her loose amongst people,' Tess had snapped. 'Only about giving her a sense of freedom. Of getting her out and about a bit. If she ends up feeling trapped here, she might as well be on drugs or locked up in an institution.'

Her father hadn't argued back — he rarely did — and since then Tess had made a habit of taking her out in the car, far from the wall and the Other One. (Though never far from Terror. *He* was always present, waiting beyond the gate in her mind.) So now there were the weekly trips to the counsellor, and regular visits to her Gran, one of their few relatives who lived in the Sydney area.

She didn't mind the counsellor too much because she kept her distance, the fear showing in her eyes, but her Gran — Tess's mother — she didn't seem to know what fear was. Like Tess when she was angry.

Once, when her Gran insisted on giving her a welcoming hug, despite all Tess's warnings, she had fastened her teeth on the wrinkled sag of flesh beneath her chin, and her Gran hadn't even flinched.

'Bite away if it'll make you feel better, darling,' she'd said, her skinny body jerking with sly laughter. 'I don't need that flap of skin anyway.'

That was the afternoon her Gran and Tess had a row over what should be done with her.

'A counsellor?' Gran said disparagingly. 'It's a fancy word for psychiatrist, isn't it?'

'Call her what you like,' Tess responded. 'She's stood by us through all this.'

'You listen to me, Tess my girl,' Gran said, shaking a bony finger under Tess's nose. 'Hot air's all you'll get from her sort. A lot of meaningless words. What we need here is action. If Mary wants to think she's some kind of dog, then let's treat her as one and see how she likes that.'

'Meaning what?' Tess asked suspiciously.

'Reward and punishment,' Gran said. 'That's how we teach animals to behave.'

'Hit her?' Tess burst out. 'Is that what you have in mind?'

'For the punishment part of it, yes. And why not? I wasn't above giving you a clout or two when you were young. It doesn't seem to have done you much harm as far as I can see.'

While they continued to argue, Mary wandered over to the mantelpiece, where Gran kept her best doilies, the ones she'd spent months on. So much fine needlework in them that they were more patterned space than cloth.

'A sharp rap or two when it's needed most, that'll soon sort her out,' Gran was saying.

Unobserved, Mary picked up the doilies one after the other and, using her hands and teeth, ripped them into shreds. The last morsel of linen was still hanging from her mouth when Gran turned and saw her.

'You'll pay for that, my girl!' she shrieked. 'Or God'll be my judge!' And she hobbled out into the kitchen and came back with a chopping board, the kind that has a wooden extension for a handle. 'We'll see how you like a bit of tit-for-tat,' she said, and raised the board threateningly above her head.

Mary felt for the collar beneath her skirt, readying herself, but Tess stepped in between.

'Put it down, Mum,' she said.

'Do you want some too?' Gran shouted, raising the board higher.

'Go ahead if it'll make you feel better,' Tess retorted, 'but you're not hitting Mary whatever you do.'

Their two faces were so close together that their noses were almost touching, Gran's face paler than the scraps of doily littering the floor. For a few long ticks of the wooden clock on the mantelpiece, Mary thought they would attack each other, and she imagined a half-open gate and the scrabble of claws on a concrete path — the hidden truth bursting out into the open, even here, in the civilised order of this old-fashioned room. Her own mouth was stretched wide in expectation, her head thrown back, her fingers hooked in under the collar. But at the very last, when it seemed that the pause between the ticks had grown so long that the clock had stopped, Gran lowered the board and started to laugh. Tess was laughing too, her arms around Gran's neck, both of them cuddling each other. And the gate clicked closed, for then, though Mary knew it would open again if she waited.

She almost believed it had creaked ajar a little later, during that same afternoon, when Tess left the room for a few minutes. They were no sooner alone than Gran reached for the chopping board and, without warning, thwacked it hard against Mary's leg, where the collar was hidden.

'That's what you can expect from me if you act like Terror,' she said, using the forbidden name.

Mary turned and lunged, but Gran hit her again, harder still, driving her back against the table.

'There are ways and ways of showing someone you love them, my girl,' she said quietly. 'Well, this is my way, and don't you forget it.'

And here was the puzzling part: there was no anger, either in her eyes or in her voice. She was as calm as *he* had been when *he'd* smashed into the stroller; and like *him*, she could have gone on hitting and hitting if she'd wanted to. Except she didn't, which was more puzzling still.

Was this how the Other One would have acted? Mary wondered fleetingly. She didn't know; couldn't find the answer, because the Other One had never spoken to her, never whispered his truths. All he'd ever done was show her things out there in the night, statues and bloodied things she only partly understood. Whereas what Gran was showing her she didn't understand at all. To hit and then just to stop, when there was no need to? Why should Gran do that? The word 'mercy' popped into her mind, but that too made no sense any more.

Even worse, it was the very opposite of what Terror had taught her. And that was reason enough to reject Gran and her peculiar ways.

All in all, Mary preferred the weekly sessions with the counsellor. There were no raised hands, no raised voices while she was there, but at least the fear in Ruth Close's eyes was familiar, something *he* would have approved of.

She ('Call me Ruth,' she'd said the first time they met) always sat on the far side of her broad desk and insisted on Tess being present. ('As a precaution,' she'd explained nervously, and given a high laugh.) There was one other thing Mary noticed: that when she entered Ruth's office, the heavy glass penholder was always at the side of the blotter and within easy reach. Would Ruth have used it? Mary decided she wouldn't. Ruth was too frightened for that. Also, unlike Gran, Ruth never again tried saying the forbidden name of Terror aloud, not after *he* taught her that all the words were his and that some of them *he* kept greedily to himself. Such as that other name, of the little boy who had been . . .

Mary gagged and banged her head violently against the concrete wall, slamming herself backwards again and again until all idea of the name was gone.

'Hey!' Bob had left the bench and was crouched beside her, both hands twisted into her hair, holding her steady. 'What are you trying to do to yourself?'

She licked the back of his hand, to show him she was all right, which is what *he* might have done, and then closed her eyes against Bob and everything, willing herself back to Ruth Close's office.

Of all her sessions there, only one stood out clearly from the rest. The last one, when there had been so little talk. Against the darkness of her closed lids she saw the room as it had appeared to her that day. Changed. The easel in the space beside the window, where the chair usually stood; and instead of pot plants on the windowsill, a neat arrangement of paints, brushes, and water.

'I want you to do a painting for me today, Mary,' Ruth said from her place on the far side of the desk (*that* never changed), and pointed to the easel with its large pad of dazzling white paper.

Were pictures the same as words? Mary thought not, but wasn't sure. She reached out hesitantly for a brush and dipped it into the bright red. *His* colour, Terror's. She hesitated again, and then painted a thin line straight across her forehead. She took more paint and was about to continue the line round through her hair to the back of her head when it struck her that *he* might think she was trying to copy the Other One. Because the Other One used paint on his face, just like this. And quickly she grabbed a handful of tissues from the box on the desk and scrubbed her forehead clean.

'You don't have to worry,' Ruth said softly. 'It's water colour. It'll wash out easily.' And then: 'Why not try again?'

She did, but not because Ruth had asked her to.

With a fresh brush she painted a big black circle on the pad; and in the middle, in creamy yellow, a tiny square gate. It was meant for *him*, to make up for her first effort. A painting that only *he* would understand.

But Ruth was much cleverer than she'd thought. 'Is that a collar?' she asked, using another of the words *he* kept for himself.

Mary turned, but Tess was faster, stepping in between as she'd done with Gran. Mary hadn't meant to leap forward, though, not this time. She wanted to make Ruth a promise, for later; another sort of picture that Ruth wouldn't be so eager to share.

Reaching for the first brush, Mary loaded it with paint, and then flicked it hard, sending a spatter of red drops across the carpet and desk and up over Ruth.

'No, Mary!' Ruth shouted, jerking sideways, but it wasn't the paint that worried her. ('It'll wash out easily,' she'd said.) It was what it meant. The same brilliant red droplets hanging from her nose and chin, clogged in her greying hair, as those that had oozed from the possum when . . .

Mary tried not to remember that, in case *he* became jealous of what the Other One had done, out there under the trees. For if that were to happen . . . !

Again she cut the thought off, and stood up, into the hard bright light of the workshop. The windows, she was glad to discover, were almost dark — dusky mirrors in which she could see the separate sections of the wall taking shape behind her. Already her father and Bob were washing their hands in the steel sink beside the benches, their shoulders hunched together as if they were whispering, sharing secrets.

There was a clatter of footsteps on the stairs.

'Dinner's ready,' Harry sang out in his high, thin voice. 'Mum says for you to come straight away or she's going on strike.'

Mary was the first one to the stairs. Harry didn't step away when she paused beside him and stared down at the cupboard in the corner. (*Her* secret.) No matter what she did to Harry, and she'd tried, she couldn't make him look at her the way Ruth did. In fear. With her parents and Bob, and even with Gran, it was more or less understandable. They were adults, they really thought they knew about everything. Until recently they'd sat in church on Sundays and listened and listened as though it were all true. But Harry, he was just a kid, years younger than her, still making up his mind about so many things, the way she'd had to on that day the gate had been left open. And yet she'd never once been able to strike a spark of fear in Harry's eyes, not even when she'd attacked him down there in the workroom and he'd cut his hand.

What did it mean, Harry's lack of fear? That some of what she'd learned outside the gate in the deceptively bright sunlight wasn't true? She trembled at her own audacity, and Harry reached out to steady her. She shook his hand away. Could it be ... the doubt also arose because of the Other One, because of what had happened last night under the trees ... could it be that Terror wasn't as all-powerful as *he* pretended? No! She mustn't let herself think that either, despite last night, and with a nervous glance at the darkening windows she hurried up to the kitchen where the round table was already set and the air was heavy with the comforting smell of food.

She would have liked to eat alone, out by the front step, but they wouldn't let her — much as they wouldn't let her wear the collar on her neck where it belonged. Maybe that was why, when the meal was served up and they were all seated at the table, she found she wasn't as hungry as she'd expected. Or maybe it was her memory of that other taste, warm and raw in the windy dark, that made her change her mind. For after the first few mouthfuls she lost all interest in eating, content to push her food around her plate, making patterns with it. Two pieces of meat for the eyes and another for the nose; a long scythe-shaped wedge of pumpkin for the mouth; a potato cut into two sharp points to represent the . . .

Bob must have been watching her out of the corner of his eye because he whisked her plate up hastily and emptied it onto his. No one else objected, which probably meant they'd also been watching. There was a long silence, and she felt their relief when she finally stood up and walked down the passage to the front door.

Her father's voice rumbled after her. 'Don't go wandering far now, sweetheart.'

Now? She agreed. It wasn't time yet. She always knew when it was time by the way the house creaked and moved, as though stirring awake in the cool stillness of the night. For now, she was happy to sit on the steps while the darkness slowly thickened. She didn't even mind when Harry sat beside her and took her hand. Of them all, he was the only one who didn't try to talk to her; who didn't try to catch her out with unforeseen questions in the hope that eventually she'd forget herself and answer.

Her hand resting listlessly in his, she gazed at the distant twinkle of Sydney's lights which peeped through the tops of the trees. Lower down there was nothing, a black swathe that even the moon, when it rose, would barely be able to penetrate.

That was how it had been last night, with stray shafts of moonlight piercing the canopy, creating tiny pools of silvery white in the blackness; pools that dimmed and glowed alternately as the moon raced through the wimpled clouds. She let her mind drift back there, lured by a strange feeling of longing, the same nameless longing that had tempted her from the house in the early hours.

Taking care to keep her face sternly impassive so as to reveal nothing to Harry, she re-enacted those events in imagined detail. The turning of the lock on the front door; the soundless flight down the steps and across the drive; the dry swish of grass against her ankles as she made for the trees. No warning bark as yet from the creek. Did that mean *he* was asleep? Was *he* ever? It was too much to ask for, she was aware of that. Glad only of the silence, of this brief delay, she ran on, resolved not to look around until she was standing beneath the outer fringe of the canopy.

The uncertain moonlight, as much as the darkness itself, made it difficult for her to pick him out. The Other One. Carefully, she searched the area to the side of the house, the long curve of the drive. Her eyes swung back as she sensed rather than actually saw him near the lower end of the lawn. A shadow amongst shadows, standing at a point where the path led down towards the creek. His naked outline seemingly as tall and sombre as the surrounding trees. She took a faltering step deeper into the bush, and he moved in unison with her. Another step and another, and a flickering shaft of silver showed her the painted pattern on his forehead and cheek. In the returning dark he was a shadow again, but she knew now that he was intent upon her, his face turned diligently in her direction.

She willed him then to follow her. Allowed herself that one moment of transgression. And straight away, from over near the creek, the barking started, as she had guessed it must.

In vain she tightened the collar about her throat. It was too late for that. Even with the buckle biting into her skin, choking her, still the barking continued. Running did no good either. *His* insistent barks pursued her as she fought the dark, crashing her way down the long, overgrown slope.

Scratched, dishevelled, sobbing for breath, she burst into a tiny, crystal-lit clearing. The brightness lasted only for a few seconds, just long enough to reveal the possum hanging from the tree by its legs. It was struggling to break free, curving its body upwards and clawing at the branch above; while a second possum, crouched amongst the gum litter, observed its plight with uncanny stillness. A ruffle of cloud rode against the moon, and as the dark rushed back, she turned and spied the Other One there behind her, the same distance away as before, his face covered by a spray of leaves. She could not go to him — dared not — and could not venture closer to the creek either, because the barking was too loud, too harsh to be a summons. Caught between hope and dread, she jumped for the inner, lower section of the branch that held the possum and climbed towards the chinks of pale sky.

Wedged between two swaying limbs, she listened past the barking and the murmur of the wind to the Other One's footsteps below. They stopped directly beneath her. Now she could hear the possum struggling frantically; hear its rasping hiss as it warned off the intruder. For a minute or more after that nothing happened, as though the Other One, like her, were waiting for the moon. It broke free of the restricting cloud and in a brief deluge of light she saw the knife flash once, twice; and the possum, its last hiss cut short, quivered and went slack, its stubby front paws folded against its chin in an attitude of prayer.

Yes, prayer! There was no mistake.

She could hardly believe what came next. It was like walking up to the open gate for the first time, not knowing what to expect. In spasms of silver clarity, she glimpsed the disembowelling — the way the Other One's head plunged towards the open wound and ripped and ripped until nothing was left inside. Hidden by dark, a shadow only, the head plunged lower still. There was a grinding, crunching noise, of teeth meeting with resistance and then breaking through. And when the moon returned, the possum's skull was a bluish-black hollow streaked with white.

'O Lord, how great ...' she prayed silently, and quickly rebuked herself for blasphemy.

But had she been quick enough? Could Terror have heard her? Or was it just the scent of blood drifting on the wind? Because over by the creek the barking grew louder. There were other voices too — her parents calling from up near the house. The wind dropped slightly, and in the lull she heard them descending the slope, crashing through the heavy bush. She looked down, to where the Other One had stepped clear of the gutted possum, his face lost in shadow, his shoulders hunched and shivering with expectation. Deliberately, he raised his hand to the dead animal in what she could only describe as a blessing. Then, with a swift tip of the head, as if inviting her to follow, he moved off into the gloom.

Mary slid to the ground. Did she dare go after him? Amazingly, the path the Other One had taken would lead them both closer to the barking, which had risen to an almost hysterical pitch. And if she stayed where she was? Her parents weren't far off now, her father pleading with Tess to slow down. Ten, maybe twenty seconds more, that's all she had.

Undecided, flustered, she was caught in yet another burst of moonlight. The limp body of the possum materialised from the shadows only centimetres from her face. She could see the gaping wound, the black drops of blood clinging to the cut edges of the fur. And on impulse she leaned forward and licked at them, sank her teeth into the pale inner flesh. Who had she done that for? The Other One? Or Terror? She was too confused to make up her mind. The crash of footsteps was right there behind her, and before the light faded she had slipped away.

There was no sign of the Other One when she reached the big clearing. She crossed it at a run and hid in a thick cluster of trees, listening to how the barking rose in pitch and rose again. So much rage in the sound that she flattened herself against the earth and stopped her breath, her eyes tight shut.

When she next peeked out, her mother was standing in the moonlit clearing and the Other One was running between the trees, heading towards the creek. *Towards* it! Her mother screamed out after him and something ricocheted off a branch and landed right beside Mary's hand. A knife. She could have picked it up if she'd wanted to, if she hadn't been so busy listening. Kevin, her mother had called him, but that couldn't be the Other One's real name or else she wouldn't have had the courage to use it. He had reached the creek, Mary could tell that from the barking which had risen to a state of frenzy. Now! she thought. Now! And again she clenched her eyes shut, waiting for what she knew *he* — Terror or *his* likeness — would do.

Except it didn't happen! The impossible occurred instead. The barking changed its note, became almost mournful, and rapidly began to fade. *He* was the one who was retreating! Terror! Mary felt as if a gate had closed in her mind and another one (a different one) had opened. A bubble of laughter welled up from deep inside her, and before it could break free and expose her to the unforgiving eyes of the night, she scrambled to her feet and made a frantic dash for the house.

A full day later, as she sat beside Harry on the front steps with the light from indoors washing around them, that same laughter again threatened to erupt into the outer dark.

'What's funny, Med?' Harry asked, and gently squeezed her hand.

Funny? She frowned and shook her head, forcing the laughter back down. Not for the first time that day, she cautioned herself against the danger of hope. The Other One couldn't possibly make the barking go away again, least of all forever. He couldn't take the words as Terror had done and keep them for himself. For himself alone. He could never replace Terror and become the master of the dance.

Could he?

9

Mary felt the bed sag as her father leaned over her and brushed the hair from her forehead.

'Stay where you belong tonight, sweetheart,' he whispered, the words more an expression of a personal wish than anything else.

She was careful not to let her eyes move in case the lids quivered and showed him she wasn't asleep.

'Rest and get better,' he breathed softly, and stood up with a sigh.

Had he gone? She peered out through finely slitted eyes and saw him standing above her, his shoulders slumped, his face buried in his hands. He sighed again, running his hands down his cheeks in a gesture that bordered on defeat, and shuffled from the room.

She didn't move. She waited, listening, her eyes staring up past the glow of the lamp. Outside the wind had dropped, replaced by an even whirr of insect noise. Nothing but that for a full hour, and another, before the house creaked and settled. A sigh as audible in its way as her father's, but with no underlying sense of defeat.

She rose stealthily from the bed then, as though the

house itself had beckoned to her. Dutifully, she wound the collar about her neck and buckled it closed. In confirmation of her action, a high-pitched bark sounded from beyond the creek, as yet faint and distant.

Barefoot, still in her nightdress, she padded out into the darkened passage and was confronted by Harry. He wasn't spying on her. His hair rumpled, his eyes only half open, he was groping his way along to the bathroom. He came fully awake at the sight of her, his pale, narrow face shocked into alertness.

'Where're you off to, Med?' he asked — whispered it to her as though it were a secret between the two of them.

She tried to push past him, but he wound his arms about her. His hair and pyjamas smelled of sleep. Closing her teeth on the loose skin of his cheek did no good. He flinched, but continued to hold on until she started to tremble, her teeth, her shoulders, her resistant hands shuddering with distress.

'At least let me come with you,' he pleaded and, loosening his hold, he stumbled after her as she flitted down the passage.

She could hear him on the steps behind her — his hissed plea that she should wait — but she was across the drive and heading for the trees at a run. The grass, in the absence of wind, was damp and clinging, cool on her bare feet and shiny in the moonlight. The barking sounded closer now, coming every three or four strides, as though urging her on.

'Med!' A last desperate plea from Harry and she had reached the cover of the bush.

The moon, almost at the full, cut bright slivers from the dark. She threaded her way between them, ducking and scrambling on all fours when she needed to, allowing the natural slope of the land to guide her — that and the faint smell which grew stronger the further she went.

Harry was far behind when she stopped to get her bearings. Quick, the barking seemed to be telling her, find it, find it — the repeated sound a kind of dance in itself. She closed her eyes and felt herself to be alone, no hectically painted face watching her from the shadows. No suggestion anywhere of the Other One. That was a disappointment, but one she was mentally prepared for. The vital issue was the dance. She knew that: knew from harsh experience how it must always attend upon the dead, like a ritual acknowledgment (*His!* Terror's!) of the nature of things.

Eyes still firmly closed, deprived even of the distraction of the moon, she turned her head slowly, her nostrils flared and quivering, seeking out the source of the smell. There! She was sure of it, further down and a little to her right.

She stole forward (Find it! Find it! *his* barking instructed her from over near the creek, momentarily blotting out all thought of the Other One — who had failed her, hadn't he?) and spied the tiny moonlit glade directly ahead.

'Where are you?' Harry's muted cry was barely audible through the barrier of thick bush.

She dismissed him with a toss of the head and entered the glade; stumbled against the rock-hard possum which gazed at her with it marble eyes. She recovered and looked up. Something was missing. She groped above her head for the rope; found the end of it, frayed and slack . . .

Slack? But the smell . . . !

One of the shadows beyond the glade moved imperceptibly and the carcass of the dead possum landed with a thud at her feet. As she started back, there was a gurgle of laughter and the shadow became the tall shape of the Other One, circling slowly about the glade.

She crouched lower, confused. Was the Other One dancing? Was he claiming the carcass for himself after all? She couldn't see him clearly enough to be sure; couldn't even make out the shape of his head and body. There were too many trees in between, and he remained a blurry presence that chuckled unpleasantly, circling in a way that made her feel trapped, as if she were the victim in the ring.

She? Had he lured her here for this? So that she could share . . . share the possum's . . . ?

She broke free with a single, desperate leap that carried her out of the glade and through the moon-streaked dark. She came upon a pool of intense black where she huddled, quivering with fright. Listening. His footsteps followed her . . . strayed to the left . . . strayed to the right . . . stopped. He no longer walked silently, carefully, as he had on the previous night, but with a boldness that horrified her. His laughter probed the gloom, seeking her out.

She bent lower, compressing herself into the smallest possible space, her face squashed into her lap. Go away, she prayed silently. Prayed! As the possum had done — her hands wedged together beneath her chin — and with as little expectation of mercy. Although she tried not to, she found herself recalling how the Other One's head had plunged down onto the carcass and ripped and ripped, and her whole body stiffened and shrank in upon itself even further.

'Please . . .' she prayed, to *him* now, who was barking frenetically on the far side of the willows.

Had *he* heard her? Was that the splash of *his* short, stocky body surging through the shallow water of the creek? The barking did seem to be growing louder. But if so, why did the Other One go on laughing? Why did his footsteps continue to probe the area all about her hiding place?

A piercing whistle rang out, and the barking rose to a long, responsive howl that ended, unaccountably, in a startled yelp. Of surprise only? Of pain? It was followed by a sharp yip-yip-yip of distress, so loud and protracted that she could hear nothing else until it died to a frightened whimper and then to nothing, and the even whirr of insect noise flowed back into the emptiness.

She hadn't meant to move, but she was on her feet, her hands still clasped in an attitude of prayer. The barking wasn't all that had stopped: so had the laughter. Where was the Other One? She turned slowly, stiffly, terrified at what she might find. The space all about her was deserted. No one moved. Nothing crossed the shafts of bright moonlight that sliced through the gloom. She blinked nervously in the light, realising how exposed she must be, and sank down, sucking in her breath in anticipation. Yet no hand, no rope, reached for her, no knife flashed from the undergrowth.

On hands and knees she crawled from cover out to where she could peer upwards and glimpse the almost-round disc of the moon glowing between black clusters of leaves. Were they playing with her, she wondered, *he* and the Other One? She crawled on, passing silently through the banded night until she came to the limits of the thick bush ... and saw it! The freshly constructed figure at the edge of the big clearing. It was arranged half in, half out of the moonlight, its head and recumbent body still slick with wet clay.

She did not think to question its identity. The prick-ears, the jutting muzzle, the strip of black about the neck left no room for doubt. But why had the Other One fashioned *him*? *Him*, of all the beings in the world? For this was surely the Other One's doing: it had the same lifelike quality as the sculpture in the glade — the make-believe possum, placed there in order to ... in order ...

The truth dawned on her slowly, the audacity of it making her draw back into the deep shadow where she could see without being seen; where she could study Terror's awesome likeness more minutely. No, she was not mistaken. The gleaming body lay stony still; the marble eyes, that stared glassily into vacant space, had a deathly look about them; the head, leaner and shorter than she remembered, was too fixed in position ever again to grasp the world in its jaws and shake it into submission. Like that other sculpture, which had been a prelude to the possum's death, the meaning of this one was all too clear.

But Terror! Could *he* truly be silenced? *His* existence snuffed out as if *he* were no more than a creature of flesh and blood? An animal in a world of animals?

The answer could be glimpsed in that glassy stare. And for the moment she was so overcome that she forgot her own dread. A distant gate seemed to click shut, and in the first flood of incredulous joy she almost cried out, almost snatched back the words *he* had taken from her. What choked off her cry was the memory of the Other One's recent laughter, of his cruel intent as he had circled her in the glade or ripped the brain from the skull of the possum.

Reluctantly the gate in her mind creaked open again, and a tall, upright shadow seemed to fall across the opening.

'O Lord, how great . . .' she intoned silently.

The order of the words, the words themselves, belonged to the Other One now. They were his by right. By might. He had made them his own. To show that she acknowledged his mastery, she rose from the bushes and exposed herself to the moonlight. With trembling fingers, she undid the buckle at her neck and tossed the collar behind her. The rest was up to him. There was little to be gained from hiding. Anyone who could fashion Terror's likeness, who could decide to silence *him*, could not be avoided for long.

'For thine is the kingdom, the power, and . . .'

Head bowed, hands pressed together beneath her

chin once more, she waited for the sound of his laughter; for the trees to divide at the far edge of the clearing and for the Other One to step forward, his naked chest streaked and splashed with gouts of black.

'For thine is the kingdom . . . For thine . . .'

Whole minutes had passed and still there was no sign of him; not a hint of laughter. Could it be . . . ? She had to cut off the thought before it possessed her.

'For thine is the . . .'

The idea forced itself back through the lengthening silence. Could it be that the Other One had placed this clay figure here for her? As a gift? A sign of what was to come? Of what was possible? As part of a pact in which she could share?

'For thine is the . . .'

He had laughed at her, it was true, but he had also tossed the dead possum at her feet. Had she misunderstood that gesture? Had he meant not to threaten her, but simply to say, 'Here, take it, it's yours?'

Mine? she thought, staring in stunned disbelief at Terror's sculptured likeness. This too?

All at once she let out a gurgle of soft laughter and hugged herself with both arms, her hands clutching at her shoulders in secret delight. Rocking to and fro, she searched her mind for some means of showing her gratitude. How? Yes, of course, the obvious way.

Somewhere in the background Harry began calling again. 'Med? Where are you, Med?' Without a light to guide him, he was floundering in the bush, beating a slow path towards her.

Plenty of time, she thought, and walked unhurriedly

across the clearing to the recently completed figure. From the direction of the creek there came a series of faint whimpers, a cowed, beaten sound. She paused, a tiny tic of doubt reflected in the sudden turn of her head, in the widening of her eyes. But the renewed silence reassured her — the phrase, 'It is finished', jostling in her mind with the words, 'Thy will be done'.

Crouching where the Other One had crouched, she ran her hands across the slick wet surface of the model and then wiped them on her face, her hair, the bare skin above her nightdress. She did that several times, until her face was a pale, inhuman mask and her hair hung down in clotted tendrils. The low hum of insect song seemed to swell out around her; the splash and drag of someone wading slowly along the creek bed provided a rhythm of sorts; and in time to that rhythm she began to move.

*

Some minutes later, when Harry stumbled from the bush, he was confronted by the sight of Mary, head and shoulders encrusted in clay, dancing around some kind of stone effigy. There was a sense of carefree abandon about her, her outflung arms making wide circles as she leaped and spun in the moonlight. She broke into quiet laughter when he caught hold of her — the first real laughter he had heard from her in weeks — and she smeared her clayey hands almost lovingly against his cheeks.

'What's going on, Med?' he asked with a grin, infected by her gaiety.

She took him by the hands and whirled him around in the moonlight, and for a second or two he half-expected her to answer. She opened her mouth and a wordless sound came out — 'Aargh' — unmistakably joyful.

Her mood altered only slightly when he tried to coax her up to the house. She frowned and broke free long enough to make a last spinning circuit of the clearing, as though completing some pre-arranged dance. Then, laughing again, and without a backward glance, she allowed herself to be led away.

When they reached the drive, Tess was just emerging from the front door, her hair and face rumpled from sleep. She looked wildly from one to the other and sat down hard on the top step, a hand pressed to her throat.

'Don't worry, it's not as bad as it looks,' Harry assured her, and wiped some of the clay from Mary's face.

Mary squirmed and laughed, as if he'd tickled her.

'What *is* that stuff?' Tess asked shakily, and came down to meet them.

'Clay,' he explained. 'She'd made a . . .' — he hesitated — 'a kind of dog. That's what it looked like anyway. She was dancing round it.'

'Dancing?'

'Yeah, really enjoying herself. Honest, Mum, you should have seen her. Happier than she's been for ages.'

'Dancing?' Tess said again, not quite taking in the idea.

To show her what he meant, he pushed Mary gently towards the moonlit lawn. 'Go on, Med, dance for us.'

Her feet shuffled, her arms rose, and with a radiant expression on her face she began to spin and twirl. Her eyes, veiled by shadow, darted towards the dark line of trees where she was sure he was watching.

'What's got into her?' Tess asked wonderingly.

'Who knows?' Harry said, joining in Mary's high laughter. 'Who cares as long as she stays like this?'

Between them they managed to get her into the house where she woke the rest of the family by dancing along the passage.

'It's like a miracle,' Tess said to Doug and Bob as they emerged sleepily from their rooms. 'This is how she was when Harry found her. Down there near the creek. Dancing round — you're not going to believe this, Doug — round the clay figure of a dog. A dog!'

Doug caught Mary as she passed and held her warmly. 'Have you come back to us, sweetheart?'

She made the same wordless sound as before — 'Aargh' — and slipped clear of his arms, dried flakes of clay falling from her face and hair as she moved away.

'Hey, Mary, disco time,' Bob said, spinning with her from one open doorway to the next.

Harry, jigging up and down on the front step, suddenly began to clap his hands and sing:

> Who's afraid of the big bad wolf,
> > The big bad wolf,
> > The big bad . . . ?

'Calm down, all of you,' Tess broke in, smiling happily. 'We'll have plenty of time to celebrate tomorrow. In case you haven't noticed, it's the middle of the night. Let me get Mary cleaned up and off to bed. Come on,' she cautioned Harry who was threatening to burst into song again. 'I know you're glad. We all are. But that's enough for now.'

'Leave it, bro,' Bob advised him, and wound a friendly arm around Harry's neck. 'Mum's right. It's cot-time for all of us, Mary included. Isn't that so, Mary?' he said, addressing her directly in the hope that she would answer.

She had stopped dancing and was standing still in the middle of the passage, unexpectedly docile, her head cocked to one side as though she were listening.

'What is it, love?' Tess asked her. 'Can you hear something?'

'Maybe it's the dog,' Harry suggested. 'It was barking earlier on. That's why I followed her.'

'If she is getting better,' Tess said tersely, 'it's no thanks to that damned animal. I'm getting on to Doris about it again in the morning.'

That was the only uneasy note struck that night, and not enough in itself to mar the general sense of well-being. Ten minutes later, Mary had showered and was safely back in bed, and the rest of the family were settling to sleep. Tess even relaxed to the extent of pushing down the off button on her alarm.

So that when Mary crept from the house shortly before dawn, nobody heard her, and no one woke when she tiptoed back along the passage in the first grey light. Bob, because his room was closest to the bathroom, turned restlessly as the insistent drumming of the shower broke in upon him, but in his drowsy state he thought it was rain on the roof, and he buried his head in the pillow and sank back to sleep.

As the sun rose, stealing between the cracks in the curtains, the only evidence that Mary had been out again that night was a faint blush of rusty stain in the farthest corner of the shower cubicle, where the jet barely reached.

PART FOUR

O the mind, mind has mountains; cliffs of fall
Frightful, sheer, no-man-fathomed.

Gerard Manley Hopkins

10

The Briggs were finishing their breakfast when the phone rang.

'That'll be her again,' Doris said.

Ted sipped unhurriedly at his second cup of tea. 'Why d'you say that?'

'Kev let the dog out again last night. I heard it.'

'Who'd have bloody kids?' he observed philosophically. 'Anyways, it's your turn to speak to her. I had an earful yesterday.'

Doris blinked hard several times. 'Do I have to, Ted?'

'Suit yourself. She can ring all day as far as I'm concerned. Kev's the one should be talkin' to her, not us.'

The phone jangled on in the dingy kitchen, harshly insistent.

'She'll know we're here,' Doris muttered unhappily. 'Where else would we be this time of day?'

'And we know where she is too,' Ted replied, unconcerned. 'What's so wonderful about that?'

'Well, it's not right, is it? Hidin' away in our own home, pretendin' we're not here, when it's a neighbour on the phone.'

Ted put down his cup with a crash. 'Look, Doris, if it

worries you so much, answer the bloody thing yourself. I've told you. I did my bit yesterday. From here on she can try knocking on Kev's door. I'm sick and tired of speaking for him.'

With a 'humph' of mild disapproval, Doris reached over to the dresser and lifted the receiver. 'Ye-e-s . . . ? Oh, it's you, Tess . . . No, no bother, I was at the front of the house, that's all.'

Ted, cup in hand again, gazing out of the grimy window as though the call were no business of his, heard the note in Doris's voice change from defensive to friendly, all within the space of a few seconds.

'Course I will, Tess . . . No worries . . . I'll give you a ring back soon as I've . . . Oh, at your place, that'll be nice . . . Yes . . . See you then.'

Doris replaced the receiver with a flourish. 'Couldn't have been friendlier if she'd tried,' she told Ted triumphantly.

'The wind must have shifted,' he said, and gave a loud sniff. 'She's all mood, that one.'

'Not with me she's not. You just don't know how to handle her. All she wants is a bit of reassurance, like the rest of us. So I told her I'd have a word with Kev. No harm in doing that.'

Ted lit a cigarette and blew a cloud of smoke up at the bare overhead bulb. 'Maybe it's the blokes she doesn't like,' he suggested, and scratched the lean of his belly through his pyjamas. 'Have you thought about that possibility? We don't hear much from Mr bloody Warner, do we? It's always her on the phone, moanin' about Kev and carryin' on about that daughter of hers.

All the girls stickin' together, if you see what I mean. That'd explain why you two get on, you bein' a woman and all.'

Doris wasn't usually given to sarcasm, but for once she couldn't resist it. 'I'm surprised you even notice these days. I might as well be another bloke for all the interest *you* show.'

'That's not fair, Doris,' he protested, and reached across the table, trying to take hold of her, but she slid her chair back and stood up.

'If it's fair you're interested in,' she said, and crooked her thumb at the sinkful of dirty dishes, 'you can try your hand at those.' And before he could answer, she swept out of the kitchen.

Alone in the bedroom, changing, she continued to mutter to herself about Ted and men in general. Kev's another one, she thought irritably, dragging a comb through her lank hair. He hardly lifted a finger around the place, coming and going as he pleased, as if he was on one of those holiday farms. Always the same, ever since he'd been a kid, expecting her to fetch and carry for him at every turn. Like now. Well this time he was in for a shock. She'd covered for him enough in the past, when the Clements had been over there. But not any more. If he wanted to go sticky-beaking while God-fearing people were asleep in their beds, then he could answer for himself or find another apron to hide behind. She'd tell him so once and for all.

In that slightly belligerent frame of mind, Doris left the house and made her way to the shack further down the hill. What she saw there only served to strengthen her resolve: the kitchen chimney cold and smokeless, the woodpile all but used up, and, to crown it all, the shotgun left outside, rusting away in the dew.

'Like father, like son,' she murmured bitterly as she knocked on the door.

There was no answer, and when she tried the handle it was locked. Locked! As if they had to worry about burglars right out here. Especially with Rory to look after the place. Which reminded her, where was Rory?

She knocked more loudly, slamming the flat of her hand against the unpainted wood and expecting Rory to set up a din inside; but all she heard was a slow shuffle of feet and a chain being slipped free. (Had it come to *chains* now, for goodness' sake!) Kev, puffy-eyed and unshaven, squinted out at her.

'Yeah?'

She pushed him aside and marched straight down the narrow passage. The merest sideways glance into the bedroom was more than enough, thank you. And the living-room-cum-kitchen! The state of it! It made her own kitchen look like one of those pictures out of Ideal Homes, and that was saying something.

'It beats me how you can live like this,' she said. 'You, a grown man and all.'

'Aw, give us a break, Mum,' he complained, and flopped down in the old armchair that was leaking discoloured scraps of stuffing. Even with one hand half shielding his face from the uncurtained window, she could see how terrible he looked. His eyes bloodshot and weary, as if he'd been up most of the night.

'A break?' she replied tartly. 'That's what I need from

the likes of you and your father. Two days I spent putting this place in order when you took off last time. And by the looks of it now, you're about ready to do another of your disappearin' acts. Well lend Rory a pair of your overalls before you go. I reckon he'll make a better job of housekeeping than you. Though that's not saying much.'

Mentioning Rory made her wonder for the second time where he'd got to. She was about to ask when she noticed how Kevin had raised his other hand guiltily to his face.

'You were with him last night, weren't you?' she said accusingly. 'You didn't just forget to lock him up. You took him over there. Isn't that right?'

'What are you going on about?' he said, peering sulkily between his fingers. 'I was asleep, wasn't I? Same as you?'

'Don't give me that,' she replied, and pulled his hands away from his face. It was what she'd always done when he'd tried lying to her as a boy. 'You've started all that peepin' Tom stuff, haven't you? The way you did with the last lot.'

She saw him hesitate — a sure sign he was guilty — before deciding to own up.

'What if I have? You were the one who got me interested in the place, remember, with all your gossip about the Clements. You can't blame me for wanting to have a look for myself.'

He pushed her aside and went to the fridge, where he took out a carton of milk, sniffed warily at it, and dropped it into the overflowing waste-bin.

'We're not talking about the Clements,' she reminded him. 'They're dead and gone, God help us. We're on about the Warners now, and for the life of me I can't see why you have to go spying on *them*.'

'Can't you?' He had spun around, looking like a boy again in his grubby T-shirt and shorts, despite his bleary face. 'Then I'll tell you. Because they're as weird as the other mob. That girl, you should see what she gets up to after dark. Crazy things. Dancin' half naked in the . . .'

'Half naked?' she interrupted. 'So that's what this is all about. The girl! I might have known. The same as last time, creepin' around in the middle of the night, spyin' on a girl only half your age. Don't you ever learn?'

Again he gave himself away by glancing wistfully at the window, as though wishing himself out of there. 'It's not like that,' he said sullenly, refusing to meet her eyes.

'Jesus, Kevin! This one's not even right in the head. She can't even string a few words together. What's got into you?'

'I told you, that's not how it is. I was just . . . you know . . . sort of curious. If you saw what she . . .'

'I'm not interested in what she does,' she cut in impatiently. 'And nor should you be. You're scarin' the livin' daylights out of the poor girl, d'you know that? You should have heard Tess Warner goin' on at your father yesterday. Damn near set the phone alight she did, and with good reason. Leave the girl alone, boy, for your own good.'

He nodded, turned completely away from her now,

his shoulders hunched, his arms crossed, his hands tucked defensively into his armpits. 'Yeah . . .' he agreed grudgingly. 'Yeah . . . awright.'

'An' while you're about it,' she added for good measure, 'make sure you keep Rory inside at night. Understand?'

He didn't move, didn't respond at all, his silhouette reminding her of some black paper cutouts he'd brought home from school years before — rows of little faceless men that he'd strung across the kitchen window.

'Where's Rory got to, by the way?' she asked, doing her best to sound casual.

His silhouette remained unnaturally still. 'Round the place somewhere.'

Doris had a sudden sense of misgiving, though she couldn't have said why. She swept a heap of soiled clothing from the nearest chair and sat down, all her earlier belligerence drained away. 'Where is he, Kev?' she asked quietly.

He shrugged, his face still turned from her. 'He ran off last night.'

'Ran off where?'

He shrugged again. 'Dunno.'

'You mean he could be out there chasin' sheep in someone's paddock?'

'Rory's no sheep killer. He's all noise.'

'You've lived in the country your whole life, boy. You know every dog's a sheep killer given the chance.'

He took another half step closer to the window, his shoulders hunched a little higher, excluding her. 'Yeah, well . . .'

Doris stood up helplessly. 'For your sake, let's hope he shows soon and there's no harm done. If there is . . . if your father gets to hear of it . . .' She left the rest unsaid and was moving towards the passage when he called her back.

'Mum. There's no dead sheep. Honest.'

She paused in the doorway. 'Where's Rory then?'

He didn't reply.

'What are you up to, Kev?'

He clung stubbornly to his silence. Out of what? Fear? Shame? She couldn't tell with the light behind him, blotting out his expression.

'You better listen to me for once,' she advised him. 'Right now I'm on my way to see Tess Warner. I'd like to tell her Rory won't be botherin' that girl of hers no more. I can tell her that, can't I?'

The dark outline of his head moved slightly in what she hoped was a nod.

'I'm warning you, Kev,' she went on, 'there'll be no more excuses from me and your Dad after this. We're washing our hands of you. Any more trouble from Rory, any more of that peepin' Tom stuff, and you can answer to the Warners yourself. You got that?'

He shuffled his bare feet uncomfortably. 'Yeah, I got it.'

'I hope to God you have.'

This time he didn't call after her until she was almost at the front door.

'Hey, Mum. Watch out for the girl while you're over there.'

'Watch out how? What're you talking about?'

'Just watch out, that's all. Don't let her get too close to you or nothin'.'

Close? She wondered sometimes what went on in that mind of his.

'It's you that's been gettin' too close,' she shouted back. 'Do yourself a favour and stay on this side of the creek.'

She shut the door firmly behind her and stepped out into a day that had clouded over. As she walked across the hillside, a suggestion of misty rain brushed cool against her cheeks and beaded her hair. The country could do with a good soaking, she thought when she reached the creek, which was lower than she'd seen it for a while. All the pools had dried up and only a thin snake of water remained. The wide banks of sand, scuffed by the wind and left high and dry for weeks, were mainly featureless except for where a margin of damp preserved a loose scattering of footprints. Here were Kev's, she noticed; and there, a little further along, were Rory's, a confused batch of them, as though he'd danced excitedly at the water's edge for some time before crossing.

As she bent to take off her sandals, she automatically searched the farther bank. Yes, that was where Rory must have splashed from the water, his prints splayed and deep, which meant he'd been lunging hard. Although they soon petered out, she could see the line he'd taken, up towards . . . She shielded her eyes from the strengthening rain in order to see more clearly. In the shadow of one of the willows, half hidden by trailing branches and more or less where Rory would have left the creek bed, there was a deep gouge in the sand. At least that's what it looked like from where she was standing. A hole of some kind, stained brown along part of the rim (or was that just a darker portion of shadow?), and with a blackish piece of driftwood sticking up.

She splashed through the creek, intending to take a closer look, but a gust of wind brought a brief shower that scored the sand all around her. She turned towards the upper end of the valley and saw how descending cloud had blotted out the skyline. Should she shelter under the willows or make a run for it? If she stayed, she might have a long wait because the cloud was dark and angry. She pulled on her sandals, undecided, and the wind and rain slackened temporarily. It was too good an opportunity to miss, and in the unexpected lull, everything else forgotten, she made a dash for the path.

The rain just beat her to the top of the hill, soaking the front of her dress before she could scramble up the steps of the house. She hadn't run so hard in years and she felt quite faint as she sheltered under the eaves trying to catch her breath. Beyond the thumping beat of her own heart she could hear a woman singing, a purely happy sound that made her feel worn and dowdy. Inarticulate childlike laughter rang through the house, accompanied by deeper, male tones. Happy families, she thought with a sudden lurch of envy, and then remembered the Clements in order to steady herself before knocking.

Tess came skipping down the passage — skipping was

how it sounded to Doris anyway, a light, quick patter of footsteps — and when she opened the door she looked strangely young and carefree, almost girlish, though she couldn't have been all that much younger than Doris.

'You poor thing, you're soaked!' she burst out and, before Doris could protest, she led her into the nearest bedroom and insisted she change into something dry. 'Here, these should do,' she said, flinging a loose-fitting skirt and blouse onto the bed, and pressing a thick bath towel into her hands. 'Just come through to the kitchen when you're ready.'

Alone, Doris looked about her. The room seemed full of mirrors and, as she changed, there was no way she could escape from her initial bedraggled appearance or from this new self that emerged like a slightly tawdry moth from its chrysalis. In freshly laundered cotton clothes and in those surroundings, she felt herself to be a fraud; and for the first time in years she noticed what a mess her hair was — unwashed, uncared for, unloved.

She opened the door and looked straight across the passage into the living room. Signs of money everywhere. No — she corrected herself — it was more than just money. Good taste, a sense of what colours and things to put together, that was what gave these rooms their special feeling. The kitchen was the same, a dazzle of varnished wood and clean surfaces that so impressed her that to begin with she hardly noticed the ring of faces turned in her direction. All she could think of was how her own kitchen must have appeared to someone like Tess: hardly more than a dingy cave. As with her hair and down-at-heel sandals, the mere idea of it made her feel ashamed and out of place.

Her former envy returned with a sickly rush, and this time remembering about the Clements didn't help at all. She really believed she would have turned tail and run if it hadn't been for the big burly man who stepped into the space between her and the door and beamed down at her.

'This is my husband, Doug,' Tess said, and touched his arm possessively.

She shook his hand and was immediately aware of how rough her own hand felt compared with his, the skin of his palm a strange mixture of hard and soft. He must have read her expression because he laughed aloud, a gentle rumble that only made the envy worse, something she could almost taste, as bitter and unproductive as her life.

'It's the wood,' he said. 'That's what it does to your hands.'

'Wood?' She was conscious of blinking nervously, but couldn't stop. She reached up to pull her hair across her face and had to force her arm back down.

'If you work long enough with it,' he explained, 'your skin and the wood start to feel the same.' He took a wooden pepper grinder from the table and pressed it into her hand. 'See what I mean?'

'It's lovely,' she murmured, and suspected that she sounded overawed and stupid.

'Keep it,' he said.

'Oh, I couldn't possibly . . .'

'No, go on, it's yours. We make them from our off-cuts. For fun. They cost us nothing.'

She held the pepper grinder to her breast, hating him and warming to him for his generosity and kindness; half resenting him for his easy, affectionate manner.

'. . . Harry you've already met,' Tess was saying, 'but not Bob.'

The same burly frame, the face younger, that was all; the same smooth-hard touch when he took her hand.

'And this,' Tess paused fractionally as though unable to contain her feelings, 'this is our Mary.'

Our? A prettyish girl of . . . How old had Tess said? She looked about sixteen, in spite of being so tiny. Even smaller than the Clement girl, Doris decided. A young woman really, which explained why Kev came sneaking over here at night. (That boy! Man! Doris wasn't sure what to call him any more.)

Mary didn't offer to shake hands like the rest. In answer to Doris's muttered 'G'day', she let out a high, wordless trill of laughter, her face not so much empty as closed upon itself, inward looking.

Doris knew she should have felt sorry for her — for the whole family because of her — but somehow she couldn't. The laugh had been too . . . too happy. Relieved. As if the girl had discovered something fresh and unexpected and was still revelling in the newness of it all, her obscure joy overflowing onto all those around her.

Tess, meanwhile, had cleared a place at the table and was bustling about the kitchen, offering Doris tea, coffee.

'We were just celebrating,' she explained obscurely. 'That's why we're so late.'

'If you'll excuse us . . .' The two men lumbered to their feet.

'Nice to meet you.' The boy shouldered a school bag and clattered off down the passage.

With another of her laughs and a dancing twirl, Mary was gone, and Doris was alone at the table with Tess.

'Celebrating?' she asked, puzzled.

Tess laughed, a sound nothing like the daughter's high trill of secret joy. 'It's a long story, but we've been under a lot of strain lately. Over Mary. And last night . . . what can I say? . . . she took a turn for the better. You must have noticed how happy she is. We all think she's starting to find her way back from . . . from wherever she was. It's hard to explain because you didn't see her before, but . . . but she's changed, that's all I can say. All the cold rage that was in her, it's gone. All the . . .' She dabbed at her eyes with a tissue and laughed again. 'Anyway, that's why we were celebrating. Maybe relaxing together would be a better way of putting it, for the first time in weeks and weeks. I can't begin to explain how it feels. To have had Mary scared for so long, and then for all the fear simply to go away — it's like . . . like a reprieve.'

Reprieve. Doris considered the word and decided that on balance it also described Mary's distinctive laugh.

'So she's not scared of the dog no more?' she asked carefully.

'I hope not,' Tess said. 'On the other hand we don't

want to take any chances. That's why I rang you again this morning. Just in case.'

Doris sipped thoughtfully at her coffee. 'An' it was only the dog that was botherin' her?'

'Yes, what else?'

'No, just askin'.' Doris waved the question aside, saw how grubby her fingernails were, and quickly snatched her hand down to her lap. 'You see, I had a chat with Kev this mornin'. He came over for breakfast. Like old times it was.' She blushed at her own lie, and the bitter taste was back in her mouth as she recalled the ring of bright faces that had greeted her when she'd stepped into this kitchen. 'He sounded real worried after I told him about your girl,' she plunged on. 'Reckons he'll make sure Rory stays in of nights from now on. His word on it. That's what he said to tell you. His word.'

There was a faint whirr as some kind of machine started up downstairs, and a few seconds later, the softer, almost furtive click of a door closing somewhere in the house. Or was it opening perhaps? Distracted by the sound, listening hard, Doris caught only the gist of what Tess was saying.

'. . . thank him . . . appreciate his help . . . I'm sorry . . . on the phone yesterday . . . terrible state . . .'

'Think nothin' of it,' she said a little too hurriedly, and finished her coffee in two noisy gulps, suddenly eager to leave this house that seemed to threaten her in more ways than one. 'Now it's time I was . . .'

'Oh, before you go,' Tess broke in, and Doris sank reluctantly back onto her chair, 'there's something I've been meaning to ask you. It slipped my mind the other day when you and Ted were being so kind to me.'

Ted? Kind? Doris's hand tightened guiltily on the silky-smooth curve of the pepper grinder.

'Ask away, love.'

'It's about the house, while it was empty. After the Clements were ... after their accident. Did you see anyone over here?'

'Anyone?'

Doris made her face go blank, a mask behind which she was furiously calculating. How many weeks ago? How many months? And how long since Kev ... ? Since she'd gone out one morning and seen smoke curling from the chimney of the shack? Had it been earlier? Later? That damned kid!

'No one in particular,' Tess answered. 'I just wondered if you saw any signs of life. You know, lighted windows at night, anything like that.'

'Why d'you ask?' Doris's voice sounded guarded even to herself, but Tess seemed not to notice.

'Well the house was smashed up inside when we bought it. Vandalised, that's the only word to describe the state it was in. And the estate agent — not the one we dealt with — said he'd had to kick out some old derro who'd taken up residence. I'm curious, that's all. I thought you might have seen him.'

'Him?' Doris had to collect herself. 'As you know, Tess, I've always found this an unlucky house. So I wasn't likely to come here sticky-beakin', was I?'

'Oh, I wasn't implying that,' Tess said, and reached over to pat her arm. 'It's just that after what you told me about working here and knowing the house and everything, I thought . . .'

'No,' Doris cut in decisively, 'I didn't see a soul. How could I? Visitin' a neighbour's one thing; goin' where you're not invited is somethin' else entirely. And as I say, this house has never been a favourite with me. Beggin' your pardon, Tess, but that's the way I feel. There's too much bad luck clingin' to it, what with Denny and . . .'

Damn! She hadn't meant to say that. She'd been so busy worrying about Kev (bloody Kev, who could never leave well enough alone!) that it had slipped out. She made another half-hearted attempt to stand up, hoping the name had passed unnoticed, then saw the question in Tess's eyes and sank back again.

'Denny was the Clements' kid,' she explained wearily. 'She was trapped in the old house when it burned down.'

'I didn't realise they'd had any . . .' Tess began. And then: 'Trapped? You mean she died?'

Doris felt herself hesitate but managed to hide it with a cough. 'Yeah, and the sweetest tempered kid you'd hope to meet. That's the pity of it. A little slip of a thing, not unlike your Mary to look at, and about the same age.'

Jesus! Why couldn't she keep her mouth shut? What was to be gained by digging it up all over again? They deserved a bit of peace after what they'd been through.

'Like Mary?' Some of Tess's lightness of spirit left her briefly, and Doris glimpsed the stressed, strung-out woman who had come knocking at their door in the early morning. 'And you say she was burned to death. Burned!' The full import of the situation seemed to hit her all at once. 'The daughter *and* the parents! All killed by fire!'

'Years apart, but,' Doris pointed out.

'Yes, but all killed by fire just the same! What a terrible story! No wonder you think of this as an unlucky house.'

'On'y for some,' Doris said by way of appeasement.

'I suppose so . . .' Tess didn't sound at all sure as she sat there fraying a paper napkin between her fingers, the torn fragments fluttering down unnoticed onto her lap. With a visible effort she managed to smile, and with the smile she seemed to recapture most of her former mood. 'Yes, you're right, only an unlucky house for some.' She smiled again, more confidently. 'Not for us, thank goodness. Not now that Mary's . . .' She broke off and laughed aloud. 'But you've heard all this before, Doris. And compared with what happened to the Clements . . . Those poor people!' Her face clouded and cleared almost instantly. 'Compared with them, our worries are nothing. All in all, we're very lucky people.'

Doris used the opportunity to stand up. 'Yeah, well there's always someone worse off than yourself,' she observed, and the sharp metallic taste of discontent and envy settled beneath her tongue again. She tried to deny it, to tell herself that she wouldn't swap places with Tess for the world, but the taste only grew stronger as she walked back through the freshly decorated house with its fine curtains and furnishings. And stronger still when Tess refused her offer to change out of her borrowed clothes.

'Why don't you keep . . . ?' Tess began, and saw the hint of bitterness break through Doris's vacant smile. 'What I was going to suggest,' she added uncomfortably, 'is that you keep them for a while. Until your dress has dried out. Or perhaps I could get it dry clea . . .'

'A good dryin' in the sun'll do nicely, thank you,' Doris said shortly.

'Of course, of course,' Tess agreed and then, to Doris's consternation, she put her arms around her shoulders and held her briefly. 'Thank you so much for coming over this morning, and for talking to Kevin. You've been very kind. Very kind indeed.'

Doris couldn't have said why that simple action brought her close to tears, yet it did.

'See you then,' she muttered, pulling free, and stepped out into the patchy sunlight that had replaced the rain.

'Bloody people!' she mumbled as she followed the path down through the bush. 'They wouldn't be so pleased with themselves and their bloody house if they understood the half of it.'

But all the time she knew she was mouthing empty words. What did the fate of the Clements matter to the Warners? Why should they care about things that had happened to another family entirely? It was all past history.

Go on, be honest, she urged herself silently, still clutching onto the silky hardness of the pepper grinder. You're just jealous, that's all. Jealous of what they've got and you haven't.

And so she was until she reached the creek. It was slightly swollen from the rain, the outer edges of the flow now tugging at the last of the visible paw prints. Had she arrived a few minutes later, they would have been washed away, in which case she would probably have waded the creek and gone straight home. As it was, the sight of those splayed marks crumbling at the water's edge reminded her of the ragged hole she'd noticed earlier, close to the willows, that she'd meant to go and investigate.

She turned and ran her eye along the upper bank. Because of the sunlight, speckled pools of shade had gathered beneath the trees, making it harder for her to see clearly. But yes, there it was, a darker patch than the surrounding shadows, with a blackish piece of driftwood sticking up from it as before.

She trudged across the rain-washed sand and, as she drew nearer, the piece of driftwood turned into something else. A strangely furred thing, familiar and at the same time repellent. A stiffened, up-jutting leg that ended . . . she started at the sight . . . in the blunted shape of a dog's paw!

Doris almost decided to turn away, and wished she had a few moments later, when she realised what the rusty-brown stains at the edge of the hole really were; when she peered into the hole itself — which proved to be a madly churned-up hollow in the sand — and saw the gaping wound, the bluish entrails speckled with flies, the . . .

She rocked back onto her heels, feeling suddenly dizzy. The tree, the sky, seemed to fall away and she sat down with a bump. The body was hidden from her now, thank God, and all she could see were the bloody stains. How had it happened? Who . . . who . . . ? Her mind flew to the image of Kevin, to the way he'd acted that morning. So evasive, refusing to look at her, refusing to explain about Rory. But why this? And to his own dog! How could he . . . how . . . ?

She squirmed backwards away from the hole, out into the warm sunlight where she felt safer. Where she stopped shivering and was able to take a few steadying breaths. Who else could have done it? She put the question to herself soberly. After all, she'd been expecting Kevin to do something bad for years. Those sudden disappearances of his, for instance, for months at a time, what did they mean? And when he was home, all that creeping around in the dark, all that spying (on the Clements to begin with and now on the Warners), wasn't it bound to lead to this in the end? Or to worse? At least this was only a dog. (*Only?* Rory?) If she had any sense she'd be thankful for small mercies.

It was a small consolation, but all she had. Now came the part she dreaded, the need to confront him with what he'd done. To challenge him with this . . . this *horror*! Well, let's get it over with, she told herself, and was about to struggle to her feet when she detected a movement within the circle of the nearest tree.

'Kevin?' she called, thinking at first that he had saved her the trouble of finding him, that she had finally caught him out on one of his spying trips.

Crawling forward on hands and knees, she pulled aside the screen of willow branches. Someone sat crouched in the deepest shade, close against the main trunk. Not Kevin at all, but the Warner girl, Mary, the laughter frozen on her lips as her eyes flicked guiltily from the dog's carcass up towards Doris.

She was gone before Doris could say her name aloud, vanishing with the stealthy silence of a wild animal. But not before Doris had registered her laughter, her unholy delight at the spectacle of Rory's mutilated body.

Doris stood up slowly, careful not to let her eyes wander down into the bloody pit only a pace or two away. Although she was horrified by what it contained, it didn't disturb her nearly as much as the expression she had glimpsed on Mary's face. Doris had to suppress a shudder of distaste. To think that she'd been fool enough to blame Kevin. To believe her own son capable of this! Or what was probably worse, to think she'd actually been jealous of the Warners! Envied them their warmth, their closeness to each other, their . . .

'And this is our Mary.' That was how Tess had introduced her. With such obvious pride, as well as love. As though she were their most precious possession, the loving centre of the whole family.

No, Doris decided, there was nothing enviable about that. And with one swing of the arm, she tossed the pepper grinder into the creek, where it disappeared with a splash, bobbed up again, and half rolled, half floated downstream and out of sight.

11

Tess sank to her knees in the sand, her stomach churning unpleasantly, and forced herself to look. Over to her left Doug was retching up the last of his breakfast, while just beyond the fringe of willow branches Doris watched her darkly, no doubt expecting her to make some kind of angry denial.

That had been Doug's first response. 'Not my Mary!' he had cried in the instant before he gagged and swung away.

But Tess, after the initial shock, wasn't nearly so certain. Now, although her stomach continued to rebel, she examined the corpse carefully, searching it for clues. In all honesty, they were plentiful enough. The tongue ripped from the mouth and fretted by ... what? A knife? Teeth? Ominously, part of it was missing.

That really made her cringe, and in spite of her resolve she flinched away for a few seconds. Steady, she told herself, it's just buried in the sand somewhere. It *must* be! She could feel Doris's eyes upon her, and she made herself act calm and look back.

To where the entrails spilled from a gash that ran from the underside of the jaw to the anus. No ordinary wound, no simple slash, but a long deliberate cut that must have required a weird degree of application, of patience. On closer examination, the entrails, too, had been tampered with. Part of the liver had been hacked off, and bore the same jagged marks as the tongue. And the heart . . . ! Or rather what was left of it!

'I should have guessed!' she moaned aloud.

She hadn't meant to show emotion in front of Doris, but she couldn't help herself. Couldn't help reaching into the pit either, in search of the last and most potent clue of all. With both hands, she rolled the carcass over, so as to reveal the top of the head. As she had foreseen, the animal had been neatly scalped, the single remaining eye staring from a ridge of whitish bone. Further back, where the head met the neck, the skull had been prised open and the brain gouged out. Greyish flecks of it clung to the velvety curve of the ears.

Doug, still trembling, crawled up beside her. 'Not my Mary!' he said again, like someone trying to deny the encroaching dark.

'Be quiet, Doug.' Her voice was suspiciously soft, sounding a warning.

'No one's going to tell me she could do this!' he shouted, and bunched both fists in the sand.

She turned on him fiercely, forgetful of Doris who, out of delicacy for their feelings, had shuffled closer to the creek. 'Use your eyes, damn you!' she hissed. 'Can't you see what this is? It's an act of vengeance! Her way of evening the score with Terror.'

'Terror . . . ?' He gazed unsteadily at her, not quite

crediting what she was saying, his heavy features shiny with sweat in the speckled shade.

'Do you enjoy hearing her laugh again?' she challenged him. 'Do you want her to go back to normal? Well so do I. And this is the price we have to pay. All of us, Mary included. Because this was the only way she could think of to get Terror out of her system. To pay him back. It's not pretty, I know, but it means she's not scared any more. And that's worth more to me than all the animals in creation. I'd put up with this ten times over if I had to, if I thought it would help. D'you understand me, Doug?'

She had wound her hands into the loose cloth of his overalls and was shaking him as she made each point.

He eased himself gently free of her and, with half-averted face, pointed down at the remains of the heart. 'Are you also saying she . . . ?'

'We don't know that!' she broke in quickly. 'Anything could have done it. Rats, a possum, a dingo, anything! There must be scavengers all along this creek.'

'But if she killed . . .'

'Leave it, Doug,' she advised him more calmly, and remembered Doris who, although standing down by the water, must still have been able to hear every word. 'Mary's on the way back to us,' she went on in a whisper. 'We all agreed about that. This is behind her now. It's part of the nightmare and it's over. When we bury this animal, we bury Terror too. Just keep that in mind.'

He nodded and ran his tongue nervously along his lips. 'I'm sorry, Tess. It's just that I can't imagine Mary

... you know.' He gestured helplessly towards the remains.

'It's all right, neither can I,' she assured him, his trembling hands held firmly in hers. 'And neither will Mary in a few weeks' time, when she's well again.'

There was an embarrassed cough, and Doris brought her face close against the screen of willow. 'My boy's just arrived,' she said. 'He's been lookin' for Rory. By rights it's his dog, so I thought you'd ... er ... you wouldn't mind havin' a word.'

The willow branches were swept aside and Kev's bulky frame appeared in the opening. 'Mum says Rory's here.'

Tess scrambled up, feeling absurdly guilty, as if she were personally responsible for what lay at her feet. 'Look, I'm sorry ...' she began, and braced herself for the inevitable show of shock and anger.

But Kevin surveyed the contents of the pit without flinching. His unshaven face, divided evenly by sunlight and shadow, revealed almost no emotion at all, as though ... As though what? Tess wondered. Had he been down there earlier, perhaps, and known what to expect? No, that wasn't possible because Doris had just said he'd come looking for the animal. Unless he was lying.

'Poor bugger,' he observed coolly. 'He got his, didn't he?'

'We think our ... our daughter, Mary, did it,' Tess said, getting the most painful part of the admission over first. 'She has a thing about dogs. That's why I didn't want Rory over here. She's terrified of them.'

'You could've fooled me,' Kevin said, and laughed.

Laughed! So that Tess, for all her guilt, was moved by a sense of outrage on Rory's behalf.

'You see, she was attacked by a dog in Sydney,' she made herself go on. 'It . . . it killed a small child she was looking after.'

'God A'mighty!' Doris murmured.

'And . . . and that's why she's done this,' Tess finished lamely.

'Well, it's only natural, isn't it?' Kevin said. 'She'd wanna kill every bloody dog she come across. I know I would.'

He was still smiling, and Tess felt torn between wanting to shout at him and thank him.

'I'm glad you see it that way,' she said, her tone tight and controlled.

'Why not?' He paused, and his smile widened as he added: 'It'll cost you, but.'

'Jesus, Kev!' Doris hit him on the upper arm with her fist.

'You bastard!' Doug growled, lurching to his feet. 'You'll not get a cent from . . .'

'No, wait a minute, Doug.' Tess took him by the wrist, restraining him. 'Maybe this is the best way.'

'My bloody oath it is,' Kevin agreed. 'Unless you want everyone around here scared shitless of that daughter of yours.'

'I've heard just about enough of this, Kev!' Doris burst out, and tried dragging him towards the creek.

He shrugged her off and stayed facing Tess. 'What d'you reckon?'

'How much?' she asked him shortly, and tightened her grip on Doug's wrist.

Kevin pulled at his lower lip, making a show of deciding. 'Well, the ute needs a face-lift. Then there's a new dog to replace...'

'That's it,' she said with finality, and brought her hand down in a chopping motion. 'We'll pay for the overhaul of your ute and get you a Doberman puppy. In exchange, you'll forget this ever happened. You'll also stay off this property once and for all.'

'Fair enough,' he agreed. 'Though there's one more thing. It won't cost you nothin', mind.'

'What's that?'

He was smiling again and pointing to the pit. 'I'll have Rory's collar back when it's convenient.'

'Collar?' She glanced down and realised it was missing from the body, the long cut running straight up the neck to the jaw. But why should Mary have taken...? She put a sharp check on her own sudden doubt. 'I... I'll see that you get it,' she promised him, struggling to keep the tremor from her voice.

'Yeah, it'll come in handy for tying the new dog up at night,' he said meaningfully.

'Leave off, Kev!' Doris protested, and shoved him from behind, so that he staggered forward and had to snatch at the willow branches to keep his balance.

For a second or two he was no more than a pace from Tess, and in that time she noticed how tired his eyes looked. They were the eyes of someone who hadn't slept for hours, perhaps for the whole of the previous night. But if so, what had he been doing? What had kept him awake?

It was yet another worry, and together with the unforeseen problem of the collar it stayed with Tess after Doris and Kevin had recrossed the creek, nagging at her while she and Doug set about burying Rory's remains.

As she scooped handfuls of sand into the hole, she kept thinking of Kevin's kinky hunting trips, the ones she'd been sure he was making. It was just possible, she supposed, that he could somehow have been involved in Rory's death. He could, for instance, have helped Mary hunt Rory down in the dark. Or held him for her maybe. That would at least explain how someone as tiny as Mary had managed to overcome a powerful animal. But why on earth should Kevin have wanted to kill his own dog? No, in all probability it was still Mary's doing.

And the gutted possum? Had she killed that too?

Tess closed that thought down abruptly, refusing to deal with more than one thing at a time.

Okay, so Mary killed Rory on her own, as a way of putting Terror's ghost to rest. Except what did she want with another collar? Her obsession with collars should surely have vanished with her fear. Unless of course, she, Tess, was expecting everything to work out too neatly.

With a troubled sigh, she smoothed her end of the finished mound. All the grave required now was a layer of stones.

Doug leaned back and dusted his hands on his overalls. 'You know, you shouldn't have offered that hoon any money,' he said quietly.

'It'll be worth a few dollars to shut him up.'

'Who could he tell? Only his mates in the pub. If

they're anything like him, they're nothing to worry about.'

'Even some hoon in a pub can make a phone call to the RSPCA,' she pointed out. 'And if someone discovered what's in here' — she indicated the grave — 'there'd be all sorts of questions asked. We could still end up losing her to an institution.'

'Not if she's well again,' Doug objected, and must have sensed Tess holding back because he turned to look at her. 'You haven't changed your mind about that, have you?'

She evaded the question by walking off between the trees in search of stones.

'Have you?' he persisted, catching her up.

She stopped on the path that wound up through the bush. 'It's mainly this business with the collar,' she confessed. 'If Mary's really free of Terror, why add another collar to her collection?'

Doug was gazing at something across her shoulder. 'Maybe she hasn't,' he suggested, and pointed through the undergrowth to a sunlit clearing, where Tess could make out a dog-like shape with a black strip around its neck.

Together, they scrambled beneath the trees and out into the open. Close up, the figure was almost exactly as Harry had described it, with blank, marble eyes and a smooth clay surface. The only difference was that now it wore a real collar. Rory's. A band of shiny black leather encrusted with heavy chromium studs.

'There's Kev's precious collar,' Doug said and laughed.

Tess would have liked to laugh with him, but something stopped her. She squatted down and ran her finger thoughtfully along the smooth surface of the leather. Why hadn't Mary used Terror's collar, the cracked, fire-blackened one she was obsessed with? And that wasn't all. Tess had assumed from Harry's description that Mary had made a sculptured version of Terror, and that in dancing around it she'd been expressing her freedom from fear. Whereas in fact this figure was decidedly more like Rory, with a longish neck and much leaner head and jaws. Also, it had exactly the same 'feel' about it as the figure of the possum.

Grudgingly, Tess admitted that she could no longer keep that other troublesome thought at bay. Well then, she asked herself bluntly, *had* Mary made both figures? The dog and the possum? Had she killed them both in the same ritual way? Or was she just following Kevin's lead? Were this figure and the manner of Rory's death no more than macabre forms of copy-cat behaviour?

Tess shook her head in bewilderment. 'What the hell's going on here?' she muttered.

'How d'you mean?' Doug was hovering over her, mystified by her reaction. 'It's pretty obvious, isn't it? She put this collar onto her model to make it look more like T . . .'

'Look at it, for Christ's sake!' Tess nearly shouted, and dragged him down beside her. 'It's not even supposed to look like Terror. It's a copy of that animal we've just buried. I'm not even sure Mary made the damned thing.'

'But she was covered in clay. You saw her.'

Tess nodded, steadied slightly by the memory. 'There's only one person who can sort this out for us,' she said at last, 'and that's Mary. Hold on, I'll be back.' And she pushed her way through to the path and ran up to the house.

'Mary?' she called from the front door.

There was no answer and on impulse she went into Mary's room and began checking through her things. She wasn't sure what she was after, but she continued searching just the same. Nothing unusual in the chest of drawers; nothing in the wardrobe. She stripped back the bedclothes — nothing there either. No sign even of the clean nightgown Tess had taken out for her during the night. Where . . . ? Tess checked again under the pillow, under the bed, in Mary's old toybox, and drew a blank each time. It seemed to have vanished.

Driven by a definitive sense of urgency now, she hurried to the bathroom and upended the laundry basket, but the only nightgown there was the one soiled with clay. Where next? The kitchen. The disposal bin under the sink.

That was where she found it. Crumpled up and hidden at the very bottom of the plastic liner. The silky-blue material blotched with reddish-brown stains.

She pushed it back into the bin as though hiding it again, and walked slowly over to the open doorway of the workshop. From there, looking sideways and down, she could see Mary, crouched as usual against the wall, in the shadowy area behind the benches. Her head was tipped back, her eyes closed, her mouth drawn into a strange semblance of a smile.

Bob glanced up enquiringly as Tess descended the stairs. 'What's happening?'

'Tell you later.'

She went and knelt beside Mary. 'I found the nightgown,' she said, whispering it to her almost tenderly as if she were imparting a secret that no one else must share. 'I also found Rory. The real one *and* the model.'

Mary responded by pressing her cheek to the solid concrete wall, like a child seeking comfort from some loved parent or guardian with whom it feels safe.

'Now I'll tell you what we're going to do,' Tess continued, watching Mary's face for the least flare of alarm. 'We're going to take Rory's collar off the model and give it back to Kevin. For his new dog, the one we'll buy him. D'you understand me?'

Mary's eyes blinked open, but that was all. She gave no sign of agitation, not even when Tess took her by the arm and led her upstairs. Placid, and wearing a contented smile, she accompanied Tess down the slope towards the clearing. As they reached the line of willows she laughed aloud, the same joyous sound she had made during breakfast that morning; and she laughed again, a high trill of excitement this time, when she saw the clay model of the dog.

Tess drew Doug to one side. 'Do you like this dog, Mary?' she asked quietly. 'Does it please you?'

Mary's only answer was to throw her arms wide and raise her face to the sun in a gesture of happy abandonment, as though offering herself to the heavens.

'Listen to me, Mary. I want you to take off its collar. Will you do that for me?'

She paused, waiting for the sullen show of resentment she had grown used to where Terror's collar was concerned. But Mary's smile didn't wane for an instant. Kneeling beside the clay figure, she slipped open the buckle and offered the collar dumbly, readily, to Tess.

'No, it's not for me,' Tess instructed her. 'You have to throw it across the creek for Kevin. You know Kevin, don't you?' Again there was no visible response. 'Leave it on the sand on his side, where he can find it.'

Obediently, she made her way through the strip of bush and down between the willows to the water's edge, where she tossed the collar carelessly onto the opposite bank. She was turning away, back towards the trees, even before it thudded limply onto the sand. Her task complete, she ignored her parents and went to sit astride the grave which she hugged with her knees and patted lovingly with both hands, her soft laughter rippling through the quiet of the morning.

'What do you think?' Doug murmured.

Tess pushed her hands into her hair and locked her fingers together at the back of her head, her attitude as tense as Mary's was relaxed. 'I think I'm out of my depth,' she confessed.

*

Tess disliked rush-hour traffic, but when Ruth Close offered her an emergency appointment late on that same day, she didn't hesitate. Now, having braved the long drive into Sydney and feeling hot and out of sorts as a result, she seriously wondered why she'd bothered. All

Ruth could possibly offer her was the usual kindness and ready sympathy, and how could that change anything?

'You mustn't let yourself get so down,' Ruth was saying. 'Feeling depressed won't help you or Mary.'

'I wasn't depressed to begin with,' she confessed. 'Not when we first found Rory. It was horrible, but it also seemed to be part of a pattern. The things she'd ...' Tess remembered Rory's one staring eye and had to take a deep breath before going on. 'The things Mary had done to him, they struck me as more than just cruel. They made a weird kind of sense. I honestly believed they were her answer to Terror. It was as if she'd decided to answer him in kind, to give him back some of his own medicine.'

'Why not?' Ruth agreed. 'It's natural enough for her to feel that way. Though don't forget that those ... those *things* she did to the animal are also an example of very disturbed behaviour. Dangerous behaviour. Whatever else, we mustn't forget that, Tess.'

Tess wondered for a moment what Ruth might have said if she'd known the full extent of Rory's injuries, if she'd seen the condition of the internal organs. Driving in along the Windsor Road, Tess had had every intention of describing exactly what they'd buried beneath the willows, but faced with the civilised calm of this room, of Ruth Close, she'd lost her nerve. How could she sit here and admit to this pleasant-faced woman that Mary had ... that she had ... ? Even within the privacy of her own mind Tess found it difficult to describe such forbidden acts in the accepted decencies of everyday language.

'I understand the seriousness of what Mary's done,' Tess said dully. 'But horrible as it was, I still thought it meant something. It seemed to be her way of ... of undoing the past. Do you know what I mean? Of cancelling it out.'

'And you don't think that any more?'

'How can I? None of it was about Terror. All she wanted to do was hurt Rory. He was the one she was dancing around. I can only suppose she killed him because he barked at her. Barking's something she's hated ever since ... since ... '

'Yes, I know,' Ruth said quickly. 'But let's get back to the pattern you spoke of just now. That interests me. I can work out how the ... er ... the *scalping* fits in.' Although she tried, she was unable to hide a slight shiver of distaste. 'What I don't follow is the part about the tongue. Why that?'

Tess stared for a while at the darkening window, at the blue of the sky gradually fading to black, and felt hemmed in by deepening shadows, by an encroaching night in which she would never find her way. Already the reasoned path that had presented itself to her down there beneath the willows had grown vague and indistinct, an illusion of a path rather than a passage through the dark.

'It seemed a reasonable idea at the time,' she said self-deprecatingly. 'You know, tongues and words, how the two go together. Well, as Terror was the one who made her dumb, because of what he did to her, I thought that maybe in taking out his tongue she was demanding the right to talk again. Does that sound stupid to you?'

Put into words, it sounded stupid enough to Tess herself, let alone to someone like Ruth, and she looked again at the darkening window, at the night pressing in from outside.

'No, why should it be stupid?' Ruth surprised her by saying. 'Now that you point it out, there's an obvious connection between the tongue and the idea of speech. I should have spotted it for myself. So, what's next?'

'There is no "next",' Tess said in a flat, uninspired voice. 'The pattern breaks down after that. If Mary was really getting even with Terror, she'd have made the sculpture look like him. Why would she have bothered making a copy of Rory? Or of . . . ?'

She had been on the point of referring to the possum sculpture, but remembered in time that she had chosen not to mention that to Ruth either. So many things she hadn't mentioned: the gnawed remains of the heart; the slaughtered body of the possum; the other, weathered piece of sculpture, made earlier (by Mary or by Kevin?); and Kevin himself, his sick hunting trips, his complete lack of surprise when he'd seen the dog, as though — she made herself face the implications squarely — as though he and Mary were in some unholy league together.

Well, were they?

She closed her eyes and asked herself again what she was doing here, why she was bothering to talk to this woman with the kindly smile. Was she merely hoping for a shoulder to cry on? A place in which to hide away for a few hours? Because she could hardly expect to be helped if she told only half the truth. But the whole truth! It made Mary sound so crazy! So totally beyond rescue! No, Tess could not imagine herself confiding in Ruth completely. Her protective impulse was too strong; as was her fear of what Ruth might say and do if she fully realised what she was dealing with.

Tess shook her head involuntarily, and Ruth, in her concerned voice, asked, 'Are you all right?'

She tried to smile. 'It's just a godawful mess, isn't it?'

'Not entirely,' Ruth answered, careful and constrained as always, but with a definite undertone of excitement in her voice.

'How do you mean?'

Ruth re-arranged the articles on her desk, her mouth closed, pensive. 'Perhaps you haven't taken the pattern far enough,' she suggested. 'If you push it a little further, it starts to make sense again. How about this, for instance?' She paused for a few seconds, as though giving Tess time to ready herself. 'Because of her trauma, Mary has come to regard Terror as a symbol of all dogs, and they in turn have come to symbolise him. For her they're all one and the same animal. Rory, Terror — as far as she's concerned, they're identical. So what does it matter which one she takes as her model? Which one she kills? Always it's Terror she's defying, Terror she's overcoming, Terror she's dancing around or laughing at.' Ruth paused again and raised her eyebrows questioningly. 'Well? You live with Mary, you see her every day. Does any of that ring true?'

Oddly, Tess found herself resisting Ruth's quiet air

of excitement, resisting her own desire to agree.

'You're the expert,' she countered guardedly. 'Right now I'm more interested in whether you think it's true.'

Ruth shrugged. 'It does tie a lot of the facts together. And it doesn't portray Mary as overly rational, which she isn't in her present condition. It interprets her behaviour in what I'd call instinctive terms.'

'Yes, but do you believe it?' Tess insisted, and again felt a surge of resistance as though, near the end of that long and trying day, she preferred to take refuge in doubt. It was less testing. Less demanding.

Ruth was watching her closely, a quirky little smile on her face. 'Believing's a funny thing, Tess. When belief fails people, they tend to feel betrayed by it. No, I'm wary of saying I believe my own theory. I'd prefer to say it has the advantage of being hopeful. And in cases like this that's important. If we're to help Mary, we can't afford to give up. Wherever possible, we have to look for genuine positives.'

Tess gave a bitter laugh. 'Are there any?'

'Before I answer that,' Ruth said seriously, 'there's something else I need to remind you of, and that's Mary's destructive tendencies. For all our sakes, I'm asking you again, let me put her onto some form of medication.'

Tess stiffened in her chair. 'No!' she said emphatically. 'I've told you before, I won't have her turned into a zombie.'

'Then at least lock her up at night.'

'Nor into a prisoner.'

'Only at night, Tess, not all the time. That's not much to ask.'

Tess relaxed slightly. 'Doug's been asking me the same thing,' she admitted.

'So why not do it?'

'At night, then,' she said, relenting, 'while we're asleep. But that's all!' she added with sudden vehemence. 'The rest of the time she stays free. I'd rather lose her than become her jailer.'

Ruth nodded, satisfied. 'I can understand that. Now, back to positives. Whether or not you accept my reading of Mary's behaviour, you still have a lot going for you. There's Mary's unexpected happiness, for one; her loss of fear, for another. Those are big gains. For all we know, the worst may be over. If Rory's anything to judge by, she's no longer scared of ordinary dogs. And even Terror may not be the threat he was.'

'Is there any way of finding that out?'

'Only by mentioning his name. By talking about him in front of her.'

Tess considered the possibility before replying. 'No, it's too early for that. I don't want to take the chance of upsetting her just yet.'

'Agreed,' Ruth said. 'It would be silly to risk what you've achieved so far. Which is why it's important to lock her in at night. No more risks, Tess. No more negative thoughts. From now on give out only positive vibes. Keep her laughing, keep her contented, act as if that Rory business never occurred. With luck she'll gradually forget the whole nightmare and slip back into a normal life. Stranger things have happened, believe me.'

Believe her? Driving away from Ruth's office, the car nosing into the moderate early-evening traffic, Tess was reminded of what Ruth herself had said about belief only five or ten minutes earlier: how, when it failed people, they felt betrayed by it. Well, she felt betrayed enough already, so much so that she was nervous about giving way to further hope, as she admitted to her mother when she stopped off there briefly on her way home.

'I don't blame you for a minute,' Meg Daniels said in her direct, practical fashion. 'When you think about it, what has that counsellor woman really come up with? After dozens of sessions and weeks of talk, the best she can do is advise you to look on the bright side of things. Isn't that what it boils down to?'

Tess supposed it was.

Meg snorted with disgust. 'If you ask me,' she said witheringly, 'it's a bit like paying to see a specialist and having him prescribe an aspirin.'

'Aspirins can sometimes work,' Tess said, trying to be fair.

'Not in this instance, my girl,' the old woman observed severely, wagging a knowing finger at her. 'A bit of common sense is what's needed here. That and a good honest look at what's really happened to our Mary. Face up to it, Tess, the only thing that's changed is that she doesn't think she's a dog any more. She's become a dog-killer instead. And maybe a killer of other things too. In your place I wouldn't waste time looking for silver linings. Not just yet anyway. I'd take double care of the rest of my family. I'd keep a sharp eye on Mary to make sure she doesn't do any more damage, to herself or anyone else. God knows I love the child dearly, the same as you, but that's the way I see it.'

It was hard, testing advice, of the kind she had come to expect from Meg. Yet during the long drive home through the warm summer dark, Tess was inclined to agree in spite of herself. Anything seemed better than raising her hopes only to have them dashed again. Or was it just her tiredness getting to her? Maybe, for she was tired, deep inside herself. On the other hand there was no escaping the fact that Mary's apparent recovery had been desperately short-lived. And after what she had done to Rory, to the possum, what possible room was there for optimism? No, the sensible thing for Tess to do now was to watch and wait, to play it safe, not to open herself to disappointment yet again.

It was in that stoical frame of mind that she turned off the highway in the late evening and unfastened the gate to their property. As she drove slowly up to the front of the house, she was puzzled by a glint of fire visible through the bush further down the slope. The house itself was in darkness, as she would have expected at that hour. She stepped from the car, keys in hand, and a tall shape detached itself from the trees and lurched in her direction. In her fright she dropped the keys and was still scrabbling for them when Doug's familiar hand fell upon her shoulder.

'You'd better come,' he murmured.

'Mary?'

He nodded and plodded off down the curving path.

Sick at heart for fear of what she might find, she followed him, the fire growing bigger, brighter, as they drew near.

It had been set near the centre of the clearing, well away from the surrounding bush, and was blazing fiercely, the flames more white than yellow near the core. At the core itself Tess could make out the dark shape of an upturned body, of stiff outjutting legs, of a head thrown back in an attitude of terrible abandonment, as though the creature were offering itself to the flames.

Doug cupped his hand around Tess's ear. 'She dug it up and dragged it over here,' he explained in a whisper.

At that moment Mary stepped from the trees with an armful of wood which she threw onto the fire. Then, her shoulders straight, her body upright, her face lit as much by inner joy as by the leaping flames, she began to dance. It was a peculiarly human kind of dance, with high, stately steps and flowing movements that carried her round and round what Tess recognised as a funeral pyre.

And suddenly, looking on, Tess almost wanted to dance with her. To rush out into the firelight and match Mary step for step, gesture for gesture. Tess had forgotten her earlier caution, her resolve not to open herself to further disappointment. Her weariness and fear of failure were swept away as she realised that Ruth Close had been right after all: that for Mary, Rory and Terror were one and the same and that what was taking place now, here before her eyes, was a true celebration, a farewelling of the dead.

Tess turned to Doug, his face a bewildered crisscross of light and shadow. 'It's him! Terror!' she whispered, her voice husky with suppressed excitement. 'That's why she's burning him! Like before. Except this time *she's* doing it! Our Mary! She *knows* he's dead!'

A fragment of her conversation with Ruth came back to her: the part where she'd asked how to find out whether Terror was still a threat. And Ruth's answer: 'Only by mentioning his name.'

Tess stepped forward into the clearing. 'Terror,' she said softly. And then louder: 'Terror!' And when Mary continued to twirl and spin: 'Terror's gone! D'you hear me, Mary? He's gone for good!'

There were no howls of anguish, no sudden flash of fear. Mary merely danced more wildly, more freely. With a throaty chuckle of delight, she lifted her arms to the faint sprinkle of stars that hovered beyond the fire's glow, beyond the dark containing circle of ancient bushland, opening herself to them.

Tess answered her with laughter of her own. Laughter that was joyful enough to begin with, but gradually grew higher and more shrill until it bordered on the hysterical. A harsh staccato sound that reverberated uneasily amongst the trees and overlaid the furtive splash and drag of displaced water in the creek.

Doug took her by the upper arms and shook her. 'Stop it, Tess! Stop it!'

She struggled to regain control, though small bubbles of laughter kept bursting through. While only paces away, oblivious of onlookers, her face and half-naked body stained a lurid yellow-red by the fire, Mary danced on, her upturned eyes intent on the distant stars. With a muffled creak the fire subsided, imploded upon itself, all but smothering the glowing remains of the corpse.

Tess eased herself free of Doug and brushed the tears from her eyes.

'It's amazing, isn't it?' she said, letting out a last bitter sob of laughter. 'I mean what people can get used to. Our daughter mutilates and then burns a neighbour's dog and we're glad. Glad, for God's sake! We actually believe the world's getting back to normal.'

Part Five

Men come, men go;
All things remain in God.

W. B. Yeats, 'Crazy Jane on God'

12

Mary first heard the voice on the night of the fire. The house was hushed and in darkness. Alone in her room, she lay teetering on the far edge of sleep when, totally without warning, the voice spoke to her, whispered its secrets into her ear. So soft and intimate, so warm and close, that it seemed to originate somewhere inside her head, the long awaited words drifting mysteriously from the dark of mind.

She sat up abruptly, momentarily convinced that it was herself she could hear, some inner part of her own mind that refused to remain silent. Then, with a distracted movement of the head, she decided otherwise, guessing straight away who it *had* to be. Him. The man. The Other One. Who else? Speaking to her from the murkiest corner of the room.

She didn't turn to look (that was forbidden), didn't actually see the words forming on His lips, but still she was sure it was Him. No one else could have spoken so knowingly or have told her things she so longed to hear.

'I am the Double God.' Those were His opening words, as indeed they had to be, though the next part came as a surprise. 'Do you hear me, little sister?'

She nodded to show she had understood.

'I am Alpha and Omega,' He said. 'The Two-in-One, the Double God. All living creatures are mine to make or unmake at will. It is my special task first to create them, to fashion them in earth, in clay, and then to destroy them, to snatch the breath from their living bodies. That is how the balance of creation, of life and death, is maintained. Is it not?'

Again she nodded, and heard murmurous laughter which, tentatively, she joined in.

'I knew you would return,' He said. 'I watched and waited and now I know it to be you. I willed it to be so. I gave breath to your pictured likeness and you stepped free. For your sake I have stopped time. All scars healed, all pain forgotten, I have remade you. That is my primary gift.'

She bowed her head in silent thanks and felt the shadows in the room stir restlessly.

'There is a further gift,' He added. 'The one you yearned for. It is waiting for us under the willow. Yours to do with as you please.'

Interpreting His offer as a summons, still careful not to turn her head, she slipped out of bed and crept along the passage. Was Tess still away in Sydney? She peered into the gloom of her parents' bedroom and made out her father's bulky form lying alone in the bed. Good. That meant there was less chance of being disturbed; she would have more time to spend with the Other One.

She stepped from the house into a moonless night, the sky lightly dusted with stars.

'Mine,' He murmured as she tipped her face to the waiting sky, His breathy voice close beside (within?) her ear. 'My ultimate dwelling place, the might of galaxies my strength.'

She felt that strength now, a surge of pure will that impelled her away from the house, her bare feet fluttering across the drive, through the cool touch of grass, and down the long curving path. He must have left her side because there were no accompanying footsteps, just a series of suggestive shadows that flickered through the bush over to her left. She nearly glimpsed Him once — as a watchful presence in the trees — and quickly she jerked her head away.

At the gap in the willows she paused before creeping forward to the stone-studded mound of sand in which *he* lay entombed, powerless and speechless, the words ripped from his mouth. She pressed her eyes tight-closed, and the Other One was there behind her, the glow and heat of His presence making her flesh tingle.

'Omega,' He murmured — Terror's death sentence, extinction, pronounced in a single word. The final proof that the Other One had taken all the words for Himself; that in truth they had never belonged to anyone else, least of all to *him*, the usurper.

Terror. She gave the name silent voice, and the sand did not erupt at her feet, a scythe of jaws did not reach for her. Terror! The name sang through her mind harmlessly, and she laughed aloud, jubilant at *his* defeat.

'We have made him and unmade him, little sister,' the Other One whispered comfortingly. 'We have kept the balance of things by recreating him in clay and then killing him in the flesh. For it is written that the Lord giveth and the Lord taketh away. Will you let him lie now? Melt back into the earth from which he came?'

He must have sensed her reluctance because He drew nearer, His overarching body like a dark, protective cloak.

'It is for you to decide,' He reminded her softly. 'Didn't I say he was my gift to you? Would I take back my word?'

She knew He wouldn't, and told Him so with a gurgle of receptive laughter.

'Judge him, then, little sister,' He urged her. 'Choose a word to shape his end.'

She tried to say it out loud, but gagged on her own tongue, the sky still too black and heartless for speech; and she stooped down instead and swept aside the stones that covered the grave. On the damp exposed sand, she inscribed the four letters she had decided upon:

F I R E

The Other One was surely able to decipher them even in the faint starlight because He sucked in His breath. She heard the hiss and sigh of it, an unruly wind that coursed along the valley, stirring the willows and the few straggly she-oaks and brushing cool with disapproval against her cheek.

Had she done wrong? Had she displeased Him? She crouched lower, aching with nervous dread. But the breeze dropped to nothing, the trees shivered into stillness, and His warmth enveloped her again.

'If that is your choice,' He breathed, 'then do it, little sister. Do it.'

Then He was gone, His footsteps merging with the splash and ripple of the creek. If she looked up, He would be there on the far bank, gauging her progress as she scooped and dragged at the sand. But she would not look up; she would reveal to Him the extent of her trust by keeping her eyes turned away. Now and forever, faith alone would bind her to Him.

Her probing fingers encountered the tough resilience of fur, skin. She plucked at it, grasped at its stiffness, and heaved backwards until the jaws broke free. She answered their bloody gape with a grin of her own and heaved again, crooning wordlessly to herself as she plucked the body from the grave. It was an easy matter for her to drag it up the bank and through the bush to the clearing — with the Other One, unseen but sensed, monitoring her every move.

She was conscious of Him observing her from the silence of the trees as she prepared the pyre; of how He tracked her up the slope to the house to which she returned for paper and matches. When she emerged, however, He seemed to have melted away. And it wasn't until she was some distance from the house and heard Doug's heavy tread behind her, that she realised why.

'Mary!' That was her father's voice (*she* knew the difference) calling to her as she sped away through the moonless dark, to where the pyre waited.

Her father, breathless, called again from the edge of the clearing, but she ignored him. 'Do it,' the Other One had instructed her, and she hauled the body up onto the pyre, stuffed paper in below and lit it.

The first tiny flames curled up through the twigs and

branches, and she hurried in amongst the trees for more fuel. The fire now was licking at the sky, the whirling sparks adding to the scattered stars. One more load and she was done, the fierceness of the heat cracking and stiffening Terror's limbs as if prompting them to keep time with the dancing flames. Much as she, Mary, intended to keep time.

Through the wavering heat haze, she glimpsed Tess's face beside her father's, but again no other presence mattered. She was thinking of a song she had learned as a child in Sunday School. The remembered image came first, of children swinging round and round in a joyous circle, and then came the title of the song itself: 'The Lord of the Dance'. Yes, that had been it, exactly the tribute she was searching for. And as she began her stately passage about the fire, she let the familiar words and tune course through her mind once again.

Dance, then, wherever you may be,
'I am the Lord of the Dance,' said He.

Beyond the crackle of the fire, beyond the ongoing lilt of the song, she could hear Tess's voice: quiet, controlled at first, but soon growing louder.

'Terror!' she was shouting. 'Terror's gone!'

Yes! Mary thought, and stared gleefully at the fire-etched figure within the dancing flames. Gone! And she lifted her legs higher, spun faster, as she hunted back through memory for the now treasured words.

I danced in the morning when the world was begun,
And I danced in the moon and the stars and the sun,

And I came down from heaven and I danced on the earth...

Tess's hysterical laughter echoed about the clearing, interrupting her.

Was the noise Tess was making loud enough to mask the splash of the Other One's footsteps as He crossed the creek and stole away? Mary hoped so, and purposely increased her own laughter to cover the sound of His departure. With Terror gone, He must be protected from curious eyes and ears. He was her secret. Hers! The Double God who made and unmade the creatures of his choice. Like now, with the flames revealing the crouched model of the dog even as they consumed the last of the gutted body.

She didn't mind them leading her back to the house. After they'd gone she lay in bed until the house creaked and settled — the floorboards in the passage whispering for her to follow... follow — and then she stole down into the darkened workshop, where she crouched in her usual place beside the concrete wall. She felt at one with Him there. The wall possessed some of His massive, immovable quality; its voiceless presence, earth-dark and secret, reminded her of the heavy silences that punctuated His words.

She had no words of her own, only those He had allowed her to retrieve from the almost forgotten past. She trilled them soundlessly now — 'The Lord of... the Lord...' — as she gradually descended into song-haunted sleep, her temple and cheek pressed to the rough concrete.

Harry was the one who woke her. His thin face

loomed above hers in the grey dawn light, anxious and oddly caring.

'Med,' he was whispering. 'Med, wake up.'

She yawned and stretched, allowing her bare arms to brush the wall comfortingly.

'Let's get you upstairs,' he said, taking her by the hands. 'They'll be happier if they find you in bed.'

Happier? That puzzled Mary. Didn't they at least understand that she felt safe here, with the hillside at her back and the windows like eyes onto the outer world? Here, where the Other One could shelter her?

At the thought of the Other One, she came fully awake and half glanced along the wall towards the dark space of the cupboard where He must surely be watching. Confident that His eyes were upon her, she jumped up and drew Harry into the dance.

He was too surprised to resist, laughing with her as he was caught up in her spinning turns which carried them between the benches and around the pieces of machinery, their dancing feet kicking up puffs of sawdust and showers of golden shavings. Out of breath, they collapsed together almost in the shadow of the stairs, and straight away her laughter died.

Too close! she thought, remembering that the Other One could also be the unmaker when He chose. And under the guise of completing the dance, she dragged Harry over to the bottom step.

'What's got into you, Med?' Harry asked, not really expecting her to answer, still laughing to himself as they climbed the stairs. 'Even before, you weren't as happy as this. Have you found out something the rest of us don't know?'

Again he wasn't really questioning her. He was merely voicing his feelings of relief, and she leaned forward and nipped him on the cheek. Not hard. A mixture of loving bite and warning which he, as blind to the true nature of things as she had once been, took only as a mark of affection. She could tell that by the way he fingered his cheek and grinned at her before going over to the sink to fill the kettle. She left him then, humming contentedly to himself, and stole quietly off to her bedroom.

Lying on her side in bed, she watched the early sunlight steal past her open door in its silent journey along the passage. Like heavenly footsteps, she mused languidly, and drifted back into sleep where the dance continued in an endless wheel of sun- and starlight. Except that now it wasn't Harry but the Other One who clasped her in His arms, His bare feet skimming across the floor with the same golden stealth as the sun's advancing rays.

She slept or dozed most of the day. One after the other, the members of the family came and crouched beside her, but she smiled vacantly at them and they went away satisfied. Tess was the most persistent, bringing food and drink which she snacked on whenever she woke — the hours drifting by and she biding her time until late evening when everyone had gone to bed.

She listened, as always, for the signal given to her by the house itself — for the way it moved restively in the cool of the night — before padding off along the passage. The front door showed as a black rectangle inset with squares of grey where glass panes let through the faint starlight. She groped to one side of them, feeling for the handle, and tried to turn it.

Locked?

But He would be waiting for her! The Other One!

She tried again, frantically now, and when it refused to budge she shook the whole door, slamming at it first with her shoulder and then with her head.

There was a shock of light somewhere behind her eyes and the sound of glass breaking on the steps outside. Warm droplets coursed down her forehead, her nose, gathered in the folds around her mouth. She licked at them and steadied herself for a fresh assault, but Tess was there beside her and she could hear footsteps on the polished floor. Quickly, she shrugged Tess off and drove her forehead at another of the grey panes, and another, each numbing impact accompanied by a crash of glass.

'Hold her!' Tess was yelling. 'Don't let her . . . ! Don't . . . !'

Stronger hands than Tess's wrestled her backwards, pinned her arms, her legs, to the floor. She tore one hand free and slashed at the pale oval of a face, snapped her teeth at the containing dark, but they had her again. So firmly that all she could do was howl. Call to Him through the shattered panes of the door.

'What the hell . . . ?'

'She's trying to get to him!' That was Tess. 'The bastard must be out there right now.'

A key rattled in the lock and the door was thrown open. The bright outside light clicked on. And Mary, her head strained upwards, stared past Tess's bare legs to where a bulky shadow was just melting back into the trees beyond the lawn.

'You're supposed to stay away from here, Kevin!' Tess screamed out. 'That was our agreement, and you've broken it. Well the deal's off. You won't get a penny from us now. Not a penny!'

One of Mary's arms was released, and for a while she was struggling so hard that she didn't notice anything else. Then a smaller, slighter figure than either Bob or her father was squirming past her. Harry! Something odd about his outline in the doorway: a long rod angled up from his shoulder.

'No, Harry!'

And all at once only her father was holding her, with Bob and her mother trying to wrest the rifle from Harry's clutching hands.

She bit into the thick forearm curved about her shoulders and she was free — ducking beneath the groping hands, pushing past the knot of panting figures in the doorway. Two, three bounds and she was onto the drive, running for the trees.

The darkness received her as a friend. Fell about her like an invisible cloak. Crouched, panting, in a nest of leaves and branches, she blotted out the cries of her family, all her senses alert to His approach. The night wind rustled the trees overhead, and He was there at her back. A dark sentinel standing above her as someone (her father? Bob?) blundered heavily through the nearby undergrowth. Tess also crashed past, her voice dying away as she descended the slope.

Mary stood up cautiously, attracted by a cast of drifting shadows over to her right. 'Come,' He instructed her, His voice like a clash of branches in the wind, and she followed Him across the hillside, her eyes downcast in case she was tempted to look beyond the disturbance of leaves and twigs that marked His passage.

She emerged near the line of dense bush that screened the property from the road. A car whined past on the far side, the wash of its headlights briefly staining the treetops.

'There,' He whispered, His voice close to her ear again, and directed her to an open space this side of the trees. She searched the darkness and saw it almost at once: the familiar outline of a wombat hole. A few paces away she could make out something else — something she had guessed must be there. An uncertain hump that hinted at a living shape.

'The cycle of creation has begun again,' He informed her. 'Are you ready for it, little sister?'

She nodded and crept over to the hummock of grass and stone that already bore the crude likeness of a wombat.

'First we must complete the making,' He said, and His voice thrilled with such pleasure that she laughed aloud at the blackness of the sky. 'Afterwards . . . ' He went on, and now He spoke with a grim fever of anticipation that made her shiver and draw in a long sobbing breath. ' . . . afterwards must come the severing. The unmaking. The cutting of the thread of life.'

Must it be cut? She raised her face enquiringly, but there was no disputing His decision.

'I am the Double God,' He reminded her. 'For every life, a death. For every creature made whole by my hand, another must be broken. That is the nature of the cycle. Or have you forgotten how the dog was dealt with? Would you have me undo that?'

She grovelled in the earth at His threat, and when next she raised her head He was gone. The night was still except for distant voices calling to her down by the creek.

She glanced sideways at the unformed hummock, as though searching its secret wombat self for some form of guidance. As voiceless as she, it awaited its breathless creation with a mixture of patience and joy — or so she suspected from its rigid stance. Letting out soft moans of delight, she ran back across the hillside to the house. Which was where Tess found her half an hour later, smiling to herself in sleep, her face and the front of her nightdress streaked with blood.

She continued to smile and laugh throughout the following day. Her cut and swollen forehead didn't bother her; not did the row later in the morning when Bob returned from a trip across the creek with the knuckles of both hands badly skinned and his face bruised.

'I fixed the bastard,' was all he said as he descended the stairs to the workshop.

Crouched at her appointed post beside the wall, the unmoving hillside at her back, Mary heard her father slam one hand down onto the bench, and then the quick patter of her mother's footsteps.

'Let's leave it at this, Doug,' Tess cautioned him.

'But this isn't the way to handle things, Tess,' he answered hoarsely. 'Not in this family.'

'What else did you expect us to do, call the police and have them warn him off?'

'Us? *Us* to do?' he took her up quickly. 'Do you mean you encouraged Bob to go over there and sort that bastard out?'

'He didn't need much encouragement.'

And Bob: 'It was the only way, Dad. Mum's right, we can't have the police poking their noses in.'

'Why not?'

Tess again: 'There's what happened to the dog, for one, and to the possum for another. Then there's whatever else Kevin's been involving her in. God knows what they've been up to out there.'

'So we become as bad as him, is that the idea? We take the law into our own hands?'

'He's the one who started it, not us.'

'We could have gone to Doris and Ted again.'

'We tried that, and they can't control him either. This was the only way. *His* way.'

'He got the story, Dad, I promise you.'

'The story?' Doug's voice, now, both angry and worried. 'Maybe you're right for the time being. But how's this kind of story going to end? You tell me that.'

To Mary, Doug's last anguished question was of no concern. Both then and later her mind remained fixed on other things. Such as how to endure the waiting;

how to hurry on the minutes and hours until that time, shortly before dawn, when the house summoned her once more.

Not along the passage to the front door. The faint creaking of the floorboards, His suggestive whisper from the forbidden corner, both steered her in the opposite direction.

'This way, little sister.'

Down the passage to the kitchen where the side window opened soundlessly; where the tangle of wild growth broke her fall to the ground. Then through the whirring and chirruping of the summer night towards the place of creation.

On this occasion she saw to the making herself. Under the guidance of the Other One (never daring to look into His riven face), she carried fresh clay from the bank further up the creek; searched for and found white chips of quartz for eyes; bent green twigs to structure the tiny ears.

'Out of the ground the Lord God formed every beast of the field,' He reminded her as she set about fashioning the blunt wombat head. And in the early dawn, while she was struggling to give a rapt expression to the face: 'And the Lord God . . . breathed into his nostrils the breath of life.'

He was there beside her once again, twenty-four hours later, during the brief and exhilarating search. The night of the hunt was how she thought of it, which ended with the live animal being strung up above its completed likeness.

'Lovingly,' He murmured as he showed her how to spill the life from its squirming body.

She placed the knife against the furry underside, eyes closed, hands clasped in prayer, and leaned forward. As the body jerked and gave before her, she imagined herself back on the Sydney street, her finger probing the warm space of Terror's skull.

'Be like a raging fire, little sister,' He urged her next, and at his insistence she bit into and then tore at the rubbery texture of the stomach wall.

Her own stomach immediately rebelled when she tried to swallow, but he was remorseless, the pressure of His darkly invisible hands holding her throat closed.

'Its death is our renewed life,' He told her, His lips all but brushing her bloodstained cheek, His fingers tightening, forcing her rebellious stomach into submission. 'We alone stand at the hub of the wheel of life. We *are* the dance. The makers and the consumers of all living things.'

Those words came back to her when she woke on the hard ground in a wash of early morning sunlight. The makers and the consumers, she intoned silently, and laughed aloud at the overhanging leaves.

Laughter was like an instinct for her now. It stayed with her throughout the tedium of the ensuing days; and at night, as she sidled between the trees in search of Him, she chuckled to herself repeatedly, a soft chirrup of sound that merged into the constant background hum of insects. His prolonged absence in no way lessened her carefree joy. She was confident that He would never desert her. Wasn't He the two-edged sword? He would return in time for the cycle to begin anew.

Meanwhile, she rose dutifully every morning during the dark hour before dawn, after Tess had made her final check of the night, and dropped silently into the now flattened bed of ferns and small bushes beneath the kitchen window. No one summoned her. The house stood rock-still in the cool of the night, and no enticing pad of footsteps whispered along the passage. All that drew her outside was the simple knowledge that He was watching, observing her readiness. She was certain that when the time was ripe . . . when . . .

Yet to her shame His long-awaited call caught her unprepared, occurring on the one night she failed to wake.

'Have you abandoned me already, little sister?' He chastised her gently, and she started up in bed, her face and body turned stiffly from the darkened corner. 'Did my gift to you mean nothing?'

She hung her head guiltily and the house, in sympathy, groaned a reply.

'Then come,' He said. 'Come, come, come, come . . .'

Each word like a footfall that led her to the rear of the house. Still groggy with sleep, she fell heavily from the window and lay sprawled in the darkness trying to regain her breath. When she looked up a sliver of moon was hanging in the sky.

'Your sign,' He said. 'The moon-wheel upon which we will make and then break him.'

Him?

He took the sharp turn of her head for a question.

'And the Lord God formed man of the dust of the ground,' He quoted in reply. 'It is written in the Book, little sister. Not just the beast of the field, but *man*. He too must be fashioned from the earth and consigned to it again.'

He left no room for refusal, and she pursued His flickering shadow down through the trees to what she immediately recognised as the appointed place.

Had He noticed the droop of her shoulders as she broke from the trees? Perhaps, because He was there beside her again, whispering, cajoling. 'Be light of heart, little sister. This is the time of making. Of merriment. In his own likeness we will create him. For half a moon he will stand free. Isn't that cause enough for celebration? Isn't it?'

She knew it was. It *had* to be, for He had said so. And she pushed her uncertainty aside and made herself laugh again. Both then, and on each separate night when she spilled from the window and looked up to where the moon was growing steadily fuller, brighter.

Carrying heavy stones from the lower creek or scooping armfuls of clay from the bank, she stayed determinedly cheerful. For His sake. Even crouched by the wall during the day, she took care to wear a fixed smile in case He was watching — His eyes probing her face from the shadowy recesses of the cupboard beneath the stairs.

As the moon drew closer to the full, however, she found it ever harder to maintain the pretence. Could He, she wondered, see past the mask of her face to her true feelings? She hoped not, her cheeks stiff from smiling.

'Courage,' He whispered, sensing her weakness. 'Out of love, we make him. And that same love must destroy him. That only. Nothing less will do, little sister. So laugh, for me. For him.'

She tried, and only failed completely on the night of the full moon. That was the night she fitted the man's eyes into the prepared clay hollows. Carefully (lovingly?) she pushed the smooth quartz pebbles into place and, with the tip of one finger, fashioned the lids around them. It was the very worst moment of them all, with that blank and yet strangely yearning gaze fixed on a spot close behind her, where she guessed He must be standing.

'Don't look at Him,' she wanted to warn this helpless creature of their making. 'To look on His face is death.'

But she had no words of her own to offer. Everything belonged to Him. And when she opened her mouth, all that came out was a half-stifled sob.

He wasn't angry as she had feared. 'This is the very love I expect of you,' He breathed, His voice filled with the gusting passion of the night wind. 'How else can we make and break the world? It is a labour of the heart. So let your heart speak for you.'

Speak? How could she? It was doubly impossible with those quartz eyes glinting emptily in the moonlight. Impossible, even though the Other One's breathy sigh of longing rustled through the trees beside the creek and lifted the hair at the nape of her neck.

'Think of the dog,' He murmured winningly. 'Think

of the peace we gave him. That same peace we'll give to this . . . '

But in spite of all that she owed to the Other One, she was not yet ready to endure such a prospect. Murder! The word flashed through her mind and was snatched away. And she turned and fled, with a new kind of terror pursuing her now. Up through the drenching moonlight to the flattened ferns beneath the window, up the kitchen waste pipe (grubby from being grasped by clayey hands), and on into the heavy silence of the house. Where, tense and fearful, all her gladness gone, she waited for His voice to reach her from the darkened corner.

The passage creaked, the deeper shadows of the night drained towards the lightening window, and briefly He was there. Her head lifted slowly from the pillow and, at the edge of vision, she almost glimpsed Him.

'I rescued you from the jaws of death,' He rumbled, the distant sound of thunder in His voice. 'I did it so we could share in everything, the creation *and* the destruction. Would you now stop short at the making of this creature's likeness? What of the rest? Would you take only the laughter and leave me with the tears?'

At the mention of tears a sob rose in her throat and she visualised the helpless man-creature they had fashioned together out there in the fading moonlight. Yes, Double God was right, as always. The wheel was only half turned. The time for laughter lay behind them. And burying her face in the pillow, she began to cry.

'Weep for him, little sister,' He encouraged her. 'Weep for his coming pain. Ease him with the water of your tears. Purify him with your pity.'

13

Everything had seemed to be going so well, as far as Tess could tell anyway. There had been that dreadful night weeks earlier, when Mary had fought to get out of the house to where Kevin was waiting for her under the trees, but since then things had settled down. Tess was convinced that Bob's little trip across the creek was what had done it. Not that she'd actively encouraged him to go over there. What she'd told Doug was true: she couldn't have stopped Bob if she'd tried. Like Doug himself, he was slow to anger, but once roused, difficult to control. And after seeing Mary's bruised and bloodied face, his mind had been made up.

'There's only one language his kind understands,' he'd said angrily, slamming fist and palm together. 'And I reckon it's time I had a bit of a talk with him in his own lingo.'

They'd been standing together in Mary's room. Mary herself still asleep, the early morning light revealing the long cut on her forehead where she'd smashed her face against the front door.

'Just watch him,' Tess had advised Bob quietly. 'He's no weakling.'

The state of Bob's own face when he came back attested to the truth of her warning. Though he'd seemed satisfied enough.

'I've fixed the bastard,' he'd said.

Predictably, Doug had made a fuss, and so to her surprise had Harry. But she didn't mind. Oh yes, in her former life she might have felt differently, in the days before all this Terror business started, but not any more. Because Bob had been right. He *had* fixed Kevin. From then on they hadn't seen any sign of him. And with Kevin out of the way Mary had made no further attempt to escape from the house at night. Ever since the fight, for instance, she and Doug had taken it in turns to make regular checks on her, and always she'd been sleeping peacefully.

As an extra precaution, and on Ruth Close's advice, she'd also put Mary on the pill. Just in case, was how she thought of it. A final defence against the possibility of Kevin still somehow managing to get at Mary — because Tess had no doubt that sex was one of the motives behind his former visits. But as the days passed, and Mary continued cheerful, happy to sleep the night through, Tess seriously wondered whether the pill was necessary. Surely, at long last, their troubled lives were beginning to come right.

Or were they? She'd honestly believed so until this morning. (Why *this* morning, for God's sake? On the eve of their planned barbecue? Of what she'd laughingly called 'the lowering of the drawbridge'?) As usual, she'd gone into Mary's room to wake her, and thought merely that Mary had been bitten by mosquitoes, because of the swollen skin around her eyes. It was only when Tess noticed the dampness of the pillow that she realised Mary had been crying.

'What is it, love?' she asked, kneeling beside the bed and shaking her gently.

Mary opened her eyes, gave a fleeting smile, and then, as though recalling something from those long hours of sleep, she shuddered away and began to cry again.

'It's all right, sweetheart,' Tess crooned, holding her, rocking her. 'You've just had a bad dream. Give it a few minutes and it'll pass. See.' She pointed to the brightness of the window. 'The day's sunny, everything's fine.'

Except that for Mary, as Tess soon discovered, the sunlit day meant nothing. All through breakfast she sat at the table with a doleful look on her face; and later, down in the workshop, she pressed herself closer than ever to the wall, as if her life depended on the solid feel of it against her cheek and hands. Watching her from halfway up the stairs, Tess was reminded of how she'd acted as a small child whenever she'd felt unhappy: the way she'd clung to one or other of her dolls with exactly the same grim determination, refusing to give it up until all was well.

'Maybe we should call the barbecue off,' Doug suggested, joining Tess on the stairs.

She shook her head. 'We can't hide her away forever. And it's only family and a few friends.'

'Postpone it then,' he added. 'Wait till she's better.'

'She *is* better,' Tess insisted stubbornly. 'This won't

last. She had a dream, that's all. She'll be cheerful again by tomorrow.'

But again Tess was wrong. For the next morning Mary had passed beyond mere dejection: more than anything else, her condition reminded Tess of the first stages of grief — her face pale and shocked; her eyes red-rimmed but strangely tearless; her mouth alternately firm and trembling, as if she had yet to grasp the nature of her own feelings. Most attempts at comfort only made her worse. Harry, in fact, was the only person she would tolerate near her. Hunkered down at her side, as wordless as she, his presence seemed to calm her slightly.

It was Harry's calming effect that persuaded Tess to go ahead with the barbecue, hoping against hope that it would lift Mary's spirits; and ironically it was also Harry, later in the morning, who caused her to regret her decision.

Returning from the small, tourist-style café down the hill, where he had been sent to buy an extra carton of cream, he took a short-cut home by clambering over the fence and then forcing his way through the thick bush that protected the property from the road. That was how he came upon the reeking fly-blown carcass of the wombat and its eery likeness crouched below, the stench of the rotting carcass making him catch his breath. He hadn't seen Rory towards the end, but he understood more or less what had happened to the dog. Enough for him to realise that the wombat had met the same fate.

The first Tess knew of his discovery was when he

burst into the kitchen, his face nearly as pale from shock as Mary's, and declared bluntly that Mary and Kevin had been killing again.

'I don't believe it!' That was Tess's initial response after listening to his account.

'It's true!' he insisted, on the verge of tears now. 'You can go and see for yourself, over by the road.'

'But she hasn't left the house at night. Not once. So how could they . . . ?' Tess stopped and gripped the edge of the table to steady herself, struck by a new and unexpected possibility. 'Christ! He's been coming over here during the day. During the bloody day! That's when they've been getting together! Just wait till I . . . !'

But she had no chance to do anything, because at that moment the guests began arriving. She could hear cars swinging around on the drive. Doug, tending the fire on the narrow strip of lawn, was already calling out a series of welcomes.

Car doors slammed and footsteps mounted the steps and entered the passage.

'Where is everyone?' It was Uncle Ken's voice, he and Aunt Maud having driven over from Lithgow. 'Where are you all hiding?'

The elderly couple entered the kitchen, their faces creased into smiles. Unlike Meg, who was following close behind, they were both bluff, thick-set figures, practical rather than perceptive, unaware in those first instants of greeting that anything was amiss. Meg, on the other hand, sensed the tension straight away.

'What's become of Mary?' she asked, her thin face raised suspiciously.

'Yes, what have you done with that beautiful young daughter of yours?' Aunt Maud joined in, depositing an armful of home-grown flowers on the table. 'I hear she's just about right again.'

'She ... she's getting on that way,' Tess answered hesitantly, and nodded for Harry to go downstairs and fetch her.

He gave her an agonised look, pleading silently to be let off that particular task, but Tess waved him away.

'Just do it!' she muttered shortly, her words reaching as far as Meg who gave her another of her suspicious glances.

As he clattered off downstairs, more guests arrived — long-term friends who were ushered into the kitchen by Doug and Bob — and for several minutes everyone was too busy with greetings and introductions to think much about Mary. Everyone, that is, except Tess. She alone remained alert in the midst of all the talk and laughter; and so she was first to detect the faint whimpers of protest that began drifting up from below. Excusing herself, she moved hastily towards the stairway, but already the whimpers had grown too loud. Others were stopping to listen, faces turning. To where Harry, his arms about Mary's shoulders, was trying to coax her up the last step and through the open doorway.

At the sight of so many people, an expression of horror flitted across Mary's face. She tried to turn and run, but Harry blocked her path, and she fell to her knees instead, her body doubled over — more like a penitent now, someone confronted by her accusers, than the grief-stricken person Tess had woken that morning.

'Come on, Med,' Harry urged her, but she refused to budge, her forehead pressed to the floor, her face hidden beneath a veil of hair.

There was a prolonged hush, people shuffling their feet in embarrassment.

'You'd better get her out of here, my girl,' Meg advised Tess in a whisper.

But like everyone else, Tess was unable to move, mesmerised by this new and unexpectedly contrite Mary who seemed capable of slipping from one guise to another with bewildering speed. And all for what? And why?

'Sweetheart!' Doug called hoarsely from the far side of the room.

That helped break the spell, though it was Aunt Maud, not Tess, who finally rescued the situation.

'There's no sin in being shy,' she said in her homely way, bustling across to the doorway. 'Shyness runs in our family, you know. It was the bane of my life when I was a girl.' With Uncle Ken's help she lifted Mary to her feet, their beefy arms making light work of her resistance. 'Don't you fret, lovey,' she murmured, kissing the hair which still fell across Mary's face. 'No one's making you stay here. You'll be better off on your own for a bit. Come on now.' And together they turned and went back downstairs.

Mary was again crouched beside the wall by the time Tess had enough presence of mind to join them.

'What's wrong with her, Tess?' Aunt Maud asked, and now a certain shrewdness had replaced her homely manner.

'That's the big question around here,' Meg broke in. 'If you could answer it, Maud, you could set yourself up as one of those fancy counsellors in Sydney.'

'Are things that bad, Tess?'

'They're not marvellous,' she confessed, and darted an unhappy glance at Mary, whose face was turned to the wall, her shoulders hunched and resistant, as though she were trying to close everyone else out. 'Until yesterday, believe it or not, she was open and cheerful.'

'D'you call laughing like a donkey cheerful?' Meg broke in again. 'I'd call it hysterical.'

'It was better than this,' Tess said defensively.

'Better? You still can't face facts, can you? Well, it's time you woke up to yourself. You've got a real problem with this girl of yours that won't be solved by hiding yourselves away. Mark my words, you'll only make matters worse.'

'If I'm so keen on hiding away,' Tess flared back, 'why on earth have I invited you all here? I *want* Mary to start mixing with other people again. Complete isolation is the last thing I need for her.'

'Then what's to be gained by skulking in the bush? You had a perfectly good home in Sydney. All she's doing here is running wild, like the animal she thinks she is.'

'You know that's not true!' Tess said hotly. 'All that Terror stuff is behind her. This is something else entirely.'

'It looks the same to me, just one stage on. What's she up to now, d'you reckon? Mourning for that poor dead child? Josh, or whatever his name was, God rest him. Is that where she's at now?'

'I don't think...' Tess began.

'That's it in a nutshell!' Meg broke in fiercely. 'You don't *think*. If you did, you'd get her away from here, back to a place she knows, amongst people she's familiar with. Where she can find herself again. Because I'll tell you for the last time, my girl, keep her shut up in this fortress of yours and you'll live to regret...'

'Hey, come on now, steady on,' Uncle Ken said placatingly. 'Arguing amongst ourselves isn't going to help Mary any. Well is it?'

He beamed at them all, seeking their approval, and Aunt Maud reached out and patted him lovingly on the cheek.

'Never a truer word, Ken,' she agreed. 'Families need to stick together in times of trouble, not tear apart at the seams.'

For Tess it was Maud's spontaneous show of affection more than her actual words that brought everything back into perspective. She looked again at Mary, at her tiny body, at her thin shoulders so curved in upon themselves, so defenceless.

'I'm sorry,' she murmured, feeling suddenly shame-faced. 'I just thought today was going to be different.'

'Most of us think that every day, love,' Meg sighed, and even she sounded chastened.

'Right, then,' Ken declared, satisfied, and rubbed both hands together as though preparing for a job of work. 'What do you say to getting on with this barbecue? A good feed'll settle us down. Mary can join in later if she wants to. Meanwhile let's give her some peace and quiet.'

'We all need that from time to time,' Maud said, nodding. 'A chance to sort things out for ourselves. And why should Mary be any different from the rest of us? Leave her alone and she'll soon get things straight in her head. Before you know it, she'll be her old cheerful self again. The Mary we all love.'

'"Leave them alone and they'll come home," eh, Maud,' Ken chanted, and let out a throaty chuckle that reminded Tess of Mary in happier mood. 'That's how it is with kids,' he added. 'There's nothing to be gained from shoving them along. You have to let them find their own way in their own good time.'

Yes, Tess thought gratefully as she led the family back upstairs and out to the front of the house, 'their own way in their own good time'. It was the kind of advice she gave herself at the start of every day, in an effort to remain hopeful; and now, hearing it from someone else — someone as homely and down-to-earth as her Uncle and Aunt — she took heart.

Chatting with people during the course of the afternoon, the sunlight pierced by the chiming cries of bellbirds, she found herself glancing up at the front steps, half-expecting to see Mary sitting there, smiling down at them. The Mary she had known before Terror had torn their lives to shreds. Or even, less hopefully, the glad-faced Mary who had filled the house with laughter.

Yet no matter how often Tess looked, always the steps remained empty: the door, with its shattered panes, like an eyeless face; the house itself as sealed off and voiceless as Mary. So that as the afternoon wore away, Tess looked less and less to the house and turned instead to the line of trees, to where the bellbirds called on, indifferent to all her worries. Was Kevin hidden in there now? she wondered. After what Harry had discovered that morning, it was easy for her to imagine him peering out at them through a screen of leaves, spying, forever spying; or biding his time, today as on every day for several weeks past, waiting for that moment when Mary, yet again, would slip away from the house and join him.

So they could do what? The inevitable question, stifled up till then, pushed itself into the forefront of Tess's mind. Kill another poor, unsuspecting animal? Is that all they were on about? And if so, why? Or was the killing merely part of some kinky ritual that she, Tess, preferred not to think about? Whatever the truth, where was the sense in it? Where was it all heading?

Tess closed her eyes — blocking out the laughing people and the bird-song, the curl of smoke rising lazily from the remains of the fire, the fading afternoon light — and pictured Mary and Kevin running together beneath the trees. Kevin, naked, his face and upper body luridly painted, loped a pace or two ahead; and Mary, slight and pale, a strangely insubstantial version of herself, was being drawn along by his shadow.

'You look as though you've seen a ghost,' someone said, and Tess opened her eyes to find Maud standing beside her.

'No, not a ghost exactly,' she replied, her voice less certain than she would have liked.

Maud placed a comforting hand on her shoulder. 'It

doesn't do to fret, lovey. All the worry in the world never achieves a thing. Why not get your mind off Mary for a while and come for a walk with us. After a meal like that we could all do with a stroll.'

'You can say that again,' Ken agreed, patting his stomach and laughing.

'And we really need you along,' Maud went on lightheartedly. 'You know what Meg's like, she'll run us off our feet if you're not there to control her.'

'Yes, come on, Tess,' Doug called out, taking off his chef's apron and dropping it on the grass. 'Let's give these city types a taste of country life.'

Tess hesitated, caught between conflicting fears. If she went with them, what was to stop Mary sneaking off in search of Kevin? Because she was reasonably certain now that Mary and Kevin *had* been meeting during the day. On the other hand, if she stayed behind there was always the chance that the walking party might wander over to where Harry had found the mutilated remains of the wombat. And even if they avoided that, who was to say what other horrors they might stumble on? According to Harry, the wombat was in an advanced stage of decay, which meant there had been time enough for more killings.

Uncertain still, Tess turned towards the house, and Maud said reassuringly: 'Nothing's going to happen to Mary in the next half hour or so, believe me.'

Believe her? Tess, who had barely smiled all day, nearly broke into laughter then, the same hysterical laughter that had overtaken her weeks earlier, on the night of the fire. The absurdity of it! Maud, elderly and kind, with no inkling of what their lives now contained, unconsciously pitting her simple faith against something as lawless and unholy as the bond that existed between Mary and Kevin!

With an effort, Tess choked back her laughter ... and was suddenly struck by an altogether different thought. Was Maud really so absurd after all? Was simple faith perhaps the only thing Tess *did* have to fall back on? Faith in the real Mary; in the loving heart that surely persisted beneath all the trauma. Yes, that was still there surely, never mind what ghastly rituals Kevin had drawn her into; and *that*, Mary's enduring identity, was still worth believing in, still worth protecting.

Tess turned back towards her Aunt, her mind made up. 'A walk is a lovely idea,' she said with a bright, false smile. Though as a precaution she called to Bob: 'Will you stay here with Mary for a while? She's been so upset for the past day or so. I'd hate her to think we'd abandoned her.'

Then she was sauntering off down the slope, linking arms with Doug and steering the party away from the roadside boundary and over towards the creek.

There had been no rain for some time and the creek had fallen almost to nothing. A mere thread of water snaked between wide banks of sand now stained a dull yellow by the late afternoon sun.

'It's like being on the beach,' Meg cried, kicking up her skinny legs and moving on ahead of the rest. 'You should bring Mary down here, this'll cheer her up. And look at those trees. What a place for a picnic.'

Before Tess could head her off, she had veered aside,

in under the willows and up over the lip of the bank.

'Hey, you!' Tess heard her shout. 'What are you doing here?'

And she and Doug together were floundering through the loose sand, hurrying over to where Meg, as indignant as only she could be, was pointing through the bush at the unmistakable figure of a man. He was standing in the clearing, as still as the dog that crouched at his side and even more lifelike.

'My God!' Doug breathed out.

'Who is he? What does he want here?' Meg demanded.

'It's not a man,' Tess explained dully. 'It's a piece of sculpture.'

'Sculpture?'

Most of the others had caught up by then, Ken and Maud panting from the exertion; and Meg, motioning for them to follow, pushed her way through to the clearing. Only Tess was left behind, as yet too sick at heart to do more than lean wearily against the nearest tree.

'Who made them?' Meg sang out. 'How did they get here?'

And after a brief hesitation, Doug's low rumble: 'Mary . . . they're Mary's work.'

'Mary? She did these? Both of them?'

'We . . . we think so.'

'Then you've a gifted girl there, Doug,' Maud said approvingly. 'You and Tess should be proud.'

'But the man!' Meg again, her voice tinged with genuine awe. 'He's beautiful! Really beautiful! Sort of . . . you know, sort of other-worldly.'

That last description, vaguely ominous to Tess's ears, was what eventually drew her through the fringe of bush to the clearing. Where, at close quarters, she was first jolted into recognition — the identity of this latest figure taking her completely by surprise — and then grudgingly forced to admit that what Meg had said was true. There *was* something other-worldly about the figure's stance, about the carefully moulded features. And also something disconcertingly beautiful, despite the fact that, beyond any doubt, what she was looking at was a model of Kevin. Or rather Kevin and not Kevin. As if the essential man, stripped of all his loutish behaviour, of all his wayward desire, had somehow been distilled into this creature of stone and clay; as if his very soul had been plucked free and planted here in this strangely pure, stony-eyed likeness.

But why Kevin of all people? And why would he have gone to all the bother of helping to model himself? Unless of course he had had no hand in this. None!

Tess experienced a sudden lurching sensation and bile spurted into her mouth, making her moan softly and reach out to Doug for support. For a few moments she tried not to think at all, to let the surrounding voices wash over her.

'The artistic temperament,' Ken was saying, wagging his finger in a knowing way. 'That's the root of our Mary's trouble. We saw a program about it on the telly. How these artist types get miserable as sin when they're working on their paintings and stuff.'

'I'd go along with that, Ken,' Meg replied. 'I've been hard on the child in the past, but I must say this puts a different complexion on things. If these figures are anything to go by, she may have been talking to us all along, through her hands, and not one of us listening.'

Tess, partially recovered, felt tempted to shout a reply, to tell Meg and all the rest of them that she at least had been listening. Too hard perhaps, especially to this purified version of Kevin that stood blank-eyed before them in the lengthening shadows of the clearing. It seemed to whisper to her now, things she definitely did not want to hear. Questions like: What if Mary, in this instance, chose to work alone? What if she did the modelling without Kevin's knowledge? What then?

Ignoring Doug, who was peering into her face with concern, Tess groped for a ready answer to the figure's silent challenge. Perhaps . . . she faltered, stricken by dread . . . perhaps Mary made the sculpture as a tribute to Kevin . . . perhaps it was a mute offering, a sign of homage, of affection, of the love she was incapable of expressing in words.

Perhaps . . .

Then again . . . then . . . !

The lurching sensation was back, the bitter taste of bile flooded into her mouth once again. Flinging off Doug's restraining hand, she flinched from the statue's blank gaze. Its delicately moulded lips were no longer tormenting her with questions. Now they were *telling* her what the figure was doing there; *telling* her what it was a preparation for. A ritual death! As much a preparation as all the earlier sculptures. A signpost directing her to what must follow. Or worse, to what may already have occurred.

'Please God, no!' Tess moaned aloud and scanned the edges of the clearing, searching for the one person who could reassure her, for the merest glimpse of his living face amongst the leaves. She knew in her heart that there was little chance of finding him, but still she went on looking.

And against all the odds he was there! In a dense clump of foliage. Partially obscured by it, but him none the less, his bulky form watching her, spying, from the shadowy cover of the trees.

She had never dreamed that the sight of him would bring such sweet relief. All that stopped her from pointing and singing out was the strangeness of his attitude. His shoulders were hunched and he appeared taller than she remembered. Nor was that all. When the trees moved, stirred by the evening breeze, he seemed to move in sympathy with them, as if he were truly a creature of the forest. And there was something else now that she looked more closely, something that explained his increased height. His feet were clear of the ground, which probably meant that he had hoisted himself up into the fork of a tree, for a better view. Either that, or . . .

Tess was not conscious of reaching a decision, yet in that first split-second of clear-eyed knowledge, as she was to realise later, she made the most momentous decision of her life. There was no hesitation. No pause for thought. Acting on instinct alone, she whirled around towards Doug and shouted at him: 'Get these people out of here!'

'What?' He was gazing at her almost as blank-faced as Kevin's unearthly likeness.

'Tess, what is it?' That was Meg, stern as always, but caring.

The others closed around her, protective, concerned.

'What's the matter, lovey?' Maud asked, and tried to take her in her arms.

She fended her off with a show of anger, even though she had never felt less angry. Right at that moment she would have preferred to burst into helpless tears or to curl up on the ground like a wounded child. What prevented her, what gave her the surge of energy she needed, was the fear that any one of these faces might turn towards the far edge of the clearing. That she could not allow, and she shouted louder than ever, a crazed edge to her voice.

'D'you hear me, Doug? Tell them to get the fuck out of here!'

Thankfully they were backing away, more bewildered now than concerned, some of them obviously affronted. Not that she cared about their feelings. She was beyond worrying about such things. All that mattered was that every eye was upon *her*. Upon her and no one else.

'Tess!' Doug murmured, but she pushed at him, too, forced him back like the rest.

'I've had you all up to here!' she screamed dementedly, making a slicing motion across her neck with the side of her hand. 'Now get the fuck out and leave me alone!'

They were trailing back through the undergrowth, shocked, hurt, insulted.

'Go!' she yelled for good measure, her voice rising out of control. 'Give me some peace, for Christ's sake!'

Meg lingered long enough for a parting shot. 'D'you want the truth, Tess? It's not Mary who needs treatment. It's you. You're the problem in this family.'

'Who wants your fucking truth? Go!'

Only Doug remained, unwilling to leave her like this — the line of bush shadow-streaked at his back, his troubled face catching the last of the sunlight.

'Tess?'

How could she go on pretending with him? She let her mask of anger slip, let all her desperation show through. He took a step towards her, but she made an odd pleading gesture with both hands and nodded in the direction of the path.

'Please,' she murmured, so softly that the sound reached only as far as him. 'Please.'

It was all she had time for, terrified that while the light lasted one of the others might come back. Yet where Doug was concerned it was enough, as she might have guessed. For still with a puzzled frown on his face, he turned and blundered off through the narrow fringe of bush.

She was so grateful to him for that, for his unquestioning trust, the tears stinging her eyes even as she also turned and made her way slowly across to the far, dusky edge of the clearing. To the dim, shadowy place roofed over with trees where Kevin — and this she understood only too well — could not do other than wait.

14

The most painful part for Doug was tightening the straps. He would almost have preferred it if Mary had struggled, had fought for her freedom, but she lay passively on the bed, gazing miserably at him. To make matters worse, Harry was crouched in the corner, crying.

'You shouldn't be doing it to her,' he kept saying. 'You shouldn't!'

'He's right,' Doug said, letting his hands drop to his sides. 'This isn't the kind of thing you should do to people. To your own daughter least of all.'

Tess's eyes flicked away from his, the way they always did when she was feeling guilty or unsure.

'Get it over with,' she said in that hard, brittle voice which he also knew well. 'Or do I have to ask Bob?'

He was aware of Bob, over near the door, shuffling his feet uncomfortably.

'I still say Harry's right,' he persisted. 'She's not an animal to be tied up.'

'Isn't she?' Suddenly Tess was on her knees before him, hissing out words, her cheeks livid. 'I wonder whether you'll go on believing that after you've been down there? You'll understand then why we can't take

Harry with us, and why we can't leave him here either, not unless Mary's restrained. Now get on with it!'

'I still don't see . . . ' he began stubbornly, and ducked as she hit out at him with the sides of her fists, her thin arms swinging desperately.

'You're such a fool, Doug!' she was shouting. 'Such a bloody fool! Do you think the rest of the world's as decent as you are? Do you? Have you any idea . . . any idea at all . . . ?'

Sheltering behind his beefy forearms, he heard hurried footsteps across the floor and felt the rain of blows stop abruptly.

'Easy, Mum,' Bob breathed. 'Just take it easy.'

Doug peered nervously at Tess from between his raised arms. Bob had her by the wrists, her face still red, the skin around her eyes strained and bruised.

'Let go,' she said, and shook Bob off. Then: 'I'm waiting, Doug.' Not shouting at him, but with the same shrill edge to her voice. 'You let me down in this and I swear . . . Christ, I swear I'll . . .!'

Even at the best of times he found it difficult to withstand her anger, especially when it was driven by despair, like now. It wasn't that he was frightened of her. He simply had no anger of his own to match hers. Also, it pained him to see her out of control, so unlike her normal self. Always he found it easier, more *right* somehow, to give in.

Bob crouched beside him, as daunted by Tess as he was. 'D'you need any help, Dad?' he asked unhappily.

He shook his head. 'No, I can handle it,' he said, and

pulled reluctantly at the nearest buckle, wincing at the way the flesh creased beneath the strap.

'Tighter!' Tess insisted, her voice hard and brittle again.

Avoiding Mary's gaze, he forced himself to tug at each of the straps in turn, sucking in his breath as they cut into the soft skin of her arms and legs.

'Does that satisfy you?' he asked bitterly. He had moved back from the bed so he wouldn't be tempted to look at Mary's face.

'It's a start,' she said, and walked over to the door where Harry, his cheeks nearly as flushed as hers, stood barring the way.

'Let her go,' he demanded tearfully.

'We can't. She's dangerous.'

'You're just saying that because you don't care about her any more. You think she's mad, and she's not. She's not!'

'We care, son,' Doug answered gently, and tried to stroke his cheek, but Harry knocked his hand aside.

'Your Dad's telling you the truth,' Tess said, her face now set and stern. 'We wouldn't be doing this to her if we didn't care. You have to believe that, Harry.'

Harry dashed fresh tears from his eyes, his bottom lip trembling and folding in upon itself. 'You're a liar!' he shouted, and turned deliberately towards Doug who wilted before him. 'You both are! Never mind what you say, I'm going to untie her as soon as you leave.'

To Doug, it was like being caught between two equally passionate forces — Tess and this younger, male version of Tess — neither of whom he had any real defence against.

'Can't we ... ?' he pleaded, and was cut short by Tess.

'I'm sorry, Harry, but Mary has to stay like this till we get back,' she said, and ushering them all out into the passage, she locked the door and pocketed the key.

They left him punching and kicking at the door, Doug almost running in an attempt to escape his broken sobs. He couldn't escape Harry's voice though. 'I hate you!' The desolate cry pursued him across the lawn where moonlight glinted on the litter of plates and glasses left over from the barbecue. 'You're liars and I hate you all!'

After the searching brightness of the moon, the blackness beneath the trees was like a sanctuary. Hunkered down, his breath catching in his throat, Doug was glad of the dark, glad that the others couldn't see his face. There was a light tread behind him and he felt Tess's hands on his shoulders. Her touch unexpectedly soft, caressing, harder to resist even than her angry demands.

'I can't do this without you, Doug. You *and* Bob, I need you both.' Her voice a whisper; she, too, partially transformed by the night.

'Give me a minute,' he begged.

But a minute for what? To gather his courage? To harden himself against his own children? Or to prepare for what awaited them further down the slope? For although he was incapable as yet of focusing his fears into one clear image, he did have some idea of what Tess had discovered.

'Take your time,' Tess whispered, her hand kneading

the tension from his shoulders. 'We'll go on when you're ready.'

He could hear them murmuring together in the darkness while they waited, Bob's voice so like his own, as if he, Doug, were doing the questioning.

'Why can't you tell us what's down there?'

'It's not something you can explain. You have to see it for yourself.'

'Is it that bad?'

'It's bad.'

Bad. The word seemed to detach itself from the conversation and descend moth-like through the dark. In a sudden preternatural vision, Doug watched it settle on Mary's upturned face, its wings shadowing the misery in her eyes, its sombre markings pulsing to the rhythm of her breath.

He lurched hastily, unsteadily, to his feet. 'We're wasting time,' he said, and crashed off through the trees, conscious of the others following close behind.

'It would be quicker to use the path,' Tess called after him.

But he didn't want the moonlit clarity of the path; he couldn't even bring himself to switch on the torch he'd brought along. He preferred this darker passage which was after all a form of preparation, a kind of descent, a blind, groping journey into whatever lightless region Mary's confusion had led her.

Who had once said that it's better to journey than to arrive? he wondered bleakly. Well it was true, because he broke out into the silvery brightness of the clearing before he was ready. The newly made sculpture (could Mary's hands alone have fashioned that?) stood directly in his path, its white-clay surface frosted by the moonlight, its quartz eyes emptied of all desire. Beautiful, that was how Meg had described it, and she'd been right. Somewhere beyond the unsteady thump of Doug's heart, beyond the fits of shivering that shook him from head to foot, a calm part of his mind saw it for what it was. Exquisite. A thing so perfect, so complete, that it seemed to have turned its back on death, like a gift from the earth itself, offered in exchange for . . . for . . .

He could sense its other self over to his left, just inside the dark line of the bush. All he had to do was turn, to switch on the torch. But still he wasn't ready.

'Look!' Tess said, her voice harsh again, and took the torch from him. 'That's what we have to deal with!'

He heard Bob moan and stagger away, gagging; and he knew then how it would be. Like Rory. The same thing all over again.

He turned, and somehow the fact that it was a man hanging up there in the torchlight didn't make it any worse. A man? Or rather what was left of a man. What *had* been a man once. One side of his face slashed beyond recognition, the mouth a vacant hole; his clothes, his flesh, ripped open from throat to crutch; the gaudy rope of his entrails spilling down to where the half-eaten remains of his vital organs made a bloodied heap upon the bare earth.

A pace or two away Bob was vomiting. 'Mary couldn't have done that!' he kept gasping out. 'Not that!'

It was, for Doug, like listening to himself, like witnessing his own earlier response to Rory's gutted carcass. And oddly, it calmed him, left him relatively free. The retching, the nausea, weren't things he needed to go through again. Although his hands were shaking, his mouth dry, he found to his surprise that he was more or less in control.

Too much in control, perhaps. Because for the moment he wasn't even thinking about Mary. He didn't dare! Couldn't bear to! That would come later. *Must* come later! Now, one part of his mind partly blanked out, negated (Oh God, not Mary!), he studied the terrible details of Kevin's mutilated form. The sheer horror of it was more than enough to cope with, inspiring in him a mixture of feelings. Revulsion, yes. But something else. Not curiosity — such butchery left little to the imagination, little to wonder at. Then what? Pushing the damp hair back from his forehead, he searched past his initial sense of shock, past the dark forbidding place in his mind, and discovered other emotions altogether. Pity. Compassion. An undeniable desire to reach out to someone so much less fortunate than himself. What moved him most, perhaps, was the terrible indignity this other person had suffered, an indignity which the body itself still needed to be rescued from.

'I'm going back for a knife,' he said in a choked whisper.

'A knife? What for?' Tess's face, pale in the deep shadow of the trees, swivelled quickly towards him.

'To cut the body down with,' he explained, indicating the rope which held it aloft, and he was about to leave when she directed the torchbeam to the heaped entrails.

'There,' she said, as if challenging him.

He recognised it straight away, despite the clotted blood on handle and blade: the long kitchen knife Tess had lost weeks before, when she'd thrown it at the fleeing figure of Kevin on just such a night as this. Equally, and with sudden dread, he recognised what its reappearance here meant, because apart from Tess, and of course Kevin, only one other person would have known where to look for it. Mary! Which in turn suggested that she *must* have . . . ! There was no more room now for doubt. That she . . . !

No! he resolved with a shudder, forcing the thought back into the inner dark where he could contain it, deny it by means of silence alone. The time hadn't yet come for that. Not yet, thank God. Hadn't he already decided to deal with the issue of Mary later? Days, months, years later, if that were even remotely possible.

Well then . . . He took a long quivering breath. First things first. Kevin, yes, Kevin. Whose remains, horrible though they were, were still preferable to thoughts of Mary. Doug made himself look at them, both fists tightly bunched to stop himself trembling. God, what a mess! After what this poor soul had been through it was surely only right and proper that his body should be treated with common decency at the last. Every creature on earth deserved that, whatever their faults.

'Get a hold on yourself,' he said to Bob, though he could as easily have been addressing himself, and he stooped for the knife.

Thankfully, the handle proved to be dry, not sticky as he had feared. He straightened up, knife in hand, and heard Tess let out a kind of sigh.

Of anticipation? Relief?

It puzzled him for a moment, and then like her he

realised what he had just done — destroy evidence; superimpose his own fingerprints on the murder weapon. Was that perhaps what he'd secretly meant to do? What he'd have done anyway, eventually, without any prompting from Tess or anyone? He wasn't sure. Couldn't decide. It was yet another thing for him to consider later. For him to force back into the inner dark.

Sidling around the body, he felt for the rope which ran from an overhead bough down to a smaller branch at waist height.

'Take the weight of the legs,' he instructed Bob who was standing out in the moonlight, wiping his mouth clean.

'I can do that for him,' Tess offered, giving way to her protective impulses even where Bob was concerned. It was her usual reaction when someone she loved was threatened. Bob, Mary, Harry, it made no difference: with her it was always the same. That was the person she would always be whenever any of them was put at risk.

And all at once Doug began to understand her basic motive for leading him down here, for insisting that he and Bob see this abomination for themselves.

'No, let Bob do it,' he said, waving her back. 'That's what he's here for, isn't it? To make sure he gets involved?'

She shone the torch full in his face. 'Are you feeling all right, Doug? This isn't like you.'

What could he tell her? That after what had happened to Kevin and the dog, nothing about them and their lives could possibly be normal again? That he had already half guessed what she was about to demand of him?

'Let's get the body down,' was all he said, and he waited until Bob had a firm hold on the legs before cutting the rope and playing it out slowly through his hands.

Afterwards, while Bob was again retching in the shadows, Doug knelt beside the body. He also felt queasy at the prospect of what he still had to do, but he did it just the same. Slowly, gently, moved by pity alone, he lifted the entrails and what was left of the internal organs and heaped them back in the body cavity.

He wasn't a particularly religious man. Back in Sydney it had been duty more than anything else which had prompted him to accompany his family to church on Sundays. Yet now, kneeling in the warm night, his hands stained with another's blood, he felt called upon to make some gesture. To wish this lost soul well in whatever journey lay ahead. For once it didn't seem to matter that he had no great faith. The fact of death was real enough, not to be denied. As was the evidence of recent suffering. More suffering, perhaps, than anybody should be called upon to bear. And taking off his shirt, he draped it over the ruined face, as though protecting it not just from the surrounding dark, but also from the cold indifference of the moon.

'God bless,' he muttered, and strode off towards the creek where he plunged his hands into the thin stream of water and scoured them clean with sand.

Like him, Tess must also have felt uneasy, almost

exposed out there in the moonlight, because she was waiting with Bob in the shelter of a tall she-oak, the thin foliage casting spidery shadows across her face.

'What now?' she asked, challenging him again, as he'd known she must.

'We should get in touch with the police,' he said, suggesting it half-heartedly because he sensed that her mind was already made up.

And his own mind? What did that tell him to do? The sensible thing? To oppose Tess for the first and only time in his life? To oppose her in something that really mattered?

'I won't let them take her away from me, Doug,' she warned him, her voice ominously quiet, worse in a way than when she shouted. 'You know what they'd do with her, don't you? They'd put her in a prison for the criminally insane. She'd grow old and die in there. And I won't have that happen to her, not for the likes of Kevin Briggs.'

She paused, expecting him to object, and seemed taken aback when Bob was the one who protested.

'Mary? Are you trying to tell me *she* killed him? Jesus Christ, you must be crazy! She'd never . . .'

'She did it, Bob,' Doug broke in, and only as he made the admission did he truly accept the fact that it was so, his voice failing suddenly.

He had been ready for grief, for despair even. But not for this. It was like a door opening onto another kind of night altogether, and for some minutes he could hardly breath, the moonlight breaking through the foliage of the tree and drenching him in its hard brightness.

Somewhere in the background he was aware of Tess whispering fiercely. To him? To Bob? A relentless monotone that overrode Bob's anguished denials, his own involuntary whimpers, reducing them both to silence.

When his breathing finally steadied, he found that he had fallen forward, his face pressed into the sand. He pushed himself up and looked at Tess. She appeared so thin, so fragile; and yet so obdurate, the exposed skin of her arms and legs a hard bone-white against the dark backdrop of the bush. Bob showed as a hunched, uncertain shape beside her, his face buried in his arms.

'... it's the only way, Doug,' she finished.

'But you saw him,' he protested feebly. 'What she did to him. How could she even have thought it? What was going on inside her head?'

'He probably drove her to it.'

'To that?'

'He was the one who started it, remember, with his models and his killings. He taught her the whole crazy process. And at the end, when he ...' She ran her fingers angrily, distractedly through her hair. 'Who knows what he was trying to make her do? Something kinky and awful that she couldn't cope with. Anyway, at the end she must have turned on him. Retaliated in the only way she knew how.'

'So it was his fault? Is that what you're suggesting?'

She took him roughly by the shoulders, her nails digging into his bare flesh. 'Think about it, Doug!' she said intently. 'Get that brain of yours working for once. She was disturbed to begin with, when they first made contact. She wasn't responsible. And that's what he took advantage of. He used her, and then tried to abuse her into the bargain. Can you blame her for turning his own weapons against him? She was only following his lead. She was like a child, for Christ's sake, doing what her elders and betters had taught her.'

'Her betters?' he asked uneasily.

'That's how she must have seen him. To her he would have seemed exciting and powerful. Don't forget he helped her kill Terror or Rory or whatever you want to call him.'

Doug shivered as the first of the night breeze drifted along the valley, rustling the overhead foliage and patterning the ground with moonlight.

'Even if you're right,' he half conceded, 'what's to stop her killing again?'

That, for him, was the hardest question of all. The one which, at all costs (even the cost of Mary herself) could not be avoided.

'Why should she?' Tess's voice was suddenly as soft and reasonable as the touch of her hands on his shoulders. 'Kevin was her role model and he's gone. In time she'll forget him. All this will become like a distant nightmare for her.'

Doug wanted to believe, wanted to keep at bay all that despairing anger which he knew lay just beneath the surface of Tess's calm. But still he couldn't bring himself to lie. Not to himself. Not to her.

'If she's so safe,' he pointed out, 'why did we have to tie her up? Why couldn't we have left her in Harry's care?'

'I said she'll settle down "in time"!' Tess reminded him, the merest flame-tip of her anger showing. 'If we're patient, we'll win her back. She'll become our Mary again. *Ours!*'

'And in the meantime?'

'We'll make sure she stays in the house. You and Bob can see to that. We'll keep her safe.'

Doug understood what 'safe' meant. 'I thought you didn't want to lock her up.'

'It'll be our jail, Doug, no one else's. And we'll be in it with her. That's the difference. That and the fact that we'll be able to let her out when the time's ripe. This way she won't be ill-treated; she won't be ignored; she won't be lost in some faceless bureaucracy.'

It was Tess's last and most direct appeal to him — he understood that as well. Which left only one other question. One that, in a sense, had already been answered, up there in the house when Tess had chosen to bring them down here rather than ring the police. A redundant question, really, though he put it to her just the same, as a test of himself as much as her.

'What are you really saying, Tess? That we should cover all this up? Pretend it never happened?'

'Yes.'

Just the one word, definite, adamant, leaving no room for compromise, for argument.

Doug was aware of Bob lifting his head, staring at them both wonderingly.

'You realise what it'll mean?' he pressed her. 'We'll have to bury the body, get rid of Kevin's ute, make it look as though he's shot through. Are you prepared to do all that?'

'Yes.'

That one word again. No hint of hesitation. And of course, being Tess, she would have thought about all those things anyway, and more. But having begun, he couldn't stop, his own conscience also an issue here.

'We'll be accessories...'

'We already are,' she said cutting him short. 'We've tampered with the body, messed up the fingerprints on the knife. As far as the police are concerned, we could have done it. It'd be our word against Mary's.'

'Kevin's blood will be on our hands,' he went on relentlessly.

'*Will* be?' she queried. 'Isn't it already? What were you washing off over there in the creek?'

He had no answer to that. Perhaps she was right. Perhaps he had really decided what needed to be done when he'd stooped for the knife? Or earlier still, before leaving the house, when he'd agreed to tie Mary up. For he had half known even then what to expect, forewarned by the desperation in Tess's face. Possibly the only real difference between him and Tess was that he lacked her honesty, her clear-eyed appraisal of her true motives and desires.

'Well?' she asked. It was another veiled challenge, her tone now as cool and detached as the moonlight.

The night wind rose and fell, carrying with it a distant promise of rain and a faint, suggestive scent of damp, turned earth. Doug shivered once again and tried to imagine an alternative, something other than the dark unlovely grave he would need to dig somewhere in the bush behind him. But all he could picture was emptiness, Mary lost and gone forever. *His* Mary! And all for what? Nothing could bring Kevin back or undo his suffering.

'Time to decide, Doug.'

The voice not of conscience, but of necessity. Of the heart. Which was odd considering how cold it sounded.

'I'll fetch a shovel,' he groaned, and stumbled heavily to his feet.

Tess turned to Bob who was still watching them, his eyes shadowy hollows that conveyed little. 'Are you in this with us?' she said, more a demand than a question.

'I think you're both mad,' he said quietly.

Tess's whole body had grown tense. 'What do you think we should do then? Give her up?'

'I didn't say that,' he protested. 'Only that you're wrong. Mary couldn't kill anyone. She's too gentle.'

'Try telling that to Kevin,' she said, as though purposely taunting him.

And he was also on his feet, swearing at them, his voice cracking. 'Fuck you! Fuck you both! You could at least believe in her! She's your own daughter, for fuck's sake!'

Doug started forward, but Tess had already scrambled up and dragged Bob urgently against her, pulling his face down into the curve of her neck. 'Hush,' she whispered. 'Hush now. We do believe in her. That's why we need your help. So she can have another chance. You want that for her, don't you? Don't you?'

He stepped free of her at last, subdued now, his face

swollen with unshed tears. 'I'll see about getting rid of the ute,' he said, and walked over to the path where he stopped briefly and gazed back at them. 'You're wrong about Mary all the same. I know her. I know she couldn't have done it. There has to be someone else. Another girl who looks a bit like her maybe. There *has* to be.'

Someone else? Another girl, like Mary but different? Someone hidden amongst the trees at that very moment, perhaps, watching them, laughing to herself?

Doug would have given anything to believe that, but when he glanced warily about him the night felt too still, the valley too deserted. A lone mopoke called from a distance, and that was all. No one moved in the shadows; nothing disturbed the cruel, revealing brilliance of the moonlight. And with Tess at his side, he turned regretfully towards the house. Towards a Mary he could hardly conceive of.

Part Six

> But after I had seen
> That spectacle, for many days my brain
> Worked with a dim and undetermined sense
> Of unknown modes of being; o'er my thoughts
> There hung a darkness.
>
> William Wordsworth, 'The Prelude'

15

'I am with you.'

That was what Mary heard Him whisper. His last words to her before her father and Bob started working on the doors and windows. Through all the noise and activity that followed, He held to His silence; and even in the deeps of the night the house failed to creak or in any other way announce His presence. Waking just before dawn, she would lift her head from the pillow and glance sideways — searching for a shape, a vague silhouette — but the murky corner of her room remained empty.

By the beginning of the fourth night she had almost begun to doubt His reality, to think of Him as a shadow cast by her own dread. Or was that what He was expecting her to think? Was this yet another trial of her faith? For the truth was that she had come close to failing Him at their last meeting down there amongst the trees.

'Laugh,' He had said, and she had cried as she was crying now, the tears welling up from a source she was powerless to control.

It had been the same a little later, the first pale streaks of dawn lightening the sky, when He had ordered her to eat. 'Ambrosia,' He had called it, 'Food for the Gods', 'The gateway to eternity'. Offering it to her as to an equal.

She hadn't meant to flinch back. That had been a reflex action occasioned by the bloodied corpse dangling from the rope above them.

'Don't let me feast alone, little sister,' He had warned her.

And she had tried. She had forced her body into that act of sharing. Though once again it had been His darkly invisible hands, the implied threat of His disapproval, that had controlled her rebellious stomach.

'Would you spurn my gift?' He had whispered/threatened.

And somehow, her whole physical being screaming a denial, she had done His bidding. While He, looming at her back in the chosen place, the place of blood, had muttered:

'The cycle is complete, little sister. Let there be no more tears until another moonswell.'

It wasn't until the following night, as she had lain strapped to this very bed with Harry crying and calling through the locked door, that He had issued His last message. A ghostly whisper that had seemed to rise from the earth itself.

'Never fear, little sister. I am with you.'

An assurance or a further warning? If an assurance, then why had He withdrawn? Why did He leave her locked here in this prison of a house?

Now, three nights later and no longer strapped down, she slipped out of bed and tiptoed through to the living room. The night was warm, the windows open, and she pressed her face to the newly-fitted bars, pushed against them until the hard angles of the iron bit painfully into her cheeks. Surely He would detect her pain. It was her only means of calling to Him, a voice He must understand better than any other.

Or was that a forbidden thought? As sinful as peering into His face, which she pictured as a vast expanse of stars; which she hoped He would reveal to her one day, if only she were patient.

Patience. It was one of the hardest things. That and faith. Both of them so difficult to sustain after what He had persuaded her to. Kneeling before the open window, she tried to lock them together like links in a continuous chain. Patience-faith-patience-faith-pa... But with her next breath they burst apart, and in a sudden frenzy she began beating at the one remaining restraint — the outer bars — punching at them until her knuckles were bruised and she collapsed sobbing and exhausted onto the floor.

Lying there, desolate, she watched the light from the waning moon inch slowly across the gleaming floorboards towards the side wall. She had lost hope by then. She anticipated nothing, least of all the sound of His voice.

'Come,' she heard Him call, so softly that she confused Him with the whirr of insect life beyond the window. Then, much louder, in a show of mercy she was unprepared for — 'Come, come, come, come, come...' — like a summoning gong sounding somewhere inside her head.

Did she dream it, the way she followed the murmur of His feet along the passage? She could no longer tell. She could not have said whether it was a real door that opened for her, or a barrier in her mind; whether the smiling faces in the half dark were truly there or merely imagined; whether the window beyond the faces was a solid thing of wood and glass or a magical casement drawn from childhood memory. And the breeze, she could have imagined that as well; or, equally, have actually felt it on her cheek, raised her face and breathed in the cool, earth-scented air.

Dreaming/waking, she walked beneath the open sky, stole through the rustling bushland with His footsteps there beside her. At the place of blood, where the grave gaped, He indicated to her what must be done.

'This isn't just another animal to rot in the sun or moulder in the earth,' He said. 'This is a man, a child of God, whose being we will purge with holy fire.'

Yet secretly it was herself she purged, each stick that she fed into the blaze also feeding her unuttered longing; the flames that crisped the helpless flesh also searing away her grief. So that once again, there in the fading moonlight, she laughed aloud, however briefly.

'Be Siva to my Vishnu,' He instructed her then, and she danced to an unheard song, each counter-clockwise circle like an unravelling, a reversal of the wheel He had set her upon.

'Forgive me,' she trilled silently, not to Him. Her song meant for other, earth-stopped ears. 'Be happy. Forget the terror and be free.'

Afterwards, back beneath the window in the living

room (had she ever moved from there?), He breathed a final warning.

'Remember, the door and window that I showed you are mine alone. In time they will be yours too, but not yet. Not until your earthly connections are purged away and you have taken the sun for father, the moon for mother, the stars for siblings. Do you understand me, little sister?'

She nodded, shivering in the pinkish-grey dawn that had replaced the moonlight.

'Now bide,' He whispered, His presence slowly receding with the shadows. 'At the next moonswell, we will begin your re-creation. We will teach you to stand where Brahma stands, and truly to dance as Siva dances.'

Then He was gone, and a long relief of early sunlight flooded the room.

'Bide,' He had said at the last. Wait. And she obeyed (what other choice was there?) for long days and nights, during which she wandered unhappily about the house at all and any hours, the whisper of her bare feet mimicking His.

Her parents and brothers she pretended not to see.

'Cheer up, Med.' That was Harry every morning, hurrying to catch the early bus, grinning encouragingly at her as he slipped out through the front door which he was always careful to lock after him.

And a little later, at breakfast, the soft rumble of her father's voice, 'How are you, sweetheart?', inviting her to another day.

A day like any other, in which she studiously ignored them all; made a practice of it hour by hour, arming herself against future grief. For hadn't He prophesied her family's eclipse, by sun, moon, and stars? She shivered as she had on the night of His announcement, hoping that He had merely been testing her again; that His mercy would eventually extend to them as well.

And if it didn't . . . ?

No, she wouldn't let that darkest of thoughts intrude upon her waiting. Better to pretend she had no family; better not to notice Tess's warm touch or the loving pressure of Bob's concern; better by far to roam her limited domain with blank, unpondering eyes.

That domain, the house itself, she now envisaged as encased in steel. A cage against which she constantly dashed her wings, fluttering bird-like, bat-like, in the rigid shadow of the bars. If she thought of Him at all in the course of her baffled flights, it was as a liberator, fixing her mind upon the image of His door, His window, and on the vague, unformulated space between.

What kind of space had it been? 'Welcome home, little sister,' He had said as soon as she entered. But it had been too dark for her to glimpse anything more than the many faces smiling down at her, all of them touched with such sweetness, such kindness; and she had flitted between them too quickly to remember the space as anything other than a suggestive hollow in the mind. An inner room of thought where kindness and creation reigned; where the faces smiled benevolently upon her; where all destruction ceased. If she could somehow find that space again; if she could burrow back through memory to the exact location in her brain where it lay hidden; if she could meet Him there and plead with Him . . .

If!

That was probably the most desperate of all her vain hopes. One she resorted to when the deep silence of the house closed in upon her and the constricting bars showed as forbidding black lines against the windows of the night.

For the rest, she attuned herself to His return, listening to the minute movements of the house, to the voiceless creaks and groans that made her heart falter. Dutifully each evening, she sat by the open window, her eyes searching the night sky for a sign of His coming.

'At the next moonswell,' He had promised. And there, one humid night, suspended above the trees, hung a sicklemoon flanked by a single star. She managed not to cry out; she held back the tears that pressed against her eyelids. Could that be Him? The star? He had once described the blackness of the sky as His 'ultimate dwelling place'. Was that where He would come from? It looked so cold, so distant, so empty.

She found consolation in the fact that He would at least arrive in His Other guise. As creator. And later that night she prepared herself for Him, sitting straight and attentive in her darkened room, her face turned from both the corner and the door.

Alert to the slightest noise, she heard the floorboards in the passage give beneath His weight, the door glide open. He passed her like a breath of wind that coiled and settled in the deepest shadows. And His voice when He spoke! Soft, beguiling, but with an undertone of steel.

'It is time, little sister.'

Time?

As always, He read the questioning tilt of her face. 'A time for making.'

And after?

He read that, too, and consoled her with a sigh. 'All things in their season, little sister. First decide where we should begin. Which tender plant shall we remake? The choice is yours.'

Her choice? She had to clamp her teeth together to stop them chattering. How could she possibly ... how ... ?

But silence was no refuge. Not from Him.

'Come,' He ordered her.

And His will seemed to lift her from the bed and impel her out into the gloom of the passage.

'Which is it to be?' He demanded. 'Is it one of these?'

She was standing in the open doorway of her parents' room. She could see the outline of their bodies in the bed, hear the even chorus of their breath. The sheets swished and they turned together, her father muttering, Tess groaning softly. For a moment Mary wondered whether they would wake and see her, recognise her not as their daughter, but as a dark angel. But they had already settled again, so trusting of the night, so it was impossible for her to walk across and point at either one of them.

'Or is *this* the one? He asked suggestively.

And she found she had moved back along the passage and was crouched beside Harry's bed. He looked so young, so vulnerable, his upturned face and throat both dangerously exposed. She reached out towards him — a quick protective gesture — and the Other One's presence seemed to swell and fill the room.

'Be clear, little sister. Is this a pointing of the bone? Is this your choosing?'

She shook her head in hasty denial and stumbled backwards — to where Bob's room, the last in the line, awaited her judgment. She tiptoed in, thinking herself alone, but his murmured questions followed her, as insidious as before.

'Is it now? Our beginning? Is this where our search ends?'

She was glad Bob's face was covered. In the poor light she could just make out his rumpled hair on the pillow. Further down the bed, one work-thickened hand dangled from beneath the sheet, palm upwards, as though begging for alms, for mercy.

'Spare him,' she prayed. 'Spare all of them. Don't let the sword descend.'

The Other One didn't answer. All she felt was the cloying breath of His disapproval, and she ran to her own room where He stalked her for the last time that night, the whisper of His footsteps circling the bed where she lay, hands pressed to her eyes.

'Eternity I offered you.' His voice a roll of approaching thunder. 'Would you reject it all for these poor cattle? They are here for your use, in order to make you God. Use them, little sister. Use them!'

She peeked between her fingers, secretly, and saw with relief the streaks of dawn light at the window. But nothing escaped Him.

'The day is no refuge, little sister, either for you or for them. And I tell you now, you *will* be purged of all earthly connections. You *will* share with me the wide spaces between the stars. You have my word.'

His word! How could she oppose that? she wondered in despair. When she herself was still wordless? Powerless? And she took her hands from her eyes, opening her face to the emptiness of the room and the early morning sunlight that probed mockingly into the vacant corner beyond the bed.

That day she refused even to listen to her family, even to hear their voices, as though by shutting them out completely she could negate their existence, render them non-people with non-lives, ghosts that could never be unbodied. She pretended other things too: that the day would never end; that the sun would linger in the sky forever.

Or so she hoped until the shadows of the trees touched the bars on the front windows, and the shadows of the bars crept across to the far wall of the living room.

She readied herself then, faced the realities of the night, preparing as best she could for His arrival. He did not come unheralded. The house, as always, announced His presence with a series of protesting groans. Whisper-soft, His footsteps traversed her room, paused near the bed where she sat with covered eyes, and padded slowly on into the obscurity of the corner.

'What has your heart told you, little sister?' He whispered. 'Which of them does it care for least? Father? Mother? Brother? Which of them will it give first to the sword?'

She could feel the tears seeping between her fingers, running down her cheeks and settling in the hollows beside her mouth. She reached for them with her tongue, tasted her misery, the onset of her grief.

'No mortal can love equally,' He went on, probing for a weakness. 'There must be one of those creatures you love least. Be brave, little sister, and ask yourself this heart-truth: which is it?'

She began to sob, muffled, choking sounds that were easily absorbed by the silence of the house.

'Must I put you to trial?' He asked sadly. 'Has it come to that?' And then, as her tears continued to splash down, warm and unruly in the moonlight: 'Ah, I see a trial is the only way.' Her sobbing faltered, momentarily displaced by fear, and He added reassuringly: 'There will be no pain involved, little sister, none beyond the pain you feel now. A short test, that is all, to help you sever those mortal strings that bind the heart.'

His talk of severing made her think of the two-edged sword, which was *Him*! Yet what He said next contained no obvious threat.

'Go to the cupboard in your parents' room,' He murmured, mellow-voiced, seductive, 'and take the camera from the top shelf. We will use it to expose the state of your heart.'

The camera? She didn't understand. How could a glass lens probe beyond the flesh?

'The steadiness of your hand,' He explained cunningly, 'that is what the camera will test, like a barometer of your deepest feelings. The greater your anxiety and care, the more blurred the photograph will be. And of course the reverse will also be true.' He chuckled softly, holding her in suspense. 'The least blurred, little sister, that is the one we must look for. The clear likeness that reveals the cool heart-truth. Now go.'

She went, because she had no means of opposing Him. His Word was law, for hadn't He dethroned Terror? He was the Double God, free to raise her up and cast the others down.

He reminded her of that as she stole along the passage. Heedless of her tears, He whispered close against her ear: 'They are the condition of your rising, little sister. Their deaths are your only road, your stepping stones to the stars.'

But she didn't want the stars. Take me, she yearned to tell Him, take me instead. But as always she had no words to plead aloud with.

Under His eagle gaze, she stole past the bed with its sleeping occupants. Soundlessly, she slid back the door of the cupboard and groped for the polaroid camera in the musty interior. The button for the flash glowed red in the dark, warning her it was ready, and she lifted the camera to her eye.

'Do it!' He instructed her, stern, imperative.

She could see her parents dimly through the viewfinder, their two heads touching. And with a sense almost of gladness — for there was nothing she could do to keep her hands from shaking — she triggered the flash.

The room sprang vividly into being and vanished, the camera whirred, an as yet blank screen of paper slid out into the tray — and through it all they slept on undisturbed. As if, even in sleep, they knew her heart for what it was and instinctively placed their trust in her.

It was the same in Bob's room, her pulse racing, sweat streaming down her face, the camera shuddering in her hands.

But when she came to Harry, suddenly and unexpectedly her heart failed her. At the last possible moment her pulse slowed and steadied and the sweat froze on her forehead.

'Hurry, brave sister,' He urged her, giving her no time to weigh the consequences. 'Eternity waits. Hurry!'

And her mouth dry with disillusion, her hands rock-steady, she completed the task.

'Wha' . . . !' Harry's head lifted from the pillow, stared at her. 'Is that you, Med?'

Before she could see his face, while she was still dazed by the flash, she groped her way frantically back to her own room. To where the Other One circled her bed in the greying light, His voice swollen with triumph.

'Has the choice been made?' He whispered knowingly. 'Has it? Come, show me little sister-amongst-the-stars, show me.'

She had pushed the three polaroids down the front of her nightdress, unable to look at them herself, least of all reveal them to His hungry gaze. She would never take them out, she vowed, Harry's sleeping face would be safe with her. As safe . . . as safe as . . . She tried to picture it now, as it had lain there on the pillow, but the only face she could see, here in the breaking dawn, was Josh's, the features bloodied, the one sightless eye staring emptily at her.

'Please God!' she begged silently. 'Please!' Clutching

the pictures to her as He continued to circle the bed.

'Come, sister mine,' He crooned as the shadows slid towards the door, drawing Him after them. 'Step free of mortal love. Bind yourself to me only.'

His voice faded with the last of the darkness. In the full glare and warmth of the early sunlight she took out the three pictures and, with her eyes averted, hid them guiltily beneath the mattress. That was where they stayed for the remainder of the day — she, inconsolable, sitting hour by hour with her face pressed to the wall, deaf to her family's worried entreaties. Harry was the only one who got through to her, her mind opening to him like an unhealed wound.

'Can you hear me, Med?' The fullness of his cheek brushed gently against her shoulder. 'Can you?'

Pretending to ignore him cost her almost more than she had to give, and a long dry sob broke into the dusty calm of the afternoon. Was that her? she wondered numbly, and looked at her hands folded in her lap, at the way they trembled.

'It's all right, Med. Don't get upset.' His words winding subtly between her defences. 'I'm going now.'

So much care in him, she thought sadly, guiltily. Whereas I . . . I . . . !

A further painful effort and she was back in control, more determined than ever to protect him. With a long sigh, she renewed her vigil which stretched on into the lonely night, when once again she heard the Other One's returning footsteps.

'Give them up!' He snarled as He prowled tiger-like

about the margins of her room. 'I am the Double God, you must obey me!'

She cringed before His anger, rigid with fright on the rumpled bed. Though still somehow she managed to resist Him, guarding the pictures as if they were Harry himself.

Much harder to resist was His despair, which occurred on the following night. And harder still was His sweet reasonableness. How many days and nights later was that? She had lost count.

Yet through it all her resolve held. Through the terrible ordeal of the days, with her family forever pestering her; and through the even more testing hours of darkness in which the Other One alternately ranted and cajoled. Only at the very last, when He resorted to threats, did she begin to weaken. The moon by then was more than halfway towards the full, its shimmering light gathering on the floor, the bed, a brimming pool in which she felt herself slowly sinking.

'Would you have me tear them all while they lie asleep?' He challenged her from the inky shadows in the corner. 'Not just the first one of your choosing, but *all* of them. Now! Is that what you desire? For me to destroy them uselessly, before their re-creation? To wrench them from the world and leave nothing in their place? No fashioned likeness to mark their passing? No thing of beauty to justify their loss?' He paused and His voice dropped to a husky whisper of pure threat. 'Or worse, cruel sister, far worse, would you have me withhold my purging fire? Keep their poor remains from the flame? Leave their spirit locked in the putrefying flesh?'

Like Josh, she thought bleakly, the tears raining down, hot on her bare legs. Like poor abandoned Josh — his the worst of all nightmares that she could never live through again.

'Would you?' He hissed, sensing her weakness. And when she lifted her distraught face to the waxing moon at the window, unable any longer to hide her indecision: 'Listen to me, sister. For the cycle of this moon I will spare them all. But on one condition. That before the moon is full, you show me the pictures and reveal the order of their undoing, from your first choice of victim to the last. Either that, or they never wake. Not with this coming dawn. Not ever.'

Not ever? It sounded so complete. A sword scything down into blackness. By contrast another month was almost an eternity. A seemingly endless stream of life, of hope.

'What is it to be, little sister?'

Crying, laughing, she scrabbled under the mattress for the pictures; laid them out in the pale moonlight for Him to see.

But someone was there in the room with them! She whirled around to where Harry, tousle-haired, pyjama-clad, was standing in the open doorway.

'Were you having a bad dream, Med?'

She almost glanced into the corner, but checked herself. Did the moonlight reach as far as that? And if it did . . . if Harry . . . if . . .

The time for painstaking decisions had come and gone. The void beckoned, and, nails and teeth bared, like the tiger He would have her be, she leaped across the room.

Part Seven

> Old faces glimmered through the doors,
> Old footsteps trod the upper floors,
> Old voices called her from without.
>
> Alfred Tennyson, 'Mariana'

16

Doris leaned across the sink and rubbed at the glass with her thumb, clearing a small circle in the grime.

'These windows could do with a clean,' she observed pointedly. 'There's more dirt on some of them than out there in the paddock.'

Ted rustled his newspaper and lifted it higher so that it obscured his face. 'Yeah, well that's a woman's department, isn't it?'

'What about the outsides?'

'It's still part of the house. That's women's work in my book.'

'Women's work!' Doris flashed back at him. 'And where's the men's work, I'd like to know? As far as I can see, there's bugger all of it around here.'

'Aw, come on, Dot, I do my bit.'

'Bit's just about the word for what you . . . !' she began hotly, and stopped herself as she realised that Ted wasn't the one she should be getting angry with. In fact there was no actual reason for her to get angry with anyone. Worry, that was her real trouble; that's what was wearing her down and making her irritable.

She gave the window another rub and peered through

the cleared space, down towards the shack. 'Still no sign of his ute, I see,' she said, trying to sound unconcerned.

'What d'you expect?' Ted answered with an I-told-you-so laugh. 'He's done a runner, hasn't he? As per bloody usual.'

'He could've told us for once.'

'Pigs might bloody fly, Dot.'

'I mean, he's not a kid anymore. A fully grown man's got no right walkin' off like that.'

Ted refolded his paper and smoothed it flat on the table. 'We're well shot of him if you ask me.'

She sniffed disapprovingly. 'It's just that kind of attitude drove him off in the first place. If you'd been more of a father to him, he'd prob'ly be a better son to us today.'

Ted turned on the gas ring and bent down, lips pursed, to relight his stub of cigarette, his eyes screwed up against the heat. 'Well you've heard the old saying, Dot. It's a wise feller knows his own son.'

'And what's that supposed to mean . . . ?' she began testily, and stopped herself once more. After all, there *had* been that young bloke in the shop where she'd worked soon after she and Ted got married. It was possible, she supposed, that he might have . . .

She shook her head, impatient with herself. What was the use of digging all that up? There were shady goings-on in everyone's past, so why should hers be any different? In any case, she wasn't the only one in the family to have had a little fling. What about that time years ago when Ted had disappeared up Queensland way? 'Walkabout', he'd called it, but she'd known better. And what about Kev's involvement with that Denny Clement just before the fire? There'd been more to that than met the eye, as she and Ted had both agreed. Though none of it warranted much looking into, not if you valued a quiet life. Let sleeping dogs lie, that was her motto.

She turned back towards the window with a sigh. 'Well he's gone off and left us anyway. There's no changin' that. I wouldn't mind so much, but I can't even get inside to see what state he's left the place in.'

'That's just as well if I know him,' Ted answered absently, studying his paper again.

'Filthy it was, last time I was there,' she went on, eyeing her own less-than-perfect kitchen with disapproval. 'The smell from the fridge enough to knock your hat off. And the stuff he'd got piled up in the sink! You should have seen it. Some of it had been there so long it was damn near taking root.'

Ted, ballpoint in hand, had begun working through the racing guide. 'Yeah, well it's his problem, Dot, not yours. Let him sort it out when he honours us with one of his flyin' visits.'

'That's all very well for you to say, Ted, but who'll end up doin' all the cleanin'? And you won't get off scot-free yourself if rats get in, 'cause you won't catch me near the place then, I'm tellin' you that for nothin'.'

'Honest to God, Doris!' He slammed the ballpoint down, almost as irritable as she'd been earlier. 'What are you on about now? Why the hell should rats get in?

This is the middle of the bloody bush, not central bloody Sydney.'

'Well there's that sink for starters,' she said, unabashed. 'All them bits of food still in the pots and stinkin' to high heaven. Then there's sure to be opened packets of biscuits in the cupboard. You know what our Kev's like when it comes to biscuits. Not to mention the . . .'

Ted pushed the paper wearily aside. 'Awright, Doris, awright, you don't have to go on. I got the bloody message. I'll give you a hand if that'll make you happy.'

'Happy, Ted?' she asked with false brightness. 'What's that? I've forgotten. Tell me about it.'

'Gawd!' was all he said as he picked up his hat from the sideboard and stomped out ahead of her.

But having sparked a reaction from him, she wasn't about to let it die. For a change, *he* could find out what it was like to be harried and made fun of. 'That's the great thing about you, Ted Briggs,' she said, laughing as she followed him down to the shack. 'You really know how to give a girl a good time.'

'Shuddup, Doris.'

'My, but you've a wonderful way with words, Ted. Didn't I ever tell you that? A real cultured gentleman, that's you. Gracious to a fault. Just like our Kev. The pair of you brimmin' over with lovin' kindness and good manners.'

She could see from the set of his skinny shoulders how he hated being laughed at, how it put him into a regular temper. Mind you, why should she care? He never worried about hurting *her* feelings. What did it matter that he scooped up the axe as they trudged past the depleted woodpile? Let him take his temper out on something else apart from her, she thought, and was still nodding with satisfaction when he attacked the door.

It was the sheer ferocity of the attack that surprised her, the way he swung at the weathered planking as if it were a mortal enemy, his face all screwed up and ugly. As the wood around the lock splintered and gave way, she suddenly found herself remembering Rory, butchered and dead in the sand; and the look on Kevin's face soon afterwards, cold and sneering as he threatened that Warner woman, with the dog (his own dog!) dead right there at his feet.

'Steady on,' she murmured shakily, and put a restraining hand on Ted's arm.

He expended the last of his anger by kicking at the door which burst open. 'That'll teach the bugger to lock it up like it was Fort Knox or somethin',' he said, but he was laughing himself now. 'Jesus, Dot, you really had me goin' there for a while. A bloody axe murderer in the makin'. Makes you wonder what we're all like underneath.'

Chuckling, more good-natured than she'd seen him for weeks, he draped his arm across her shoulder and drew her into the passage.

'Whew!' He pulled a face, waving a hand at the unpleasant, closed-up smell that greeted them. 'I see what you mean about the rats, love. This'd be a bloody paradise for them. Look, you hold on here and I'll do a bit of a recce.'

She turned aside into the bedroom while he continued along the passage. Through the flimsy framing of the wall, she could hear him giving her a running commentary.

'God A'mighty, Dot, a bloody pig'd live better than this! I shouldn't wonder if it scared the bloody rats off. You should see it! I'd rather live in a bloody garbage truck, it'd be a sight healthier.'

She vaguely registered his complaints, but didn't really take them in, most of her attention focused on the bedroom. On the unexpected neatness of it. (Kev? Neat?) On its emptiness. The bed was stripped back to the mattress, and nothing littered the lino floor, not so much as a sock or a pair of underpants. She opened the wardrobe ... empty! Even the hangers had disappeared. It was the same with the chest-of-drawers, with the bedside cupboard. Not a sign of him left.

For a moment or two she couldn't decide whether to feel stricken or relieved. Then her body decided for her. Her legs gave way, so that she sat down on the bed with a thump, and tears welled up into her eyes.

'Hey!' Ted was kneeling beside her, gently rubbing her back with his hand. 'It's just old-fashioned dirt, love. We'll soon get it cleaned up. No need to do a tragedy-queen number on me.'

'He ... he's gone,' she said brokenly, smearing at her tears. 'Our boy ... we've seen the last of him.'

'Christ, love, you're overdoing it a bit. He's probably just on the run from this lot. The bloody awful smell in that kitchen's enough to drive anyone out.'

'No, he's gone for good this time. He's never taken

everythin' with him before. This is different.' She gave a loud sniff and managed to collect herself, a trace of resentment replacing some of the sadness. 'He's bloody pulled up sticks and left us, that's what he's done. Hiked off as if . . . as if we was a coupla nobodies, people he'd met on the side of the road. Thirty-odd years and that's all we mean to him.'

'Not a chance,' Ted assured her, shaking his head, though she could sense him looking around the room, taking in its emptiness just as she'd done. 'He knows where his bread's buttered. A few months in rented rooms and he'll be knockin' at the door again. You'll see.'

She wiped her eyes and forced back another wave of tears. 'You know, I was pretty sure that Warner girl'd keep him here for a while, the same's Denny Clement did years ago. You remember what he was like then. You'd have needed a crowbar to prise him off the place.'

'Yeah, but that was Denny,' Ted answered sadly, and she could tell that he'd also read and accepted the silent message of the room. 'From what you've told me, I'd say she was a cut above this other girl. At least she had all her marbles.'

'The Warner girl has Denny's look about her, though,' Doris insisted. 'A little scrap of a thing with the same wild streak, only worse. I reckon that's what attracted him. What kept him going back there. It was no good tellin' him to stay away. He never would listen to me, not where that place was concerned, nor to you neither. And then when . . .' She hesitated briefly, as though making up her mind about something. 'Then when he walked into the kitchen one mornin' last month, with his face all knocked around, I thought...'

'His what?' Ted broke in. 'You mean someone gave him a bit of aggro?'

'I didn't mention it at the time,' Doris confessed, 'because of the way you carry on, but yeah, he'd had a bashin'. Not that it worried him, mind. You know Kev, he don't scare easy. Anyway, when I saw his face, all cut and bruised, it was like turnin' the clock back. I thought, oh-oh, here we go, Kev's got it bad again. But...' She had to fend off another wave of tears. 'But as it turned out I was wrong, wasn't I? He didn't care about her either. Not enough to stay.'

Ted didn't answer straight away. 'No, love,' he said at last, nodding thoughtfully at the empty room. 'Maybe you weren't so wrong after all.'

She turned to look at him, his face shrewd and calculating in a way Kev's had never been. 'How d'you mean?'

'Well, if those Warner blokes gave him a hidin', and that's how it sounds to me, then that'd account for him runnin' off. Think about it. The door's slammed in his face, he gets the big N.O. from Dad, and what's left for him here but bad memories? So it's into the ute and off into the wide blue yonder.'

Doris considered the possibility before answering. 'No, I've met Doug Warner and he's not that sorta bloke. And nor's Kev. He wouldn't run away just because someone bashed him. He's too obstinate for that. He'd more than likely stay right where he is, if only to make a nuisance of himself.'

'Awright,' Ted conceded. 'But what if it was the girl

who gave him the old heave-ho? What about that? Wouldn't that make a difference? You know what these young blokes are like. Some girl throws them over and they think their heart's broken. All they wanna do is clear out and leave it all behind. Till they've done their dough, at any rate. Then it's back to good old dependable Mum, the one girl they can trust. What d'you say to that, Dot?'

She drew in her lips, not completely convinced. 'It sounds fine except for one thing. The Warner girl can't talk. So how could she send him packin'?'

Ted gave an oddly reminiscent smile, his eyes almost squeezed shut as if he were gazing inwards or back through memory. 'Plenty of ways for a girl to say no, Dot, without puttin' it into words. One look'll do the trick. You see that glint in her eye and you know straight off you've got your flamin' marchin' orders.'

It was on the tip of her tongue to ask him if that was what had happened to him in Queensland all those years ago, but she said instead: 'Yeah, I s'pose the girl could be behind it all.'

'Bloody right, she is!' he answered vehemently. 'Same's that Denny Clement was before. Stands to reason, don't it? After all, he only started this runnin' off lark after Denny dipped out on him.'

Doris wiped the last of the tears from her cheeks, feeling suddenly more resolute, less defeated. Kevin was hardly the ideal son, but still he was all she had apart from Ted, so why should she give him up without a struggle? Who were the Warners and their batty daughter to deprive her of him?

'What do we do about it then, Ted?' she asked, her voice steady, businesslike.

'Do?' He pulled his collar tight about his scrawny throat and fastened the top button, as though preparing to go out and greet the world. 'We don't stick our heads in the sand like last time. We get to the root of the bloody problem. We pay the high-and-bloody-mighty Warners a visit and find out what's been goin' on.'

*

Their first sight of the house came as a shock to them both.

'Jesus bloody wept!' Ted exclaimed. 'What've they been up to? It looks like bloody Long Bay prison!'

Doris had to agree with him. The change in the place was extraordinary — all the windows were heavily barred, including those to the basement room, and a close-meshed security door protected the main entrance.

'Seems to me we're not the only ones with worries,' she murmured, thinking how like a masked face the front of the house had become.

'Well there's your answer, Dot,' Ted added. 'They've locked their darlin' daughter in and locked poor old Kev out. No wonder he's done a runner. Harry bloody Houdini couldn't get in there.'

But Doris, standing thoughtfully on the path between the trees, had her doubts. If the Warners had wanted to stop their girl seeing Kev, there'd surely been simpler ways of doing it. Such as coming to talk to her and Ted. Tess especially had every reason to believe they would have listened sympathetically to her. And that big gentle husband of hers, he just didn't fit into Doris's notion of a prison warder, which was how he had to be feeling inside that fortress. So why start off by going to these lengths? And to all this expense? Because Doris could see at a glance that it must have cost them a pretty penny.

'I'm goin' up there anyway,' she said, and continued along the path.

Tess was the one who answered the door, her face, like the front of the house, half-shielded by the security grille. Even so, there was no mistaking the uneasiness of her smile; nor the reluctance with which she greeted them.

'We've come about our Kevin,' Doris said determinedly, not to be put off.

'Kevin?' she answered, and although her voice was vague, Doris noticed how her gaze darted past them, out into the vacant blue of the day. 'I . . . I'm afraid I haven't seen him.'

'If it's awright with you, love,' Ted said, friendly but firm, 'we'd like a few words just the same.'

'Just to put our minds at rest, if you see what I mean,' Doris added, and reached for the security door so that Tess had no option but to open it and invite them in.

'Perhaps . . . perhaps the kitchen . . .' Tess suggested half-heartedly, but Doris was barely listening. She was more attentive to the faint whimpering that originated somewhere in the house. An almost animal sound, dull and wordless, which grew steadily louder as they proceeded along the passage.

Tess, hurrying on ahead, pulled one of the side doors closed and stood with her back against it, waiting for them to pass, her face so seamed and knotted by concern that she was hardly the same carefree woman Doris remembered from her last visit.

'Havin' trouble with a dog, are you?' Ted asked conversationally. 'A whelpin' bitch by the sound of things.'

'Hush your nonsense!' Doris muttered, and dug at him with her elbow.

'I was on'y askin',' he protested, all innocence.

Or was he putting on an act? Doris wondered. Manoeuvring himself into the driving seat, so to speak? She looked again at his open expression, and couldn't decide either way.

'In point of fact . . .' Tess began, and took a deep breath as though summoning her resolve, '. . . it's Mary . . . our daughter. She's not at her best at the moment.'

'What, poorly, is she?' Ted persisted, so much the wide-eyed innocent now that Doris felt sure he was up to something.

'She . . . she's upset,' Tess confessed.

Ted shook his head understandingly. 'Boy trouble, I wouldn't mind bettin'. That's usually what it is with these young kids nowadays. They're that headstrong you can't hold them. I expect she wanted to run off after him, eh? Am I right?'

It was too good an opportunity for Doris to miss. 'Which reminds me, Tess, I s'pose you know our Kev and your Mary were seein' a bit of each other. They were pretty keen from what I can gather. Funny how it all stopped after you put up these bars. Bit of a coincidence, wouldn't you say? I mean, here's your Mary mopin' away, and there's our Kev God knows where. You wouldn't — and I'm on'y askin', mind — you wouldn't happen to know where he's headed off to, would you?'

'Just so's we can check he's awright,' Ted explained, more friendly than ever. 'A bit of parental concern, you might say.'

Tess, her grip tightening on the door handle, glanced quickly from one to the other, her face registering . . . what? Outrage? Alarm? Again Doris wasn't sure, and while she was still trying to decide, Tess swallowed hard and steadied, a polite smile replacing every other expression.

'Look, I think we'd all better sit down and talk about this,' she said calmly. 'So if you'll just excuse me a minute . . .'

And she was gone, running along the passage and leaving them to find their own way to the kitchen.

'She's got a cool head on her, that one,' Ted observed grudgingly. 'She don't let on much when you . . .'

'Shush!' Doris cautioned him, aware now of a whispered discussion drifting up to them from the downstairs workshop. It stopped before she could make out what was being said, and a few seconds later Tess reappeared with her husband and son in tow — the two men as big, their faces as good-natured, as Doris remembered them.

Tess didn't bother with introductions. 'You wanted to know about Kevin,' she said, coming straight to the point in a way Doris couldn't help but admire. So different from her own habitual dithering.

'Yeah, we'd take it as a favour,' she said, softened by Tess's openness.

'Well, Bob was the last one to see him. He can tell you what he knows. Though . . .' She paused, out of delicacy alone it seemed to Doris, as if sparing of their feelings. 'Though I might as well warn you, it's not good news.'

She stood aside, but Bob, with none of his mother's confidence, lingered in the doorway, his face partly obscured by shadows, so that for Doris it was a bit like listening to a voice coming out of nowhere, telling her things she had always dreaded she might hear some day. The self-same story Kev himself had threatened her with years before, when she'd made the mistake of standing between him and Denny Clement. And all for what? It had been pure selfishness on her part, that's all. If she hadn't been so blindly possessive, she would have realised straight off that he'd never stood a chance with Denny. What had he ever been over here but a peeping Tom? Denny wasn't the kind of girl to be interested in him — why not admit it? — never mind all his talk of running off with her. And after the fire? What did it matter that he'd gone on snooping around the place? She, Doris, should have minded her own business. Again, if she'd had any sense, she would have recognised that he could never have been really interested in what was left of . . . in what the fire did to . . .

These unwelcome reminiscences coursed slowly through Doris's mind as she half listened to what she had guessed already, from the moment Tess had stood aside to let Bob have his say. Fragments of Bob's account, halting, strangely hesitant (was he also sparing her feelings? and why?), reached her through a mist of self-recrimination and regret.

'... saw him in the village ... loading up with supplies ... a girl with him ... pretty much in love I'd say ... said they wanted to make a new start together ... up north, I think, or out west ... can't remember exactly ...'

Yes, Doris thought bitterly, yes! This was how she'd always known it would be eventually. Kev to a tee. Off with the old and on with the new. Some girl or other had crooked her finger at him, and he'd been away, chasing after rainbows. And why not? What was there for him to stick around for? Failure, first with Denny and then with the Warner girl, that's all he'd come up with here. And she had to be honest, he'd had scant support from her and Ted. Not the kind of support he'd needed anyway. All they'd ever told him was to steer clear of this place, to keep his nose clean. Never a word from either of them about the way he might be feeling. Yes, a fresh start, that's what he was looking for. She should have realised ... should have spoken to him while she ...

'Hold on a minute,' Ted said suddenly, breaking into both Doris's thoughts and the uneven flow of Bob's account. 'You're talkin' as though you and Kev was mates. Since bloody when? Far as I knew, you'd never set eyes on each other.'

Bob seemed to Doris to draw back further into the

shadow of the doorway — natural delicacy again, she supposed, an unwillingness to be the bearer of bad tidings. In fact that was the sense that Doug Warner gave her too, his face pained, darkened by what his son was saying. Only Tess appeared unmoved, her features set and closed, giving no hint of her inner feelings.

'We ... we met in the pub,' Bob explained, even more halting than before. 'More than once. We ... er ... chatted and had a few drinks. Not mates, you're right about that. Just sort of ... er ... acquaintances.'

'Then tell me this,' Ted answered, obviously not convinced. 'What was his face like? I mean, how'd it look when you last saw him?'

'His face?'

Ted was bristling beside her, his wiry body thrust forward aggressively. 'You heard me, young feller.'

'Tell him, Bob,' Tess prompted her son, her voice as hard as the set of her mouth.

'Well ... er ...'

'You haven't got a bloody clue, have you, mate?' Ted interrupted again.

'Give him a chance,' Tess said levelly.

'Go on, Bob,' Doug rumbled, the softness of his voice somehow settling the atmosphere in the room and reminding Doris once again of how he'd made her feel during her first visit here.

She looked up into his eyes and was strangely discomfited by the sadness she saw there. Unaware of her, he wiped one of those silky palms of his across his mouth and then nodded encouragingly, and straight away there was a rush of words from the shadowy doorway.

'Kevin looked pretty knocked around if you must know,' Bob said, talking fast, as though eager to put the whole explanation behind him. 'His face all cut and bruised from where he'd been bashed. He reckoned it was the girl's brothers. They'd tried to see him off, but he wasn't having any. That's partly why he and the girl were heading up north or wherever. He said her brothers had really finished him with this area and that . . . that he and the girl'd had it with families generally and wanted to get away on their own, where no one could bother them. They were never coming back, that's what they said, more than once, both of them.'

Doris let out a loud sob, a sound which embarrassed her almost as much as everyone else. Why now? she asked herself. But she knew the answer. It was what she'd just heard: a simple confirmation of her failure, of how Kevin had run from her as much as anyone else. She sobbed again, and again, explosive expressions of grief, of disappointment, that she could not prevent. Kevin's departure, the manner of it, like the departure of the last vestiges of youth, of hope.

'I knew it!' she said brokenly, her eyes dry as yet, all the unshed tears contained within her strangled whisper. 'When I saw his room, I knew he'd done with us. With *us*! We're the ones that drove him off. Us as much as them blokes, whoever they are.'

'Don't upset yourself, love,' Ted was saying, a leathery hand on her arm.

But it was that other, silkier touch that worried her; the way Doug Warner crouched beside her chair and took her hand in his. His face, when she glanced up furtively, appeared sadder than Ted's would ever be, as if he were to blame for all that had happened, not her or Ted.

'If it's any consolation,' he murmured, 'our Mary's also grieving for Kevin. You must have heard her when you came in. She can't bear the idea that . . .' He hesitated, just like the son a little earlier. '. . . that Kevin's run off with someone else. She'd have gone chasing after him if we hadn't secured the house.'

'And I thought . . .' Doris responded between sobs, '. . . I thought she was the one that gave *him* the shove. It never entered my mind that he . . . that he . . .'

'You mustn't blame him,' Doug assured her softly. 'He was a good man really, he had a kind heart. You have to believe that. Not only now, but always.'

What was it she found so hard to take? Doug's kindness? Or the way he spoke to her, as though she were literally bereaved and Kevin were dead and gone forever. Whatever the cause, her pent-up tears came flooding out.

'It's this place,' she sobbed. 'It's always been unlucky, for the Clements *and* us. First one son, and now another. There's a curse on it I shouldn't wonder.'

'Two sons?' That was Tess, her voice, like her face, empty of any discernible emotion. Oddly desolate.

So much so that Doris, in spite of her grief, was immediately on guard, immediately conscious of having let slip something that was better not spoken of. Enough, she chastised herself firmly, and throwing off Doug's detaining hands, she scrabbled in her pocket for a tissue.

Yet as she should have realised, there was no stopping

Tess once she'd started on something. Just like a bloodhound on the scent, she was, never leaving anything alone. Not content even to let the dead lie at peace.

'Wasn't it a *daughter* you said the Clements lost?' Tess was asking now. 'Denny, you called her. I remember that distinctly.'

Ted was just as bad, and he at least should have known better. There he was, jabbering away before she, Doris, could dry her eyes or blow her nose.

'Yeah, they lost Denny awright, but they lost their boy too. Young Will, about fifteen he was.'

'So they had *two* children killed in the fire?'

'Well not in the fire itself,' Ted answered more cagily, suddenly alert to how little the Warners knew. 'As a *result* of the fire you might say.'

'You mean they died afterwards?' Tess pressed him. 'Of their injuries?'

Ted shifted uncomfortably on his chair. 'Yeah, kind of,' he said with a vague wave of the hand.

'How long after?' Tess insisted.

It was then that Doris decided things were going too far. Wasn't it bad enough having all that tragedy behind them, without inviting the ghosts back into their lives with loose talk? God knows, opening those well-sealed doors to the past could only make this place worse than it was.

'What Ted's trying to explain,' she said quickly, wiping at her nose with an already soggy tissue, 'is that poor Denny lasted till six months or more after the fire. As for young Will . . .' Even she had to pause there, choosing her words with care. 'He followed soon after.'

She would have preferred to leave it at that, with the ghosts safely locked within the vaults of history, but she could see another question forming on Tess's lips and she hurried on, to a slightly less daunting topic, to what no one who'd been there to witness it all could possibly doubt.

'You can hardly blame us for seeing this place as unlucky,' she sighed. 'Kevin, the Clements, it's claimed them all one way or another, the same's it claims anyone who has any dealings with it.' She forced herself to meet Tess's coolly appraising gaze. 'It'll claim you too if you hang around here much longer. If I was in your shoes, I'd get my family back to Sydney while I had the chance. That's stickin' my nose in, I know, but it's how I see it, and I'd be less than a good neighbour if I didn't say so. That girl of yours f'r instance . . .'

But she was the one who was going too far now, as she could tell from the crinkling of the skin around Tess's eyes, and she let her last suggestive half-statement hang there in the strained silence of the room.

'I see,' Tess said at last, the corners of her mouth quivering so that Doris wasn't sure whether she was trying not to laugh or cry. 'As I understand it, you're saying this house, or at least the land it stands on, has had some kind of hex placed on it.'

'Hex?' Doris had never heard the word.

'A curse then. The house, the land, they've been cursed. Is that right?'

'Didn't I say so before?' Doris countered. 'The first time we met? I warned you about it then. And if the truth be told, it all goes back to one of them Aboriginal stories. Or maybe it's older still.'

'I dunno about that, love,' Ted said uneasily. 'Bad luck's one thing, but all that old legend stuff . . .'

'Well it's here, isn't it?' she said, turning on him. 'You've seen it at work. How much proof d'you need?'

He patted her shoulder placatingly. 'Don't get me wrong love, I know bad luck when I see it. It's just all that old legend stuff I don't go along with.'

'What's the difference?' she snapped back, fighting off another outbreak of tears. 'It got our Kev, didn't it?'

Ted scratched at his stubble, with no ready answer for once. 'Yeah, well . . .' he mumbled.

And there was that Doug Warner again, looming over her, acting as if it were *his* son who was lost and gone. 'You mustn't . . .' he began, and she could see the line of sweat on his upper lip, smell the strong wood-scent of his clothes and skin. 'I mean, you mustn't worry about him. He's probably fine wherever . . . wherever . . .' He shook his head in obvious distress. 'I'm sure he's found peace in his . . . his new life. He deserves that after . . . after all he . . .'

Listening to him stumble on, the hurt in his voice almost as distracting as his big gentle hands, Doris found to her surprise that she felt more sorry for him than she did for herself. And why not? Kevin was away and free, making a fresh start somewhere, whereas that daughter of theirs! What could you say about her? Mad as a hatter most likely. Doris could hear her now, a faint background whimper that seemed to originate in the very bowels of the house.

The house! She suppressed a slight shudder, glad that it wasn't hers for all its gleaming woodwork and fine furnishings. Her own home wasn't much — she was painfully aware of that, especially here in this modern kitchen — but at least there was no cloud hanging over it, no curse or whatever it was that continued to afflict this property.

'Well I s'pose we all have to make the break sometime,' she said philosophically, cutting short Doug Warner's stumbling efforts. 'An' that includes Kev. The fact is, he was gettin' a bit long in the tooth to go on livin' off us. It was time he snipped the apron strings.'

She stood up, motioning for Ted to follow suit, and glimpsed an unmistakable flicker of relief on Doug Warner's face.

'If there's anything we can do . . .' he muttered, but he was covering up, she was certain of it, in spite of his show of sympathy. He was pleased she was leaving.

'Yes, anything at all,' Tess agreed, and behind the tightness of her mouth, Doris could detect that same sense of relief.

She swung towards the opening to the basement, but Bob's face remained veiled by shadow as it had been all along.

'We'll be off home then,' she said huffily, and led the way down the passage, past the room where the whimpering continued, muffled now as though the girl had pushed her face into the pillow.

Was it that sound, the pathetic quality of it, that made Doris pause at the front door and act as she did? Was she genuinely concerned for the welfare of the family? Or was she just being spiteful, responding to their barely disguised relief with a parting shot of her own? Even afterwards she wasn't able to separate her motives, to disentangle the honest caring from the malice. All she could console herself with was the fact that she had spoken truthfully, told them what they needed to hear from someone, sometime.

'I know I'm just stickin' my nose in again,' she said, turning on the top step, 'but if that was my daughter in there, I'd spare her another night under this roof.'

'Now, now, Dot,' Ted cautioned her, but she ignored him — ignored too the peculiarly hangdog expression on Doug Warner's face and the tight, hard look on Tess's.

'You probably think I'm a silly old woman,' she added, 'and I can't really blame you for that. But I've seen this place at work, I've seen what it does to people, what it did to the Clements. And yes, I'll admit it, what it might've done to my Kev. I'm not just talkin' about dyin' or runnin' away. There's worse things in life than that. Well if you give this place the chance, it'll do the same thing to your Mary. Her just for starters. You'll be next, or more likely those two boys of yours. It'll take them one by one . . .'

'Take?' Tess queried, and Doris could see that she'd got through to her, the unfeeling mask of her face slipping slightly, a hint of real anguish revealed in the depths of her eyes.

'What I'm tryin' to say,' Doris plunged on, 'is that this place'll change you, until you don't know yourselves. Until you end up doin' things, terrible things, that . . .'

'Button your lip, Doris,' Ted cut in, and linked his

arm firmly through hers. 'The Warners can't afford to stand around yarnin' the day long.'

'Things?' Tess asked, and all at once she was clinging onto Doug as though she needed him for support. 'What sort of things?'

But Ted was clattering down the steps, dragging Doris after him.

'Get Mary away from here while you can,' she said over her shoulder. 'That's all that matters.'

She failed to see what effect her closing words had on the couple in the doorway. She was too busy trying to keep up with Ted who was hurrying her away. They were already well down the slope, partly shielded by the trees, when Tess called after them.

'We're sorry about Kevin, Doris. We really are.'

It was an oddly tearful, almost regretful cry that caused Doris to yank her arm free and stop in the middle of the path.

'What's she got to be so sorry about?' Ted commented drily.

Through a speckle of gum leaves, Doris could just make out the facade of the house, the grim face of it barred against what she thought of simply as fate.

'Maybe everything if she stays around here much longer,' she answered, and astonished Ted by grabbing his hand and running headlong down the path, urging him on until, red-cheeked and breathless, they emerged on the far side of the bordering creek.

17

It was the closest she'd ever come to having a row with Doug. Normally he was too easy-going, too docile to start or sustain a fight, and if there were any hard words between them they came from her. But that morning was different. She'd never seen him quite so upset — upset almost in the literal sense of that word. He looked as though he'd been knocked off balance, the way he had to steady himself against the side walls as he staggered back down the passage and collapsed into the nearest chair.

'Don't you *ever* put me in that position again!' he shouted, mopping the sweat from his face.

'What position?' she asked, acting dumb, hoping his anger would pass.

He crashed his fist down on the table. 'You know damned well what I'm talking about, Tess! And I'm telling you now, I'm never going through something like that again, not for you or anyone. D'you hear me?'

'Don't start pointing fingers, Doug,' she warned him, her own voice rising. 'You're in this as much as I am. You have been ever since you agreed about Kevin. You were the one who buried him, remember. Your hands are as dirty as mine.'

She expected him to back off then, chastened by the memory of that terrible night, but all he did was hit the table again, so hard that it jolted against her hip.

'Christ, Tess! What's wrong with you? Are you made of steel or something?'

That accusation hurt her almost as much as the recent sight of Doris's grieving face. 'You know I'm not,' she said quietly. 'I'm only doing it for Mary.'

He barely seemed to hear her. 'That poor woman!' he groaned. 'And the three of us just standing there! Lying to her! Pretending that . . . that . . .'

He buried his face in his arms, his shoulders shaking, and Tess thought for a moment that he was crying. Yet when she put out a hand to comfort him, she realised immediately that the trembling in his body was the result not of anger or grief, but of shame.

She bent down and wound both arms around him, buried her face in the sweaty hollow of his neck. 'There's no other way, pet,' she whispered tenderly. 'Not if we want to keep Mary safe.'

That had no effect either, and she went over to the bench and busied herself making coffee. Down below, she could hear the high whine of the bandsaw, an irritating sound which none the less blotted out Mary's whimpering and told her that Bob was losing himself in work. That at least was a good thing. Work, distraction, they were what Bob needed right now, and what Doug needed too if he was going to get over this business.

And herself? What did *she* need? How, for instance,

did she propose to forget not just Doris's distraught face, but her closing words, out there on the front step.

'... this place'll change you until you don't know yourselves. Until you end up doin' things, terrible things ...'

And then: 'Get Mary away from here while you can.'

While she could? Was it perhaps too late for that already? Had the 'change', the 'terrible things', already overtaken them? Or was she simply putting too much store by the words of a woman distracted by grief? Doris was, after all, a woman whom she, Tess, would not have gone to for advice even at the best of times. Did that sound snobbish? It was a fact all the same. Also, those self-same 'terrible things', or rather the fear of them happening, was what had driven her out of Sydney in the first place, what had persuaded her to come here. So where else could she and her family run to? Especially now, with that unmarked grave down there amongst the trees.

She shook her head, undecided, and took the steaming cups of coffee over to the table.

'Bob did well this morning,' she said, doing her best to sound normal, relaxed.

Doug still didn't respond, didn't look up, though his shoulders had stopped shaking.

She sat down opposite him and sipped slowly at her coffee. She had intended to give him as much time as he needed, but after only a minute or two of having Doris's warnings go round and round in her head, she was the one who couldn't stay silent.

'Do you think there was anything in what Doris said?' she asked. 'About this place being jinxed?'

He straightened up, saw the coffee before him, and pushed it away with the side of his hand. His face, always slightly florid, looked unnaturally flushed, and his eyes refused to meet hers.

'It's not the place, Tess,' he said softly. 'It's us. Us and Mary. We're the ones to blame.'

She reached out to grasp his hands, but he snatched them away and sat with both fists thrust down into his lap, exactly like Bob as a child when he'd been caught out over some wrongdoing.

'I'm not suggesting we're innocent,' she replied. 'Only that there may be something in what Doris had to say.'

'It's a piece of ground, Tess, some wood and a few bricks. Nothing else.'

'Even houses and patches of ground can have a feel about them,' she countered. 'And after what happened to the Clements . . .'

'We're not the Clements,' he broke in. 'They have nothing to do with us.'

'But all four of them, burned to death,' she persisted. 'First the two children and later the parents. Think about it, Doug. Doesn't that make you wonder about this place? Whether there isn't something bad here?'

'Bad?' He at last raised his eyes to hers, and she almost wished he hadn't. The whites were discoloured, as though bruised by shame. 'If there's any evil here,' he reminded her, 'we brought it with us.'

But she wasn't having that. 'Mary isn't evil,' she

said, a hint of outrage in her voice. 'She's disturbed, that's all.'

'D'you call what she did to Kevin a disturbance?' he challenged her unhappily.

Below stairs the bandsaw paused and then whined into motion as she lurched to her feet. 'We've been through all this, Doug,' she said, leaning over him. 'Kevin started it, with his dangerous games. He taught Mary, not the other way round. So don't give me all that evil crap. She's mixed up. She doesn't know what she's doing.'

'All right,' he conceded, waving her back into her chair. 'Maybe Mary's not evil, maybe we aren't either. Probably evil's the wrong word. Call it what you like, but it's still something we brought here. You can't blame it on a piece of ground.'

'And the Clements?'

He shrugged and stood up, buttoning his dust-coat as he moved towards the top of the stairs. 'The Clements? Whatever happened to them, it wasn't caused by this property. Underneath the house, under all the grass and trees, there's just dead earth. You of all people shouldn't need me to tell you that.'

He was right, of course. Sitting alone at the kitchen table, Tess knew she was being irrational, knew that Doris's warning was pure superstition. How could lifeless bricks and mortar or the earth itself exert any power over people? It was impossible. Or was it? There had been whole cultures that believed the very opposite. There was that modern theory about Gaia. And right here in Australia many Aborigines still placed their faith in the power of the land. What was it she'd heard an Aborigine say once on the radio? How it wasn't the people who possessed the land, but the land that possessed the people. That made perfect sense when you thought about it. So why shouldn't this particular piece of land have . . . ?

No, she shut herself off from the possibility. Or tried to. But throughout the morning the same thoughts kept erupting through the ordered, rational set of her mind. Like inner voices that she had no control over, they seemed to whisper to her, to insinuate themselves continually, regardless of what she was doing. *Suppose*, they suggested, *just suppose that Mary really is in the clutches of this place; suppose that it wasn't Kevin at all, but something older and crueller and more enduring that was directing her. What then?*

'Yes, but why only Mary? Why not the rest of us?'

She had spoken aloud before she realised it, standing still and pensive at the desk in the living room, having just finished entering the week's invoices. Yes, why? she repeated inaudibly. And straight away the answer was there, uttered with a confidence that matched anything her conscious self could lay claim to:

Because Mary was the vulnerable one; so traumatised by her encounter with Terror that she was exposed, defenceless before whatever lay coiled within the dust.

And with that voice, like an echo effect, there came another. Doris's. Something else she'd said out there on the steps:

'You'll be next, or more likely those two boys of yours. It'll take them one by one and . . .'

Tess started from her reverie and folded up the front of the desk. This was absurd. It was only guilt that made her vulnerable to Doris's suggestions. For she *did* feel guilty about Kevin, even though she'd hidden it from Doug, and about Doris too. Horribly guilty. She'd been close to breaking point when Doris had started to sob. If it hadn't been for Mary, whimpering in the background, she'd have given in and started sobbing herself. Or done something sillier perhaps, like telling Doris the truth.

But that was the problem. What was the truth? What really lay behind those butchered figures, animal and human, found abandoned out there under the trees? Was it simply Mary's memory of Terror, a memory that drove her on from one act of vengeance to another? (But then why the sculptures?) Was it Kevin himself, the final victim of his own kinky behaviour? Or . . . ?

That one word was like a summons to her other, less reasonable self which seemed to swim up out of the dark, badgering her, tempting her to listen:

Or was it something about this place? This house? This land? Some ancient identity that never passed away?

'No,' she murmured, a hand to her throat.

And once more the perfect answer was there, as clear as if she'd spoken it aloud:

What about the Clements? All killed by fire! All four of them. And now this. This!

She closed her eyes, and when she opened them again the room looked solid and real, as did the trees beyond the window, their upper branches stirring in the morning breeze. Things were what they were; they couldn't be something else as well. How could she believe in ancient spirits or identities that dwelt within the land? God, He was another matter, someone she had given little thought to since their troubles began. (So much for her faith and her years of churchgoing!) But the idea of a cruel and enduring power somehow wedded to a single place ... How could she believe in that?

How?

Mary's continual whimpering, seeping through the closed door and along the passage, gave particular force to that question. A question which continued to trouble Tess all through lunch. Doug and Bob, locked in their sullen, guilty silence, didn't help matters; they only made her feel more alone, more prey to doubt. On the spur of the moment, she heard herself saying:

'I think I'll pop into the village this afternoon. There are a few things I need to do.'

She hadn't consciously decided on any plan, yet she knew instantly what she was going there for. To try and resolve the issue. To make up her mind one way or the other by finding out as much about this place as she could. Obviously it had an unfortunate history; and just as obviously Doris and Ted had been unwilling to go into detail about it. They hadn't acted as though they were hiding anything: they'd merely shown a normal reluctance to rake over an unpleasant past. Even Ted, who didn't seem particularly sensitive, had gone vague when she'd pressed him. Which meant that things must have been pretty bad here. But bad enough for an otherwise sensible woman to believe in a curse? That was the issue, and one that Tess had firmly in mind an hour later when she parked outside the office of the estate agent from whom they'd bought the house.

She was in luck (if that's what you could call it, she thought wryly) because Ann Guthrie was just farewelling a client when she walked in. Moreover, she was greeted warmly enough to begin with.

'Always a pleasure to see a former customer,' Ann said, giving her a well-practised smile and showing her to a chair in the inner office.

The smile grew a little stiff, however, when Tess explained why she was there.

'Ah, yes, the Clements,' Ann said carefully, and her expression became as vague and evasive as Ted's earlier in the day. 'Well, perhaps I'm not the best person to talk to. You see, the property wasn't really on my list. I was handling it on behalf of another agent. Mike Jensen, he's the person you should . . .'

Tess reached across the desk to a pile of papers and pointed to the firm's letterhead. Immediately below the name of the company were the words: *Serving this area faithfully for thirty-five years*.

'That's long enough to know what's going on here,' Tess said quietly.

Ann Guthrie's manicured hands were folded defensively across her stomach. 'I still think you'd be better advised to . . .'

'Hold on,' Tess cut in, 'I'm not here to make a scene. We bought the house and that's it as far as I'm concerned. All I want to find out is what kind of house it is I'm living in.'

She could see the process of decision at work in Ann

Guthrie's well-made-up face. A frown formed between her eyes, her nostrils drew almost closed, her lips narrowed; and then, with an exhalation of breath, she relaxed, her hands falling loosely onto the desk.

'It doesn't have a wonderful history,' she confessed.

Tess nodded. 'Yes, some of it I know about, from the Briggs.'

'Ah, the Briggs,' Ann said, and gave her a thin smile. 'Then you'll have heard about their son's involvement with the girl. What was her name . . . ?'

'With Denny?'

'Yes, that's it. With Denny Clement.'

Tess experienced her first cool shock of the afternoon, a feeling immediately accompanied by a disquieting sense of *déjà vu*. 'No,' she said, keeping her voice level, 'the Briggs haven't mentioned that.'

'Oh, I see.' And the frown was back between Ann Guthrie's eyes, a snaking flaw in the smoothly powdered skin.

Again Tess was able to detect the silent passage of decision across the woman's face. She helped it along by leaning forward and covering those tensed hands with her own. A simple gesture of assurance, from one woman to another.

'This isn't an official meeting,' she said, her voice dropped now to a confidential whisper. 'Whatever you tell me, I'm not going to hold you to your word. Nor will I get hysterical, I promise. And as the owner of the property, I'm not likely to shoot my mouth off outside this office, now am I?'

She waited, and there was that same exhalation of

breath, the hands growing slack within her own loose grasp.

'Well all I can tell you is the local gossip,' Ann explained reluctantly, 'because nothing was ever proved. But there were some around here who claimed that the Briggs' son had something to do with the fire.'

'You mean he lit it?' Tess bit her lip, too late. Clearly that had been the wrong thing to ask, the woman's face surprisingly expressive of her feelings. 'No, don't answer that,' she added hastily. 'Forget I spoke. Just go on with what you were saying.'

This time the pause, the frown, were short lived.

'It was just talk anyway,' Ann went on. 'Some said he was angry because Denny had given him the flick. Others said she'd never really been interested in him in the first place. Others again claimed that the one behind the fire wasn't the Briggs' boy at all, but the Clements' son ... um ...'

'Will?'

'Yes, that's it, Will. He was very young at the time. Fourteen or so, I can't remember exactly, but young enough for most people to ignore that sort of gossip. It was only ...' She faltered momentarily. '... only afterwards that they took it more seriously, though again nothing was ever proved.'

'Afterwards?' Tess asked, and she could tell from those eyes, from the familiar frown, that it was the question Ann Guthrie least wanted to answer.

'After what?' she prompted her gently.

Ann drew her hands away, not defensively, only to

grip the edge of the desk as though bracing herself. She cleared her throat and took a slow breath.

'After he killed his sister.'

Tess rocked back in her chair, her fingers to her mouth. She wasn't feigning shock: the cold sensation in her stomach was all too real. And yet in a strange, almost macabre way, it was this kind of news she had been ready for; precisely this order of grim truth she had already half divined from Doris's dire warning. 'Cursed', Doris had said of the house and land, and perhaps she was right. Perhaps . . .

'After Will did *what*?' she whispered, just to be sure.

But Ann wasn't going to say it again.

'It's not as bad as it sounds,' she explained quickly. 'Really it isn't.'

'Not as bad?'

Now Ann was holding *her* hands. 'The papers said he did it out of pity, love.'

'How can you kill someone out of love?' Tess objected, and she was thinking as she spoke of Kevin, hanging there amongst the trees with the evening shadows gathering about him.

'The girl was seriously burned in the fire. She nearly died. And when they eventually released her from hospital she was horribly disfigured, half blind and scarred down one side. I never saw her, but I gather she wasn't a pleasant sight.'

'I still don't see . . .'

'No, listen to me for a minute,' Ann insisted, and she was no longer acting the polished salesperson, her voice now husky and intense. 'Will took it all very badly by all accounts. The parents had to stop him going to the hospital, it upset him so much. He must have been in quite a state because all the time they were living on the Central Coast he was in the care of a psychiatrist. That's what it said in the papers after the inquiry.'

'The Central Coast?'

'Yes, they had a weekend cottage there, and a boat. It's where they stayed while the house up here was being rebuilt. I think I'm right in saying that Denny was taken there for a while after she came out of hospital.'

'So Will didn't . . . ?' Tess began hopefully, but fell silent as Ann shook her head.

'No, he did it up here. I'd like to tell you otherwise, but that's the way it was. Evidently the girl was very depressed, understandably I suppose, and he couldn't bear seeing her like that. So . . .' Ann shrugged helplessly. 'So he took matters into his own hands. He put his sister out of her misery and then . . .'

Tess thought she had had her share of shocks for one afternoon. She wasn't prepared for anything else. She was already too raw, too exposed. That's enough, she longed to say. I don't want to hear the rest. Except, of course, she did. One part of her mind was hungry for every detail, for anything that would release her from uncertainty — hungry even for what this woman said next.

'. . . and then he committed suicide.'

Doris's various warnings came rushing back, their force redoubled. *This place'll change you, until you don't know yourselves. Until you end up doin' things, terrible things.* This place! *I've seen this place at work,*

I've seen what it does to people. Yes! It was true! To Denny! To Will! To the parents! *It'll do the same thing to your Mary. Her just for starters.* Tess closed her eyes, trying to shut out her vision of Doris standing there on the doorstep, her back turned resolutely to the wooded hillside she was denouncing, but all Tess saw instead, in the darkness behind her closed lids, was the bloodied, desecrated figure of Kevin. *Terrible things!*

'Are you feeling all right, Mrs Warner?' someone was asking.

A mug of warm tea was pressed into her hands and she clung onto it, gulped down its hot sweetness in an effort to melt the icy fist that had fastened on her stomach.

When she looked up — her hands, her face, her mind once more under control — Ann Guthrie was gazing guiltily at her, reminding her, absurdly, of Doug.

'You must think I'm a real bastard,' she said, 'selling you a house like that.'

She even spoke like Doug. All this talk of blame! Of being wise or sorry after the event! What did it matter? The place itself, that was all she cared about, and what had happened there — what was still *happening*, for God's sake! The rest was just words, pointless breast-beating. After all, how could this woman possibly have known what the place was really like? Even she, Tess, hadn't yet finally made up her mind about it, in spite of all she'd heard. Was it truly cursed, a place of ancient and enduring evil, or just an ordinary hillside on which people had acted out their darkest thoughts?

'No, I'd probably have done the same thing in your

position,' she said truthfully, and was astonished at how steady her voice sounded.

'That's very kind . . .' Ann began, but Tess waved aside all talk of gratitude, impatient now to get back to what really counted.

'There's one thing I still don't understand,' she admitted. 'How could Will commit suicide and also die of the injuries he received in the fire? Did he do something to make his injuries worse?'

She guessed she was on the wrong track even before Ann answered — that expressive face of hers again.

'Who told you Will was injured in the fire?'

'Well, I rather got that impression from the Briggs.'

'You must have misunderstood them. You see, he drowned himself.'

Death by water! The pattern of fire broken! Which meant . . . what? Compared with the four human torches she had imagined, a watery death sounded almost gentle. Merciful. Is that how it had been in his case? No agony? No flaming dance of death like the one Mary had celebrated in the clearing? Just a gentle quenching of the spirit?

'Are you sure?' she pressed Ann, feeling as though she were about to be reprieved, though from what she couldn't decide.

'Absolutely. He drove his parents' car to the coast, took their boat out to sea, and went over the side. He and Denny both died within a few hours of each other.'

So! Drowned! To that extent at least the house, the land, were innocent. Or were they? Wasn't it the events out there — Kevin's jealousy, the fire, the agony, the murder — that had pushed Will to the edge? It was arguable that where he actually took his own life was beside the point. The root cause, the miasma of violence and tragedy which seemed to seep from the very hillside, that was what counted.

'And the parents?' Tess asked shakily, and even as she put the question, she felt disconcertingly close to that unknown couple, as if all these years later she were standing in their shoes, facing the same brooding forces that had beset them. 'How did they cope with their loss?'

'I hardly knew them,' Ann confessed. 'After the inquiry they lived like hermits out there. Never had visitors, or not that I heard, never spoke to anyone. I only ever saw them when they came into the village for supplies.'

'But you must have some idea of how they took it all,' Tess pressed her. 'People don't go through that sort of experience and stay the same.'

Ann Guthrie glanced towards the front of the office, where a young couple were speaking to the woman at the desk, and Tess guessed rightly that she was growing weary of this intense conversation. It was too far removed from her workaday world, and the sight of prospective clients was enough to distract her.

'Really, I'm not unsympathetic,' she began, half rising. 'I do understand your position, but afternoons are a busy time for me and I do have to . . .'

'I won't keep you much longer,' Tess said stubbornly, not budging from her chair. 'Just tell me about the

Clements and I'll leave you to your work. I won't bother you again.'

Ann sank back, not quite managing to suppress a sigh. 'I'd help you if I could, honestly, but there's so little to tell. All I could judge by were their faces, the way they looked.'

'Wasn't that enough?'

The woman at the desk was signalling through the glass partition, and this time Ann rose resolutely to her feet.

'Their expressions,' Tess insisted, still not moving, 'what were they like? What did they make you think of?'

From the corner of her eye Tess could see the young couple waiting out in the corridor beyond the glass-panelled door. Ann took a step in their direction and stopped, a smile of welcome frozen on her lips. As she turned briefly towards Tess she was the salesperson again, cool, professional, bidding goodbye to a client. Except that what she said belied her appearance, her voice a husky whisper, the words themselves totally out of keeping with the modern, glossy look of the office.

'If you must know, they looked haunted. Like people who . . . who lived with ghosts . . . with spirits of some kind.'

'Good or evil spirits?' Tess asked quickly, and Ann hesitated as she reached for the door.

'I'd say . . .'

'Yes?'

'I'd say . . . both.'

Then they were shaking hands and smiling as if they'd

done no more than transact some matter-of-fact business, and moments later Tess was standing out on the pavement in the hot sunlight.

Like people who live with ghosts . . . with spirits . . . Good or evil . . . ? Both.

As she drove slowly home through the undulating heat haze of mid-afternoon, those words, like Doris's, stayed with her. Opening the car windows did nothing to dispel them. The blustery wind, which snatched greedily at her hair and dress, ridding the car of its hot stagnant air, failed completely to clear the uncertain spaces of her mind.

The sight of the house perched up there on the hillside only made her feel more closed in, more trapped within herself. With its heavily barred windows and door, it was like a blind-faced keep designed to hold at bay whatever invisible forces ringed it in.

She plodded wearily up the front steps and was greeted by Mary's whimpering, a sound that had become as regular and monotonous as the ticking of the kitchen clock. Was Mary also haunted, Tess asked herself, just like the Clements? Was *that* her problem? Was she also visited by ghosts, by 'invisible forces' which the bars at the windows were powerless to exclude? That was certainly how she looked when Tess opened the door to her room. A clenched, terrified figure, no less blind-faced than the house itself, her legs folded beneath her on the rumpled bed, her head stiffly averted from the farthest corner.

'What is it, darling?' Tess whispered, kneeling beside her. 'Is there something in here with you? Is there?'

Her eyes tightly closed, her cheeks tear-stained, Mary flinched from Tess's touch, her face suddenly furrowed by a bewildering mixture of emotions — misery, yearning, grief, guilt...

Guilt? Tess leaned back and studied her features keenly, wondering for a moment whether Mary had begun to understand what she'd done to Kevin. Had she? Or was there some other, unknown cause of all this heartache? Was Mary perhaps already alive to sights, to sounds, to *forces*, that she, Tess, had only the vaguest inkling of?

'Is there something here that's frightening you, sweetheart?' she asked gently. 'Is it making you do things you don't want to? If there is, you must find a way of telling me. You *must*. And I'll take you far away from here, where you'll be safe.'

She waited to see what effect her words would have, but all Mary did was turn her shoulder as well as her face from the corner, as though pretending that that part of the room didn't exist.

'Is that where it's hiding?'

Tess made as if to go over there, and all at once Mary was grappling with her, tearing dementedly at her hair and clothes, almost tigerish in the manner of her attack. Normally the stronger of the two, all Tess could do was shield her head from the slaps and punches that drove her rapidly back. She managed to keep on her feet as far as the door, and then fell sprawling into the passage.

Winded, shocked, she curled up, braced for a fresh onslaught, but as suddenly as it had begun, it was over, with the house uncannily silent all about her, no sounds coming even from the workshop. There was the barest shuffle of footsteps, the creak of bedsprings, and when she looked up, Mary, having cleared her room, was again seated on the bed, her head turned adamantly from the corner.

Other, much louder footsteps approached along the passage and Tess, still shaken and confused, flinched away just as Mary had done earlier. Someone loomed above her, huge, his features strangely golden, and she let out a choking cry before she realised it was Doug, his face covered with a bloom of sawdust.

'Are you okay?' His voice all concern. 'What's going on?'

She didn't answer until they were seated together on the living room couch, the door firmly closed behind them.

'I don't want you laughing or pooh-poohing what I have to say,' she warned him.

'Have I ever?'

'I mean it, Doug.'

He sighed as Mary's whimpering started up again in the background. 'There's nothing left to laugh at around here anyway,' he said sadly. 'Not any more.'

She took his hand and held it warmly against her. 'All right then, this is what I think. That ... that Doris Briggs is right and that ...'

He eased his hand away from her before she could finish. 'This isn't worthy of you, Tess. It's superstitious nonsense.'

'Is it?' she challenged him, and quickly she recounted what she'd learned that afternoon in the village.

All the time she was speaking she watched his eyes, searching there for the beginnings of doubt, but even when she came to the parts about Will's suicide and the haunted appearance of the Clements, there was no detectable change in him. That down-to-earth quality of his, which she'd always admired, which she'd relied on throughout their married life, held steady now, and as she completed her account all he did was shake his head sorrowfully.

'What a terrible story,' he murmured.

'Story?' she took him up. 'Is that what you think it is? Just a story?'

'You know that's not what I meant,' he reprimanded her gently. 'I'm not putting it down. You're right, it's awful. But I still don't see what any of it has to do with Mary. It all happened years ago. It's finished with, Tess.'

'No! You're wrong. There's something here!' She stabbed downwards with one rigid finger. 'It affected the Clements and now it's affecting us.'

When he didn't answer, she stood up impatiently. Why was he so stubborn? Why couldn't he *see*? Left to herself Mary was basically gentle. She wouldn't ... couldn't possibly ... And yet ... Tess could feel her face crumpling, the tears pressing at the backs of her eyes, and she had to suck in her breath to stay in control.

'Here,' Doug was saying, and he drew her back down on the couch and nestled her against him.

'It has to be this house!' she said desperately. 'It *has* to!'

He waited for her to grow calm before he spoke. 'I want you to listen to me for once,' he pleaded.

'Don't I always?'

'No, not always, Tess. Over that Kevin business I listened to you. Now it's your turn.'

'All right, I'm listening,' she said dully.

He drew her closer still, as though by containing her physically he could also contain her in spirit, or at least contain the worst excesses of that spirit.

'I'd like to blame this place,' he began, 'and that's the honest-to-God truth, but I can't. There's just no comparison between the Clements and the way Mary's acting now. You must be able to see that, Tess. What Will Clement did . . . well, there's a kind of sense to it. It can all be explained in terms of ordinary human emotions. Feelings like jealousy and grief and love. Whereas with Mary it's different. There's no sense in what she's doing, not unless we . . .'

'So Will Clement was sane and Mary's not,' she interrupted him plaintively. 'Is that it?'

'That's not what I'm saying. All I'm pointing out is that you can explain his actions. There was too much love there, or the wrong kind of love or something. And that's not how it is with Mary. To make sense of her actions you have to trace them back to Terror. That damned dog was the one who started all this. If you ask me, she still sees him everywhere. She'd have acted just the same even if we'd stayed in Sydney.'

'Would she? How can you be sure this place hasn't made her worse?'

'Oh come on, Tess. Terror's the issue where Mary's concerned, not this house or this hillside. In your heart you know that as well as I do.'

Did she? What *did* her heart tell her? Earlier, when she'd listened for those inner promptings, all she'd heard were the voices of Doris and of Ann Guthrie, both of them in their own way warning her against dangerous and invisible forces. Now, nestled in Doug's arms, it was his voice, his brand of common sense, which seemed to hold sway. Was she then so fickle? Couldn't she decided on a course and keep to it? Or earlier had she merely been clutching at straws, ready to believe anything but the worst about Mary? Was it time, as Doug suggested, to face up to the truth and somehow learn to live with it? *Their* truth, not what might have been true for the Clements or anyone else.

'She's safe here, Tess,' Doug murmured enticingly. 'As safe as she'll be anywhere.'

Tess let herself sink back against him. 'So what do we do?'

'We stay where we are. We've got too much invested here to do anything else. We give her a chance to heal. And she will if we're patient, I promise.'

He had promised. And who was she to say he was wrong? What had *she* done that had been so right? Wasn't it time that she relied on him, trusted him more? Not without misgiving, she let the reins of decision slip from her own uncertain grasp into his big capable hands.

'Yes,' she breathed, 'maybe it's best if we stay.' And she rested her head on his shoulder, ignoring the tiny qualm that persisted somewhere at the back of her mind.

Yet like a faint dissenting voice, it refused to be silenced, nagging at her throughout the remainder of the day and on into her dreams, where it eventually became so strident, so demanding, that she woke in the middle of the night and sat bolt upright, shivering. And still it went on, or so she half believed, until her head cleared of sleep and she realised that what she was hearing were other voices entirely. Demented shrieks and the shouted protests of someone desperately afraid.

'Wha'?' Doug was struggling up from his pillow.

She didn't wait for him, but leapt for the door, groping for the outer switch. In a sudden glare of light she saw a tangle of bodies halfway along the passage, arms and legs kicking out or twined madly about each other. Bob, pale and bleary-eyed, was already hovering above them.

'Leave him!' he yelled, and before Tess could rush forward, he stooped and plucked Mary free of the struggling mass.

Beneath her Harry lay perfectly still, his pyjama top torn down the front. His eyes were open, but he seemed too shocked to move. There was blood on his face, and deep scratches on his chest and neck.

'Uh! Uh!' Mary continued to let out formless shrieks as she fought to break free, her hooked fingers clawing the air.

'That's enough!' Bob demanded, and hit her with the back of his hand, so hard that she went slack for a moment, with saliva drooling from one corner of her mouth.

Tess by then had scuttled forward. Although it was Harry she scooped up and crushed against her, it was Mary she was looking at, her expression almost as fierce as her daughter's.

'We've got to get her out of here!' she shouted, her head raised as though she were addressing the house itself.

Doug crouched beside her, breathing heavily, his cheeks mottled from stress. 'We can't, love. Look at her. She's too dangerous.'

As if to prove his point, Mary convulsed violently and tore herself free. Though not in order to renew her attack on Harry. Ducking aside, she scurried into the farthest corner of her room where she turned at bay like some feral animal, the darkness draped about her.

Tess jerked her head away. 'No, it's not Mary!' she protested with a shudder. 'I don't care what you say! It's what this house is making her into!'

'Look at her, Tess,' Doug repeated quietly. 'Then tell me that . . .'

But she wouldn't let him finish. Still clutching onto Harry, she lunged at him with her free hand, almost as demented in that first split second of abandonment as Mary herself. He flung up his arms to protect his face, but her moment of madness had already passed, and she collapsed against his chest.

'We have to take her away!' she sobbed.

'Hush,' he whispered, hugging them both, rocking them gently.

He was holding her as he'd held her that afternoon, the circle of his arms warm and secure, but still she could sense a tough knot of resistance in him. This time she matched it with a hardness of her own, the tears that spilled from her eyes as hateful as any she had ever shed.

'She can't stay here!' she insisted, no more capable of

looking down into Harry's staring eyes than across at Mary. 'If she does, it'll destroy . . .' She left the rest of that unsaid, adding only: 'We have to take her away.'

There was a brief period of silent struggle, soon over. As always, she felt him give before her, the strength in him dissolve.

'All right, sweetheart, if that's what you want.'

'You know it is.'

He began rocking them again, one hand reaching protectively for Harry whom she still clutched in her arms. 'As soon as it's light, then,' he murmured reluctantly. 'First thing tomorrow . . . tomorrow . . . tomorrow . . .'

The repetition of that word, meant to lull her, sounded like a dull bell through the silence of the house, while Mary, a caged animal backed by shadow, swung her face slowly from side to side, keeping time.

18

It was like that other time, with Tess and Bob holding her down on the bed while he, Doug, fixed and tightened the straps. Except that now he found it easier to meet Mary's fierce gaze. Anything, even this, was preferable to having Harry end up like Kevin. Also, Harry wasn't crying and denouncing them this time. His face still bloody, his torn pyjama jacket held closed at the throat, he was standing by the door, watching them silently.

Doug checked the last strap to make sure it was tight enough, and left Tess to cover Mary with a light rug.

'Try and get some sleep, my pet. Rest now, and I'll take you away from here in the morning, I promise.'

That was Tess, murmuring lovingly behind him as he went across to Harry. 'You all right, son?'

Harry nodded, his eyes fixed on Mary who had begun to struggle against the constraint, small gasps and grunts of effort breaking from her lips.

'She didn't . . .' Harry faltered uncertainly, and was interrupted by Tess who ushered them all out of the room and drew the door closed.

'She didn't mean to . . .' he began again, tears showing

in his eyes, and Tess pressed her fingers gently to his lips.

'We all know that,' she answered. 'She loves you really. She loves all of us.'

Doug cleared his throat uncomfortably. 'The boy's in danger, Tess. Face up to it. He deserves to know the truth.'

She swung around, her face set and determined, nothing left of the softer self she'd exposed to him that afternoon. 'What I've told him *is* the truth!'

Doug would have preferred to let her have her way, but with Harry caught in the middle of all this he couldn't just back down.

'What about the other one out there?' he said meaningfully, not wanting to be too explicit in front of Harry. 'Did she love him as well?'

'Dad's right,' Bob said in a quiet voice.

Not for the first time, Doug was reminded of Mary by the way Tess gazed aggressively from him to Bob and back again — a disquieting thought which he quickly smothered.

'That had nothing to do with this,' she protested. 'She had a weapon then.'

'Yes, and it was an animal,' Harry joined in, not understanding.

Tess patted his cheek and went on less confidently: 'This . . . this was different. She was only . . . only . . .'

'And I think I surprised her,' Harry added, coming as much to his mother's rescue as to Mary's.

'Yes, that's what it was,' Tess agreed, and it saddened Doug to see how eagerly she snatched at any possibility. 'It was the same when she rushed at me yesterday. We both caught her off guard, that's all. She was defending herself. Everyone has the right to do that.'

'You don't strap people down just for defending themselves,' Doug pointed out, and braced himself for the next outburst.

But before Tess could answer, Bob came between them. 'We shouldn't be arguing about this now,' he said. 'Things always look worse in the middle of the night. Let's wait till morning.'

It was a suggestion even Tess seemed thankful for. 'Come on,' she said to Harry, leading him off to the bathroom, 'let me see to those scratches of yours.'

Doug squeezed Bob's arm in silent thanks and returned to the bedroom where he tried to compose himself for sleep. It seemed a remote possibility at that moment, with his heart still clamouring uncomfortably and the morning only a few hours away. And what then? If they were to leave this place, as Tess demanded, where were they to go? Where were he and Bob to work? Their old house and their former workplace in Sydney were rented out, which effectively closed off that avenue. So where? And for the present did he really want them all to stay together, for Harry to go on being exposed to Mary? The obvious solution was to have Mary committed, but he knew Tess would never agree to that, and he wasn't sure he could come at it himself. Which meant the problem remained.

He was distracted briefly as Tess came back to bed. She stretched out beside him without a word, without so much as a goodnight peck on the cheek. Is this what we've come to? he wondered miserably. Are we so far apart that we can't even comfort each other? He reached for her hand, but she shook him off and turned away, leaving him to his own lonely vigil.

He sighed and pulled the sheet higher. There was, he knew, one possible answer to their problem: for Tess and Mary to go to Meg's, and for him to stay on here with the two boys. That way he and Bob could continue working, and Harry would be safe. But what about Meg's safety? No, that was a silly question: Meg could look after herself; and she'd help them out if they asked her.

There was one other thing too. After how they'd acted over that terrible Kevin business — hushing up the death, burying the body secretly down there amongst the trees, lying to Doris and Ted — he was loath just to walk away. It was as though his part in those grisly events had somehow tied him to the place. Perhaps it had, he thought wearily. And perhaps, for similiar reasons, Tess would feel the same once she'd discovered that Mary's trouble had nothing to do with the property itself. That would at least be a bond of sorts, something to hold them together through whatever trials still awaited them. Not like the old closeness, but better than nothing.

With the immediate future more or less settled, he was mildly surprised to find himself feeling sleepy. As he moved to a more comfortable position, the house stirred restlessly in the cool of the night, the creaking of its timbers like an involuntary response to the pressure of ghostly feet. It was a sound he had heard so often before that it failed to disturb him. In his present sombre frame of mind he almost took comfort from the familiar creaks and groans, carrying them effortlessly into his dreams where unseen presences moved from room to room in a house he only half recognised, and where Tess told him over and over again that they had arrived at a fated place from which there could be no escape.

He awoke with a start in the early dawn and rolled over onto the other now empty half of the bed. Tess? He raised his head and saw her outlined in the open doorway, her hair in wild disarray, a long kitchen knife clutched in one hand.

'Jesus!'

He was out of bed and flattened against the far wall, his heart palpitating madly. Tess hadn't moved. In her black nightdress and with her shoulders hunched, she looked to him almost like an angel of death, like some fate figure stepped straight from his dream.

'She's gone,' he heard her whisper.

She? What was Tess talking about?

'It's Mary.' Tess held up the knife for him to see. 'She must have had this hidden under the mattress. She's cut herself free and disappeared.'

As his heart slowed to a governable pace, he tried to make sense of what Tess was telling him. Disappeared? How could Mary disappear? The windows were barred, the front door locked, secured.

He lurched forward and had to clutch onto the bed-end.

'She must be in the house somewhere,' he said.

'I'm telling you she's gone!' Tess shouted, and out of sheer desperation she drove the knife into the doorframe.

He was about to go to her when a sudden chilling possibility occurred to him, worse in its way than those first shocked moments of awakening. If Mary wasn't in her room, if she had a knife, then . . . then . . . !

The shortness of breath, the palpitations were back, and it was all he could do to mouth a single word:

'Harry . . . ?'

'Don't you think I thought of him first?' Tess snapped. 'He's fine, and so is Bob.'

Again he steadied, his strength returning, his normal calm spreading like warmth through his body and limbs. He stood away from the bed, the thump of his heart reduced to an almost imperceptible murmur.

'She must be hiding,' he said.

'I've looked.'

'We'll look again.'

He noticed the two boys then, standing together in the still shadowy passage, one side of Harry's face swollen from the night's attack. Bob had already pulled on some tracksuit pants and runners.

'Shall I check outside?' he asked, and was moving towards the front door, key in hand, when Tess stopped him.

She was back in control now, wearing that hard unremitting expression which always caused Doug's heart to sink. 'Not yet,' she said shortly. 'We'll make another search of the house first. You, Doug, downstairs, we'll look up here.'

He didn't argue with her, not while she was in that mood. Taking Harry with him, he padded as silently along the passage and down the stairs as his bulk would allow.

He had never been to the workroom so early in the morning. The grey dawn, spilling down from the bank of east-facing windows, gave to the low-ceilinged space an eery quality that was vaguely unsettling. For reassurance as much as to see better, he groped for the light switches. The fluorescent tubes stuttered and blinked on, casting a harsh white glare in which nothing moved, the benches and machines standing rock-still in the silence, like dumb witnesses to the room's emptiness. No, not just empty, Doug thought, looking about him: there was a feel here of desertion, as though someone or something had recently fled with the dawn shadows. Mary perhaps? Or was his imagination, fired by all Tess's wild talk, merely playing tricks on him?

Although he sensed that it was useless, he searched every possible hiding place — under the benches, in the cupboards, anywhere that a human being could conceivably hide. Always with the same result: nothing, no one. All he encountered, even in the shadowiest corners where the light barely reached, was that same weird feeling of desertion.

He looked across at Harry who was sitting hunched on the bottom stair, half concerned, half sleepy.

'D'you think she's been here?' Doug called softly.

Harry raised his head, his damaged face strangely pale and sensitive in the harsh glare, like a young animal testing the nonexistent breeze. 'Yeah, I think so.'

It was the same when they returned upstairs. There, too, Doug felt haunted by the sense that they had just missed her. He felt it especially strongly when they joined Tess and Bob in Mary's room. The open cupboard and drawer, the nightdress lying almost in the doorway, all suggested a hasty departure, as though she'd rushed out at the first hint of dawn.

'So what now?' Tess asked.

She was sitting nonplussed in the old armchair which Mary had claimed years before as her own.

'You said she hid the knife under her mattress,' Bob said. 'How do you know that?'

'We're looking for Mary,' Tess answered impatiently, 'not the knife.'

'I still want to know,' Bob insisted.

Doug saw the flush of anger rise in Tess's face and then subside. 'Where else could it have been?' she said in a tight, contained voice. 'That was the only place she could have reached.'

'Is anything else under there?'

'I haven't . . .'

Doug and Bob both lumbered forward together, but Tess was quicker, grabbing at the side of the mattress and levering it up and back against the wall. On the timber base there was a scattering of papers, three photographs amongst them. All three had been taken by flash, but the pictures were so blurred that they meant nothing until Harry pointed at one and said simply:

'It's me.'

The other two sprang to life then. Through a shimmer of overlapping images, Doug made out his own face and Tess's: set side by side, with an expanse of white between, they reminded him unnervingly of death-masks. As did the third picture which, despite the excessive blur, was almost certainly of Bob.

'What the hell's going on here?' he asked, bewildered. 'Where did she get these?'

'We were asleep,' Tess said, and she sounded as though all the hard determination had been drained out of her. 'She must have taken them in the middle of the night.'

'But what for? What did she want with them?'

Tess didn't answer, her head bent over the other pieces of paper.

'Listen to this,' she said at last, and in a voice as dull and defeated as before, she read from the topmost sheet:

Dear Double God, have mercy on my weakness and show me Your other face.

'Dear what?' Doug asked incredulously.

He took the page from her and stared at the handwriting. Like the photographs, it was shaky, uncertain, but recognisable for all that, as Mary's.

'There are lots of them,' Tess said, and began reading one after the other, letting the finished pages drift down to the floor:

Dear Double God, lead me now from the valley of the shadow of death.

Lord, lift thou up the light of Thy countenance upon me.

And out of His mouth went a sharp two-edged sword; and His countenance was as the sun. Dear Lord, show me only the sun.

These are the words You have given us: For I desired mercy, and not sacrifice. Hear them, Lord.

Double God, be One for me.

The heavens are Yours, Lord. Your sister-star wishes only for the earth.

Let pity soften Your . . .

'I don't get it,' Bob interrupted. 'Half of them sound like quotations to me. What's she on about?'

Doug wiped distractedly at his mouth. There was an icy hollow in his chest, but he couldn't have said why. For the first time, it seemed, he noticed the Bible on Mary's bedside table, with paper markers sticking out from one end.

'They're her prayers,' he explained in a whisper.

'Yes, but what's she praying *for*?'

Tess opened her hands and the unread pages fluttered down to join the others. Before they had all settled, the icy space in Doug's chest was growing larger. He recognised it now for what it was — the beginnings of panic.

'I don't know,' he said hoarsely, 'but I think we'd better try and find her while we can.'

As he ran to the front bedroom for shoes and a key, he half expected Tess to call after him — to object that Mary couldn't possibly be outside — but for once they were of one mind. 'Here!' she said, and snatched the key from his hand before he realised she was there beside him. She was gone just as quickly, the inner and outer doors crashing open one after the other while he was still struggling with his shoes.

'Wait!' he cried, and followed her out into a day so startlingly fresh and still — the early morning sky rising white and unblemished from the dense green of the hillside — that it was hard for him to imagine this as a place where prayers, of whatever kind, were even remotely necessary. All that disturbed the utter peacefulness of the scene were Tess, running bare-footed along the path, her hair flying, and his own laboured breaths as he struggled to catch up.

Down near the willows his feet suddenly tangled in his untied laces and he fell heavily, winding himself. Christ, he thought, his face pressed into the sandy soil, I'm too old for this. Too old to go tearing through the bush in search of God knows what. He sat up slowly, intending to rest until he caught his breath, and noticed something between the trees. A suggestion of movement. He listened hard and heard a muffled cry.

'Mary?' he called hopefully.

But when he pushed through to the clearing, it was Tess whom he found kneeling in the dewy grass. She was searching through the remains of a fire, picking out what was obviously an assortment of bones. That puzzled him for a moment, until he glanced around and saw the site of the first fire up there at the far end of the clearing, between the now crumbling figures of the man and the dog.

'She must have got out somehow and burned Kevin's body,' Tess said, holding a blackened skull.

All the terrors of that night seemed to invade the morning, staining its brightness.

'Are you sure?'

'Come and see for yourself.'

She led him into a thick knot of bush, to the place where he'd sweated and cried over the digging of the grave; and where afterwards, his hands soiled in a double sense, he'd pounded the earth flat and strewn it with branches. Now there was only a gaping hole with earth scattered untidily all around.

'The savage little bitch!' he heard himself groan, his bunched fists trembling before his face, the taste of sweat and tears on his lips. 'Is this what she was praying for? This?'

'Get a hold on yourself, Doug.'

But he couldn't. The image of Mary lugging the decomposing corpse from the grave was too vivid, worse in a way than what she'd done to Kevin in the first place. So calculating, so deliberate.

'Why the hell should I?' he broke out, aware that he sounded like a child, but unable to stop. 'She's the fucking murderer, not me!'

Tess slapped him then, a stinging blow that he almost welcomed — that he knew he deserved.

'You walked into this with your eyes wide open,' she reminded him grimly. 'There's no backing out now.'

He nodded, ashamed. 'What's she trying to do to us, Tess?' Not a complaint this time, but an appeal.

Tess put her arms around him, held him tightly against

her as if he were Harry, or even Mary. 'It's what she's doing to herself that worries me more,' she murmured. 'When she wakes up one day and looks back on all this, how's she going to cope? How will she live with herself?'

Again Tess was right, and he kissed the top of her head, glad to have her pressed warmly against him, their locked arms, bodies, somehow defying the grave that gaped at their feet.

'You'll be there for her,' he said softly. 'You're there for all of us when you're needed.'

She gave him a last reassuring pat and drew away. 'Come on,' she said, heading off in the direction of the path, 'let's get back to the house. She could be anywhere by now. There's no point in wandering around.'

He trailed after her. 'So what do we do, just wait?'

'For a while anyway.'

After their closeness back there in the bush, he dearly wanted to stay silent, but the sight of the second fire ring, with its scattering of bones, served as a reminder of what had to be said.

'We can't afford to wait too long, Tess.'

He saw her back stiffen, yet she didn't turn on him as she had earlier that morning.

'An hour or two,' she called over her shoulder, 'that's all I'm asking for. After that we'll contact the police.'

'The police? Are you crazy?'

He had stopped abruptly at the edge of the path, and she came back and linked an arm through his, urging him on.

'Mary's not wanted for anything,' she pointed out. 'We may know what she's done, but no one else does.

As far as the police are concerned, she'd just be another missing person, a young girl who's a bit slow and can't speak.'

'So you wouldn't tell them . . . ?'

She said it for him this time. 'That she's dangerous? No. Would you?'

It was more of a challenge than a question, both of them so confident of the answer that there was no need for him to speak. And after all it was true what Tess said: the dark knowledge, the suspicion, existed in *his* mind, not out there in society at large.

He could just see the house through the trees by now. Bob, sensible as ever, had stayed behind with Harry, the two of them sitting out on the steps in the early sunlight. They waved as he and Tess approached, the house rearing up behind them like a fortress.

He stopped again, on the strip of lawn, and looked upwards. The way the upper line of bars continued around the sides of the house lent to the facade its appearance of a masked face, with the straight line of the lower bars for a mouth. It was a stern, forbidding face; one that gave nothing away, its secret character locked within.

'I still don't see how she managed to get out,' he muttered.

'What about the roof?' Tess responded, thinking aloud rather than actually making a suggestion. 'Could she have got out that way somehow?'

Doug ran his eye across the roof, searching for signs of disturbance, but there was no visible break in the pattern of the tiles. 'It's not likely,' he said, 'She'd first have to climb into the attic and then . . .'

Tess must have caught a whiff of his excitement because suddenly she was clutching at his arm.

'Doug, what is it?'

'The attic! She could be hiding there!'

For once he was ahead of Tess, forging past the astonished eyes of the two boys who flattened themselves against the railing, and on into the passage, his own morning shadow striding before him. Caught within that shadow, half obscured by it, was a smaller shape, a startled face that vanished even as he recognised it.

'Mary! Sweetheart!' he sang out.

Tess was trying to push past him. 'Where? Where is she?'

They reached the end of the passage together, in time to hear the last of Mary's scampering footsteps on the downstairs floor. There was a double click, of a door or window opening and closing, and after that silence.

'Sweetheart?' he called again, and was drowned out by Tess.

'Wait for me, Mary! Wait!'

He was shoved roughly aside and Tess ran down the stairs ahead of him. Too relieved to hurry, he searched the space below as he moved slowly from step to step. The workroom was bathed now in the soft light of morning, a light marred only by the shadow of the window bars which sprawled across the floor. In the absence of the harsh fluorescent glare, the whole room looked very different. Yet still, to his dismay, there was that strange air of desertion about it which he'd detected earlier. As though Mary, who could surely be nowhere else but here, had managed magically to slip away once again.

Remembering the double click he'd heard from up in the passage, he paused on the bottom step and watched Tess as she moved frantically from cupboard to cupboard, shouting as she went.

'Where the hell's she hiding now? She can't just disappear into thin air!'

He waited until she had given up and was standing there baffled and frustrated in the middle of the room.

'Where else is there to look, Doug? You work down here, for God's sake!'

'There has to be another door,' he said quietly.

'D'you mean to the outside?'

Is that what he'd meant? He glanced at the three outer walls, all of them made of solid brick. No, nowhere for a door there, and if one did exist they'd have spotted it long ago, from outside the house. That left the inner wall — solid sections of concrete set in an unbroken row. Could one of those be false, or hinged perhaps? It was possible, though for Mary to get out of the house that way there still had to be another door or window beyond. And there simply weren't any.

Or were there?

Hastily, he tried to visualise the ground plan of the house. It was basically a rectangle, with the living area and two of the three bedrooms built over this workroom. And beyond the workroom? Beyond this concrete wall? What about the space beneath the kitchen, bathroom, and third bedroom? He had assumed that it was taken up by the natural curve of the hillside. But was it?

'Wait here a minute,' he said, and ran quickly up the stairs.

Bob and Harry met him halfway along the passage.

'Have you got her?' Bob asked.

'Not yet, but I have an idea where she might be. Come on, I need a hand.'

He led them down the steps and around to the southern side of the house, the shadiest and therefore the least overgrown area. All three together forced a passage through the ferns and bushes, searching the damp-streaked wall beneath the bathroom and third bedroom for some kind of opening. When they drew a blank, they tried the other side, directly under the kitchen, where Harry soon found a low, tunnel-like passage through the undergrowth. Even Doug, once it was pointed out to him, was able to crawl along it quite easily.

It brought him to a deeply shadowed section of wall immediately below the kitchen. A window had been set into the wall almost at ground level. Still on hands and knees, he pressed his face to the pane, which was filthy, and immediately started back in alarm as he glimpsed a gigantic face. More cautiously, he looked again and realised that what he had seen was a huge photograph fixed to the inner wall beside the window. There seemed to be another photograph beyond it, and another, all of them the same perhaps, though it was hard to see clearly through the dirt and the interior gloom.

The window, he now noticed, was slightly warped, the upper edge protruding just far enough from the frame for him to grasp it with his fingertips. One sharp jerk was enough. There was a splintering of wood as the catch tore free, and the window swung open, carrying with it the smell of dust.

'Mary?' he called. 'Mary? Are you there?'

The only answer he received was from Tess, her voice faint and indistinct, filtering through to him from the basement which was on the same level as this secret room.

'Doug? Is that you?'

'Hold on,' he called back. 'I'm coming.'

With Bob's help, he lowered himself through the opening, his feet feeling for the floor. What they encountered instead was the unmistakable softness of a bed. He looked down and received his second shock within the space of a minute, for there beside his feet was the pale oval of a face.

'Jesus!' he cried, and half-fell, half-toppled from the bed, his hands scrabbling frantically along the wall for a light switch.

Amazingly he found one, the sudden glare from the overhead bulb revealing to him first that it was Mary who lay on the bed, her eyes too tightly shut for her simply to be asleep, and then that he was standing in a narrow sliver of a room whose every surface was thick with dust. The room itself was so narrow that it struck him as hardly more than an antechamber to the workroom beyond. Either that or a chapel, a shrine even, because all around the walls, reaching from chest height up to the ceiling, were hung identical monochrome photographs of a young woman about Mary's age. Although grainy from overenlargement, the outsize face that stared out from them was prettier than Mary's — even Doug had to admit that — and tipped back in an attitude of carefree laughter which contrasted sharply with Mary's closed expression as she lay there on the dusty coverlet. Apart from the photographs there was very little else in the room: just the bed, with a small chest of drawers beside it, its top littered with trinkets and knickknacks; a bookcase set into the wall at the foot of the bed, most of its shelves filled either with books or more childish knickknacks; a door in the middle of the narrow inner wall that separated this space from the workroom; and a dense film of dust over everything, with a single track worn through it from the door to the foot of the bed and along to the side of the window.

Somewhere in the background — beyond the cocoon of astonished discovery that still held him — Doug could hear Tess calling, her voice muffled by the closed door.

'Are you there, Doug? Answer me, for God's sake!'

And much nearer, clearer, his head and shoulders framed by the window opening, Bob's surprised exclamation:

'What the hell's this?'

'It's a shrine,' Doug said, and knew straight away he was right. That's precisely what it was: a space set aside by the Clements in memory of their lost daughter; a secret room excavated from the hillside and hidden away behind the concrete wall of the workroom. It had clearly been built to house all those things that were deeply personal to her — her bed, her books, her many china and glass trinkets, their lustre long since dimmed by dust, and most important of all, her likeness, caught in a fleeting moment of joy. Yes, a shrine, a holy place, in which he felt an instinctive need to duck his head and speak in whispers.

He turned slowly towards the door, which opened, as he had guessed, into the back of the built-in cupboard beneath the workroom stairs. Tess must have guessed the truth, too, because she was already standing there on the other side, the cupboard doors open, ready to scramble between the generously-spaced shelves.

As he helped her through, she seemed to absorb in a single glance both the details of the room and their hidden meaning. Except that when she straightened up and faced him, there was in her eyes no sign of the wonder or even the astonishment that he expected to find there. Only a hard certitude and an antagonism which warned him that for her this room was either much more or much less than the faded shrine he had taken it to be.

'So it's her!' she said, and she no longer appeared angry or overexcited. Her voice was low, almost menacing, and conveyed an air of utter conviction. 'It's Denny Clement! She's the one behind it all!'

At the sound of Denny's name, Mary flinched and curled up tightly on the bed, as though protecting herself from imminent attack by some unseen assailant.

'Behind what?' Doug asked, mystified, looking from Tess to Mary and back again.

'Behind what's been going on here. Don't you see?

It's not just the house or the land as we thought. It's Denny, damn her! It's been her all along, ever since the fire.'

Mary covered her face with both hands and let out a shrill whimper of terror.

'D'you hear her?' Tess added. 'Mary understands even if you don't. And so does Denny.'

'Denny?' Doug gestured futilely towards the huge photographs, noticing as he did so that the eyes, screwed up in laughter, were mere black slits in the grainy texture of the face. 'But she's dead! She's been dead for seven or eight years!'

'That's the point!' Tess explained, in a tone that shut off all further discussion. 'That's why she needs Mary. How else could Denny have got back at Kevin? How else can she do anything?'

PART EIGHT

Why did I laugh tonight? No voice will tell:
No God, no Demon of severe response,
Deigns to reply from Heaven or from Hell.

John Keats, 'Why Did I Laugh?'

19

It was a lot of nonsense. That was what Meg Daniels thought. She also thought Tess should have known better. Wasn't it bad enough having a crazy granddaughter? And now for her own daughter to go the same way! Well...!

Mind you, she had guessed it was in the wind some time ago. Like that day she was invited out there for a barbecue — having the red carpet unrolled for her one minute, and being bundled unceremoniously off the place the next. And at a moment's notice! She'd told Tess the truth then: 'It's not Mary who needs treatment. It's you. You're the problem in this family.' She still couldn't bring herself to repeat Tess's answer. The language! Afterwards, back here at home, she'd even shed a tear or two, the first since George had died. Because that's how it had felt, like another loss.

And then weeks later, out of the blue, just when she'd washed her hands of the whole affair, there was Tess on the phone again:

'Can Mary and I come and stay for a while, Mum? Only the two of us. We won't be any bother. I need a break from this place, that's all.'

'And what about Doug and the boys?' Meg had asked accusingly. 'Don't they need a break too?'

'They . . . they've decided to stay.'

That slight hesitation had spoken volumes. So there was trouble between her and Doug now. Not that Meg was surprised. Doug was an easy-going person most of the time, but push him too far and he'd dig in his heels like anyone else. In the present instance you could hardly blame him: a saint would have jibed at Tess's latest mad idea.

Meg herself didn't realise quite how far over the edge Tess had gone until she and Mary turned up on her doorstep.

'I suppose it's for me to take you in now, is it?' she said, blocking the doorway just long enough to remind Tess that, strictly speaking, there were no favours owed.

'We'd be grateful, Mum.'

'Well, luckily for you, my girl, blood's thicker than water,' she said grudgingly, ushering them in.

What else could she have done? Especially with Tess looking so browbeaten and nervous. Tess! Who usually took a backward step for no one. She and poor Mary about as woebegone as each other.

Not until she'd helped them unpack and they were having a candid chat over tea did Meg begin to appreciate precisely what she'd allowed into her home.

'Let me get this straight,' she said indignantly. 'Are you telling me that the . . . the spirit of this Clement girl is haunting the house out there?'

Tess lowered her eyes, shamefaced, yet as stubborn as ever. 'More than that, Mum.'

'More?'

'She's affecting Mary. Sort of . . . *using* her. That's why I had to bring her away.'

'Are you out of your mind, girl?'

Tess sat there fumbling with her hands, almost as distracted as Mary beside her. 'I know it sounds crazy . . .'

'For once you're talking sense,' Meg interrupted, and pointed straight at Mary. 'Look at her. Has bringing her away made any difference? Go on, look!'

Of course Tess didn't so much as turn her head, because she knew in advance what she'd see. The same disturbed face; the same empty eyes; in a word, the self-same unhappy girl she'd packed into the car a few hours earlier. Mary even obliged her by choosing that moment to let out one of her frightened whimpers, but still it made no difference. Not to Tess. As Meg was all too sadly aware, her mind was made up.

'She'll start to get better here, Mum,' she insisted quietly. 'It'll take time, but it'll happen. You'll see.'

In fact, Meg soon noted, the very reverse happened, to begin with anyway. Those first few days were terrible, with Mary whimpering or crying for hours on end, and alternately withdrawing into herself or acting downright aggressive.

In a way Meg preferred the aggression to the constant animal noise. It was something she could deal with. A good case in point was the first evening they all spent under the same roof. She was knitting in the living room soon after dark when she heard furtive footsteps on the stairs. (Her hearing was still perfect, thank God.) 'Tess?'

she called, and receiving no answer she ran into the passage in time to prevent Mary sneaking out of the front door. 'You stay right where you are, my girl,' she warned her, and for a minute there she believed Mary was about to leap at her throat, her young face bright red and furious. She soon put a stop to that little caper. A good hard slap was all that was needed and the battle of wills was over.

Between her and Mary at least. She still had to deal with Tess, who was down the stairs in a second.

'Don't you ever hit her again!' she shrieked, her face almost as furious as Mary's had been. 'Not *ever*! D'you understand?'

But Meg wasn't Doug or the boys to be cowed by Tess's show of temper.

'I won't have a child threatening me in my own home!' she flared back. 'In *this* house we have a few civilised rules, and don't you forget it!'

Once all the fuss had died down, Tess was more conciliatory. 'She wouldn't have hurt you, Mum. She's not dangerous, not any more. Honest.'

Honest? In that case, Meg wondered later that night, why did Tess go to all the trouble of dragging her bed across the door of the bedroom she chose to share with Mary? And not just on that night, but on all the nights that followed. The faint rumble of the castors on the carpeted floor soon became a regular part of the late evening ritual. (Like locking-up time at the zoo, Meg caught herself thinking once, and felt immediately chastened by her own unkindness.)

That nightly practice was partly what prompted her

to ring Maud and Ken and invite them to stay. She had a big house after all, with plenty of bedrooms, and Ken's stocky presence would give her an added sense of security. It wasn't so much that she was frightened of Mary — God knows she loved the child, in spite of all. No, what she dreaded far more was the inconvenience that might result from being hurt. What if she were to fall? Her hips were stiff and tender enough already. What would she do at her age if . . . ? But it was better not to think about that; and it would be better still to have Ken there, in case of trouble.

Though as Meg was to appreciate afterwards, when she thought back over those trying few weeks or so, Mary actually went through her worst spell before Ken and Maud arrived. All that grief or anxiety or whatever it was that afflicted her! All that gazing at the moon! From the moment it got dark in the evening, there was Mary prowling restlessly around the house, forever peeking between the closed curtains. And when the moon rose on that first night . . . ! It was a wonder the rellies didn't hear her up in Brisbane! At the first long wail, Meg went rushing along the passage, convinced that something awful had happened; yet all she found was Mary alone in the kitchen, standing in the dark by the window, staring out. Her face was brushed with yellowish moonlight and she looked more truly miserable than Meg had ever dreamed of being in all her eighty years. Agonised, that was the only word to describe her.

What's more, it was how she stayed right up until the full moon.

On that particular night, her bedroom floor awash with moonlight, Meg was woken a dozen or more times by Mary's muffled sobbing. In the end she gave up trying to sleep and just lay there listening. She couldn't help feeling for the child, and for Tess too, never mind her nonsensical ideas about that dead Clement girl. If the truth were told, living with so much heartache day in and day out was enough to give anyone silly ideas. Anything — even a belief in some ghostly figure risen from an unquiet grave — was preferable to sitting by and watching your own flesh and blood sink deeper and deeper into misery. Or so it appeared to Meg in the closing hours of the night. No kin of hers deserved to suffer to that extent, she concluded, as the dawn etched out the tree beyond her window, and nor would they if she had any say in the matter.

She acted on that conclusion at breakfast by doing what for her was the hardest thing of all: admitting she'd been wrong.

'Never mind what I've said in the past,' she said, taking Tess's hand in hers. 'There's nothing more we can do for the child, not on our own. She needs outside help. Professional help. The best money can buy.'

Tess's eyes were swollen and bloodshot, her face puffy. From crying? From lack of sleep? Both probably.

'Mary's already getting help,' she pointed out. 'From Ruth Close.'

Meg waved the name aside scornfully. 'We've seen what good *she's* done! No, it's time for a change, my girl. If I were you, I'd find someone else for the child. There must be some big names in that line of work. And if it's a question of money, you know I'm not mean about the things that matter.'

Meg was convinced Tess would jump at her offer, but all she did was return the pressure of her hand and give her a watery, evasive sort of smile. 'It's too complicated for that now, Mum.'

'Too complicated? I don't see why.'

'Believe me, it is.'

As if to show her how true that was, Mary took a turn for the better that same night. They were all together in the living room, Tess making her evening call to Doug and the boys, Mary watching her mother intently from over by the window where the newly waning moon was just showing above the house tops. How long had the phone conversation been going on? It was hard for Meg to remember because she was half watching the television with the sound turned down. But all at once Mary started to laugh. Loud, hysterical laughter which somehow veiled the emotion behind it. Rather like those fairground figures Meg remembered from her younger days, that chortled and bellowed and rolled around in their glass case when you put a penny in the slot. Under other circumstances Meg would have closed her ears and turned away, but after witnessing nothing but abject misery for days and nights on end, she found herself joining in out of sheer relief. Tess was laughing too, and holding out the phone for Doug to hear.

'Listen to her!' she kept saying. 'Just listen!'

Mary, bless her (and Meg prided herself on never doing anything less), grasped the phone in both hands, as though Tess were offering her some form of gift. Or did she genuinely want to communicate with the people at the other end of the line? As always, Meg was hard pressed to work out what really went on in Mary's mind.

'Your Dad sends his love,' Tess told Mary minutes later, before ringing off. 'So do the boys.'

Which, for reasons that Meg was again unable to fathom, only made Mary laugh louder.

Naturally it couldn't possibly last. Meg guessed as much while Mary was still chuckling to herself, her back now turned to the window through which the moonlight shone palely. And sure enough, as the evening wore on Mary grew steadily more subdued, a frown puckering her forehead. A frown that signified what? Meg asked herself, watching her across the room. Anxiety? Indecision? Bewilderment?

Whatever its cause, the frown was still there the next morning when Maud and Ken arrived, bringing with them some normal laughter and good cheer. Meg was more grateful for that than for the inevitable bunch of late summer roses that Maud pushed into her arms, the scent of them like heaven.

Tess, of course, was looking daggers at her from the other side of the kitchen, but what did she care? Come one, come all. The more the merrier after the past few days of being shut up with Mary. And besides, the extra company might do the child some good, especially now that she seemed to have turned the corner.

Mary drifted into the kitchen while they were busy putting the roses in water, Meg's own Bible pressed to her chest. The Bible Meg always kept in her bedside cupboard! Which meant that Mary had been into *her* room, hunting through *her* things! If it hadn't been for Ken and Maud, Meg would have obeyed her initial impulse and snatched the Bible away; but fortunately the smiling couple got in between, giving Mary hearty hugs that she endured passively. And with time to reconsider, Meg decided that on balance it was probably better to say nothing and for Mary to keep the Bible. Who could tell what might come of it? Some of the truths contained in those pages might well do her more good than all Tess's worrying or any number of weekly sessions with that Ruth Close woman.

'What? We've found religion, have we?' Ken exclaimed, tapping the Bible with one broad knuckle as he let Mary go.

'Don't make fun of the girl, Ken,' Maud cautioned him.

'Who's making fun of her?' he replied, and gave Mary a last reassuring pat. 'A bit of religion never hurt anyone. It's only when people overdo it that it does harm.'

Was Mary overdoing it? That was a question Meg couldn't help putting to herself a week or more later as she stood in the living room doorway and watched Mary poring over the old-fashioned, closely set text. The child didn't seem to do much else these days, that same frown always there, creasing her forehead. What was she looking for? Or had she perhaps found it already? Was it the book itself that she needed? Were those sacred words her chosen path back into the world of speech and ordinary decent behaviour? As far as Meg was concerned no better path existed. (In moderation, of course, and that was the worry.) It was the path she herself had followed (or at least tried to) throughout a long and not always easy life. So why wasn't it good enough for Mary? Didn't all this reading suggest not fanaticism, but a real turning to the light? A kind of — she hunted for the appropriate words — a kind of *clinging on*? Yes, that *had* to be it. Surely.

She was startled from her uneasy reverie by a sound in the passage behind her, and when she looked around, there was Tess, peering at Mary over her shoulder and clearly no less concerned than she. In an attempt to reassure Tess as much as herself, she said in a whisper: 'It does my heart good to see her turning to the word of God.'

'It depends which God you have in mind,' Tess murmured in reply.

'There's only one true God in the Bible *I* read,' Meg reminded her sharply, 'and that's the loving Creator of the world and of everything in it.'

'I wish that was so, Mum.'

'Shame on you, Tess. It hurts me to hear you saying things like that.'

And it did. It was one of those moments, rare with her, when she wondered what her life had been for. Was this the net result? This? Her only daughter plagued by doubt, and her granddaughter barely clinging to the edge of sanity?

'I can't help what's written there,' Tess said softly, and pushing past her, she went over to Mary and took up the Bible. 'Listen to this,' she said, and began reading from the open page:

His head and his hairs were white like wool, as white as
snow; and his eyes were as a flame of fire;
And his feet like unto fine brass, as if they burned in a
furnace; and his voice as the sound of many waters.
And he had in his right hand seven stars; and out of his
mouth went a sharp two-edged sword . . .
And when I saw him, I fell at his feet as dead. And
he . . .

During the course of the reading Mary had scurried
off into the corner where she crouched with her face
hidden, her shoulders trembling.

'Can't you see you're frightening the child?' Meg
broke in, and quite unaccountably, her eyes flicking
across to Mary, she had to still a sudden tremor of fear
in herself.

Tess, Meg noticed particularly, didn't so much as
glance in Mary's direction as though, fool that she was,
she wanted to undo all that had been achieved in the
past week; as though she were trying to thrust the child
back into a state of hopeless misery.

Replacing the Bible on the low table, she looked up
at Meg and said, 'Does that sound like your "loving
Creator"?'

Her own daughter asking a question like that! Putting
everything she'd been taught into question! Well what
did that passage sound like? Who *was* that God who
dwelt in fire?

'It's our Father in Heaven,' she retorted — and felt
as if she were defending her whole life.

'Yes, but is He loving?'

'I don't care what the words say!' Meg answered fiercely, and punched herself on the chest in the region of the heart. 'In *here* He's loving! And that's all that counts with me.'

Mary, meanwhile, hadn't moved, her face still pressed to the corner.

'You're probably right, Mum,' Tess conceded unexpectedly, and this time she looked at Mary as she spoke, as if willing her to listen. 'But do you know what Mary calls Him? For her He's Double-God.'

Mary slammed her hands over her ears and held them there.

'Double-what?' Meg could feel herself sliding out of her depth.

'She's terrified of him,' Tess went on, and there was no doubt in Meg's mind that Tess's voice was raised a notch or two for Mary's benefit. 'And shall I tell you something else? This Double God of hers isn't really God at all.'

Mary responded with a sob and thrust her head down between her knees.

'He's someone else entirely,' Tess continued. 'He's not even a "he". Do you know who she's confusing him with? Who she's looking in this Bible for? Shall I tell you? For Denny Clement. That's who her precious Double God really is. Someone who can't rest until she's taken revenge on everyone who ever . . .'

But Meg had found her footing at last and wasn't prepared to stand there and be bombarded with any more of that nonsense. She would have spoken out even without Mary's low moan of distress to spur her on.

'Have you gone stark raving mad, girl?' she shouted at Tess. 'Your daughter turns to God and you mock her for it! You do your best to fill her head with all that balderdash about ghosts! Well there's one place apart from this house where she won't be exposed to such rubbish. And that's the greatest house of them all. Come Sunday, she's going to church with me. She'll get some real guidance there, and we'll see then about your Double Gods and your Denny Clements and all the rest of it.'

She could see straight off how *that* knocked the stuffing out of Tess.

'You can't take her there, Mum,' she said, and she didn't sound nearly so high and mighty now. 'Really you can't. She's not . . . not ready for something like that yet.'

'Oh isn't she?' And Meg marched down the passage to the kitchen where Maud was pretending she hadn't heard a thing. 'What do you say, Maud?' she demanded. 'Tess here reckons Mary's not fit to go to church with us on Sunday.'

'That isn't what I meant . . .' Tess began, but Meg shushed her with a toss of the head.

'Let's hear Maud's opinion,' she insisted. 'We're all family, and she deserves a say as much as anyone.'

'Well . . . if she was mine . . .' Maud said hesitantly, 'I couldn't think of a . . . a better place for her.'

'There you have it!' Meg cried, and wondered why she hadn't thought of this solution earlier. Maud was right. Given Mary's interest in the Bible (even in mysterious passages like the one Tess had read out), a church was the perfect answer. Somewhere more than just quiet and restful. A place of sanctity where she could begin to heal her soul.

That conviction stayed with her right up until Sunday morning, when the five of them set out together through streets that were almost empty compared with the teeming traffic of weekdays. Tess, for all her opposition to the trip, had insisted on coming along, walking grim-faced at Mary's side. Meg, who always enjoyed her Sunday walk, tried not to look at her, determined that Tess shouldn't spoil their outing with her dark mood. Where Mary was concerned it was another matter: she wasn't responsible for her blank expression or for the way she had to be urged on with kind words from Ken and Maud. She was astray, poor thing, still clutching onto the Bible which had become her only anchor in a bewildering world. Well that was one blessing at least, a single ray of light in all the darkness of the past months. And the church would be another, preferable to any psychiatrist's couch Meg had ever heard of.

She could see the spire now, a finger of worn sandstone soaring above the red gums that lined the street. A sight for sore eyes, and enough in itself to bring comfort to the heart of any true believer. Turning to Mary, she put an arm around her shoulder and pointed it out.

'There it is, pet,' she said fondly. 'God's dwelling place. He's waiting in there for us at this very moment, ready to . . .'

She didn't finish. She felt the child start to tremble, and then she was gone — the Bible landing at Meg's feet as Mary ducked rapidly beneath her arm. She'd have been off down the street if she hadn't slammed into Ken, bouncing off him like the little slip of a thing she was. That gave Meg time to grab her again.

'There's nothing to be scared of,' she whispered, holding on for all she was worth. 'It's just God's . . .'

As a girl, Meg had once seen a fallen baker's horse trapped in its shafts. She retained a vivid memory of the way it had rolled its eyes and tossed its head in panic. Well she glimpsed the same panic in Mary now, the same wild movement of the eyes and head. As though Meg's arms were the shafts trapping her; Meg's frail body the one obstacle between her and freedom.

Meg tried to step back and let go, but already Mary was fighting her; whirling her around in crazy, staggering circles that forced her to cling on or fall. She, Meg, fighting as hard as Mary now, in a desperate attempt to keep her balance; the faces of Maud, Ken, Tess, swinging past; her arms, and finally her legs, so entangled with Mary's that they both went crashing down.

'You wretched child!' she heard herself scream, convinced that the pain in her hip, where she had struck the pavement, foretold the worst.

Eyes closed, her breath coming in quick, uncertain gasps, she tried to prepare herself for the inevitable: for the long months of discomfort, of helpless confinement in some pallid hospital ward. It was a vision as nightmarish in its way as her image of the horse, and she needed time to get used to it. But there were hands out there that refused to leave her alone, that insisted on hauling her to her feet. Where she discovered to her amazement that she was able to stand! The pain in her hip undoubtedly real, but bearable, the result of a bruise, nothing more.

'Are you all right, Meg?' Maud enquired in a worried voice.

She opened her eyes to see Mary struggling in Ken's powerful grip. And to be confronted by Tess, her face, blotched with anger, barely a hand's breadth from her own.

'Didn't I warn you!' Tess hissed at her. 'Didn't I tell you she was terrified of him!'

Meg blinked, confused. 'Terrified? Of . . . of . . . ?'

'She thinks her Double God's in there waiting for her! Denny Clement!'

And from Mary, at the mention of that name, a last high whinny of terror that thrust Meg back in time to those far-off Sydney streets where she'd first heard the frantic clatter of hooves and the crash of a heavy body striking the ground. Her own body? No, thank God! But still close and fearful enough for her to pull irritably away from Maud and scurry back along the street, the church resolutely behind her.

Did Mary's condition begin to worsen again after their abortive outing? That was a possibility which worried Meg, nagging at her through long sleepless hours in which her bruised hip throbbed painfully and she waited, like the nervous child she had once been, for a dawn that seemed to take so long to arrive. The magpies, carolling in the grey light, were always a welcome sound, banishing the loneliness of those night-time vigils. Yet still, even in the midst of the daily bustle, the same questions remained. Was it her fault that Mary searched the Bible ever more frantically day by day? Was it because of her that the poor child had begun, once again, to peer between the curtains after dark? And most pressing of all, if it hadn't been for that Sunday morning, would Mary have cried out quite so shrilly when she caught her first glimpse of the new moon through the kitchen window?

'Don't take on so, Meg,' Ken and Maud both advised her. 'It's none of it your doing.'

But what did it matter even if they were right? The sight of Mary's growing distress still wrung her heart. Far more testing than the pain in her hip was the pain of seeing Mary's face pressed to the kitchen window each night, her frown deepening into something else, something oddly indecipherable, as the waxing moon grew fuller, brighter. And no less painful for Meg were the hours Mary spent with her head bent over the Bible, her fingers riffling so rapidly through the now brittle pages that sometimes she tore them in her haste. To Meg, there was more than a hint in both these activities of a looming disaster; of some forthcoming event that Mary was either desperately anticipating or just as desperately trying to evade.

Or was she perhaps trying to do both? Meg couldn't make up her mind. All she knew — knew it as intimately as the persistent ache in her hip — was that Mary's troubles were moving towards some sort of climax. More than ever before she needed to be watched, helped, taken care of. And feared? Yes, that too. Something inside the girl — an unfathomable rage or grief or resentment — was clamouring to escape.

That was why Meg felt so incensed when Tess announced her intention of going out alone.

'There're some things I have to talk to Ruth about,' she explained vaguely. 'Things I don't want Mary to hear.'

Meg didn't ask what those 'things' might be. During the past weeks she'd been exposed to more than enough claptrap about ghosts and the like. Her only concern now was for Mary.

'It's not right to leave the child at this stage,' she said disapprovingly. 'You know full well I can't handle her on my own.'

'She'll be all right, Mum. Really. I'll only be gone a few hours. And if she does give you trouble, there's always Ken to help.'

Ken. Yes, that was true. That was why she'd invited him in the first place, not just for his smiling good nature, which was more of a bonus. Still, there was a principle at stake here, not to mention her sense of disquiet, neither of which she was prepared to ignore.

'She's your responsibility, my girl,' she pointed out. 'Leave her with us and I won't answer for her.'

But she might as well have spoken to the air. Tess had never been one to take advice. She'd always been too headstrong for her own good, or for anyone else's come to that. And as Meg might have foreseen, she'd barely left the house when Mary let out another of those wordless cries of hers.

This one didn't sound stricken, as on the night of the full moon, weeks earlier; it was more of a yelp, reminding Meg of the cries made by children playing games like hide and seek. And not just any children either. Standing there, startled, in the kitchen, Meg was surprised by the vividness of the memory that the cry evoked. Herself as a child, hidden in the bushes, and her brother's voice ringing out above her as he parted the leaves and discovered her there.

She had to give herself a shake to dispel the vision. And by then Mary was pounding up the stairs, flinging things around in her room.

Meg didn't want to find out what was going on. This, she sensed, was the climax she had been anticipating. And, typically, Tess was nowhere to be seen, relying on others to clean up after her. Meg wasn't going to waste time on anger, however. There was too much to do: Maud and Ken to be called in from the garden; the front and back doors to be secured; Ruth Close to be phoned...

Damn! she swore mentally — a strong word for her — as the ringing gave way to a faint tape hiss and then to the practised drone of a voice on an answering machine. Of course, Ruth wouldn't want to be disturbed during her sessions.

She slammed the receiver down, and immediately above her head the stairs creaked.

'You can't go out on your own, lovey,' she heard Maud call from the passage, and the stairs creaked again.

She was about to leave the phone when she remembered Tess mentioning another number, a private line that Ruth always kept open in case of emergencies. Yes, but had Tess made a note of it? With trembling fingers, she hunted through her dog-eared address book. C? No, nothing under C. Nor under R. Damn! Tess again, leaving everything . . . everything . . .

There was a gasp, and when she looked along the passage Maud was sitting on the floor, her back to the wall and a surprised expression on her face; while Mary, in a track-suit and runners, tugged dementedly at the front door.

Ken, bellowing as he ran, rushed through from the kitchen, but Mary easily evaded him by slipping under his outstretched arms. She was onto Meg before she realised it, brushing her aside as she made for the back door. Meg heard her fists hammering on the stout timber, and again the house rang to one of her shrill screams. Then she was back again, darting now into the living room where there was a splintering of glass and a sudden gust of air along the passage.

'Oh my God!' Meg breathed, and hurried towards the living room herself.

Ken was there ahead of her, already wrestling with Mary in the middle of the floor, a great jagged hole in the main window behind them.

'You young vixen!' he shouted, and tried to pin her down, but for all his superior size and strength she was again too quick for him. With a sudden twist of her body, she squirmed out from beneath him, leaving him floundering on the carpet. Before he could rise, she had snatched up a spindle-legged side table and swung it hard.

Meg didn't see the actual impact. She was busy making for the window in order to cut off that line of escape. When she turned, arms outstretched, Ken was still on his hands and knees, blood pouring down his face. Either he was dazed or blinded by the blood because he didn't seem able to get up. He was groping with one hand, snatching feebly at the empty air, while Mary, just out of reach, hefted the table back with both hands.

'Get away from him!' Meg screamed.

To no effect. There was a loud 'thock' as the wooden table-top caught him full in the forehead, and he went down, his body twitching.

Mary turned her attention to Meg then. The table had slipped from her hands, as if she understood that she had no further use for it. Her eyes were weapon enough. Or that at least was Meg's conviction. Frail and exposed before the shattered window, returning Mary's fixed gaze, she came as close to despair as she would ever be. The child's eyes! The things contained within them! Hunger, desperation, hope, hatred . . . and something more. A thought or emotion, or perhaps even a way of surveying the world, which Meg had no words for, no means of describing. All she could have explained at that moment was how *she* felt. As though . . . as though she were staring into the eyes of God. Not a loving saviour, but another, more primitive deity, the one who dwelt in fire.

For her, as for the prophets of old, that burning regard was more than she could endure. And in the brief second or two of stillness before Mary came at her, she fell to her knees and hid her face in dread.

20

Tess had never felt quite so isolated. She wouldn't have believed it possible to be so alone in a city of nearly four million people. She was always most keenly aware of it at night. Lying in bed, roused by stealthy movements in the darkness, she would watch as Mary's silhouette appeared before the window, her face tipped up yearningly towards the waxing moon, for all the world like ... like what? An animal seeking solace there? A mad woman fixated on the shining symbol of her body's deeper rhythms? Tess couldn't say. All she was sure of at such times was the vast gulf that separated her from her daughter.

For Mary had not improved here in Sydney as Tess had hoped. Away from that house, from Denny Clement's malevolent influence, she had merely begun to act the part of the lost soul: her days spent in a fruitless search for meaning in Meg's old Bible; her nights devoted to a puzzling study of the heavens. As though Denny Clement, like some god of old, were able to inscribe a message for her in the mysterious configurations of moon and stars.

There was, it seemed, nothing that she, Tess, could

do to help her, to get through to her. Mary gave every sign of being as alone as Tess herself, the two of them possessed of the same secret, but unable to communicate it to each other.

Certainly there was no way of communicating it to Doug. Oh, he was understanding enough. 'Stay on there if it makes you feel better, sweetheart,' he assured her time and again on the phone. 'You need a break anyway.' But as to *believing* her ... that was another matter. Always, when she begged him to join her in Sydney, he found some excuse for delay: either it was Harry's school term, or the difficulty of moving the workshop at short notice, or the lease on their Sydney house. Always something. And if she came right out and warned him about the dangers of what she now thought of as the Clements' property, all he did was fall silent, his obvious embarrassment only accentuating the distance between them.

There was no such embarrassment where Meg was concerned. She seemed almost to enjoy telling Tess how deranged she'd become. Tess had tried describing that secret room to her, how it had felt in there — the dust, the photographs, the personal knickknacks, *everything* — but Meg had pooh-poohed it all as superstitious nonsense. Perhaps she'd have been less dismissive if she'd also known about Kevin and Mary and how they'd reworked history. How they'd been drawn to each other by the same kind of destructive infatuation that must once have bound Kevin to Denny; an infatuation that had ended once again in death, though this time Kevin's. Would that terrible story of revenge have convinced

Meg? Possibly. Or, like Doug, would she have preferred to go on believing that Mary was single-handedly capable of the horrors that had been perpetrated out there? Clearly Tess would never find out, because the truth was something she could no more tell Meg than she could Ruth Close.

Ruth, of course, was another matter. Oddly, and to Tess's surprise, she had emerged as an ally over the past few weeks. Not that she actually believed in the possibility of a haunting. She didn't. And said so when she was challenged. On the other hand she was at least ready to listen, to sympathise. She didn't just look embarrassed or switch off impatiently the moment Tess raised the topic.

'This is something we have to talk through', she'd said on more than one occasion, while Mary, mute as ever, had sat watchfully on the sidelines.

Even more to the point — and this had further surprised Tess — Ruth had been prepared on Tess's behalf to find out more about the history of the two Clement children.

Tess had no illusions about Ruth's motives. Behind all the sympathy and help lay a professional desire to coax her back to 'normality'. Still, the fact remained that Ruth had gone to the lengths of tracing and then contacting the psychiatrist who had treated Will Clement up on the Central Coast all those years before.

'It wasn't easy getting her to talk,' Ruth confessed on the phone. 'She was worried about the question of confidentiality.'

'But as far as she's concerned the Clements are all

dead,' Tess objected. 'There's no one left to protect.'

'Even the dead deserve some privacy,' Ruth pointed out. 'In our line of work we only reveal what's in their files for a very good reason.'

'There is one,' Tess insisted. 'There's Mary.'

'There's you, too, Tess,' Ruth said quietly. 'You and Mary both.'

It was a rare instance, in those lonely weeks, of any embarrassment between them.

'Did you tell her that?' Tess asked at last, and listened as Ruth chose her reply with care.

'Let's just say that . . . that I persuaded her to speak openly.'

'And?'

'I think you should hear what she told me. It might help you to get the Clements in perspective. Though it's for your ears alone. I especially don't want Mary to hear any of this.'

'Why not Mary?' She was conscious of the sharpness, the suspicion, in her own voice.

'Don't misunderstand me, Tess. This has nothing directly to do with Mary. It's not a pleasant story, that's all, not the sort of thing you'd want to expose her to.'

Tess managed an ironic, unhappy smile. *Not a pleasant story.* As though, after what Mary had witnessed (and *done!*) she needed to be protected from anything. Mind you, Ruth wasn't to know that. Not now. Not ever. Which was largely why Tess didn't argue. Why she broke her word to Doug about never letting Mary out of her sight, and left her in Meg's unwilling care (what, after all, could happen in a few short hours?)

while she drove through the afternoon traffic to Ruth Close's office.

It was only the second time she had been there alone. The first occasion had been during the summer. Now, already, it was autumn, with a softer, gentler sunlight bathing the African violets and tiny ornamental cactuses that sat clustered on the windowsill. Autumn. A fitting season, Tess suspected, for what she was about to hear.

'Well?' she asked expectantly.

'This isn't a story about vengeance, Tess,' Ruth began by explaining.

'So what is it about?'

'A poor little boy called Will Clement. Well, not "little" exactly. Although he was younger than Denny, he was big for his age. Very big, I gather. And when he was first taken to see Doctor Raf . . . No, let's leave names out of this. When he first saw the psychiatrist he was already deeply disturbed, torn between . . .'

'He had to be disturbed if he was going to murder his sister,' Tess cut in impatiently. 'I know this stuff already. It's Denny I want to know more about.'

'The two of them were in this together, Tess. You can't discuss one without the other.'

'Why not?'

Ruth Close drew back slightly in her chair, as though putting more distance between herself and what she had to say.

'Because Will didn't just decide to murder his sister. He only did it because Denny begged him to.'

'*Begged* him? Are you sure?'

'I told you, Tess, this has nothing to do with vengeance. It's all about the tangle those two kids got themselves into.'

'She *wanted* to die?' But it wasn't really a question. All Tess could think of as she spoke was of Mary's grief-stricken face and of her more recent scrutiny of the Bible and the night sky. Could it be that, having identified herself with Denny, Mary was preparing herself to meet the same fate? That she might on any day, at any moment . . . ?

'Yes, but Will wanted her to live,' Ruth answered. 'And that was the problem. That was why they both died in the end.'

'I don't see why . . .' Tess began vaguely, still thinking only of the link between Mary and Denny.

'The point is, he was religious,' Ruth broke in.

'D'you mean like Mary?' Tess asked, and felt the icy touch of a new and disquieting fear.

'No, not like Mary,' Ruth assured her. 'He'd been religious since he was very young and had first gone to Sunday school. You know how it is with some people. They seem predisposed to a religious point of view. Well, Will Clement was one of those people. Already, at the age of fourteen, he believed devoutly that only God could give or take life. And there was his sister, the person he loved most in the world, begging him to put her out of her misery.'

Tess shivered slightly as her sense of disquiet grew stronger. 'So what did he do?'

Ruth shrugged, as though her answer followed inevitably. 'What else could he do? Caught between the demands of his God and his sister, he had a breakdown. That's when the psychiatrist first saw him. By then he was convinced that anyone who took a life dethroned God.'

It was the last thing Tess wanted to hear. 'You mean he thought a murderer was a kind of God?'

Ruth shrugged again. 'Or a kind of Devil. He was too mixed up at that stage to see anything straight. That's probably the reason he bungled his first attempt.'

'His what?'

'He made two attempts on Denny's life,' Ruth explained. 'The first while they were still at the Central Coast. Denny, as you probably realise, was receiving a lot of medication, partly because of the pain she was in, and partly too because of her depression. She was horribly scarred and she just couldn't cope with it. Well, Will forced open a locked cupboard where her pills were kept, mixed them into a cocktail, and gave them to her. Of course it didn't work. All he did was make her sick.'

Tess nodded, already half aware of what she had discovered here today, but determined now to listen to it all in the vague hope that her new-found fears were groundless.

'Did anyone apart from the psychiatrist know about the murder attempt?' she asked.

'The parents must have suspected the truth. The trouble was, Denny swore blind she was the one who'd broken into the cupboard. That was virtually impossible given her physical condition, but no one could make her change her story. As things turned out, that's a pity, because if Will had taken the blame they might have restrained him earlier.'

'Earlier? Was he restrained at all?'

'Yes, but only after he'd badly mutilated himself.' Ruth held up one hand, anticipating Tess's next question. 'It appears that he wanted to look like his sister. He cut himself around really badly and even damaged the sight in one eye. When the psychiatrist saw him, soon after it happened, Will said something very revealing. At least in retrospect it sounds revealing. He said, "Now we're both Gods", meaning, I suppose, himself and Denny.'

Tess *knew* then: knew the wholeness of the truth she had only half grasped weeks earlier, when she had stumbled into the secret room decked out as a shrine to Denny Clement. Yet still she forced herself to sit there quietly, to hear it all through to the end. In the hope that . . . ? No, it wasn't hope she was after now, but cold, hard surety. *Know your enemy* were the words that came into her mind, though all she said aloud was:

'He meant more than that.'

'More?' Ruth was already sitting less stiffly in her chair, as though relaxing after a difficult task.

'He meant that he and Denny had a pact. They'd both agreed to die. They'd placed themselves above God by taking their lives out of His hands.'

Ruth nodded reluctantly. 'Yes, I expect you're right. Anyway, as you've probably guessed, he acted more or less normal after that. They let him out, the whole family went to live in the new house, and a month or two later . . .' She made a helpless gesture with both hands. 'You know the rest.'

'Not quite,' Tess said. She was sitting forward on her chair, gripping the edge of the desk. 'No one's told me how Denny died.'

'Aaah.' Ruth suddenly looked uncomfortable. 'I was hoping you weren't going to ask me that. It's pretty grisly stuff, and I don't see any point in . . .'

'Just tell me,' Tess insisted softly.

Ruth cleared her throat and shuffled some papers on her desk. 'Well, he did it with a knife if you must know,' she said, avoiding Tess's eyes. 'He . . . he bled her at the throat to begin with, the way they do in some forms of traditional sacrifice. At least that's how Doctor . . . how the psychiatrist described it. And then . . . then he gutted her.'

Tess didn't flinch, her body locked into an unnatural stillness. 'And the innards? What did he do with those?'

Ruth pushed herself sharply away from the desk. 'For God's sake, Tess!'

'Tell me what he did with them.'

'I don't know.'

'And the body? What did they do with that? Did they cremate it?'

'I don't know that either. I don't *want* to know, and nor should you. They destroyed each other, they're dead and gone, that's the point.'

'No, it's not the point,' Tess whispered.

Ruth looked at her peculiarly. 'Then what is?'

Tess's knuckles were white from where she was gripping onto the desk, her face drained of colour. She hadn't meant to say anything else, but she couldn't help it, the word pushing itself out past her lips.

'Double God,' she breathed.

'What?'

She said it again, louder, unable to contain it: 'Double God.'

'That's Mary's word, not theirs,' Ruth reminded her gently. 'You said yourself that Mary seemed to be using it to describe the two faces of God, the merciful and the destructive. There was that piece of paper, one of Mary's prayers, with the quotation on it. How did it describe God? As a two-edged sword, yes, that's it. *Double*.'

'It means them as well,' Tess answered, and although the room was warm enough, she gathered her jacket around her. 'Will and Denny. "Now we're both Gods." Isn't that what he said?'

'Yes, but it had nothing to do with Mary. It all happened years ago.'

'What do years matter?' Tess cried out, and suddenly she was almost shouting. 'They're *both* out there! Not just Denny, like I thought. *Both* of them! After what happened, they can't leave that house. And now . . . and now . . . !'

'Be sensible, Tess.' Ruth leaned across the desk and tried to take her hands, but Tess snatched them away. 'There're no such things as ghosts. There's no possible link between now and then. It's not as though Mary has gone around killing people. Sacrificing them. If that were . . .'

'Hasn't she?' Tess interrupted, in such an agonised voice that Ruth jerked back in her chair.

'Is there something you haven't told me?' she asked carefully.

Tess never understood where she found the resolve to contain her feelings, to dredge the anguish from her face and appear calm again.

'No . . .' she stammered, and made a further effort to gain control of her voice. 'No, there's nothing like that. It's just the coincidence of it all. Mary and the Clements, all of them disturbed. And in a similar way.'

Ruth came around the desk and insisted this time on taking her hands. 'It's not such a coincidence, Tess, not if you consider the number of people with mental disorders in our kind of society. If you were to delve into the history of any house in any street, there's a reasonable chance you'd unearth a sad story or two. Mental problems simply aren't uncommon. People sweep them under the carpet, that's all. The Clements' case is extreme, I'll grant you that, but it's only a matter of degree. And there's nothing at all unusual about disturbed people turning to religion for help or guidance. It's almost the natural thing for them to do.'

Tess willed herself to nod, as if in agreement, her hands slack and clammy in Ruth's firm grasp.

'There's just one more thing,' she began, her voice completely steady now, almost a monotone.

'I think we've talked enough for today,' Ruth suggested.

'The fire,' Tess continued, 'the one that destroyed the original house. Does the psychiatrist have any idea who lit it?'

Ruth pursed her lips, clearly deciding whether or not to reply. 'It could have been an accident,' she said at last. 'The insurance company never pinpointed the cause. Equally, it could have been lit by either Will or Denny's former lover, if that's what he was. The man on the adjoining property . . . er . . .'

'Kevin Briggs.'

'Yes, him. We'll probably never find out. If you ask me, it's best that way. The past is important, Tess, but not when it threatens to overwhelm the present.'

'And the parents,' Tess pressed on in the same monotone, 'how did . . . ?'

'You said just one thing, Tess,' Ruth reminded her. 'And this isn't doing you or Mary or anyone else any good. It's *over*.'

'. . . how did *they* feel about what had happened?' Tess finished, as though she hadn't registered Ruth's interruption.

Ruth sighed and, releasing her hand, moved back behind the desk. 'What do you want me to tell you, Tess? That they also believed the house was haunted?'

'The truth will do.'

'What truth? After all they'd been through — the fire, the constant worry, the double bereavement — they were almost as confused as their children had been.'

'You haven't answered my question,' Tess said evenly.

'Okay then, Tess. The last time the psychiatrist spoke to them, on the phone, they said they couldn't come down and see her because . . . because God needed them. Don't ask me what they meant. Like I said, they were in grief. Just two more bewildered people to add to the list.'

Tess stood up, ready to leave, her hands clutching

onto her bag to stop them shaking. 'You've been very kind,' she said, backing slowly towards the door. 'You've gone to a lot of trouble and I'm grateful.'

'Are you all right, Tess?'

'Yes . . . yes, I'm fine.'

'Truly?'

'I promise.' Her hand groping feverishly behind her for the door handle.

'Well don't forget what I told you, about the past being done with. If you put the two cases side by side, there are no clear lines to be drawn between Mary and the Clement children. Believe me. Even the religious thing isn't a real connection. It's commonplace in these instances.'

'Yes, I understand that now,' she said, pulling the door open.

'So you'll give me a call if you have any problems?'

'I will.' The door like a shield which, thankfully, she could swing between them.

'Until next week then, Tess.'

'Until next week.'

She wasn't conscious of leaving the outer office or of descending in the lift. She was too taken up with holding herself together, with keeping at bay the invisible pressure of the walls and ceilings, the curious glances of other people. Her control lasted just long enough for her to reach the car, and then her whole body rebelled, her hands locking onto the steering wheel as she sat there shivering uncontrollably, her face screwed up in dry-eyed desperation.

So it wasn't only Denny, she thought — and in spite

of the shivering she felt perfectly lucid. No, there was Will to contend with, too, and there always had been. Denny *and* Will. Both of them! Why hadn't she realised that earlier? *Why?* And in her frustration she beat on the steering wheel until the sides of her hands were sore. *Why?* It was all so obvious really. Denny was not the only one who had suffered because of Kevin's crazy jealousy. Not the only one who wanted vengeance. Together, in spirit at least, they were Double God, with Kevin as their sacrificial victim, and Mary as their agent in the here and now. And after Kevin, what then? Why had Mary written out those prayers, begging Double God to have mercy? Mercy for whom? For what? Were the Clement children again pressing her to act on their behalf?

That consideration, more than anything else, helped to bring her rebellious body under control, leaving her outwardly cool and calm. She had been foolish to leave Mary behind, she could see that now. If anything were to happen . . . ! She looked quickly at her watch, calculating as she rummaged through her bag for the key and started the car. She'd been away a little under two hours. Say another half hour or so if she had a clear run through the traffic . . . no, longer than that because it was a Friday. Three hours altogether then. What could happen in so short a time? Nothing surely.

Or so she pretended to herself until she drew up outside the house an hour later and, with a sinking sense of dread, saw the gaping hole in the front window. She ran inside and found Meg and her Aunt drinking tea together in the kitchen — Maud still visibly pale and shaken. Ken, she learned, was in bed upstairs, awaiting the arrival of the doctor.

'She was like a mad thing,' Maud observed, and fingered a pinkish bruise on her cheek.

'There was no holding her, Tess,' Meg explained, her voice uncharacteristically subdued, shocked almost, as though she had been the one attacked. 'She nearly killed poor Ken when he got in her way. And God knows what she'd have done to me if I'd tried to stop her. Like I told you, she's your responsibility and you should have been here.'

Tess sank down onto the nearest chair, feeling momentarily beaten.

'So where is she now?' she asked weakly.

'That's anyone's bet,' Meg answered. 'You can see for yourself, none of us was capable of chasing after her. She was gone before I could so much as get to my feet. I tried reaching you, but that was no good, so I rang Doug instead. What more could I do?'

Doug! Tess wondered guiltily what he was thinking at that moment. She could almost hear his voice. *You promised me, Tess. You promised.* Those accusing words, coupled with her deep anxiety over Mary, robbed her for the moment of all energy.

'What did he say?' she asked.

'Well he was disappointed in you, for one thing.'

She waved that aside wearily. 'What else?'

'He said to give her until dark in case she turns up there. He'll ring us if she does.'

'And if she doesn't?'

'To contact the police. Though in your shoes I wouldn't wait until...'

Tess wasn't listening. The police? No, she wanted to avoid them if possible. Not because of the awkward questions they might ask, but because of what they might find — because of what Mary, under the malevolent influence of the Clement children, might already have done.

'... she's more than a danger to herself.' Meg's voice drifted back into Tess's consciousness. 'She's a hazard to the world at large. The streets aren't safe with her out there.'

'D'you think I don't know that?' Tess replied sharply and saw that her ready agreement had taken Meg by surprise.

'Well what do you propose to do about it?'

'We wait, like Doug said.'

Meg shook her head. 'It's not advisable, Tess. What if she does something we'll all be sorry for? Imagine how you'll feel if...'

If! To escape Meg's dire warnings, which merely echoed and amplified her own inner dread, she wandered through to the front of the house.

The living room was a mess. The couch and coffee table were overturned; a smaller side table lay smashed beside the hearth; there were books and magazines and other small items strewn everywhere; and in the middle of the carpet she could see a reddish-brown stain that looked suspiciously like blood. She bent to inspect it more closely and noticed something else: Meg's old Bible, that Mary had been studying intently for days, now lying abandoned and crumpled amongst the debris.

She picked it up carefully, so as not to dislodge the bookmark still protruding from the top edge. Parting the pages, she found it marked a chapter in Genesis which told the story of Abraham and Issac. One verse had been underscored with pencil:

And they came to the place which God had told him of; and Abraham built an altar there, and laid the wood in order; and bound Isaac his son, and laid him on the altar upon the wood.

The reference to burning, to sacrificial death, was too obvious, too pressing to be ignored. Hastily, she turned the page and found that several more verses had also been underlined:

And Abraham stretched forth his hand, and took the knife to slay his son.
And the angel of the Lord called unto him out of heaven, and said, Abraham, Abraham: and he said, Here am I.
And he said, Lay not thine hand upon the lad, neither do thou any thing unto him: for now I know that thou fearest God, seeing thou hast not withheld thy son, thine only son, from me.

Tess closed the Bible slowly. What did it mean? That Mary felt she was being tempted by her Double God? To use the knife again? That she, like Abraham, had decided to trust the voices, confident that they wouldn't make her commit the act herself? Is that what she was thinking? Is that what had driven her from the house? A desire to put herself on trial? And if so, who was her intended victim?

As if in answer to that final question, the telephone rang in the passage. Tess reached it before Meg could emerge from the kitchen.

'Yes?'

'Mary's here,' Doug's voice said. 'She must have hitched. She's just wandered up from the gate.'

A few minutes earlier Tess would have been overcome by relief. Now, she experienced an instant of blind panic.

'Where's Harry?' she blurted out, and only acknowledged her latent fear after she had spoken the words aloud.

. . . and laid him on the altar upon the wood.

'Harry?'

'Yes, where is he?' she shouted.

'Take it easy, Tess.'

. . . and took the knife to slay . . .

'Tell me, damn it!'

'He's not back yet,' Doug answered, and a distant, detached part of Tess's mind simultaneously recognised and dismissed the hurt in his voice. 'It's one of his afternoons for sport.'

That at least was a genuine relief, like someone releasing a tight band of pressure from around her head.

'Listen,' she began more calmly, and could tell straight away that the line was empty, with no one at the other end — the same faint rushing sound on the phone as when she held a seashell to her ear.

'Doug? Are you there?' The panic surging back again.

There was a faint clink, followed by the rasp of his cheek against the mouthpiece. 'I thought I heard a noise, that's all.'

'What kind of noise?'

'Nothing. One of the machines switching off probably. Or Bob may have gone back to his carving. You know that ornamental panel he's been working on.'

Her breath steadied. 'Listen,' she said again, 'I want you to strap Mary down until I get there.'

She heard him sigh. 'There's no need for that, Tess.'

'No need? You should see what she's done to this place!'

'Maybe that's because you weren't with her.'

'This is no time for recriminations, Doug. Just do what I ask.'

'I can't. Not again.'

'You *have* to!'

'I'll watch her,' he said doggedly. 'Bob's with her now, in the workshop. We'll keep her with us until you arrive.'

'That's not good enough, Doug. You have to strap her down. D'you hear?'

'Yes I hear,' he said, but she knew he didn't, that he was just humouring her.

'I'm relying on you,' she said, feeling suddenly tearful, stretched almost to the limit. 'Don't let anything happen. Please. I'll be there as soon as I can.'

She replaced the receiver, only to be confronted by Meg.

'What are you going to do, Tess?'

'I'll bring her back . . .' she began, and sensed the refusal on Meg's face. 'Just for tonight, Mum, that's all I'm asking. I'll find somewhere else tomorrow.'

Meg shook her head, as stern and unbending as only she could be. 'I have no more room for her, not even for a night. It's not because I've run out of love for the child. You didn't see what she was like, Tess. There's a . . . a wild beast inside her, one we'll never tame on our own. I'm telling you, for the good of everyone, get her committed.'

Tess didn't stop to argue. Snatching up her bag from the phone table, where she'd left it, she began backing away along the passage, mindful as she did so that she was fleeing from this house much as she had fled from Ruth Close's office.

'Mary needs us, Mum,' she said from the front door. 'All of us. They'll destroy her if she's committed to one of those places.'

'They?'

But she couldn't explain. If Meg hadn't accepted her ideas about Denny Clement, what chance was there that she'd believe her now? Double God. Stated simply, it made her sound almost as deranged as Mary.

'You know what you have to do, Tess,' Meg called after her. 'I don't want to hear from you again until you've done it.'

She slid into the car and started the motor, Meg's voice following her as she pulled away.

'No more calls, Tess. I mean it. Not till you've done your duty by the child.'

Her duty? What was that? To lock Mary up for what

those two Clement children were doing to her? To punish her for their malevolence? No. She put such ideas, like Meg's threats, firmly behind her, concentrating on the road, already working out times, distances, possible routes. The length of the trip, she knew, depended on how many people were leaving Sydney for the mountains and the Central Coast. With luck she might...

But on that particular day luck seemed to have deserted her. Within minutes she was caught up in a tedious stream of weekend traffic that soon slowed to a crawl and often stopped altogether. 'Come on! Come on!' she urged the cars ahead; but no amount of anger or silent pleading had any effect on the long tailbacks. Like everyone else she had to bide her time, so that it was nearly dusk before she broke free of the worst congestion, and after dark when, weary and disheartened, she finally turned off the highway onto their property.

The house, surprisingly, was in darkness, Bob's ute gone from the front. But gone where? And why on this night of all nights?

Cautiously, she let herself in at the front door and clicked on the passage light.

'Doug? Bob? Anyone here?'

When no one answered, she stole along the passage to the kitchen. Predictably, it was an uncared for mess, with dirty dishes piled in the sink and on the draining boards, and with used pots and empty packets and leftovers littering the other surfaces. She opened the fridge and, just as predictably, it was empty.

So, she thought with relief, they must have gone to

buy food. Probably takeaways. And Doug *had* promised that they wouldn't let Mary out of their sight. It was, after all, better for Mary to be away from this house, to be *anywhere* rather than here. In fact the moment Mary arrived back — Tess settled the matter finally — she would transfer her from the ute to the car and drive off. She wouldn't listen to any arguments from Doug or Bob. Or offer any explanations either. What would be the use? They'd never believe her. Like Meg, they were convinced that all the evil (what other word was there for it?) sprang from the murky depths of Mary's mind, not from the insane forces at work within this house. No, Tess resolved, come what may Mary would never cross this threshold again.

In the meantime Tess felt oddly grateful for this brief pause in the headlong rush of the day's events. It gave her time to unwind, to rest before the trip back to Sydney. Or should she perhaps forget about that trip for tonight and stay in a nearby motel? She'd have to use a motel or hotel anyway, even if she made the long drive, because she knew from experience that Meg was always as good as her word. If she said she'd have no more contact with Tess until Mary was committed to an institution, then that was what she meant, and it was no good turning up on her doorstep. Tess shook her head regretfully. Meg was just one more problem for her to deal with, but not tonight. A quiet room out here in the country, that was the short-term answer. God knows, she could do without the immediate prospect of another punishing drive through city traffic. All she wanted right at that moment, for instance, was to put her feet up and relax.

With that in mind, she made herself a cup of coffee and drifted through to the living room. It was shadowy and restful in there. The only light came from the passage, a faint wash of it spilling in through the half-open door. Cup in hand, she sank back in the most comfortable chair and closed her eyes. For a few seconds only, she wondered whether that was wise, knowing as she did what dwelt within these walls. But what could the Clement children do to her? She had no fear of them, not for herself. She wasn't a child to be influenced by their malicious whisperings. Nor was she disturbed in spirit, as Mary had been. She was a grown woman — sane, assured, determined — with no place in her life for crazy notions like Double God. The only way Denny and Will could get to her was through Mary, and that she would put a stop to, whatever the cost.

'Take care, you bastards,' she murmured aloud, and placing the cup on the floor beside her, she sank back once again.

She hadn't meant to sleep or even to doze. She believed all along that she was listening for the ute, and she carried that belief into her dreams — turgid, confused affairs in which, trapped behind the steering wheel of a car, she followed the endless serpentine twistings of an ever-darkening road.

What roused her eventually wasn't the rumble of wheels on the pot-holed drive, but the familiar creaks and groans of the house settling in the cool of the night. Half awake, she wondered what time it was. Didn't the house usually contract like this in the early hours? And in that case where could Doug have ...? With a start she remembered something else, something she would have recalled earlier if she hadn't been so tired. The ute! It seated only two people! Three at the most, because Doug refused to let anyone travel in the back. Whereas there had been four of them. Four! Doug, Bob, Harry, and Mary. So how ... how ...?

Her eyes snapped open onto a room flooded by moonlight. The moon itself, almost at the full, gazed blankly at her through the heavily barred window. The shadows of the bars formed a criss-cross pattern at her feet, strangely cage-like and disturbing. Behind her, the house creaked yet again beneath the cool weight of the night. And as she lurched forward in her chair, moved by an impulse to run to the front door and fling it open, something or someone snatched at her throat.

Who ...?

Breathless, choking, pinned to the back of the chair, she groped desperately for the unseen hands that held her, her own hands encountering only a tightly stretched cord that bit ever more deeply into her neck.

Who ...?

Already it was impossible to breathe, her head forced back, her fingers clutching at the emptiness behind the chair.

Emptiness? Then ... then ...!

'Plea ...!' she gurgled helplessly. 'Plea ...!'

Her voice died to a strangled whisper as the pressure increased; her tongue seemed to swell and fill her mouth, her throat, the cavity behind her eyes.

Double God? she thought in fearful wonder, struggling violently against the deepening night. Could it really be that . . . ?

Although her eyes were wide, staring, straining against her sockets, she could see so little. With each involuntary spasm, each tic of an arm, a leg, the moonlight grew dimmer, the shadows spread out from the floor and up through her feet. And the path of light from the passage — where was that? Gone? Swallowed by the black roaring in her head?

She fought her way back to a fleeting consciousness and glimpsed the dark space of the half-open doorway. No light beyond. Nothing. And yet she had turned the light on herself. So other hands, *real* hands, must have . . . must have . . .

She heard it then: the hoarse breathing of someone behind the chair. Someone! Not a ghost at all, but a living being! An actual assailant, voiceless and intent, who . . .

Voiceless?

The even breaths were disrupted by a grunt of effort that brought the darkness swarming back. It enveloped her like a smothering blanket, but not before she realised who was strangling her. Realised it with a stab of purest grief. Only one person in this house who strove in silence. Only one. Tess would have wailed out loud if she had been able to. How could her own . . . her own . . . ? That, her last grieving thought as she surrendered to a moonless dark.

PART NINE

> Dragons of the prime,
> That tare each other in their slime,
> Were mellow music match'd with him.
>
> Alfred Tennyson, 'In Memoriam'

21

She woke to the same moonless dark, to a blackness so close and dense, so suffocatingly complete, that it made no difference whether she opened her eyes or kept them closed. She stirred and tried to swallow, and tiny knives seemed to slice into her throat, worse than the painful bite of the cord which she suddenly remembered with a start of terror.

'Mary . . . !' she tried to cry, but all that came out was an unintelligible croak.

Straight away the hands had her again. The hands themselves this time, solid and real, reaching out of the blackness; and once again she was fighting . . . fighting . . . until it filtered through to her that she wasn't being attacked. The hands were soothing, stroking her now, and Doug's voice was whispering urgently.

'It's all right, sweetheart, it's all right.'

She clung hard to him then, each stifled sob lacerating her throat. When she could bear the pain no longer, she managed to mutter a single word:

'Drink.'

And he helped her up, the faint squeal of springs telling her that she had been lying on a bed. Held close against him, she shuffled slowly through the pitchy dark, both of them guided by the rasp of his hand against an unseen wall. When he turned her slightly, edging her through a narrow gap of some kind, it occurred to her that he must have explored this space earlier.

So how long had she . . . ?

But for the moment she could concentrate on nothing but the searing pain in her throat, on the need to ease it with a drink.

They had stopped and (oh, heaven!) she heard a tap being turned, followed instantly by a gush of water. She stooped greedily, and his cupped hand, cold and wet, pressed against her lips.

'Easy now, easy,' he breathed.

The first swallow was like fire, but thereafter the pain rapidly subsided, leaving her sore, but able to speak, able to think past her own discomfort.

As though a barrier had been lifted, all the events leading up to the attack rushed back into memory. The hard, unrelenting fact of the attack itself was suddenly and vividly *there*, like another presence in the darkness. And with it came a question.

Why was she still alive? Why? Even as the cord had tightened about her neck, she had known what was happening to her. Not just that Mary was her assailant, but that she, Tess, had been chosen as the next sacrificial victim. The next figure, after Kevin and Rory, to be placed upon Abraham's pyre.

And Abraham stretched forth his hand, and took the knife to slay . . .

Or had someone perhaps interceded after all, as in

the Bible story? But who? Double God? Had the dead Clement children pleaded for her at the last, like some divine voice from heaven? And if so, why? After what had been done to Kevin, the idea of mercy seemed so improbable. Far more likely was the idea that she had misunderstood her role; that she wasn't a victim at all, but merely someone to be got out of the way; that the real victim was another person entirely. Someone younger and more trusting, like the Isaac of the story, someone less able to defend . . . more exposed . . . !

She jerked up so abruptly that the back of her head slammed against Doug's chest.

'Harry!' she blurted out. 'Where is he?'

'He's just . . .' Doug began.

But it wasn't words that she needed: it was Harry himself. Pushing Doug aside, and in spite of the darkness, she started forward, only to crash into something solid. She reeled backwards, her breast and shoulder smarting from the impact.

'Harry?' she cried tearfully, sure that she had lost him somewhere in this bewildering night. 'Where are you?'

'I'm here, Mum.'

It was his voice, thank God!

'Where?'

'Over here.'

She traced the sound, radar-like, through the dark, her hands groping past the door frame and along a rough brick wall until her onward path was blocked by a series of bars.

Bars? Had she somehow felt her way to one of the outside windows?

She moistened her lips, testing the air for freshness, for any hint of a breeze. No, there was none. A clammy, closed-off feeling pervaded this space, as if she were trapped within a cavern.

'Are you still there, love?'

'Yeah, Mum.'

'Can you come closer?' Her own arms reaching through the bars, out into another vista of obscurity.

'I can't. There's a chain thing. It's fixed to the wall.'

His voice sounded thick, congested. With tears? How long had he been alone and crying out there? And out where?

'Listen to me, love,' she said, trying to sound calm, confident. 'Feel along the wall, as far as you can and in this direction.'

There was the rattle of a chain, a shuffled footstep and something brushed her knuckles. She stretched further and located his groping hand, their fingers locking together.

'It's okay,' she murmured comfortingly, tightening her hold, 'I've got you.'

Yet the firm grip of his hand in hers only opened her to another anxiety.

'Bob? Is he . . . is he . . . ?'

Doug rumbled a quick reply. 'He's in here too. He hasn't come round yet, not properly.'

With a whispered assurance to Harry, she slipped her hand free. Already Doug was there beside her, guiding her through black space: along the bars that brushed their shoulders as they passed, along another length of brick wall, the surface rough on her groping hand, to the far corner where someone (Bob? yes, the solid feel of his limbs reassured her) lay curled up on what she guessed to be a folded blanket.

She touched his arms, his shoulders, his face, using her fingertips like eyes — eyes that told her so little until she located the warm stickiness in his hair, which she recognised instantly as blood. As she probed the wound, he let out a soft moan and stirred restlessly on the blanket, but when she felt again for his face, his eyelids remained closed.

'What happened to him?' she asked, keeping her voice too low for Harry to hear.

'It was after you phoned,' Doug explained in a whisper. 'I went back to the workshop and he was lying on the floor. She must have got me too, while I was bending over him.'

'Got you? How?'

'She hit us with something. Christ, Tess, she must have moved like a cat! I didn't even see her coming. I woke up in here, the same as you except my hands were tied. And so were Bob's. She didn't cut us free until she dragged you in. I tried to get hold of her, but it's so bloody dark, and my hands . . . they were still numb . . . and she . . . she . . .'

Tess could sense him crying there beside her, his big body shuddering in distress as she took him in her arms.

It's all right, she wanted to say, but couldn't. Because nothing was all right any more. The months of violence and brooding threat, which she had told herself over and over would end in happiness and relief, had brought them only to this. This *nightmare*! This lightless cage or cavern which she knew in her heart was the closest she had ever been to hell. What made it so was the realisation that their own precious child had become their hellish keeper. How was it possible? Mary! Sweet, quiet Mary! Could she really have abandoned them, *damned* them at the behest of those crazed voices from the past?

'She's mad, Tess,' Doug groaned, confiding his bitter secret to the warm hollow at the base of her neck. 'She's capable of anything!'

She continued to hold him, all her feeling for him and the children combined in that one fierce embrace.

'It's not really Mary, not our lovely girl,' she whispered, matching his secret with one of her own. And quickly, while she had him there in her arms, close to her in every sense, she told him what she'd learned in Sydney. About Will and Denny and the idea of a Double-God; about how they were directing Mary and had been all along; about the marked passage in the Bible and what it meant.

He didn't pull away, not even when she finished. If anything, he seemed to move nearer to her, as though shrinking from whatever invisible presences shared this darkness with them.

'You don't really think . . . ?' he murmured uncertainly, and she hushed him by pressing his face hard against her neck.

This, she knew instinctively, was no time for voicing aloud their doubts, not with Bob lying unconscious beside them and Harry chained like an animal to the wall. Were she to give way to doubt now, in this mysterious and forbidding nowhere, she might easily end up as mad as . . . as mad . . . She managed to stop herself in time, before she could commit herself to what, here especially, had become the unthinkable. As mad as Mary? No! She would never accept that.

'It's not her fault!' she hissed passionately, as though the sheer force of her assertion could make it true. 'Never mind what she's done. It was their doing, *theirs*! Denny and Will Clement's. In her heart she wants to save us. I swear it, Doug!'

Her vehemence must have unsettled Harry who began to sniffle and whimper somewhere off in the dark. It was a desolate, upsetting sound, yet for the moment, caught up in her own harsh struggle, she could find within herself no soft words of comfort.

'Don't fret now, son,' Doug called out to him. 'We'll soon get you . . .' With an effort that only Tess understood, he corrected himself: 'Mary'll get us out of here soon. Just try and be patient.'

The whimpering died down. 'Why's she doing it to us, Dad?'

There was a long, uncomfortable pause. 'It's one of her . . . her games. You know what she's like these days.'

'Yeah, but where are we?'

Tess silently echoed the same question.

'It's hard to say. Under the house, I think, somewhere beyond the back wall of the workroom. In another of those secret rooms the Clements must have dug from the hillside.'

Tess pounced on the idea. 'You see! They told her about this place! Will and Denny! They *must* have! How else could . . . ?'

She didn't finish. Without warning the blackness dissolved, the surrounding space flooded with light — the suddenness, the brightness of it, making them all cry out in pain.

Tess lurched back against the wall and flung an arm across her eyes, but not before she had glimpsed the nature of their prison. Even with her eyes closed she could still see a crude outline of it, a ghostly negative that lingered on the blackness of her retina. A pale grid of bars; a crouched, blurred shape which she took to be Harry; and over to his right . . . !

Good God! Surely it was a mistake! A trick of the light, of the darkness! Either that or a mote, a suggestive speck of dust trapped in her field of vision and now imprinted on memory. It *had* to be! Surely! For how could other . . . ? How could they have . . . ?

With both hands shielding her face from the light, she forced her eyes open, just a fraction, and squinted through a hazy fringe of lashes. For the first few seconds she could make out only those things near at hand. The concrete floor between her feet; Bob, his hair bloodied, lying insensible beside her on a tartan rug; Doug, still in his work clothes, crouched on her other side, the palms of both hands covering his eyes. In spite of the painful glare, she made herself look further: to the divan bed over to her left; to the door in the other corner.

(A door to what? Just the tap she had drunk from? A bathroom? Fleeting questions that barely impinged on her consciousness.)

She could see more clearly now, her gaze moving around towards the bars. Solid, upright, no more than ten centimetres apart, they ran from the floor right up to the low concrete ceiling, forming an impassable barrier between her and the space beyond. That other space was less brilliantly lit, receiving only a wash of light from the bare bulb directly above her, its floor strewn with shadows cast by the bars. As though caught in the net of shadows, Harry sat hunched and disconsolate against the wall, a loop of chain running from his waist to a steel hoop set into the brickwork above his head.

Slowly now, reluctantly, making herself do it, she swung her eyes over to the right, to where she had glimpsed . . . to where . . . !

In that same instant she was on her feet, scrambling backwards, almost stumbling over Bob in her haste. No, she had not been mistaken! There they were, unchanged, exactly as she had glimpsed them against the dark of her retina. Two groups of people huddled together at the far, shadowy end of the other chamber! Their faces were turned watchfully (wistfully?) in her direction, their bodies passive and still.

'Doug!' she cried out.

And as he grunted with surprise and half rose, so her vision cleared completely and she saw the figures for what they were. Sculptures! Wonderfully made, lifelike, but sculptures just the same. Each of them, like those other figures in the clearing, filled with a strange, radiant beauty. As though they had been fashioned in a spirit of love, devotion even, a whole world of care and attention lavished on their making.

But what were they doing here? And had Mary made these as well? Were these yet another mysterious side to the daughter Tess once thought she knew?

She stumbled forward and pressed her face to the bars. Immediately one aspect of the mystery was solved. At close quarters it was obvious that Mary could not possibly have made all the figures, for the nearer of the two groups depicted people Tess had never seen before. They had been carved out of wood and painted, their eyes made of whitish glass, their heads topped with real hair. There were four of them and they were looking at her with a strange attentiveness. Directly at *her*! Or whoever had once stood where she was now standing, behind this screen of bars. As she returned their fixed gaze, staring into the uncanny emptiness of their eyes, she knew intuitively who they were. The Clements. All four of them clustered close together and hidden away here in the dark. There was nothing particularly remarkable about them that Tess could see. They appeared quite ordinary really: the kind of family she would have passed in the street without a second glance. The parents middle-aged and rather dowdy; Denny, a small, prettyish girl, positioned between them; and at their backs the hulking figure of the young son, Will, already a head taller than the father in spite of his boyish face.

This, then, was the source of Mary's obsession with making life-sized figures of the doomed and the dead. This was the legacy Denny and Will had passed on to her — yet further proof that the Clement children had taken her over, that they were directing her every move.

Harry's voice, an awed whisper, broke in upon Tess's troubled thoughts. 'What are they doing here, Mum?'

She shook her head at the distraction and shifted her gaze to the second group of figures. These weren't quite finished, all but one of the heads eyeless, hairless, their wooden bodies still to be painted. She recognised them just the same, their features so familiar to her that her hands tightened about the bars until her knuckles shone white. One of the figures was unmistakably herself, the mouth straight and hard, unyielding, as were the clenched fists held rigidly at her sides. Another was Doug, with a big brooding body and sagging cheeks. A younger, thinner version of the same figure, which could have been no one but Bob, stood a little behind him. While crouched at Tess's feet, his unseeing eyes lifted questioningly to the light, was the figure of Harry. Of the four, only Harry looked complete, the face startlingly lifelike, the narrow shoulders typically hunched and tense.

It took her only seconds to work out what that one complete figure truly meant.

And Abraham built an altar . . . and bound Isaac his son . . . and took the knife to slay . . .

'No, not Harry!' Tess breathed, and became conscious of Doug there beside her, his broad hands gripping the bars as tightly as hers. Even in profile his face was a wilderness of dread, his eyes clenched shut against what he too had seen and understood.

'It that supposed to be me?' Harry asked nervously.

She waited for Doug to reply, and when he stayed silent, she made herself speak, her voice breaking under the stress of the moment.

'It's just part of . . . of Mary's game, love.'

'What sort of game?'

There was only one answer Tess could think of: the God game, which consisted first of making a lifelike sculpture in clay or wood, and then of ritually killing whoever the figure represented. Mary had obviously learned this intricate and cruel sport from her Double God. And having already practised it on man and beast alike, she was now preparing . . . preparing to . . .

'Why're you crying, Mum?' Harry asked, and the whimper had crept back into his voice, coupled now with a note of alarm.

Crying? She squeezed the tears hastily from her eyes and managed to control the quivering of her lips. Though still there was Doug, right there beside her, his clenched features revealing the unspoken truth.

'I'm upset about Mary, that's all,' she said in a tone of forced calm. 'She shouldn't be doing this to us.'

Tess was saved further explanation by a groan from the corner as Bob, his face pale and bewildered, tried to sit up. She went to him and pressed him gently down onto the rug.

'Where . . . ?' he muttered, his eyes skittering from side to side. 'Where . . . ?'

'Just rest for a bit longer,' she whispered, and brushed the bloodied hair away from his forehead. 'You'll feel better later.'

Her voice alone was enough to reassure him, and he sank back into an uneasy half-sleep, his eyelids flickering in response to troubled dreams.

'Hush now,' she murmured consolingly, but didn't try to rouse him. Whatever his dreams were like, she suspected that they were preferable to this place and what awaited him here. For if she was right (and, oh God! she prayed that she wasn't), then it was better for him to be concussed; better for him not to have to witness what was to come.

Or was she just being unduly pessimistic? Mary was her own flesh and blood after all. Tess *knew* her. Or did she? Yes! She knew the *real* Mary! The Mary who had hunted desperately through the Bible for a way out of the God game; who, when it came to the point, would choose her family, her loved ones, rather than those demented spirits of the dead. When the voices of her Double God instructed her this time, she'd refuse them. She'd stay her own hand. She *had* to! If she didn't, then ... then ... !

Once more Tess found herself struggling for control, her back turned resolutely towards the bars in a desperate attempt to hide her feelings from Harry. Yet somehow he still seemed to sense her panic.

'What's going to happen to us, Mum?' he called plaintively.

She had to resist the temptation to whirl around and scream for him to leave her in peace. To scream at Harry! The one most in need of her protection! To cry out against his questions that she had no allowable answers for. Questions which only served to start into life those ghouls of dread ever ready to stalk her from the shadows.

Deliberately, she bent down and kissed Bob's flickering eyelids, to steady herself, to concentrate her mind, her body, on something other than her own rising hysteria. Then, apparently relaxed, she sat down on the rug beside him and turned to face not just Harry — nor just Doug, still hunched forlornly against the confining bars — but also those silent blank-eyed figures who watched her from across the dividing line that separated sanity from dementia.

'Nothing's going to happen to us,' she said evenly. 'All we have to do is bide our time. Mary'll get tired of her game soon and give it up. I promise.'

She promised. But whom? Harry? Herself? Those clustered figures poised expectantly in the half-dusk beyond the direct influence of the light? They were the ones she really had to answer to. She understood that well enough. And all she could answer them with was Mary: the Mary who had walked out one day with a little boy called Josh; the Mary who, in spirit at least, had never arrived at that half-open gate; had never been plunged into the same tongueless silence as the figures over there in the shadows; had never been exposed . . . no, *prepared* in those few Terror-filled moments for the dark whisperings she would later encounter in this fortress of a house.

In a sense it was that younger, more innocent Mary whom Tess set herself to wait for now. In faith alone. For hope would have been too demanding, too wearing. It was easier simply to trust, to fix her mind on the belief that when the shadows parted, down there at the far end of the chamber where she could just make out the shape of a barred doorway, the Mary who walked through the opening would be fresh-faced and smiling. Their liberator, not their jailer.

Meanwhile, Tess tried not to notice the dragging hours; tried not to wonder how long this ordeal would continue. Moment by moment she filled the time with small mundane duties — with a comforting touch whenever Bob came tremblingly half-awake; with fetching the occasional drink for Harry, in a plastic mug she found in the bathroom which, unaccountably, had also been built into this secret underground part of the house; with a show of sympathy when Doug, his face hollowed out by misery, stumbled across the cell and nestled against her in the cruel glare of the overhead light.

'Where did we go wrong?' he whispered wretchedly. 'Where?'

His doubt, like a sudden breath of winter, caught her unawares. To ward it off, she pictured Mary poring over Meg's old Bible, searching through those gilt-edged pages for the Godly face of mercy. But with that picture came another, one almost as unwelcome as Doug's whispered doubt: a picture of Mary, night after night, peering between the closed curtains at the moon. Like some werewolf who fed upon its pale glow.

She hadn't wanted to remember that. The same wintry breath of doubt touched her once again, right inside this time. The moon! It was almost the last thing Tess had seen, up there in the living room, before she had succumbed to Mary's attack! The great pale disc of it staring at her through the window like some baleful eye; its light flooding between the bars and striping the floor with shadow. So bright! So like the night they had cut Kevin's body down from the trees. The same sharp contrast between light and shadow on that occasion too. And on other occasions, such as that long trying night at Meg's when Mary had sat upon her moonwashed bed and sobbed uncontrollably for hour after hour.

The moon had been at the full then. And last night? Had the disc at the window been a perfect circle or had . . . ?

Tess pulled quickly away from Doug and looked at her watch. Five o'clock. But surely it must have been close to that when she woke in the living room.

'Doug!' she said in a tense whisper. 'How long have I been down here?'

He shook his head muzzily, as though stupefied by his own despair.

'Think!' she hissed fiercely at him. 'It's important!'

'It was so dark,' he complained. 'I couldn't keep track of time, and you were out for hours.'

'How long was I out? A rough estimate, that's all I want. More than twelve hours? Less?'

She could see him struggling to concentrate, his full lips pulled in hard against his teeth. 'Less probably,' he said at last. 'Not more than that anyway.'

'So!' she said. 'It's late afternoon. And tonight's the full moon. The *full moon*! No wonder she wanted to get back here. Christ! Why didn't I think of this before?'

She pulled away from Doug, feet gathered beneath her, her whole body tense and ready.

'Think of what?' Doug asked in a dull, defeated voice.

She didn't bother to answer, her eyes scanning the

upper level of the confining walls. Apart from some air bricks, there were no signs of any opening. Which meant that the only means of escape, once out of this cage, was through the barred doorway at the end of the chamber. But how to reach it? She hurried across to the bars that stood between her and the silent, glass-eyed figures that seemed to observe her every move with unearthly detachment. Yes, now that she looked carefully, there was also a door of sorts set into the bars over near the right hand wall: a separate section of bars that slotted unobtrusively into the rest, and with something attached to them on the outside. A raised plate positioned so close to the wall that she hadn't noticed it until now. Without a mirror she couldn't see what the face of the plate was like, but her groping fingertips told her that it had a keyhole in the centre. And when she put her ear to the back of it, she could detect a faint ticking.

A bomb?

She pulled sharply away. No, on reflection a bomb wasn't very likely. There was some kind of clock in there all the same. But for what? A timing device? A lock that could be set for a specific period? Yes, that was probably it. Except why should something like this ... this prison ... have been built beneath the house in the first place? And why had it been hidden behind the blank inner wall of the workroom? What the hell had the Clements been playing at? How many more secrets did she yet have to discover about that weird and unhappy family?

'What are you up to?' Doug called, rousing himself and coming over to her.

'We have to get out of here, Doug,' she said, and found that she was whispering, as though fearful of being overheard; as though those watchful figures were really a guard, placed there to make sure no one escaped.

'It can't be done, Tess,' Doug said regretfully. 'Whoever built this place knew what they were doing. It's all concrete and steel.'

'I don't care,' she cried, flinging the words at the figures like a challenge, and she grabbed the bars and tugged so hard that they hurt her hands. 'We have to find a way out. We *have to!*'

'I'm sorry, sweetheart,' he mumbled, as if it were his fault that they were trapped. 'All we can do is wait for Mary.'

For Mary! Suddenly she felt so exasperated by him that she wanted to scream.

'That'll be too late!' she shouted, punching ineffectually at his chest. 'Look at the time, for Christ's sake! It's after five. And once it's dark . . . once it's dark!'

He had caught her against him, holding her hard and sure. 'What does the dark have to do with it, Tess? Tell me!'

And from Harry, whimpering and dragging at his chain as he struggled to his feet: 'I'm scared, Mum! I don't want to stay here any more.'

She knew that for Harry's sake she shouldn't voice her fears aloud. The problem was, over the past few minutes those fears had hardened into near certainty. It was no longer a case of what *might* happen, of holding threatening possibilities at bay through a willed act of faith, of clinging with stubborn tenacity to a belief in Mary's essential purity of heart. Within the space of a few searing breaths, it seemed she had moved beyond all that. Remembering Rory, Kevin, the unnatural beauty of their sculptured likenesses in the brilliant moonlight, remembering also the night Mary had spent sobbing on her moondrenched bed, Tess finally gave way to bitter acceptance. There, in that garish light which cast skeletal shadows even over Doug's fleshy face, the terrible cycle of events presented itself to her with a starkness and a clarity that placed it beyond all question.

'It's the moon that triggers them,' she murmured, relying now on Doug's supporting arms.

'Them?'

'The Clement children. It's when they make her do things.'

For once he was ahead of her. 'And tonight . . . ?'

'I think so.'

Had Mary been watching them all along? Listening? Tess often wondered about that afterwards, but never dared to ask, perhaps as tender of her daughter's fragile happiness as the Clement parents had once been. Whatever the truth, at that precise moment a rectangle of light suddenly appeared at the far end of the chamber.

Like Doug, like Harry who had stopped crying and tugging at his chain, Tess swung around and stared at the barred opening. Through it she could see a high-set window, a bed with a dusty coverlet, and beside it a chest-of-drawers whose top was spread with tiny glinting shapes. There was something else not quite in view:

a section of a face — a laughing eye, the corner of a mouth — attached to the wall that flanked the window.

'Denny Clement!' Tess breathed, her finger digging into Doug's shoulders. 'Her shrine! That's how you get in here. Through her room.'

She almost expected Denny herself to step into the opening; Denny's long-dead hand to unlock the barred gate — the self-same hand, Tess now realised, that had already slid aside the bookcase that served as a concealed door.

'Med?' Harry called, no less expectantly. 'Is that you Med?'

And Doug, with a passionate ring of conviction in his voice: 'Mary, love! Don't listen to what they're telling you! Don't!'

But neither Mary nor any suggestion of Denny's unquiet spirit darkened the opening. It was as if the bookcase had been moved aside only so that the prisoners could see for themselves, in the muted light of the outer chamber, how the evening was already approaching.

'Are you there, Med?' Harry began calling again, and Tess silenced him by slapping the bars with her open hand, the hum of the vibrating metal filling the space with uneasy vibrations.

'Keep quiet, Harry,' she added sternly, her features hard and inexpressive, telling him nothing.

And she went back and sat next to Bob, her face turned towards the far end of the chamber.

Doug lowered himself down beside her. 'D'you think she'll listen to them?' he whispered.

But Tess shushed him, too, with a quick, dismissive

gesture. How could he expect her to answer such questions? If he'd come round to her way of thinking days, weeks earlier, if he'd accepted the existence of a Double God when she'd first put it to him, of twinned voices that spoke to Mary from the past, then things might have been different. They might have had time to . . . But no, it was too late for recriminations. All she could do now was sit and wait, her eyes fixed on the barred opening.

The light seemed to fade with excruciating slowness, dimming to pale grey and finally to nothing. It was only when the doorway showed as a black rectangle in the shadowy far wall that she heard a noise — the merest hint of a footfall which reminded her all at once of the familiar creaking of the house as it settled in the cool of the night. Leaning forward, stiffly alert, she sensed a movement out of there in the dark. There was a clink of metal on metal, the sharp click-click-click of a dial being turned, and the barred door swung inwards.

Someone followed it. Someone small and slight. Mary? Surely it had to be Mary! Who else? Yet still it was hard for Tess to be sure because the face was covered by a mask that had been divided vertically in two: one half as pale as moonlight, the other a lurid flame-red.

'Dear God!' Doug muttered, scrambling up onto his knees; while Harry, with an inarticulate cry, shrank back against the wall, both hands clinging onto the chain that bound him.

Only Tess hadn't moved, transfixed as Mary (Who else *could* it be?) paused just inside the threshold, her body trembling like a dancer's. After one searching sweep of the mask, she took a cautious step forward, causing the shadows to stir alarmingly at her back. Another step and she was inside the chamber, drawing in her wake . ... But how could she? *How?* . . . drawing in her wake the vast spirit of the night itself.

Or that, at least, was how it appeared to Tess's totally bewildered gaze.

22

Harry was shouting somewhere in the background, an oddly breathless sound. A kind of 'Aah-aah-aah!', as though he were struggling for air. Nobody was hurting him. Not yet. He was merely scared. (Merely?) Tess understood that even as she yelled for him to be quiet.

Gradually his panting cries died away, allowing her to order her scrambled thoughts, to confront the one question uppermost in her mind:

How could they *both* have come back?

Because there were two of them down there. She was sure of it. To make doubly sure, she shaded her eyes from the dazzle of the overhead light and peered keenly into the gloom at the end of the chamber. Yes, two. Shadowy and indistinct, but two just the same. Actual physical presences. Yet how? Denny, yes, her presence made sense — a horrible, ghoulish type of sense, but sense all the same. She was here in the person of Mary, their separate identities blurred by the use of the mask. But for *both* the Clement children to take bodily form! *Both!* Who could possibly be standing in for Will? Not Kevin. Not Bob, who was lying concussed and semi-conscious beside her. So who? There was no one left. No one Tess could think of. Unless . . .

The simple truth hit Tess with almost physical force, so that she sank back onto her heels. Yes, of course! *Who else?* What other explanation could there be? *He* was the reason for this dungeon, this keep, this place of concrete and steel. And also the reason for so many other things: for the regular creaking of the house in the small hours of the morning; for the appearance of the sculptures, both here and out there in the clearing; for the voice of Double God that haunted Mary's waking hours and filled her life with nervous dread; and, most important of all, for the terrible atrocities in which Mary had been involved. Rory and Kevin had died not because of some mad streak in Mary herself; nor because she was haunted by the vengeful spirits of the dead. Mary (thank heaven!) was no monster. She was as sane as anyone else. The insane one, the driving force behind all their tragedies, all their heartache, was *him*! *Him!* This looming shadow, huge and menacing, that hovered at Mary's shoulder! This, the crazy Double God that she prayed to; that she now looked to for mercy, foolishly hoping he would relent, as in the story of Isaac.

'Will!' Tess said aloud, her voice at first a mere breath, and then gathering force, becoming a strident cry of accusation: 'Will Clement, that's who you are!'

'What?' Doug turned bewildered eyes in her direction. 'But he's . . .'

Tess reached out a hand to silence him.

'You were supposed to be drowned,' she plunged on, addressing the sombre shape who all but filled the far doorway. 'The trouble is, no one ever found a body.

Not that I heard of anyway. Drowned! How bloody convenient! And all the time you were hidden down here by your parents. Isn't that right? Isn't that how it was?'

A shadowy arm eased Mary aside; a voice, surprisingly deep and resonant, didn't so much answer Tess as declare itself to the space they shared.

'Will Clement is dead. I am the Double God. In my right hand I bear the seven stars, in my left the two-edged sword. And this' — he touched Mary's shoulder lightly, delicately — 'this is my sister moon.'

Another, even simpler truth occurred to Tess at that moment. One that explained so much — Mary's whole involvement with this Double God, no less.

'Mary isn't your sister,' she said harshly, clambering to her feet. 'Denny's dead. You killed her. Don't you remember? And nothing can ever bring her back. Nothing, d'you hear?'

Tess could see how Mary's hand — the one holding the mask in place — had begun to shake.

'Mark how the mortal earth spews forth its lies,' the deep voice pronounced clearly.

'No, not lies!' Tess shouted, and darted towards the bars, her shadow, now spreadeagled across the outer chamber, reaching almost to Mary's feet. 'You're the liar, for pretending that Mary can take Denny's place. She can't. Nobody ever will. Denny's gone for good. She was a poor young woman who suffered and died, that's all. She's not a God who can be reborn.'

'Lies!' the voice insisted, though with a tremor in it now.

'And you're not a God either,' Tess went on, her face pressed to the bars, her eyes trying to penetrate the shadows about the doorway. 'Inside, you're just poor little Will Clement. A bewildered little boy who couldn't accept what he'd done to his . . .'

With a bellow, the shadows themselves seemed to erupt, sweeping Mary aside. Tess caught a glimpse of vivid red and white, of a weirdly streaked arm scooping Harry up in passing and hurling him against the wall, and then a massive body slammed into the bars mere centimetres from her face. The impact knocked her down, the light dimming momentarily as her head thumped onto the hard concrete floor.

'Harry!' she screamed, her head ringing from the fall.

And heard him answer from a long way off: 'I'm okay, Mum. I'm okay.'

She could hear Doug, too, shouting angrily in the near distance. So unlike Doug to be angry. So out of character. So . . .

She shook her head to clear it and looked up at something she had never anticipated, had never dreamed of, not in her wildest confusion. An immense figure totally naked and towering above her, the right side of his head and body shaved of all hair and painted with hundreds of tiny curls of flame. She blinked and looked again, and saw things that even the care and beauty of the painting could not hide. What had Ruth Close told her? Not just that Will had mutilated himself, but that he had tried to make himself look like Denny after the fire. And here was the result. His right eye opaque and white and unseeing; the remains of his right ear a mere blackened shred of flesh; one side of his scrotum hacked away; and in amongst the curling flames, from the crown of his head right down to his feet, the livid weals of healed scars, where he must have slashed himself repeatedly with a knife.

Poor little Will Clement, she had called him, and so had Ruth. Yet there was nothing pitiable about him now. He was like a figure who had stepped straight out of hell, with the flames of those unquenchable fires still clinging to him. No wonder Mary had sobbed and grieved and finally done his bidding. Challenged by this monstrosity — this Double God, with his human and his demon faces halved into one — what choice had she had? What choice, what hope, did any of them have?

Tess rose gingerly to her feet, never taking her eyes from Will's uncannily divided face. Doug, she realised, had stopped shouting, his hand reaching, fumbling for hers. The two of them like lost children. As lost as Harry and Mary, marooned out there on the other side of the bars.

'Mum,' Harry whispered plaintively, but she pursed her lips, cautioning him to stay quiet.

She allowed herself just one quick turn of the head. Where was Mary? Ah, there, in the barely lit area around the door, the mask clamped in place with both hands, as though she were terrified that it would slip and reveal the human face beneath.

Will, meanwhile, was still pressed against the bars, the top of his head almost brushing the ceiling, his one good eye fixed, it seemed, upon some infinite space far beyond the confines of the chamber.

Gazing up at him, Tess wondered despairingly how she could appeal to someone so far removed from the real world. Someone who had pursued the path of torment to a point where torment itself no longer mattered. For that was how he appeared to her now: as a being wholly encased in his own mad delusions; as a man-god who had set himself the dual task of destroying the world in order to create it anew in the form of those glassy-eyed family groups at his back. What possible weakness could such a being . . . ?

Tess paused in mid thought. No! There was one flaw in his mad scheme. Loneliness! Or was it guilt? One or the other had driven him to recreate Denny in a living form; to perceive Mary as his dead sister. Mary! She was the key, in every sense. The one person he acknowledged as an equal, whom he truly valued. If they were all to get out of here alive, it had to be through her.

Pulling free of Doug, Tess forced herself to sidle up to the bars, to within reach of those huge hands.

'No one wants to take Denny away from you,' she said in a wheedling tone. 'If you let us out of here, you can still go on seeing her. I give you my word on that. You can stay on here in the house like always. You and Denny together. Nothing will change.'

She was watching his face for some sign of response, but there was none, his gaze unwavering and purposeful. It was as if she hardly existed, as if she were some insignificant microbe, unworthy of attention.

With a sinking heart, she tried again. 'Denny loves you,' she crooned, speaking exactly as though she were comforting Harry, coaxing him from an unpleasant dream. 'But she loves us too. She'd be unhappy if anything happened to us. And you don't want her to be unhappy like before, do you? Wishing she was dead? I can't believe you want that. So why not let us go? Then we can all live like a family again. Do you remember how it was? You and Denny together?'

His hand shot through the bars so quickly that she had no time to leap back. His fingers had closed around her neck before she could even fling up an arm, his grip just tight enough to reawaken the pain in her badly bruised throat, and to reawaken also the terrifying memory of that moonlit scene upstairs in the living room, when she had genuinely believed she was about to die.

'Let her go!' Doug shouted, and dived forward, but Will had already released her, the impress of his fingers on her bruised skin serving as a warning.

Of what? Tess asked herself as she rubbed gingerly at her throat. And knew the answer. He had told her, without recourse to words, that he wasn't a child to be coaxed, and nor was he stupid, someone she could appease with empty promises.

'Are you all right, sweetheart?' Doug was asking, but it was Will she was listening to, his lips moving almost imperceptibly in that ravaged face.

'I am Double God,' he murmured, reminding her once again of what she really had to deal with.

Having given her a second warning, he half turned towards Mary, so that the light fell only on the unblemished side of his body, the other side hidden in shadow. And in that instant Tess saw him as he might have been. Not monstrous at all, his fair hair falling softly across his forehead, his face as ordinary as the faces of those figures behind him, the skin of his legs and chest covered with a sheen of blond down. Here was the Will Clement he could have become. No, more than that, the Will Clement he was still! A part of him anyway. Half of him at least still human. It *had* to be! Still capable of human responses, of hearkening to the promptings of his heart.

'Let us begin, little sister,' she heard him say, and was conscious of Mary cowering back even further, a mere wisp of greyish shadow against the blackness of the door.

'Let us begin,' he said again, but in the same coaxing tone that Tess had used.

And encouraged by his unexpected gentleness — the softness of his voice echoing the more human half of him, the unblemished half, spotlighted still by the garish light — Tess slumped to her knees. She hardly noticed Mary flitting away through the far doorway. Driven by sudden hope, she reached through the bars and grasped his leg with both hands, his flesh reassuringly warm, the even beat of his heart pulsing through her clutching fingertips.

'Please!' she implored him. 'Please! We haven't done anything to hurt you. We wouldn't. Not ever. For Denny's sake, I'm begging you, let us go. For her sake, please . . . please!'

He couldn't ignore her, could he? This creature of flesh and blood like herself? This man with a heart and emotions and tender skin that throbbed between her hands? His sane, human half must surely know how she was feeling. He too must have pleaded once, for Denny. Begged, just like this, for her to be treated mercifully. How, then, could he refuse?

Tess lowered her head, waiting, hoping, for his hand to reach down and touch her hair, stroke the tender nape of her neck, for him to give her a sign that he had heard, that he understood and sympathised.

'Please,' she murmured once more, clinging onto him, willing him to relent.

But there was no gentle touch; no whispered assurance. Only the slow drag of Mary's returning footsteps and the sudden tensing of his leg muscles which grew rock-hard within her pleading grasp.

'Good God, sweetheart!' Doug broke out hoarsely. 'What are you thinking of?'

And almost simultaneously Harry was shrieking: 'Don't give it to him, Med! Don't!'

Tess's head jerked up, first towards Mary, who was standing at the outer limit of the light, her mask still in place, her free hand clutching one of the long-bladed kitchen knives. Already Tess had guessed what she would find when she raised her eyes to Will: his head now tilted in such a way that all she could see were coiling flames, the burned stump of an ear, a sightless eye.

'My God!' she burst out, snatching her hands away.

'You have spoken,' he lisped knowingly. And then to Mary: 'It is time, little sister. Time for you to ascend to the heavens. For you to take up your rightful place there. Only these lives of clay bind you to the earth, measuring you with their mortality. Cut yourself free. One swift stroke will place your foot upon the stair. Do it, little sister. Join me, up here amongst the stars where you belong.'

The mask in Mary's hand had begun to shake again, so violently that it barely concealed her face.

'Don't listen to him!' Tess hissed, her face pressed to the bars, her arms reaching out now to where Mary lingered in that fringe area of shadow and light. 'He's mad! He doesn't know what he's talking about. All he wants is for you to be as mad as he is.'

But again it was as if she hardly existed.

'Do it, little sister,' Will repeated, and pointed to the sculpture of Harry. 'See, the hand of Brahma, of Vishnu, has done its work. Now he must feel the burning touch of Siva. Of the Terrible One.'

'Mum!' Harry wailed, and Tess scurried towards the corner and stretched for his hand which she clasped protectively in both of hers.

'Don't worry, love!' she whispered urgently. 'I won't let him hurt you.'

'Nor will I, son,' Doug said, and he was there at her side, stretching past her, their hands twining together.

'We'll keep you safe,' she added, tightening her grip.

Yet silently, in the desolate regions of her mind, she was screaming out: *Safe?* What did it mean? What did anything mean, with these bars biting into her cheek, her shoulders? With Will Clement out there pointing at Harry's likeness? And with Mary moving slowly, hesitantly, into the circle of light, the blade of the knife pressed flat against her breast?

Tess turned her head slightly, flinching away from Harry's terrified expression, from his boyish features, screwed up in anguish, that tore at her inside. It was easier (or harder? she couldn't tell any more) to look at Mary's red and white mask, its two halves mirroring Will's weirdly divided face.

'Listen to me, Mary love,' she said, her voice trembling with emotion. 'He isn't God. You don't have to obey him. He's just a madman. And he isn't just tempting you, like that story you found in the Bible, about Abraham and Isaac. He's going to let you do it, I swear. The same as with Kevin. The same as with Rory.' She could feel her voice spiralling out of control, but there was nothing she could do to rein it in. 'Are you listening to me, Mary?' she shrieked. 'He wants you to kill him, damn it! He *wants* you to!'

'Help me, Mum! Help me!' Harry shrilled.

And with two swift strides Will had plucked him from their hands.

'You bastard!' Doug bellowed, beating his forehead and fists against the bars. 'You fucking bastard! I swear I'll kill you! I'll kill . . . I'll . . . !'

With blood streaming from a gash along his hairline, he broke down, sobbing, as Will lifted Harry to the full extent of the chain.

'Leave him!' Tess cried. 'Can't you see he's just a child? Just a boy?'

But her pleading, like Doug's threats, meant nothing. Through a rain of tears she watched, helpless, as Will bent open the clasp of the chain which fell with a dull rattle against the wall. Harry, his eyes squeezed shut, his face barely recognisable, had gone rigid with fright, hanging there, speechless, from Will's clenched fist.

'Now!' Will breathed, beckoning to Mary. 'Now is the testing time, little sister.'

From behind Mary's mask there came a low moan. And another. Sounds that awakened in Tess a last germ of hope.

'Harry loves you, Mary,' she whispered brokenly. 'He's your brother and he loves you.'

The mask twitched in her direction and the white half briefly caught the light. But only briefly. It was immediately eclipsed by the half-moon of red as the mask was twitched back towards Will.

That was Tess's last attempt at intercession. As with Mary, months earlier, it dawned on her then that all her words were useless. They were empty, formless noise that had no power to change the world. Will alone, this self-made Double God, had access to the language of power, to words that could bend things to his needs. And he employed those words now, whispering them enticingly, using them like invisible magnets to draw Mary towards him.

'The first is the hardest, little sister,' he murmured, holding Harry up for her to see. 'Always. The pain of it will be a fire in your heart, a blazing furnace of grief, but a furnace that will burn away all human passion and leave you free. Trust me, little sister, for I too have endured its heat. You will rise from the ashes like the Phoenix, knowing your true destiny.'

Tess watched in dread as Mary, her mask quivering, took a hesitant step forward. No! Tess yearned to cry out. Don't go any nearer! But her lips refused to open, refused to form the sounds trying to burst from her body. Beside her, Doug was making inarticulate choking noises, as bereft of words as she, his big hands reaching out for support. She pulled him against her almost absently, her eyes flicking from Mary to Harry as Will resumed his insidious whispering.

'Here, I give him to you, little sister,' he said, and held Harry out towards her as though he were a gift — Harry's face now so blank and pale with shock that Tess moaned aloud, like Mary minutes earlier. 'Take him. He is the first of those that bind you to your mortality, each a link in the same earthly chain. Remember that all must be severed within this quarter of the moon, for that is our agreement, but this one first . . . this one first.'

He paused and waited for Mary's next hesitant step. As did Tess, the heel of her hand jammed between her clenched teeth. She had stopped crying, had stopped straining against the bars. Strangely dry-eyed, she knew with an awful bitterness of heart that there was nothing she could do to halt that slow advance. Only Mary herself could do that. And here was the bitterest part: Mary, mesmerised by the slow dance of his voice, seemed as powerless as any of them.

'He was *your* choice, little sister,' Will murmured confidentially, and to Tess's horror Mary shuddered like someone reminded of a guilty secret. 'Yes, *yours*! Would you point your finger and then draw back your hand? No! Be like Kali . . . like Siva . . . like me. Feed on his pain. Savour the passing of his breath.' He shook

Harry as if he were a puppet. 'Let this mortal trash nourish the God in you.'

Nourish? A nerveless sigh escaped from Tess as a vision of Rory's desecrated body, of Kevin's, seemed to pass before her eyes. Nourish? Surely Will couldn't mean *that*, she told herself. Surely not *that*! Yet already Mary had taken another step, one that brought her into the full blaze of the light, the red of her mask matching the intensity of those tiny coiling flames that adorned Will's face and body. And now, it seemed to Tess, he was speaking differently. No longer trying to lure Mary towards him; no longer gentle and cajoling. A hard edge of threat had crept into his voice.

'Choose, little sister. Which is it to be? His death or yours? A place beside me amongst the stars, or another scrap of blood-sodden earth? No other path exists. Just these two. And one of them must be chosen. *Must*, little sister. There is no middle ground. As you discovered in the good book, those who are not for me are against me. Which are you then? Which?'

Tess guessed the answer before it was given, and forgave Mary in advance. Or believed she had until the mask was finally lowered and she saw the face behind it. No anguish there, no pity, no visible sign of grief. The features as lustreless, as devoid of emotion, as the pale half of the mask itself; the eyes as blank and unseeing as those glass-eyed figures that looked on so dispassionately.

My poor baby! That was Tess's one thought, though she could not have said whether it was meant for Mary or Harry. Both her children, at that moment, seemed equally lost to her. My poor baby!

Somewhere beyond the silence that closed her in, Will's voice droned on, but she no longer cared. Or rather she cared too much for other things — things she couldn't pinpoint. With her fingers buried in Doug's hair, in the fleshy part of his heaving back, she caught only snatches of what Will was saying, his words weaving through the emptiness.

'For God so loved the world . . . do it with love, then little sister . . . let the blade caress him . . . kiss him . . .'

Tess raised her eyes with agonising slowness, and saw Mary, with identical slowness, lift the knife to a point above her shoulder. But why? To keep it from Will? To ready herself for a sudden thrust? It was all too difficult to work out. And besides, Will had already snatched at her wrist with his other hand. Mary's hand and his both locked about the knife; the tip of the blade brought quiveringly to within a hand's breadth of Harry's throat.

'Let me be your guide, little sister,' Will was saying now, cooing the words at her, almost like a lover. 'Let me light the path that you . . .'

Tess herself was incapable of speech, of movement, but all at once she was surrounded by noise and confusion.

Harry, jolted from his frozen state by the gleaming menace of the knife, exploded into a wild frenzy of resistance. 'No, Med!' he screamed out, his head thrown back, his mouth a black circle of denial, his arms and legs raking the air in a desperate attempt to break Will's hold on him. 'No! No! No! No! No!'

Doug had again hurled himself at Will. 'Bastard!' he was yelling, the veins standing out on his swollen throat. 'Bastard!' His head and fists pounding dementedly at the restraining bars, his blood spattering the floor at Will's feet.

And Bob, roused from his semiconscious state by all the din, had staggered up from his makeshift bed, his eyes vague and unfocused. 'Wha'?' he broke out, his arms lifted against the glare of the light. 'Wha's happen . . . happen . . . ?' His gaze wavered and then settled on Tess, and he came at her in a lurching run.

She gathered him in just as Will, with a bellow that silenced even Doug, shook Harry into submission.

Doug turned helplessly towards her, his bloodied face like a distorted mirror image of her own misery. 'Why?' he muttered distractedly, his bruised hands held up in a childlike gesture of bewilderment. 'Why?' And she reached out an arm and gathered him in too.

Crushing them both hard against her, their two faces buried in her shoulders, she stared out at a scene almost as still, almost as fixed in time and space as those groups of glass-eyed witnesses standing off in the shadows. Will, a sheen of sweat glazing the lurid flames that half enveloped him, was now holding Harry by the hair. Harry himself hung down slack-limbed, only his face registering the pain and torment he was enduring. Mary, not a flicker of feeling in her eyes, her mouth, in the smooth round of her cheeks, was leaning slightly forward, the knife poised above her shoulder, her hand and Will's still locked about the handle.

'Let me make this journey with you, little sister,' Will

murmured in the same loving voice he had used before. 'Let us share in this as in all things henceforth.' And slowly, deliberately, with not a murmur from Mary's parted lips, he brought his two hands together.

Tess had steeled herself to go on watching, if only as a means of saying goodbye, but at the last her nerve failed and she winced away, hating the all-revealing light and shutting it out.

She couldn't shut out the sounds though. The faint hiss of the knife slicing through flesh. The even fainter hiss of Harry's escaping breath, which was partly overlaid by Doug's 'Whau!' of mute refusal. The terrible tearing sound of skin and cartilage and cloth and bone, its seconds-long passage measured by Doug's shuddering sobs that broke, muffled, into the hollow of her shoulder. And last, the most horrifying sound of all, Will's voice as he whispered intimately:

'Eat, little sister. Eat.'

How long did she wait until she looked again? How many other sounds did the roaring in her ears save her from? She had no idea. In the returning silence her eyes seemed to open of their own volition, and she saw Harry still dangling from Will's bunched fist. No, not Harry. Only the husk of Harry, his face a smooth white and at peace, his life — his very being — tumbling down between his legs in multi-coloured profusion. And beyond Harry she saw Mary, her mouth and chin smeared with blood, her face tipped up blankly towards Will.

But no, again Tess was wrong. Mary's face wasn't

quite blank. Something was working within it, the muscles of the jaw tensing, the cheeks creasing, the lips quivering. With a violent convulsion of her features, the thing inside Mary broke free. A single word.

'Terror,' she breathed, her voice husky and uncertain after months of disuse. Then once again, much louder, firmer, a look of triumph lighting her eyes: 'Terror!'

And that look, the repetition of that one word, finally, was more than Tess was able to bear.

Part Ten

O body swayed to music, O brightening glance,
How can we know the dancer from the dance?

W. B. Yeats, 'Among School Children'

23

'See that she puts on a jumper or something,' Tess said distractedly. 'You know how cold these autumn nights can get.'

Although it was airless and warm there in the brightly lit basement, Tess herself was shivering, her bare arms clamped across her breasts. She was lying on the bed, her back turned to the bars, her half-open eyes staring at the brick wall, as though intent upon some shadow play that Doug was unaware of.

'I'll see to her,' Doug answered, his voice still muffled by tears, and patted her shoulder.

She didn't respond, the coarse lines of bricks and mortar holding her attention, and Doug guessed that she hadn't even heard him, her mind wandering somewhere he couldn't get to — some less testing place than this, where Mary hadn't yet crossed that unthinkable borderline into . . . into what?

He rubbed at his cut and swollen forehead, still struggling to take in what had happened. His Mary! *Her* hand on the knife as well as Will's! The two of them together, equally mad, equally heartless, as they . . . as they . . . !

Doug stifled a fresh outbreak of sobbing, his shoulders hunched with effort as he blocked out Harry's face, his voice, his last rasping breath. For *that* to happen to their youngest! For Mary to do *that* to him! To the baby of the family! Not just someone *out there*, some remote figure like Kevin, but her own brother whom she'd once loved!

Doug smeared clumsily at his eyes with the back of his hand.

Love? What did it mean any more? He longed to consign it, with Mary, with Harry, to the unquestioning dark. Perhaps he might have done precisely that — taking refuge in denial, distraction — if it hadn't been for Tess. This Tess whom he barely knew, lying confused and forlorn beneath his hands.

Hours earlier, surfacing from that first terrible plunge into grief, he had reached out for her, knowing she would be close by, like always. And he had discovered instead that he was alone, kneeling over there by the bars, the reek of blood his only companion. Tess, withdrawn, unreachable, had already been curled up here on the bed, muttering incoherently, closed against him, pushing him off as if he were some stranger.

That had shaken him almost as much as the loss of Harry. To have Tess crack under pressure! To have her break down completely! The tough, unbending Tess he would have trusted with his life. It was like the end of everything. And like all endings, it was also a strange and unforeseen kind of beginning. For confronted by this new, unfamiliar Tess, he had been forced to take her place, somehow to keep his presence of mind, to deny the chaos that awaited them all out there in the shadows. His face turned obdurately from that other, confusing world beyond the bars, he had occupied himself with the ordinary necessities of the moment, just as she would have done.

Bob he had dragged over to the rug in the corner and coaxed into troubled sleep. Tess he had pleaded with for hours, using words, touch, shared memories, anything that might reach her. At one point in the course of that long and fruitless appeal, he had heard the whisper of bare feet on the concrete floor behind him, the grating noise of a tray being slid beneath the bars. He had guessed it was food from the smell, but he had drawn the line at trying to tempt her with that. His mind, his heart, his stomach had rebelled at the idea of their eating anything prepared by *those* hands. He hadn't even been able to turn and see who it was — Mary or Will — a part of him lamenting silently that it no longer mattered.

Tess stirred now on the bed beside him, as though reacting to the words he dared not speak aloud.

'I don't feel well,' she complained, and picked at a jagged piece of mortar in the wall, pulling so hard at it that she tore her nail right down to the quick.

He grabbed her hand and cradled it in his, but she hardly seemed conscious of the pain.

'I'm not up to cooking tonight,' she went on. 'You and your father will have to do it.'

You? He didn't have the heart to ask whom she meant.

'Don't worry, sweetheart,' he whispered. 'We'll see to it.'

That appeared to satisfy her because she finally closed her eyes, her body twitching slightly as she drifted away.

Gently, Doug released her hand. Even in sleep she continued to tremble, and he stripped off his shirt and draped it over her. In just his singlet and trousers he felt oddly exposed and alone. More alone than he could remember, with half his family utterly lost to him, and the other half astray somewhere, leaving him abandoned here in this pit of harsh brightness.

He stood up uneasily and half turned. Without actually looking to his right, he was aware of the cloth-covered tray on the floor, of the splash of bright red over near the chain, of those blank-eyed groups of figures watching him silently. And of something else! He swung hastily towards the bars and saw Will, his body rock-still and far more garish and unlikely than any of the figures around him. He was standing close to Denny's sculpture, one hand resting possessively on her shoulder.

'Where is she?' Will demanded.

'She?' The word was out there, bridging the gap between them, before Doug could prevent it.

'Little sister,' Will said, as though talking to an empty room. 'Now that the moon has risen, this is where she belongs.'

Doug glanced towards the open door. Dark again! Had another day gone by already? No wonder he felt so empty, so dry. He blundered into the bathroom and put his head under the tap; drank his fill as the shock of the cold water revived him, snaking down his neck and body in icy runnels.

When he emerged, dripping wet, Will hadn't moved, the painted flames, electric bright, swarming up one side of his body. Both his eyes, shaded by heavy brows, seemed equally blind, and his head was tipped at a peculiar angle, like someone who has genuinely lost his sight and come to rely more on hearing.

'This is her place,' he went on, speaking as if there had been no interruption. 'Siva cannot dance again until the creation is complete. She knows that, and yet she hides from me. From me!'

Doug had decided earlier never to answer him, never again to feed his madness with more words, but now the temptation was too great — especially with the bloodstain, a sombre brown, still clearly visible there on the concrete floor just beyond the bars.

'Can you blame her?' he half shouted. 'Look at you! You're not God. You're a fucking freak! Anyone in their right mind would hide from you!'

In their right mind? Mary? But it wasn't the truth he was interested in any longer. All he really desired was to get back at this creature, to make him pay for every agonising second of Harry's mute suffering. Crying again, in spite of himself, he stumbled over to the bars and kicked at the tray, sending shattered fragments of crockery clattering out beyond the circle of light.

'D'you know what you are?' he snarled, barely recognising his own voice, but unable to change it — he, as much as Tess, transformed by their ordeal into something he wasn't. 'You're a . . . you're . . .'

He paused, eyes closed, his throat clogged with anger, and realised in the sudden dark that he was directing all his pent-up rage at the wrong person. For all his size and strength, there was something pathetic about Will: he was like an overgrown child playing games with deadly intent; games which, in his savage and misguided innocence, he had mistaken for reality. No, it wasn't Will whom Doug really hated. It was Mary. His own daughter! Whom he hated and loved all at once, the two emotions tied into a knot that he could no longer unpick or even cut through.

'Can the earth accuse the heavens?' Will was demanding loudly. 'Is it fitting that the fuel for the fire accuse the flames?'

Fuel, flames, what was he talking about? Doug opened his eyes and Will was towering over him. Before he could step back, Will had him by the wrists, his grip unbelievably strong. And there was a strange smell. Of woodsmoke! Is that perhaps what he was . . . ? Or . . . or . . . ?

In a flash of memory Doug saw the fire in the clearing, the body of the dog lying stiff-legged at the white heart of the flames. And he knew immediately what the woodsmoke signified. That pungent odour, clinging still to Will's bare skin, was the last lingering remains of Harry's funeral pyre!

He let out a broken sob, imagining Harry trapped within a crackling blaze; and Mary, her eyes twin jets of flame, dancing round and round him in an ever-tightening circle. Mary again! Her dancing image once more clogging his throat with anger, an anger mixed now with grief and desperation.

'God help her if she comes near me!' he gasped out

in that same barely recognisable voice. 'I swear I'll kill her! I swear it!'

Momentarily he had almost forgotten Will, caught up by emotions not his own, but those hands hadn't forgotten him, their grip tightening until he thought his wrists would break, crumble under the pressure. He wasn't even aware of his legs giving way. He was down on his knees, his face pressed to the bars, and he could hear that other voice of his begging for mercy.

'Mercy!' Will bellowed. 'You speak against sister Moon, against the heavens themselves, and you ask for mercy? You! A piece of kindling fit only for the fire!'

From behind him someone else was calling out. Bob? Harry? No! Dear God, not Harry!

'Dad? Is that you? What's going on?'

He moaned with relief as Will released his wrists — his hands, dead things without feeling, hanging slackly between his thighs. Through the receding pain he heard a dull ring of metal, a sharp click-click-click, and with a clang Will was inside the cage. He staggered up, but one flame-covered arm caught him across the eyes and he fell again, onto hands too numb to bear his weight. Sprawled on the floor, he looked up as Will stooped above Bob and hoisted him to his shoulder with the same effortless strength that had felled Doug moments earlier.

Doug wanted more than anything else to cry out that he was sorry, that Will should take him this time — *him!* — but that foreign voice, uncontrollable, spoke for him yet again, filling his mouth with invective.

'You fucking bastard!' he yelled, his tone high and

demented so that even to his own ears it sounded as though he were the maniac. 'Let him go, you fucker! Put him down!' With his hands flapping uselessly, he ran at the hinged section of bars just as it clanged shut, his already bruised forehead slamming into the unforgiving steel.

Dazed, outraged, his body heavy with defeat, he watched as Will fastened the chain about Bob's waist.

'Dad?' Bob called faintly, but he was still only half-conscious, his wavering eyes struggling to focus on Will's weirdly divided face. He slumped down as Will released him, his head lolling drunkenly, the heel of one shoe scoring an uneven line through the brown stain on the concrete.

'You asked for mercy,' Will said, speaking with such detachment that he might have been addressing the dark hillside that lay just beyond the walls. 'Well, here is my only mercy. The peace that must follow all earthly striving. The long sleep that undoes every particle of the created world.'

For a few breathless seconds Doug thought he was about to lose Bob as well; to have him snatched away before his eyes. He only understood the grim promise behind those words when Will turned disdainfully towards the door, dismissing this cell and its puny occupants as though they hardly existed.

'Take that chain off him!' Doug shouted as Will disappeared into the darkness. 'Take it off or I'll . . .'

Or he'd what? What did he have left to threaten Will with? Only Mary. The same unknown Mary that Will was now searching for. Doug could hear his muffled cries sounding through the house overhead: not the cries of a would-be God, but, once again, of the pathetic child.

'Little sister, I need you here beside me,' he wailed. 'Don't reject me for these things of the earth. Don't let me rule alone in the heavens. I am lonely without you.'

Lonely! It seemed strange to Doug that he should share any emotion with that monster, yet the longing in Will's cries definitely stirred something in him. A solitary sense of himself that grew out of emptiness. Out of lost faces, lost or strayed identities. Was this, perhaps, what had also afflicted Tess? This sense of being totally alone, as Mary and Harry both receded from her? As Bob wandered in confusion, and he, Doug, grovelled helplessly at her feet? Had the isolation been too much for her to bear? He turned and looked at her. She was still lying with her face to the wall, but the hunched shape of her shoulders told him that she was awake — that she had probably been awake all along, listening. And he shuffled over to the bed and lay down beside her, holding her while their animal warmth gradually mingled.

The last of Will's fading cries reached him just before he fell asleep, and he thought distinctly: Don't let him find her; don't let Mary come back here again. She was Doug's greatest fear, he had no doubt of that.

'Please,' he murmured drowsily. 'Spare us.' Those few slurred words, as he sank slowly into the dark, like prayers proffered to some unimaginably merciful God.

Prayers that received no answer, for when he woke and sat up, Mary was crouched at the far edge of the lighted circle, watching dispassionately as Will worked at one of the incomplete figures.

Doug didn't have to look closely to see which figure it was, his eyes flicking automatically towards Bob who still lay sprawled at the end of the chain. Beyond him, at the limit of the shadows, the open doorway showed as an uncertain rectangle of light. Day again! The hours sliding by so fast!

Tess stirred and moaned beside him. 'I'm so dry! Ask Harry to bring me some tea.'

He stumbled to his feet and into the bathroom, fleeing as much from Tess's delusions as from the sight of Mary seated there so calmly; and fleeing too from the sight of Will, engrossed in his strangely beautiful creations. As before, the cold water spilling over his neck and shoulders helped to revive him, and he emerged, mug in hand, feeling steadier.

'Here,' he murmured, and propped Tess up while he held the mug to her lips.

She clutched greedily at his hand until she had finished, and then, suddenly cool and dismissive, as though he were some stranger bothering her, she waved him away.

He turned back towards the bathroom, intending to refill the mug for Bob, but noticed that someone had already given him a drink, one of the cups from the kitchen standing beside him. Someone had also left a plate of food there for him, and pushed another cloth-covered tray beneath the bars. Someone? Mary perhaps? Had she begun to feel some pity? For Bob in particular, who had always been her favourite? Bob, still badly concussed, lying slack and still on the hard floor like a wounded animal. Had his present condition perhaps touched her? Awoken some of the real Mary — *real?* — the Mary they had all known and loved? Did she still exist somewhere behind that cold mask of indifference?

More uneasily curious than hopeful, Doug approached the bars.

'Mary?' he called softly, pronouncing a name only, unsure as yet who would answer. 'Mary, can you hear me?'

She leaned forward, moving out of the uncertain penumbra and into the wash of hard light, her face giving him his answer. It was no longer simply the face of his daughter, even in outward appearance. Her right temple and cheek were badly bruised; the flesh around her eye so swollen that the eye itself had disappeared; and red scratches, like tiny coiling flames, licked up from her neck and over the line of her jaw.

Doug clutched at the bars with both hands. 'Who did this to you?' he whispered hoarsely, knowing that he was asking the most telling question of all, one that might well decide all their fates. 'Was it him? Or did you do it yourself?'

Mary herself said nothing, her one good eye gazing blankly before her. Will, straightening up from his delicate work on the face of Bob's likeness, turned ever so slightly.

'She has chosen,' he said, answering for her.

'But she can't!' Doug protested — his hands, more cut and bruised than Mary's face, heaving ineffectually at the bars. 'Not like this! She isn't you! She never can be!'

'There is a place for her at my side,' Will answered absently, and handed Mary a pair of scissors. 'His hair,' he said, indicating Bob's recumbent form. 'We need it for the work to be complete.'

And to Doug's dismay, she knelt obediently beside Bob and began cutting off clumps of his hair, placing the thick brown curls carefully on the concrete floor.

While she was still busy, Bob came half awake and gave her a crooked half-smile. 'Mary? Is that you, love?'

She placed her open hand over his eyes. To pacify him? To hide from him her identity? Doug, straining at the bars, could decipher nothing from her impassive expression. Only the damaged side of her face, so like Will's, seemed to speak to him. To whisper to him dreadful things he would have preferred not to hear. And long before she had finished her task, he limped back to the bed, to Tess, burrowing back into sleep, which was the only refuge left to him.

It was Will's plaintive cries that woke him this time. He sat up, dreading what he might find, and saw that Bob was still there, lying coiled at the chain's end, his head oddly naked, with dark stubble where his hair had been. Doug's initial feeling was one of gratitude, a warm rush of it, followed just as quickly by regret as he realised that the ordeal was still to come. And soon! For Bob's likeness, staring at him across the circle of light, had taken on the same weird beauty as Harry's.

Those two sets of glassy eyes, harder to read even than Mary's impassive features, were more than he could cope with, and he looked away, towards the door.

Dark! Night again. How many hours had passed? He inspected his watch, but the positioning of the hands meant little to him any longer. So little that he undid the strap and ground the watch under his heel, as though asserting his mastery over time. As though, through that simple action, he could defy the passing of the hours and prevent the darkness, out there in a world gone mad, from ever blossoming into moonlight. It was a pointless gesture — he knew that. Trapped within this cage, unwashed, unshaven, dressed in a singlet stained with his own blood, and with bruised, enfeebled hands, he understood just how powerless he was. No match for either Will or Mary, or for the relentless thrust of time. Yet still, with no other outlet for his stifled feelings, he ground away at the watch, deriving some small comfort from the soft crunch of glass and metal.

Will sounded much nearer now, a lost child again, his complaint the same as before, but with a desolate, even desperate ring to it, as though he had almost given up hope of being heard.

'Come to me, sister Moon. Come. It is time for the undoing. For the severing of earthly bonds. Don't refuse me. Don't leave me here amongst the stars.'

Braced for Will's entrance, Doug studied the open doorway and detected there a hint of grey. Dawn already? Had one more night passed? Did he have to endure another day before . . . before . . . ?

'Where's Harry?' Tess mumbled from behind him, her voice thick with sleep.

He reached out and patted her. 'He's safe,' he

answered softly, stifling an upsurge of the old grief, striving to believe in the fullness of his own words.

She sighed contentedly, sinking back into her dreams of the past, and he turned again to the doorway, where the hint of grey had taken on a pearly quality. So! Definitely not moonlight. True dawn. He stood up, as if to meet the unknown challenge of the day, and all at once Will was there in the opening, the kitchen knife clutched in one hand.

Doug tried to shout a warning, and when that failed, his mouth opening onto silence, he fell to his knees, wanting only to plead. But that other, ungovernable self had him again, spewing out a torrent of rage and hatred, the words issuing from some dark and alien identity he had no knowledge of.

He was breathless, grovelling and spent, before he realised that Will — *this* Will — had no interest in the prescribed rituals of death. Not yet. His divided face appeared haggard and bloated with tears; a rictus of grief tore at the corners of his mouth; the painted flames on his cheek were blurred at the edges and beginning to run.

'What have you done with her?' Will demanded, and although he spoke in the petulant tones of a little boy, there was a weight of misery in his voice that matched anything Doug had endured there in that hard ring of light; a misery, Doug sensed, more dangerous than any rage or dementia.

'She's abandoned all of us,' Doug answered, and meant every word.

'Never!' Now it was Will who was clutching onto the

bars, as though the world at large had become his prison and he was yearning for the safety and solitude of the cell in which he had spent so many years. 'She can't leave me here! You can't take her away from me again. Not again! I won't allow it!'

The knife was rattling so hard against the bars that Doug had to raise his voice to be heard.

'She's taken herself away,' he said bitterly, restricting himself to the absolute truth. 'She doesn't need us. Any of us. She doesn't even need you.'

'That is a lie!' Will shouted, speaking through the harsh rattle of the knife. 'I am the Double God! I have recreated her from the detritus of the past! Without me she is earth! Without me she is clay!'

'You're wrong,' Doug said, pitting himself against the persistent noise of steel on steel. 'She recreated herself, the same as you. She . . .'

Doug noted a flicker of movement behind Will, and Mary stole through the doorway. Why, he wondered, didn't Will turn and see her? Was it the sharp clang of the knife that distracted him, drowning out her footfalls? Or was it Will's own voice, raised in desperate denial?

'I am the Lord of Hosts!' he was shouting, and the rattling stopped abruptly as he strode over towards Bob. Still without turning, he lifted Bob by the chain and held the knife to his throat. 'All things are mine!' he thundered. 'Give her back to me or I write her name in blood.'

A single drop of that blood leaked from the tip of the knife and splashed down onto the concrete. And although Doug knew that he was bargaining only for minutes, he very nearly shouted in reply, 'There! There!'; very nearly pointed to where Mary crouched silently in the shadows.

What stopped him was her attitude, so wary and secret, like a hunter. And there was also the hammer, pressed almost lovingly against her breast. His own hammer, taken from the peg board above his bench. There were other things about her, equally mystifying — her lank hair, shimmering with sweat; the filthy state of her face and hands and clothes, as though she had been reborn of the earth itself; the hard focus of her eyes, her former blank gaze replaced by a glint of purpose.

He took in every detail with a glance, sensing immediately that he mustn't give her away. *Mustn't!* Not just for Bob's sake — Bob, now dangling helplessly at knife-point. There was Harry's memory to consider too. And his own darker self which he had discovered down here in the earth-silence of the cell. That self also deserved some consideration, demanded it!

'You want her back?' he asked Will quietly, amazed at how calm he sounded, at how he managed to look only at Will, as though Mary weren't there, gliding stealthily into the light. 'Then give me something in return. An hour, that's all I ask.' He paused, hunting frantically for words, for anything that would divert attention from Mary's slow progress across the outer cell. 'Less than an hour if you like,' he went on, stilling the tremor in his voice and somehow preventing his eyes from skittering towards the hammer now lifted above Mary's head. 'A minute will do. Or even less than that . . . less . . .' Words! More meaningless words to be plucked from nowhere! Any sound at all to span the silence while Mary drew steadily nearer. 'How about twenty seconds? Or fifteen? Just fifteen short sec . . .'

That, in the end, was all she needed — Doug grunting with approval as she brought the hammer crashing down onto the back of Will's skull; Doug's snarl of delight matching her fixed grin as the first gout of Will's blood hit the wall. She struck again, with the same joyful ferocity, and Will folded at the knees, like someone about to pray. A third blow almost felled him, but not quite. With a mystifying gentleness, he placed Bob on the ground beside him; and then, the undamaged half of his face turned to the light, he toppled backwards and lay still, his breath coming in noisy gasps.

'Sweetheart!' Doug bawled, so much unfamiliar passion burning through him that he could barely contain it. 'Sweetheart!' And he ran to the bars as if to welcome her back.

He didn't welcome what she did next, though. Without even glancing across at him, she took a long nail from her pocket and pressed its point to the closed lid of Will's right eye — the eye that was already blind.

'Terror!' she muttered. And again: 'Terror . . . Terror . . . Terror!' The word puffing rhythmically from between her lips as, with each blow of the hammer, she drove the nail through his eyelid and eye and into the soft tissue of the brain.

Will, his noisy breath surging on, responded only with a tremor of the hands and feet, his slightly parted eyelid leaking tears of watery blood. And it was left to Doug, all his unholy joy squandered in those first moments of relief, to groan and beg for mercy.

'That's enough, sweetheart!' he implored her, searching her bowed head — her hair clotted with earth and clay — for some sign of the Mary he thought he had rediscovered. 'Leave him now! It's enough! For God's sake, sweetheart! Please!'

Yet for all his pleading, he still didn't know the Mary who finally looked up at him; and she, he suspected, didn't know him either. Or else she failed to see him, Will's heaving chest, his snorting breaths, rising like a wall between them. Doug flinched away as, with undisguised malice, she lifted the hammer yet again and struck at the face, smashing in the nose and mouth, so that now Will's tortured breath bubbled up through a mess of ruptured tissue.

'Enough!' Doug sobbed, pleading more for Mary herself than for Will. But still she didn't acknowledge him, as though she and Will and no one else shared this stark arena of light.

'Terror!' she repeated, and reaching inside her filthy blouse, she took out a cracked and coarse strip of leather.

In spite of its buckle, in spite of the fire-blackened studs all down its length, Doug took some time to see it for what it was — a dog collar — and by then Mary had already fastened it about Will's throat.

'Terror!' she muttered for the last time, and flitted away through the dawn-grey opening.

Where? Doug rushed in a sudden panic to the hinged section of bars and shook them. Was she going to leave him there? Desert them all? Or had she struck Will down only to take his place? Only in order to . . . ?

That thought, the worst possible, froze Doug into the same unnatural stillness as those ever-watchful figures beyond the bars. His own likeness, with its placid air of contentment, stared mockingly back at him. Was that blank gaze right? Had nothing changed? Could it be that Will, gasping out his life on the bloodied floor, was just one more in a line of victims? With Bob soon to follow?

But if so, why had she chosen to fasten the collar about Will's throat? No ordinary collar, but the one that had belonged to Terror; that Harry had rescued for her from the fire. What possible reason could she have for producing it now?

It was that cracked, discoloured piece of leather which released Doug from more than just his frozen state; which gave him his first real insight into Mary's obscure purpose. Yes, of course! Terror's collar! What else? And ignoring Bob, who had begun to groan as he slowly regained consciousness — ignoring Tess who was calling to him from the bed — ignoring even the promptings of his more tender self, Doug shook the bars with renewed force.

'Mary!' he cried stridently, her name rising above the sound of Will's laboured breaths and carrying clear across the cellar and up through the house. 'Mary!'

As if at his special bidding, she reappeared, panting under the weight of a full can of petrol.

'Mary,' he repeated, speaking lovingly to her now, no longer troubled by her closed expression or by the gasping, bloodied figure of Will. In a voice nearly as full of dark need as Mary herself, he whispered thickly, 'Do it, sweetheart! Do it!'

And she did. Taking Will by the shoulders, she strained backwards, panting again as she dragged him into the centre of the room, well away from both Bob and the grouped figures. Will sighed when she released him, his bubbling breath struggling on, a snail-trail of blood marking his passage across the floor.

'Now, sweetheart!' Doug urged her, in the same passionate whisper as before. 'Now!'

And strangely intent, like someone acting out a prescribed role, she uncapped the can and upended it.

To Doug's ears the soft gurgle of the petrol sounded almost playful as it splashed down over Will's head and shoulders, as it slopped over his massive body and legs and spread in an iridescent pool all around him. Glistening on the blond hairs of his unscarred flesh, it ran in broad rivulets across his painted half, dissolving the tiny coils of fire and smudging them into a crimson wash. Yet enough of them remained to join the real fire that leapt up when Mary struck the match.

Within moments Will had become a ghostly outline at the heart of the blaze. An outline that shuddered and rippled and seemed to dance as the yellow-tipped flames reached up to lick at the concrete ceiling and then swirled towards the far door, drawn there by the natural draught. Caught at the base of this curving path, Will's shadowy arms lifted one by one in ready sympathy, as did the dark blur of his legs, his body responding Siva-like to the fire's interlacing patterns. The bright halo of his face, stripped of all deformity by the searing heat, appeared to detach itself from the gross flesh and spiral upwards in a dancing plume of light. Until all that remained of his old self was a blackened hulk, stolid and inert, fit only to feed the twisting flames.

But still the dance went on as Mary, undeterred by the choking fumes, pirouetted slowly before the fire. No longer expressionless or stern, she was laughing openly, joyfully, her swollen face bunched into a lopsided grin, her dirt-streaked features marked by rapture. And Doug, looking on, one arm raised to shield himself from the heat and smoke, glimpsed again the Mary he had lost all those long months ago on a quiet street in suburban Sydney; the young woman, innocent and open, who had walked out into the beguiling sunlight of a bright spring morning.

Over to his left, Bob had come groggily awake. Coughing and calling feebly, he crawled as far from the fire as the chain would allow. Tess, having staggered up from the bed, clung shakily to Doug's arm.

'What's Mary doing?' she asked in bewilderment, her voice muffled by the sleeve drawn across her mouth and nose. 'Why is she laughing?'

He eased her away, not unkindly, knowing there would be time for Bob and Tess later. Now it was Mary's time.

As oblivious of the choking fumes as Mary herself, he called softly, 'Dance, my baby, dance.' His own feet twitching in response as Mary continued to twirl and spin in the dying firelight.

Part Eleven

Tumult and peace, the darkness and the light —
Were all like workings of one mind.

William Wordsworth, 'The Prelude'

24

Doris looked up at the calendar. The fly spots as much as the month itself told her that it was early summer. Not that she was particularly interested in either the season or the month: only in one of the days which had been crossed through in blood-red ballpoint.

'Isn't it the fifteenth today?' she asked over her shoulder.

There was a rustling noise as Ted consulted the top corner of his newspaper. 'That's about it, love.'

She wished in a way she'd been wrong.

'Well you know what's happenin' today, don't you?' she said with forced carelessness. 'The Warners are movin' out. Runnin' back to Sydney.'

Ted's newspaper rustled again. 'I thought those buggers'd run off months ago.'

'That's what I heard too,' she said vaguely, because she didn't want to admit even to Ted how she'd gone over there and peered through the barred windows at the undisturbed rooms with their carpets and fine furniture; or how she'd rung the real estate agent and asked whether the Warners ever planned to come back.

'So what's all this about movin' then, Dot?' Ted pressed her.

'Well they left all their gear behind, didn't they? All that machinery and stuff. That's what they reckon in the village anyway.'

She could feel Ted's eyes on the back of her neck. 'You been sticky-beakin' again, Doris?'

'What d'you think I am?' she flared. 'Go down the village if you don't believe me. Everyone's sayin' the same thing, how the Warners plan to move their gear out today.'

Ted gave a 'humph' of disgust. 'Beats me why they didn't clear their bloody stuff out months ago. What's the good of it sittin' there doin' nothin'?'

'Yeah, I s'pose you could be right,' she said non-committally.

'"Could be"?' Ted took her up. 'I bloody am! It don't make sense, lettin' good gear rot away in an empty house.'

'Not to you maybe,' Doris said with a sniff.

Ted's chair clattered backwards. 'An' what's that mean, Doris? Come on, get it off your bloody chest.'

She remained turned away, taking courage from the blood-red cross scrawled over the number fifteen on the calendar.

'There're some people in this world,' she said stiffly, 'that might not wanna rush straight back into a house like that one. They might need a bit of . . . of healin' time.'

She heard the newspaper being crushed down onto the table top.

'You stickin' up for the Warners now, Doris?'

She held firmly to the jutting edge of the sink. 'I'm just tellin' you that not everyone's as hard-hearted as you are, Ted Briggs.'

That, she knew, was enough to start any row, yet surprisingly all Ted did was sigh.

The chair creaked as he sat down again. 'Listen, love,' he said quietly. 'I'm not gonna fight with you over them buggers. If they're clearin' out of here, then it's not before time. It's good riddance to bad rubbish, that's what I say.'

And that's what Doris had said, too, during the months leading up to the enquiry, and for a while afterwards. In recent weeks, however, she had begun to feel differently. As if . . . as if . . . She shook her head, baffled, still unable to define exactly how she *did* feel about the Warners now.

'I dunno,' she said, genuinely confused. 'Tess wasn't a bad sort. An' they did lose that young son of theirs.'

'What about *our* son?' Ted came back at her, speaking with a bitterness she wouldn't have believed if she hadn't heard it there in his voice.

'Yeah, there was poor old Kev,' she agreed, the tears prickling at the backs of her eyes.

'He'd be alive today if it wasn't for the bloody Warners!' Ted broke out, and she realised with a shock that she wasn't the only one crying. Ted, of all people! Fancy him going soft on her now, after staying so cool and dry-eyed throughout the inquiry.

She dabbed at her eyes with a crumpled tissue. 'It

wasn't really their fault, love,' she said gently. 'We was all losers.'

'Not their bloody fault?' This time the chair slammed backwards onto the floor. 'Whose daughter was it lured him over there? Who was it stood by and didn't lift a finger while that nutter did him in? You answer me that, Doris.'

But she didn't want to think about Kevin's last moments. Not again. She'd already rehearsed them too many times in those long sleepless nights during the previous winter. Often, it seemed to her now, each act of memory was like a fresh betrayal, a fresh act of suffering. As with the Warners, she found it easier simply to avoid the ghostly rooms of the past.

'Leave it alone, Ted,' she advised him. 'You heard it all at the inquiry, same's me. You know it's no good blamin' people like Tess and Doug. They were as much in the dark as us.'

'Don't give me that bullshit!' Ted answered belligerently. 'They knew about Kevin all right. What? All that killin' and burnin' going on under their noses and they didn't notice a thing? I wasn't born yesterday, Doris, even if you was.'

She turned towards him. He was standing at the table, a skinny old man smearing at his tears with the grimy cuff of his checked shirt.

'There was plenty went on under *our* noses back in the time of the Clements,' she reminded him. 'Plenty. And I don't remember *us* sayin' much.'

'Such as?' he challenged her.

'Such as the fire and what happened to Denny. You're

not gonna tell me our Kev — God rest 'im — was squeaky clean on that one, 'cause we both know different. If it comes to turnin' a blind eye to save your own, we're as guilty as the next.'

Ted took a cigarette from the pack on the table, his hands shaking as he held a match to the tip. His first lungful of smoke coiled and drifted across the kitchen towards her.

'Well, Kev paid the price,' he said in a steadier voice. 'An' that's a bloody sight more than you can say of that Warner girl. She's no bloody hero in my book, never mind what the court said.'

'She did save the rest of her family,' Doris pointed out.

Ted dragged on his cigarette, angry again. 'Yeah, but not our Kev, did she? An' you can bet your bloody life *she* knew about Will Clement creepin' around the place even if her parents didn't.'

'Aw, come off it, Ted,' Doris objected mildly. 'She was half daft most of the time. You were over there that mornin'. You heard how she . . .'

'Heard? What's "heard" got to do with it?' he interrupted, his eyes red-rimmed and unhappy behind a cloud of smoke. 'Like lotsa people, she was on'y daft when it suited her. An' it suited her to give our Kev up to that fuckin' mongrel of a Clement!'

Had Mary really given him up? That was a question that had vexed Doris's mind throughout the lonely winter. The court had dismissed it out of hand. And faced with Ted's bitter rage, so at last did Doris.

'You reckon?' she said sceptically.

'I bloody reckon!' he nearly shouted at her. 'I tell

you, Doris, there's an old sayin' and a true one, about the mills of God grindin' slow but fine. You mark my words, when those mills finish grindin' away at Mary bloody Warner, she won't be smellin' of roses. Underneath that goody-goody look of hers, she's no better'n that mongrel Clement kid. An' no different neither. Two screwball peas from the same bloody pod, that's what they are.'

To emphasise his point, he threw down his half-smoked cigarette and stamped on it. So angry and vengeful that Doris glanced again at the scarlet cross on the calendar and made up her mind there and then. She was done with hatred and resentment. They'd all been losers — the Clements, the Warners and themselves — and it was time for a bit of forgiveness and understanding. For all their sakes. Time, too, for whatever evil forces had been at work over on that hillside to be laid to rest.

'Well, you can sit around waitin' for your mills of God if you want to,' she said with a toss of the head. 'Me? I've been ground down enough, thank you very much. I'm about ready for a change.'

'Change?' he took her up. 'What sort a change?'

'A change of heart, for starters,' she said, and walked resolutely over to the door.

'Where you off to then, Dot?'

'Where else?' she called over her shoulder. 'To say goodbye to the Warners. To get rid of some of that bad blood between us.'

'Them?' he howled after her. 'You're goin' over there! After what they done to Kevin!'

She didn't even bother to answer that.

'D'you hear me?' he yelled from the open doorway, and when she kept on walking: 'May God forgive you, Doris, 'cause I bloody won't!'

God? she thought ruefully as she picked her way down the overgrazed hillside. What did Ted know about God? Or about forgiveness, come to that? If there really was a God at work hereabouts, she was reasonably sure He wasn't the vengeful being Ted had in mind. How could He be? Someone as vengeful as that would hardly have allowed a slip of a kid like Mary Warner to get the better of big Will Clement. Now would He? No, only a loving God could have made that happen. Only a God who cared. The very opposite of that crazy Double God idea that had driven Will to do all those terrible things.

Buoyed up by that thought, Doris looked about her with a fresh appreciation of the summer day. The heat on her scalp, the wafts of warm grass scent from underfoot, the mob of grubby sheep huddled in the scanty shade of the willows, even the bone-dry bed of the creek seemed at that moment to be aspects of some benevolent plan. There was, she felt certain as she gazed up at the unblemished blue of the sky, some kind of overseeing power that kept everything in balance. And what better name was there for it but Love? A Love that cropped up in the most unlikely forms: in Kevin's obsession with Denny and then Mary; in Will's mind-twisting grief; and in Mary's brave defence of her family. Yes, despite all their trials, everything made loving sense in the end. Doris had little doubt of that — at least until she reached the top of the winding path and, through a screen of summer-dry leaves, caught her first glimpse of the house.

That, she had to admit, shook her confidence somewhat. The sheer unloveliness of that blunt facade! Like a grimly barred face, it only half revealed itself to the hillside, as though it still had things to hide. But what things? Surely all its secrets had come to light at the enquiry: the seven years Will had been a prisoner in the basement; the revenge he'd probably taken on his parents after his escape; the months during which he'd lived in the very midst of the Warners without their knowing it. What a situation! Just the idea of it made Doris shiver. It also made her pause, there in the cover of the trees, no longer sure that she wanted to go on; no longer quite so convinced that simply by proffering her hand to the Warners she could lay all the ghosts of the past.

All? What about those she had no knowledge of? How could she bring peace to them? Or was she just being paranoid? Imagining things that didn't exist? Had she allowed herself to be unnerved by that mindless heap of bricks and mortar up there?

Still hesitant, she drew into a deeper patch of shade and watched the activity outside the house. A large semitrailer stood parked on the drive, and by the looks of things the moving-out process was all but over. Doug and Bob, having folded up the ramp at the rear of the truck, were securing the back doors; and Tess was stowing a last few items in the ute.

And Mary?

'Come on, sweetheart,' Doug called.

Doris's eyes swung back towards the house just as Mary stepped into view. A slight, almost childlike figure, she lingered at the top of the steps and surveyed the hillside below, giving it a long slow perusal that was oddly calculating in its effect, like someone confirming the exact nature of their surroundings. Doris squinted through the sunlight, trying to bring Mary's face into sharper focus, but at that distance Mary's expression was no less difficult to read than the barred exterior of the house.

'I have the keys,' Tess called up to her. 'Just pull the door to after you.'

The sharp click of the lock carried all the way down to where Doris was standing, the sound bell-clear in the lazy heat of the day. And then the Warners were gathered on the drive, talking and laughing together before starting on their journey home, snatches of their conversation drifting out over the silent hillside. As Doris understood only too well, now was the time to go and say her goodbyes. Now or never. A few minutes more and they would be gone, with only the dust of their passing left hanging in the air.

Yet once again she held back, constrained not simply by the brooding appearance of the house, but also by the sight of that tight family group. By what it made her feel — simple, stark jealousy. The same feeling she'd had that first time she'd visited them, and just as difficult to resist.

Earlier, she'd consoled herself with the thought that the Warners, like everyone else involved in the saga of Will Clement, had been losers. All three families, after all, had lost a son. But were they all really equal in their suffering? The Clements had been wiped out completely. She, Doris, had only Ted left, and he was small comfort to her most of the time. Whereas the Warners still had so much — their money, their fancy possessions, their second house in Sydney, their tight family group which seemed to have grown tighter, warmer, since the death of Harry. Even as Doris watched them, Doug encircled Mary's neck with his arm and kissed her on the cheek; and she, responding to some remark from Bob, threw back her head in carefree laughter, a sound as bell-clear as the final click of the lock.

So much!

And with her jealousy deepening into something worse — into the bitter taste of envy — Doris turned and scurried off down the winding path.

'Bloody people!' she muttered to herself as she crossed the dry, shimmering sand of the creek, unaware that she had used those same words once before and in a similar circumstance. 'They think they're too good for everyone else, that's their trouble.'

But it was Doris's trouble, too, the memory of Mary's laughter rankling anew as she paused, just as Mary had done, and surveyed her own derelict property. It wasn't much to look at, she had to admit that: a parched hillside, a few scruffy sheep, a ramshackle house that seemed to be sinking back into the soil. And the biggest eyesore of all, Kevin's down-at-heel old shack, its roof nearly rusted through, its weatherboard cladding half rotten and unpainted.

She hadn't visited the shack since the morning of

Kevin's disappearance. She hadn't wanted to. After learning from the Warners that he was never coming back...

Doris paused in mid thought. Now *there* was a story! For instance, had that boy of theirs really seen Kev with a girl? Had the girl really failed to come forward because she'd been scared off by all the publicity? Had Kev genuinely meant to leave, but been waylaid by Will Clement during one of his last spying trips across the creek? And where had Kev's ute and gear got to? Were they dumped somewhere in the bush by Will, the way he'd also dumped the Warner's ute on the night of the attack? So many questions, and so few reliable answers. No wonder Ted was still angry.

Doris sighed and pulled her hair back from her forehead, reminding herself yet again that there was nothing to be gained by raking over old coals.

Now, what had she been thinking of a bit earlier? Ah yes. About the Warners and how they'd told her Kev had shot through. After that, she'd had Ted nail up the door of the shack, as though trying to close off his memory forever.

She wondered now why she'd bothered. You couldn't hide from the past. She'd learned that much at the enquiry. Nailing up a door hadn't changed anything, because even then Kevin had been dead and gone, and that was that. And here was the Warner girl still alive and well, and like it or not that was also that. There wasn't a thing she, Doris, could do to bring Kev back or make any of it any different. So what was she moaning about?

She waved the flies from her face, drew herself up straight and smoothed her crumpled dress — the withering sunlight all the while beating down on her.

All right then, she decided, she'd show the Warners that they weren't the only ones who could make a fresh start. She might not have a family around her, she might not have a husband with silky-warm hands and a heart to match, but she still had a place to call her own, and she was still capable of using a hammer and a paint brush. And where better to begin than the shack? There, she could sweep away both the real cobwebs and the cobwebs of the past, all in one go.

Gathering up a lump of quartz that jutted from the thin soil, she approached the shack door, meaning to bash it open, only to discover that the nails had already been torn out, the door hanging crookedly on its hinges. It creaked as she pushed it inwards.

'Ted, is that you?'

As if it could be! She could hardly get him to lift a hand around the place these days. The racing guide, the cricket and the football — that was about the limit of his interests.

Tentatively, she edged along the passage. Not much point in taking risks, not with Sydney's burglary rate starting to spill over into the bush. Or so they were saying in the village. She reached the bedroom doorway and peered hastily inside. Nobody in there, thank heavens. Empty, just the way Kev had left it. Slightly more confident, she crept on, far enough for her to see the breakfast area to the left of the kitchen. By the look of it, there was no one in there eith . . . !

She reared back, her heart hammering, as she glimpsed a giant shape against the window.

Dear God! What the . . . ?

When nobody followed her, when not the least sound reached her ears, she peeked again. Yes, it was still there, but not alive. No living thing could stand so straight and still.

Both hands clutching the front of her dress, she crept forward, hugging the wall. She could see the thing clearly now, outlined against the shabby kitchen cupboards. Not a real man, as she had feared, but the life-sized model of a man made out of stones and clay. Not just *any* man, but someone quite specific. Someone she hadn't seen for years, not since he was a great lumbering lad over there in the old house, in the days before the fire. Yet still she recognised him, despite the fine cracks that now scarred the clay surface. How could she help but know him? The likeness was so complete. His heavy features, the swell of his limbs, had all been perfectly and lovingly modelled. Yes, *lovingly*! There was no avoiding that. The damaged eye and ear, the painted flames all down one half of the body, only served to confirm his identity. Will Clement. Unmistakable. His one good eye, a sliver of clear glass, gazing emptily at her.

Having attended the many sessions of the enquiry and heard all about the notion of Double God, Doris realised at once whose hands had fashioned him and for what dark purpose. Mary! She was the only one who could have made this life-sized likeness; made it, moreover, as a prelude to murder.

A hero, they'd called Mary at the enquiry. Doris had heard them say it. A hero! As though what Mary had done to Will had been no more than an act of brave rebellion, a way merely of severing herself from a grief-crazed past. That and nothing else! Whereas in fact... Doris swallowed hard, digesting this sudden unpalatable truth... in fact Mary had acted just like Will, first modelling the person she had decided to destroy. Which surely meant that she had seen herself as taking Will's place! As the new... as the new...

But Doris, already in a mild state of shock, baulked at that idea. For the present at least. Nervously, she backed away across the kitchen, noticing for the first time the clayey footprints on the floor. Small, delicate shapes, in keeping with the small, delicate young woman who had stood up at the enquiry, tears in her eyes, and explained her final destructive action. An impulse, that was how she had described it, carried out on the spur of the moment, with the sole intent of defending her family. 'He was mad and had to be stopped,' she'd said. The same young woman, equally believable, who had stood on the sunlit driveway that morning, a picture of innocence, relaxed and carefree in the midst of her loving family.

Innocent? Carefree?

Lingering uneasily at the entrance to the passage, Doris was reminded of something Ted had said only that morning. Something about the mills of God. How had he put it? 'You mark my words, when those mills finish grindin' away at Mary bloody Warner, she won't be smellin' of roses.'

She won't be smellin' of roses!

It was all Doris could do not to break into bitter laughter. What stopped her was Will's glassy, one-eyed stare which seemed now to survey the room with all the melancholy of a dethroned God. Returning that icy gaze, Doris was struck by the realisation that for Mary to have made this model so lifelike, so perfect, she must have worked with all the passion and fervour of Will himself. Nothing less would have sufficed. A chilling enough thought that sent Doris scuttling off down the passage and out into the reassuring sunlight.

From the front of the house she could see the creek bed immediately below her, a band of yellow-white sand that lay like a desert between the two properties. She felt glad it was there. Relieved almost, even though in all likelihood the Warners would never return. For Ted had been right after all. The mills of God! She couldn't have put it better herself. Mills that were probably still at work, at least if Will in there was anything to judge by; mills that would soon be grinding slow and fine at the heart of some quiet, unsuspecting suburb in Sydney.

Grinding? Now what did *that* remind her of? Ah yes, the gift Doug Warner had pressed upon her all those months ago. The pepper grinder she'd later hurled into the creek. That would have been after she'd come across the mutilated body of Rory and glimpsed Mary's watchful face through the fringe of willow.

Come to think of it, she hadn't felt envious of the Warners then either.

Also available from Mandarin Paperbacks

STEVE MORGAN

Before I Wake

Amy St Clair has got problems. She's a widowed mother of two young girls, she's got a high pressure job in a big New York hospital and nagging fears that she's being followed by a mysterious man. Perhaps worst of all is the series of mysterious deaths that have dogged her emergency room for several weeks – fatal heart attacks in low-risk patients, all bankers, all in their sixties, all grey-haired, blue-eyed, all fit, all just like her father in fact . . . is he too a likely victim?

'Spine-chilling suspense in a medical thriller that never falters in its pace or telegraphs its secrets.'
Publishers Weekly

MICHAEL MOLLOY

Cat's Paw

Hold the front page.

On the brutal Brent River estate, the mutilated naked body of a young woman is found. For Superintendent Colin Greaves it is all in another day's grisly work. For newspaper journalist Cat Abbot, it is the clue to a story that could boost his flagging career.

Cat's big break comes when a clairvoyant reveals to him in a trance the location of the body of another murdered girl. Soon the story hits the headlines, and Cat is plunged with fellow reporter Sarah Keane into a world more seedy and dangerous than any they expected to find. A world of rival gangs and vice wars. A world that Colin Greaves might not even be able to crack . . .

Michael Molloy is back with a front-page story in this tough, gripping tale of hard news and the London gangland underworld.

'Mr Molloy knows it all from the inside out'
Irish Independent

'A thoroughly unsavoury but no less palatable feast of crime fiction'
Birmingham Post

A Selected List of Fiction Available from Mandarin

While every effort is made to keep prices low, it is sometimes necessary to increase prices at short notice. Mandarin Paperbacks reserves the right to show new retail prices on covers which may differ from those previously advertised in the text or elsewhere.

The prices shown below were correct at the time of going to press.

☐	7493 1352 8	**The Queen and I**	Sue Townsend	£4.99
☐	7493 0540 1	**The Liar**	Stephen Fry	£4.99
☐	7493 1132 0	**Arrivals and Departures**	Lesley Thomas	£4.99
☐	7493 0381 6	**Loves and Journeys of Revolving Jones**	Leslie Thomas	£4.99
☐	7493 0942 3	**Silence of the Lambs**	Thomas Harris	£4.99
☐	7493 0946 6	**The Godfather**	Mario Puzo	£4.99
☐	7493 1561 X	**Fear of Flying**	Erica Jong	£4.99
☐	7493 1221 1	**The Power of One**	Bryce Courtney	£4.99
☐	7493 0576 2	**Tandia**	Bryce Courtney	£5.99
☐	7493 0563 0	**Kill the Lights**	Simon Williams	£4.99
☐	7493 1319 6	**Air and Angels**	Susan Hill	£4.99
☐	7493 1477 X	**The Name of the Rose**	Umberto Eco	£4.99
☐	7493 0896 6	**The Stand-in**	Deborah Moggach	£4.99
☐	7493 0581 9	**Daddy's Girls**	Zoe Fairbairns	£4.99

All these books are available at your bookshop or newsagent, or can be ordered direct from the address below. Just tick the titles you want and fill in the form below.

Cash Sales Department, PO Box 5, Rushden, Northants NN10 6YX.
Fax: 0933 410321 : Phone 0933 410511.

Please send cheque, payable to 'Reed Book Services Ltd.', or postal order for purchase price quoted and allow the following for postage and packing:

£1.00 for the first book, 50p for the second; **FREE POSTAGE AND PACKING FOR THREE BOOKS OR MORE PER ORDER.**

NAME (Block letters) ....

ADDRESS ....

....

☐ I enclose my remittance for ....

☐ I wish to pay by Access/Visa Card Number

Expiry Date

Signature ....

Please quote our reference: MAND